MEET SWEET

Appleby grabbed Ashvarinda by the throat and began to choke him.

"Rinda! Rinda!" Vernon Sweet cried, and reached out between the bars with his long thin arms.

Ashvarinda saw the motion and his dark skin paled. "No," he rasped through the choke hold. "Vernon . . . no . . ." He attempted to pull Appleby away from the cage, but the larger man saw this as an attempt to dislodge his grip and so he fell back against the bars, dragging Ashvarinda with him.

Appleby heard Sweet cry, "Rinda," once again, and then another voice, a lower, darker voice, cried, "Rinda!" and then the snarl of an animal barked, "Rinda!" Appleby turned to see Vernon Sweet smiling at him through the narrow bars of the cage. Their faces were inches from each other as rows of narrow dagger-like teeth burst out from between the thin lips of the geek and buried themselves in Appleby's forehead, buzzing as they vibrated and burrowed through the bone into the brain.

THE DEMON

Jeffrey Sackett

BANTAM BOOKS
NEW YORK · TORONTO · LONDON · SYDNEY · AUCKLAND

THE DEMON

A Bantam Spectra Book / February 1991

ISBN 0-553-28596-3

Published simultaneously in the United States and Canada

This book is for those who lived through the 1960's, and for those who did not survive the era; for Mario, Lenny, Tom, Artie, Carl, and Rod; for Carol L., Helen, Scotty, Ted, Dave N., and John; for Nancy K., Nancy S., Barbara, Linda, and Susan; for Ken and Dave B.; for Cindy, Jennifer, and Samantha; for Russell, Peter, Buzzy, Eric, and Freddie; for Rosie, Edie, Ingrid, and Streek; for Bob, Cathy, Jamie, Jim, and Aardvark; for Valerie, Abby, and Mary; and for Dr. Dankner and the Mighty Kronk.

A special thanks to Indrani Abumusallam, Vishna Puri Chandra, and Eugene McDonald for their research assistance.

THE DEMON

Preface

My name is Arthur Winston. That may or may not mean anything to you, but you've probably seen my face on your television screen a number of times. I am what is usually described as a "character actor," and I am a reasonably successful one. I mention this right up front because the story I'm about to present to you is unbelievable, and I want to make it clear that I am a real person with a real career and a real reputation to protect.

No, wait. I think perhaps I'm getting ahead of myself. Let me introduce my story and my problems a bit differently.

When I was a child in the late 1950's, I spent a good deal of time watching horror movies. The Saturday matinees back then were wonderful, with twenty-five-cent admissions, two features, five cartoons, Coke for a dime, and popcorn for fifteen cents. The movies made for the horror fans of the age were classics of low-budget nonsense, and my ten-year-old eyes drank in each and every one of them. I was properly terrified, of course, by the giant ants and spiders that atomic radiation had produced, by the absurd special effects (3-D, Smellorama, William Castle's special specter glasses, the skeletons that came floating out over the audience), by the clay and catsup makeup, and by the dozens of enraged prehistoric monsters who periodically destroyed Tokyo.

I often wondered why people continued to live in

Tokyo, what with all those damned prehistoric monsters lurking about.

A film was released in 1959 that scared the hell out of me, gave me many sleepless nights, and made me shudder every time I passed a cemetery. The film, *Plan 9 from Outer Space*, was standard fare for 1950's horror movies. A race of alien superbeings, having decided that mankind's creation of atomic bombs and missiles had made the human race too dangerous to be permitted to exist, decided to wipe us out by resurrecting dead people from our cemeteries as bloodsucking zombie vampires who would wander around on their stiff limbs and kill people at random. The bloodsucking zombie vampires were played by Tor Johnson (who reminded me of Nikita Khrushchev), Vampira (the apparent inspiration for both Morticia Addams and Elvira, Mistress of the Dark), and Bela Lugosi, in what was unfortunately his last role. Lugosi died during filming, and the budget for the film was too low to afford to rewrite or reshoot anything, so he was replaced by a much taller guy, who wandered around with his face obscured by a Dracula cape. I seem to recall that the aliens were ultimately thwarted by a muscular young man with a pompadour and a brunette with tits like torpedoes.

The whole thing certainly made sense to me.

What impressed me particularly about this movie was that Criswell, a world-renowned mentalist (remember "Criswell Predicts"?), was the narrator of the film, and he appeared on screen at the beginning to assure the audience that the story he was about to tell was true, that it was derived from sworn testimony, and that each and every incident about to be related was absolutely factual. Of course, I believed him completely. (I mean, he made his statement in public, in a movie, on the screen for all to see and hear. It simply *had* to be true!)

Bloodsucking zombie vampires from outer space. The very concept terrified me.

My older brother Gary, with whom I saw the film at the Drake Theater on Woodhaven Boulevard in Queens, New York, tried to make me understand that the idea of alien superbeings creating bloodsucking zombie vampires was, to say the least, unlikely.

Years were to pass before I realized that my brother was right and that Criswell was probably fibbing.

There is a point to this rambling reminiscence. Ever since I realized that *Plan 9 from Outer Space* was fictional, I have been skeptical of any book or film that assures me that it is based upon fact. I do not believe the well-known sentences that preface books and films, "The story (or film) you are about to read (or see) is true. Only the names have been changed to protect the innocent."

Balderdash, say I.

I assume that you, Mr. or Ms. Reader, share my prejudice. I am an actor who has appeared in numerous horror films, and you, presumably, are a reader of horror stories. I have been in movies dealing with resurrected mummies, witches, vampires, werewolves, and sundry other things that go bump in the night. I do not believe in resurrected mummies, witches, vampires, werewolves, or night bumpers, and I assume that you don't believe in them either.

But all of that notwithstanding, the story you are about to read is true. Only the names have been changed to protect the innocent.

I can almost hear you chuckling, saying to yourself, What an amusing if rather hackneyed literary and cinematic device. Allow me therefore to repeat myself.

The story you are about to read is true.

There once was a creature, a demon, named Grogo the Goblin. He really lived. I sat in the ramshackle ruins of his house in the foothills of the Catskill Mountains on a cold, dark night in January of 1969. I saw his photograph, read his sideshow handbill.

I have felt his inhuman presence, and that intuitive feeling sent chills up my spine and made my blood run cold.

Perhaps I should explain. . . .

First of all, I did not write this book. Oh, sure, I added a few things, deleted a few things, renamed the characters, and tossed in an adjective here and there, but I am not the author. The author was someone I knew back in the 1960's. The author is dead. The author committed suicide.

The author would never have sent the manuscript of this book to me were it not for the fact that I am an actor, not a star by any means, but with a face you will probably recognize the next time you happen to see a film I am in. My acting career resulted from my college experience, for two reasons. For one thing, I was in the Drama Club for four years, and did quite a bit of acting on campus, so I wasn't exactly new to the trade when I graduated. The second thing is that, well, that I did indeed graduate, and had to figure out some way to make a living.

The problem was that like many other people of my generation who went to college in the late sixties, I had been psychologically conditioned to be unemployable. Half of my friends from college had decided to "hang out" until the revolution came (after which no one would have to work), and the other half decided to dedicate themselves to the improvement of the human condition. The latter group are now teachers, social workers, and nurses. The former group are now lawyers, stockbrokers, and chiropractors.

I never believed in the revolutionary rhetoric of the

time, but I didn't really feel like having a conventional career either. I was a pretty decent guitarist and singer back in those days, and for a while I contemplated trying to be a full-time musician. My brother Gary, whose opinions I always have and still do respect, talked me out of it, saying that as good as I was, good singer/guitarists were a dime a dozen. He was right, of course. This was the late sixties, remember, and everyone, absolutely *everyone* played guitar. Though I was reluctant to face the facts, I eventually abandoned all hopes of being another Arlo Guthrie. But soon after graduating from college with a meaningless degree in sociology, I decided upon a career that made even less sense than singing, for much the same reason: I decided that I wanted to be a full-time actor. I will not flatter myself by claiming any high artistic motivation for my decision; it just seemed a nice idea to sit around with my girlfriend, watching TV, drinking beer, smoking pot, and waiting for the residuals checks to arrive in the mail.

It turned out to be a lot harder than that, needless to say. I spent the customary number of years waiting on tables and unloading trucks, until in 1978 I landed a role in a Sam Peckinpah film. It was a small role, but it was also the kind that gets noticed, and my agent was able to get me increasingly bigger and more lucrative jobs. In short, it probably would have been less laborious for me to go to law school or something like that; but nonetheless, while nowhere near rich or famous, I am today relatively comfortable financially, and a name known and respected in the industry, if not known to the general public.

My friends are all aware of my films, of course. Even people whom I haven't seen or heard from for years know about me. It was for this reason that I received the following letter in the mail a few months ago:

Dear Artie:

I see that you've finally made a name for yourself in cheap, low-budget movies! All those years of effort have not come to naught, and you must be feeling pretty proud of yourself.

I have written a book, and I am sending you the manuscript. I am not, I repeat, not asking you to send it to any agents or anybody you know in show business or anything like that. I just want you to read it, and then do with it whatever you want. It contains the story of Grogo the Goblin, and Clay and Rebecca and Sean, and that crazy old bartender Alex, and all the misery and tragedy that I am sure you remember so well.

You'll notice immediately that I've taken a few liberties with the facts and the sequence of events and all that shit, but I think you'll find it tells the story pretty much the way it all happened. Of course, I doubt that you'll believe my presentation of what Grogo actually was . . . or should I say, actually is; but remember, more things in heaven and earth, Horatio, and all that.

Don't bother to send the manuscript back to me, or even to write or call to let me know how you liked it. By the time you get this in the mail, I'll probably be dead anyway.

Enjoy the book, you son of a bitch.

The letter was unsigned, and the handwriting was unfamiliar, but the name and address of the sender was clearly written on the upper-left-hand corner of the large envelope. I recognized the name immediately, and I remember remarking to myself how odd it was that this person would contact me in this manner after more than twenty years. The comment about the writer being dead by the time I received the book seemed so characteristically self-indulgent and melodramatic that I disregarded it. I shouldn't have.

The book you are about to read reproduces the manuscript pretty much as I received it. I have changed the names of the people and the places only to protect the anonymity of those characters who are still alive.

I'll return at the very end of the book to let you know how everything ended up, and to distinguish for you between the factual and fictional elements of the story. Perhaps "fictional" is the wrong word. Exaggerated, perhaps, or hyperbolical. Reader, I must ask you to keep an open mind; there is more fact here than you might believe possible. Don't look for the standard type of story line, with clearly defined protagonists and antagonists, linear plot development, neat and clean conflict resolution, and all that. Reality does not fit easily into standard literary packages, after all.

Here now is a tale of the late 1960's, an era possessed of less idealism and more narcissism than we survivors like to admit. Here now is a tale of tragedy and sorrow, of cruelty and loneliness, of tortured lives and bitter, horrible deaths. Here now is the strange tale of Grogo the Goblin.

The story you are about to read is true. Only the names have been changed to protect the innocent.

ARTHUR WINSTON

Prologue

November 9, 1968

"The MYSSSSSSteries of the Orient, ladies and gentlemen, the dark and terrible SEEEEcrets of the Eassssssst, kept here under lock and key and presented for your amusement. Only fifty cents, my friends, one simple half of a siNNNGLE dollar. Step rrrrrright up, ladies and gentlemen. . . ."

It was a tableau of romantic Americana, a tawdry vignette from an age of squalid innocence long past. The heavy thud of poorly fastened canvas slapping against the tent poles in the cool wind of the late-autumn evening; the wide-eyed children, the gruff, silent men, and the slightly unsettled women listening to the sideshow barker as he invited them into the world of the arcane, the bizarre, the safely perverse that awaited them within the tent; behind the barker, the crudely drawn posters, their once vibrant colors now faded and dull, offering the viewer a glimpse of the unnatural and the abnormal, the subhuman and the deformed, drawn in the absurd hyperbolical manner traditional to the trade. All the atmosphere and imagery that traveling freak shows carry with them and exude almost as miasmic vapors, seemed to intoxicate the crowd, and the intoxication was made all the more potent by the utter anachronism of the scene. It was 1968, not 1868. This was not one of the many traveling freak shows that once wound their ways from town to town across rural America, but rather one of the last of its breed. And the crowd stood on the midway at the south end of the New York State Fairgrounds in Syracuse, not in a clearing in some rustic village in the American hinterland.

"SEEEEE them all, ladies and gentlemen," the barker cried, tipping his straw hat slightly back upon his balding head and wiping his jowly face with an old gray handkerchief. "See them all for only FIFFFFFty cents. See Maharaja the Rubber Man. See him twist his body like a serpent and tie himself into knots which would confound the experTEEEEESE of a sailorrrr. Let Ahmed the Wizard read your minds, ladies and gentlemen, let him discover your innermost secretsssss. See Konga the Gorilla Girl, captured by Jungle Jim himself while on a safari in the heart of DAAAAArkest Africaaaa. See Grogo the Goblin, the ugliest man in the world, the circus geek parrrrr EXCELLeeence." He spoke in his best singsong barker banter, attempting to sweep the crowd along with the lilting cadence of his exhortation.

He needed the lilt and the sweep, for if left to themselves, no one in the crowd would part with fifty cents to see the tired old commonplace acts he was so melodramatically describing. They knew that the so-called rubber man was nothing but a contortionist, that the wizard was just a mentalist doing an old vaudeville routine. They knew that Konga the Gorilla Girl was just someone wearing monster makeup, with fake fur spirit-glued to her skin. They knew that there was no such person as Jungle Jim, that he was just a character from the adventure movies of the 1940's. They knew that the myth of the "heart of darkest Africa" had been long ago dispelled in a hundred thousand elementary-school classrooms. They knew that Grogo the Goblin was most likely some poor deformed unfortunate, or perhaps even just another product of the makeup case.

But on a more basic level, none of this mattered. The barker was attempting to seduce the crowd into a willing suspension of disbelief, and the mood, the atmosphere, and the peculiarity of a freak show itself combined to make the crowd willing to be seduced.

The New York State Fair had been held in Syracuse every summer for over a century, but by 1968 the event had long since shed its original purpose and had become essentially an enormous flea market. The tractor pulls and livestock exhibitions were still presented, of course, but few of the visitors expressed any interest in them. The large fairground was host to a thousand merchants and a hundred food booths, and only the area designated for the cheap mobile carnivals retained any of the ambience of preindustrial America.

Most of the rides and attractions in the midway carnival section were owned by amusement companies that made the annual circuit from fair to fair and from church bazaar to church bazaar; but Dr. Miracle's Freak Show was a small operation, working on a shoestring budget, constantly in the red and at the end of its long tether. Dr. Miracle himself—Norman Appleby—was the owner, manager, bookkeeper, paymaster, and at the moment, sideshow barker, and he knew that he was collecting his last fifty-cent admissions, that this would be the last performance. And so also did the few elderly employees who were still with him, who still paraded their useless skills or their personal tragedies before the eyes of the curious, impassive audiences.

This was the last evening for Dr. Miracle. Appleby was unwilling to continue to dip into his savings to meet the bills, such as the fee for the space he had rented at the fair. No more appearances had been booked because no one seemed interested in the small company of freaks. Ashvarinda Patanjali, known as Maharaja the Rubber Man, would give a public demonstration of yoga positions, his *asanas*, once more, and then be done with it. Ahmed the Wizard would relive vaudeville for one final performance, and then resume his life as Bernie Sherman and retire to live with his daughter Dawn in Boca Raton. Florence Jackson would remove her Konga makeup and then do God knew what for a living, whatever an uneducated middle-aged black woman could do. And Vernon Sweet, Grogo the Goblin? What about the elderly freak whose childlike mind had come up with the greatest carnival illusion Appleby had ever seen?

Appleby had plans for Vernon Sweet. He had already negotiated a deal with Emilio Tagliotti, the famous stage and television magician. All he needed was Sweet's signature on an agency contract, and he could start collecting a percentage of the take when Sweet joined Tagliotti's act. Ten, maybe fifteen percent?

Nah. Twenty, twenty-five. Why not? Without me, where would Sweet end up going? Into some mental home someplace?

"Don't delay, ladies and gentlemen." Appleby urged, "you may never again have the chance to witness the wonders awaiting withinnnnn. . . ." A few people approached the rickety podium behind which Appleby was standing and began to pay the admission fee. "Thank you, thank you, right through there, thank you . . ."

Two and a half . . . four . . . six and a half . . . seven and a half . . . be surprised if we took in in fifty bucks for the whole goddamn day, Appleby thought dismally. And me owing the Fair Commission fifteen hundred! He could pay the debt with no problem. He just did not want to, and he certainly had no intention of incurring any further debts trying to keep the tired old freak show alive.

Appleby was a large man in every sense of the word. His stomach was large, his mouth was large, his dreams were large. The only thing about him that was small was the level of his achievement. It had all been so romantic and exciting back in the early 1920's, when he had actually done that about which most little boys only dream: he had run away from home to join the circus. It had been an absolutely delightful existence for so long, he recalled as he continued to usher people through the entrance flaps into the dark and musty interior of the freak tent. An elephant boy until he was fourteen, shoveling a ton of shit and carrying an ocean of water for a dollar a day plus room and board; from fourteen to eighteen, a shill and a barker at the games of chance; and then the high point of his life, his career as a strongman and acrobat with the stage name of Henry Faber.

God, did I get the girls back then, he mused as the last of the curious onlookers entered the tent and the rest of the crowd outside wandered away toward other midway attractions.

But the ignorant optimism and profligacy of youth had shifted into the cautious, penny-pinching realism of middle age. Appleby was now in his midfifties, and all his dreams of grandeur and fame had long since faded before the cold realities of life. He was nearly forty before his increasingly tender back and incipiently arthritic arms told him that his days as a strong man were numbered. It was then that he began to plan for his future . . . better late than never, he had reasoned . . . by making the move from performer to manager and then to owner. It had taken every cent he could beg and borrow to buy the Dr. Miracle Freak Show from Wayne Kessler, the previous Dr. Miracle, and over the years he had seen profits from his investment. But he knew that the show had had its run, and now it was time to bring down the curtain and fold up the tent.

Appleby had saved and invested wisely, and he had no fears for his financial future. Hell, he had even paid into Social Security long before he had to. But that was not the point. He would miss this life, miss the traveling and the circus people with whom he had spent his life. Of course, with Tagliotti and Sweet, there would be more money to be made, and that never hurts; but he felt an undercurrent of bitterness and anger nonetheless.

Typical of my luck, he thought as he closed the tent flaps and walked to the small stage at the rear of the tent, that I invested in the branch of the circus industry which was the first to die. No one is impressed by my mundane horrors anymore, not when they can switch on the TV news and watch people bleeding to death in Vietnam or being attacked by police dogs in Alabama.

He recalled bitterly the confrontation he had had with a group of college students just two months before. The Konga the Gorilla Girl act was racist, they had told him. It was cultural imperialism for him to degrade the religion of India by presenting the yogi Ashvarinda as a rubber man. And in a socialist system, a handicapped person such as Vernon Sweet would not have to parade his deformity in order to survive. He would be cared for by society.

Socialism, for Christ's sake! Goddamn kids today. Bunch of spoiled, lazy little brats.

And they don't buy tickets to freak shows.

When Appleby now addressed the audience, he spoke in soft, low tones, a stark contrast to the booming voice with which he had urged them to enter the tent. The contrast was intentional and calculated, for the atmosphere within had been designed to be mysterious and mystical. The interior of the large tent was lighted by a few oil lanterns whose flickering flames created shadows that danced upon the dark canvas. The audience sat upon a few rows of wooden benches, and two large cages stood on either side of the small stage, hidden from view by curtains that reached from ceiling to floor. An incense burner sent wisps of aromatic smoke to provide an exotic haze, and from an unseen record player came the tinny twangs of a Ravi Shankar sitar raga. Norman Appleby would not know a raga from a rug; but the music was weird and gave him a headache after a while, so he figured it was good background for the show.

"And now, ladies and gentlemen," he said with a tense solemnity, "Maharaja the Rubber Man!"

Ashvarinda Patanjali walked onto the stage as Appleby left it, and proceeded to sit down into the lotus position, placing each foot sole upward upon the opposite knee.

"*Tat Vishnum vareniam*," he whispered to himself. "*Bhargo devasya dhimahi dhiyo yo nahk pracodayat. . . .*"

Let my meditation be on the glorious light of Vishnu. . . .

May this light illume my mind. . . .

Ashvarinda was a small, wiry man, but he had a presence about him that made him seem large and strong. His long white hair reached down to his shoulders, and the tip of his thick gray beard almost touched his navel. He moved at times with the quickness of a bird and at other times with the grace of a gazelle, with no hint of the slow stiffness so common among people who had lived as long as he. He paid no attention to the audience, for he was not a showman. He was a yogi, and he performed the *asanas* of hatha yoga for himself alone, not for the crowd that sat gaping at him.

He had come to America thirty years before, hoping to teach Vedanta and hatha yoga to Americans, but America in the late 1930's had little interest in the arcane mysteries of the East; the Great Depression and the impending world war had been of more immediate importance than achieving *samadhi*, enlightenment.

And so Ashvarinda had survived as best he could, eventually becoming the rubber man in the freak show. Here at least he could devote his time to the physical and mental disciplines that were at the heart of his religious practice without having either to starve to death or beg. Only Buddhist monks beg; Hindu yogis work. And only Jains see virtue in starvation.

Ashvarinda shifted with methodical grace from *asana* to *asana*, with no break in movement and no apparent strain. The simple *asanas* first, the cobra *asana*, the plow, the triangle, the salutation to the sun, little more than stretching exercises; and then the more complex *asanas*, the full spinal twist, the full locust *asana*, the balancing tortoise, the shooting bow. A few amusing chuckles emerged from the audience by the time he reached the final *asana*, the *dwipada sirasana*, as he rested his weight before him on both hands and wrapped both legs behind his head. He then flowed back into the lotus posture. "*Om, shanti, shanti, shanti,*" he whispered, ignoring the sporadic applause, and then departed from the stage.

As Appleby introduced Konga the Gorilla Girl, who waited in the curtained cage to the right of the stage, Ashvarinda went behind the curtain on the left. Here Vernon Sweet waited quietly in his cage for his part in the performance, the finale of the show.

"Are you all right, Vernon?" Ashvarinda asked.

Even in the pitch darkness behind the curtain, Ashvarinda could see Sweet's crooked teeth as he smiled. "Vernon good, Rinda," Sweet replied.

"Just one more time, Vernon, and then we go home."

"Go home," Sweet agreed. "Big house."

"Yes, yes, I know, Vernon," Ashvarinda said. "Your mother's house, your father's house, way off in the woods, far away from here. There we can rest and be left alone."

"No eat chicken," Sweet said.

"No," Ashvarinda whispered. "You will not be a geek anymore, Vernon, not after tonight."

"New friends for Vernon!" Sweet insisted.

Ashvarinda laughed softly. "Yes, Vernon, we will have many new friends, if we want them. And if we wish to remain alone, apart from other people, we shall be able to do that as well."

"No mean face?" Sweet asked hopefully for the hundredth time.

"No, Vernon, no audience. No one to stare at you. No one to make fun of you. No one to laugh at you."

"Vernon go home!" Sweet chirped. "Rinda go, too!"

"Yes, Vernon, yes. But now we must prepare for the last time, the very last time." He paused. "Can you see my eyes, Vernon?"

"Vernon see."

"Good. Look at my eyes, Vernon, and pray with me." His already soft voice sank even lower. "*Hei Bhagawan Vishnu, merey iss kurum sey koiy bura nutiyja na nikley kyo kiy joh kurna hei vo ho kur hiy ruheyga. . . .*" Lord Vishnu, let no bad karma result from this act, for we do what we must. . . .

The night wore on. Mirrors and flashing lights effected the change of Florence Jackson into Konga the Gorilla Girl, a cheap special effect that elicited a few laughs and not one bit of applause. Bernie Sherman's mentalist act was more of a success, primarily because he was a seasoned comedic performer who joined the audience in not taking himself seriously. He was simply enjoying himself, and his own sense of fun was contagious.

As Sherman left the small stage, Appleby reentered and said, "Ladies and gentlemen, our last exhibition will

shock and disturb many of you. Before we reveal to you
the horror which waits behind the curtain—"and he
gestured to his left—"we want to give the fainthearted,
the very young, and the very old, a chance to leave." Of
course, no one left the tent. Appleby's melodramatic
warning did nothing but amuse some of the onlookers
and irritate others. Appleby waited a few moments and
then shrugged. "Well, we've warned you." He paused.
"Ladies and gentlemen . . . Grogo the Goblin!"

The left-hand curtain parted, and an audible intake
of breath came from the audience. After Maharaja and
Konga they had expected another cheap excuse for a
thrill. They had not expected the monstrous deformity
that stood before them in the cage.

Vernon Sweet was clad in a simple white gown, a
curious hybrid of a hospital dress and a kaftan, and the
simplicity of his clothing was designed to draw as little
attention to itself as possible, so better to accentutate his
bizarre and twisted body.

Sweet stood some four and half feet tall, and his
diminutive stature seemed all the smaller for the enormous, round, almost bald head that was perched upon
his long thin neck. His shoulders sloped downward
because he had no collarbones, which made his arms
seem to grow directly from his throat and reach down
until his hands were even with the knees of his short
legs. His spine was bent in the shape of an upside-down
question mark, and thick tufts of dark hair grew upon his
large, gnarled feet.

His eyes were small and close together, and his
teeth, some of which protruded over his upper lip, were
broken, bent, and as yellow as his sallow, wrinkled skin.
His mouth was abnormally wide, his nose sharply
pointed, his chin nonexistent. Only his hands seemed
properly formed, and they were exquisitely beautiful,
with thin, delicate, almost artistic fingers; and these

fingers now scratched spasmodically at his knees as he looked out at the gaping faces.

He was absolutely hideous. The audience was delighted.

Appleby waited for a few moments before continuing to speak. He allowed the eyes of the audience to drink in the living grotesquerie in the cage, watching with some amusement as he read their thoughts in the facial expressions too flabbergasted to be guarded. Is that real . . . ? Is it makeup . . . ? That can't be real. . . . My God, he really looks like that! And so forth.

Vernon, my boy, Appleby thought, I think I'm gonna see some real money in a few weeks, thanks to you.

"The most reMARKable circus geek in the world, ladies and gentlemen," he said. "Grogo the Goblin has powers which science itself cannot even begin to understand. Watch him carefully, my friends. You are about to think that your eyes are deceiving you. Stay in your seats, please, during the performance. It's dangerous to get too close to this creature."

A nervous giggle drifted through the small assembly. The people in the audience were neither unsophisticated nor cruel, and each of them felt embarrassed and just a bit guilty at having gawked so unreservedly at "Grogo the Goblin." None of them would have stared callously at a victim of cerebral palsy or paid admission to see someone whose legs had been lost to diabetes; and yet here they were, paying fifty cents for the privilege of staring at a deformed man.

Appleby knew how audiences reacted to freaks, and he measured his words accordingly. One minute, no more, for them to realize what they were looking at; and then, before the shocked and perverse fascination changed to disapproval or disgust or worse, back to the show, back to the act, back to the circus world. It's all a show, folks, all a game; and you don't think he really looks like that, do you . . . ?

"We all know what the geek does, my friends. We all know about the time-honored tradition of people accepting money in exchange for doing outrageously disgusting things. Do any of you here remember the muck jumpers back during the Depression?" A few low laughs were the response. "Yes, indeed, my friends, the muck jumpers, the homeless, unemployed men who, for five lousy cents, would let you watch as they dove into cesspools." A few disgusted groans arose from the audience. "Well, the circus geek is an old member of that unique fraternity. The geek devours live chickens."

Appleby watched as a few women turned to their companions and whispered urgently. He could hear bits of what they were saying. "I'm not going to sit here and . . . We're going home right now, Harry . . . ! I think we should call the police and . . . This is the most sickening . . ."

And he could hear bits of the men's responses as well. "Karen, it's all an act . . . You don't think he's actually going to . . . Special effects, just special effects . . . I mean, how realistic was that stupid Gorilla Girl bit . . . ?"

"But Grogo the Goblin," Appleby said loudly, "is, may I say, a unique geek." His booming voice quieted them and focused their attention back on the stage. "This creature is"—and he paused for effect—"a shape-changer!"

"Right, just like Konga," someone in the audience said in a stage whisper.

Appleby pretended to ignore the remark and the ensuing laughter, and the pretense was as calculated as everything else he had said so far that evening. By pretending to ignore the comment, and by making it very clear that he was only pretending, he could give the appearance of an irritation he did not feel.

It was the oldest technique in the sideshow barker's repertoire. Shock them, offend them, then lull them into security and confidence and let them think they've got the upper hand.

And then clobber them with something incredible and leave them openmouthed.

"Judge for yourselves, ladies and gentlemen." He turned to the cage. "Maharaja, if you would do the honors?"

Ashvarinda had ceased whispering to Vernon Sweet, and he now took a small metal cage from the ground behind the large cage in which Sweet was standing. He looked at the chicken in the cage and muttered, "You serve, small life. It is your dharma to die, and your karma to be reborn." As he took the chicken out and pushed it through the bars of the goblin's cage, Appleby went around the tent and lowered the flames of the lanterns. He then moved to the side of the tent farthest from the cage and stood waiting.

The people in the audience were straining to see as Vernon Sweet picked up the chicken and appraised it for a moment. The chicken clucked and fluttered and scratched at the delicate hands that were holding it fast, and then Sweet brought the chicken's head to his open mouth and tore it off.

Exclamations of disgust burst from the audience and a few people made motions as if to rise from their seats, but then complete silence descended as Vernon Sweet began slowly to move about within the cage. At first his movements were slow, a measured turning from left to right in a full circle; but then his motions grew more rapid and frenzied, a whirling gyration in the center of the cage. The people in the audience gaped as Sweet's body seemed to begin to shrink as it spun about, and they squinted their eyes through the dim lighting and the incense haze as Sweet's sallow skin grew bright yellow, as feathers began to thrust out in all directions from his rapidly diminishing form.

Their staring eyes inevitably blinked; and in the center of the geek cage were two birds, two chickens. One was clucking and pecking at the floor. The other was lying dead and decapitated.

Ashvarinda allowed the spectators to gaze at the phenomenon for a few more moments, and then he lowered the curtain and shut the cage from sight.

"That concludes our performance, ladies and gentlemen," Appleby said from the other side of the tent. "Thank you for coming, and we hope to see you again soon. . . ."

A few minutes later the rest of the spectators had left the tent, and Appleby walked over to the cage and stepped behind the curtain. Ashvarinda Patanjali was conversing with Vernon Sweet in soft, low tones, and they looked up as Appleby approached. "Damn it, Ash, that's the best goddamned illusion I've ever seen in a carnie, and I've seen 'em all!"

"Thank you, Norman." Ashvarinda smiled as he unlocked the cage, took a rake and burlap bag from the floor behind it, and proceeded to remove the dead chicken. Sweet looked at Appleby blankly.

"And you too, Vernon," Appleby said. "Jesus, I'd never have thought it! I never knew you could come up with . . . well, what I mean is that it never occurred to me that you could learn to . . . what I mean is . . ."

"Vernon understands, Norman," Ashvarinda said. "In many ways he is not as simple as he seems."

The conversation was polite and amicable, but Appleby was, as always, slightly irritated by the clipped, precise, educated English of the Hindu. It was a constant reminder of his own lack of formal education, and he always felt that Ashvarinda's manner and tone seemed a bit condescending. But this was the moment of farewell, and Appleby smiled almost affectionately at the aged yogi and said, "You know, Ash, I've already spoken to Florence and Bernie about this, but I haven't had a chance to talk to you. . . ."

Ashvarinda held up his hand. "No need, Norman. Bernie told me last week that the show was closing down. I understand, really."

He nodded. "Uh-huh. Good. Did he tell you about the severance pay?"

"That there will not be any?" Ashvarinda smiled. "This much I surmised. It does not matter. All my needs are provided for."

Does that mean you saved your money, or are you saying some weird religious thing? Appleby wondered. "Well, Ash, it's been great working with you over the years." He knew better than to initiate a handshake. Ashvarinda had once explained caste prohibitions to Appleby, and even though he had not really understood it, he put up with it.

"It has been pleasant for me also, Norman. I wish you well."

Appleby nodded again. "You given any thought to what you're gonna do now?"

"I think it is what Bernie calls retirement."

"Oh, good, that's good. What are you, about sixty now?"

Ashvarinda laughed. "Goodness, no, Norman. I am eighty-seven."

Appleby's eyes went wide. "Eighty-seven! That's nuts, Ash! You don't look a day over sixty!"

The Hindu shrugged. "Seventy-five years of yoga can do wonders for the human body, Norman. It is not too late even for you."

Appleby did not know if that was an insult or a

witticism, so he ignored it. "Well, best of luck to you. You going back to India?"

"Oh, no, we are going to Beckskill, New York State, to live in Vernon's family home."

"Vernon's . . . what? What are you talking about?"

"Do you not remember, Norman, when Vernon received a telegram five years ago?"

"Oh, yeah, sure, that. It was about taxes or something."

"Yes. Vernon's sister Edith had died, leaving him the family home with all of the tax debts. The telegram told him that taxes on the land needed to be paid immediately, or—"

"Yeah, yeah, I remember that. So what?"

"So I paid the taxes. I have been paying the taxes for Vernon ever since."

"You been paying . . . ! Where the hell'd you get the money to pay taxes on property? You make a lousy thirty-five bucks a week!"

"Yes." Ashvarinda nodded. "And I have been making so modest a sum for many years. And how much of it do I spend?"

Appleby blinked. The Hindu lived on nuts and vegetables. He didn't drink or smoke. He never had any women. The only clothes he ever wore were those stupid sheets and blankets he wrapped himself up in, even in winter. Why, except for books, the son of a bitch hardly ever buys anything! Appleby tried to do some mental calculation. Ashvarinda Patanjali had been with the Dr. Miracle Show for decades before Appleby bought the troupe . . . say an average of thirty a week . . . fifty-two weeks a year . . . say maybe thirty years . . .

"You got a bank account?"

"Oh, yes indeed. Mr. Kessler many years ago suggested . . ."

Simple compound interest . . . three percent before the war . . . about five now . . .

He gaped at Ashvarinda. "You got over a hundred grand in the bank?"

"I believe that is the approximate sum, yes."

Appleby was impressed, and just a bit envious. "Well, I'll be damned! And so you're buying Sweet's house from him?"

"Oh, goodness, no, Norman! Vernon and I are going to live there together."

Appleby's eyes narrowed. "Hold on a minute there, Ash. I got plans for our friend Vernon."

"Plans?" Ashvarinda frowned slightly. "What do you mean?"

"You've heard of Emilio Tagliotti, haven't you?" Ashvarinda shook his head. "The magician?" Another shake. "Well, he's famous and he's rich, that's the important thing. Him and me have made a deal about Vernon here. . . ." He turned to Sweet. "We'll talk about contracts and percents later on, old buddy, okay?"

"Norman, I don't under—" Ashvarinda began.

"Vernon and I stand to make a bundle from Tagliotti," Appleby interrupted. "That chicken bit of his is a surefire draw for the nightclub crowd, and Tagliotti—"

"No!" Ashvarinda said firmly, with just a hint of panic. "It is out of the question!"

"Now, wait just one goddamned—"

"No, Norman, absolutely not!" Ashvarinda said even more firmly. "Tonight was the last . . . the last trick. Vernon shall never—"

"And who the hell do you think you are, his goddamned mother?" Appleby demanded, his face growing red. "I can make this guy rich! Who the hell are you to stand between him and money?"

"Or between you and money," he responded icily. "He is not in need of money. Between us we have more than enough for—"

"I've been waiting for years for something like this to come along, goddamn it! If he'd a started doing this trick fifteen years ago, I wouldn't be in the situation I'm . . . " He paused. "I get it. I get it. You found out about Tagliotti, and now you want a piece of the action, right? Well, that's fair. I know you figured out the trick. Vernon sure couldn't have—"

"Norman, the show has closed, Vernon's work has ended. He is over seventy years old, and he has been doing this for forty years. Now he can rest."

Appleby was too self-centered to be able to conceive of altruism in another man's breast. All he saw was his future income being lowered, vanishing receipts and a future of poverty and want, and in his fear for himself he grew furious. "Yeah, sure, right," he spat.

"And two months after you two walk out of here I turn on the TV and see you on the 'Sullivan Show,' with Tagliotti waving his wand over Vernon while he does his chicken trick and you pick up your percentage! Why, you son of a bitch!"

The nostrils of the aged yogi flared slightly. "You forget yourself, Norman," he said evenly.

"You son of a bitch!" Appleby shouted again, and swinging a closed fist around in a furious arc, struck Ashvarinda in the face, sending him sprawling onto the ground.

A yelp of frightened concern burst from Vernon Sweet as he rushed to the bars of the cage and wrapped his long fingers around them. "Rinda!" he cried.

Ashvarinda Patanjali struggled to retain his composure as he pulled himself to his feet and wiped a trickle of blood from the corner of his mouth. This is maya, maya, he told himself, the net of sense perception. This man is trapped in the web of illusion, he suffers from the weight of his karmic chains, he—

"Get the hell out of here, you goddamn jungle bunny!" Appleby shouted, pushing the Hindu forcefully against the cage.

Though Appleby outweighed him by at least a hundred pounds, Ashvarinda attempted to hold his ground. "Vernon's destiny is not yours to decide, Norman," he said, his voice shaking from the rage he was attempting to suppress. "He must not continue to do this thing. You do not understand what you are—"

Unlike Ashvarinda, Appleby made no attempt to restrain his anger. He grabbed the elderly man by the throat and began to choke him, screaming. "You goddamn bush nigger, you fuckin' thieving bastard!"

"Rinda! Rinda!" Sweet cried again, and reached out between the bars with his long thin arms.

Ashvarinda saw the motion and his dark skin paled. "No," he rasped through the choke hold. "Vernon . . . no . . . " He attempted to pull Appleby away from the cage, but the larger man saw this as an attempt to dislodge his grip and so he fell back against the bars, dragging Ashvarinda with him.

Appleby heard Sweet cry "Rinda" once again, and then another voice, a lower, darker voice, cried "Rinda!" and then the snarl of an animal barked "Rinda!" Appleby turned to see Vernon Sweet smiling at him through the narrow bars of the cage. Their faces were inches from each other as rows of narrow daggerlike teeth burst out from between the thin lips of the geek and buried themselves in Appleby's forehead, buzzing as they vibrated and burrowed through the bone into the brain.

"No, Vernon . . ." Ashvarinda screamed. "*NUHIY YEY NUHIY KUHRO!*" Don't do it!

It was too late. The aged yogi squeezed his eyes tightly shut and prayed, trying to ignore the shrieks of agony and the guttural sounds of pleasure.

A dark and horrible silence descended upon the tent.

At last Ashvarinda Patanjali opened his eyes and looked sadly down at Appleby's corpse as it lay in a pool of blood at the foot of the geek cage. Then he looked up at the Appleby-thing that was standing impatiently within the cage, its balled fists resting upon its hips, the ripped tatters of the now-much-too-small white robe hanging in shreds from his large frame.

"Goddamn it, you goddamn bush nigger, get me the hell out of here!" the Appleby-thing shouted.

The entrance flaps of the tent whipped open and Florence Jackson and Bernie Sherman rushed in. "What the . . . ?" Sherman began, and then stopped as he saw the two Applebys. "What the hell is going on here?"

Florence Jackson swallowed hard. "Norman, that . . . that guy is dead!" She frowned. "Hey, that guy is *you!*"

The Appleby-thing laughed. "Well, how do ya like it? Me and Ash've been working on a new bit. Whataya think? Looks real, don't it?"

They walked toward the cage so as to view the body more closely. "Is that wax?" Sherman asked.

"Rubber," the Appleby-thing said calmly. "Hey, come here, both of you. Let me show you the rest of the bit."

Ashvarinda tried to shout a warning, but he was weak and numbed, and his cry came too late. The Appleby-thing reached out between the bars and grabbed Jackson and Sherman in either hand. The Hindu closed his eyes and covered his ears against the shrieks, knowing that if he watched, he would see the Appleby-thing become a Jackson-thing and the Jackson-thing become a Sherman-thing.

A few minutes passed. Two screams became one, and then again there was silence.

"So, ah, Ashvarinda," the Sherman-thing said. "You know what you gotta do, right?"

"Yes," Ashvarinda said softly.

"You get rid of these bodies. But get me outta here first, okay?"

He nodded and rose slowly to his feet. "Yes," he said again as he took the key from Appleby's corpse.

By the time he had unlocked the cage, the Sherman-thing was once again Vernon Sweet. The old geek emerged from the cage and tugged shyly upon Ashvarinda's arm. He looked up at the aged yogi with a look of childish eagerness.

"Vernon go home now?" he asked.

Ashvarinda Patanjali sighed, "Yes," he said for a third time. "Now we will go home."

I

Home Sweet Home

Let me speak to the yet unknowing world
How these things came about: So shall you hear
Of carnal, bloody, and unnatural acts,
Of accidental judgements, casual slaughters,
Of deaths put on by cunning and forced cause,
And, in this upshot, purposes mistook
Fall'n on the inventors' heads. . . .

—HAMLET, V. ii

Chapter One

November 20, 1968

Alex Brown slowly eased his weary body down upon one knee and brushed the leaves off the small plaque that covered the grave of his wife. The dying leaves of late autumn had been falling for weeks in the small rural cemetery, and they were sporadically removed only by the occasional visitor or the buffeting of the indifferent wind. Beckskill, New York, was not an affluent town, and the position of cemetery caretaker had long ago been abolished by the town council as an unnecessary expense, an unjustifiable strain on the town budget. Alex was a member of the council and he had approved of the idea, as he always voted in favor of anything that either lowered taxes or at least inhibited their rise. Still, it pained him to see the cemetery so unkempt, to see the boundary hedges untrimmed and the plaques covered with leaves and twigs. The older gravestones stood upright and were thus spared this indignity, but the newer ones were rectangular markers that lay flat upon the ground, and most of them had been covered by the red, brown, and yellow signatures of the impending winter.

Alex flexed his stiff fingers as he brushed away the leaves and uncovered the inscription. "Paula Brown, *née* Riasanovsky . . . 1920 – 1946 . . . Whosoever liveth and believeth in me shall never die."

"Paula." He sighed. "I'm sorry about the leaves."
He looked around to make certain he was alone, and
then he sat down awkwardly upon the withering grass
beside the grave. He sat in silence, gazing at the name of
his wife, and then he muttered, "You think maybe I
shouldn't have changed my name, Paula? You never
changed yours, except by marriage. Your whole family,
still the Riasanovskys, just like back in the old
country . . ."

The old country. No pleasant memories or nostalgic
bonds tied him to the old country, to the Ukraine he had
fled as a child, leaving a dead family on a newly
collectivized farm in Stalin's Soviet Union. He had come
to America possessed by the same vision that had
possessed so many millions of European immigrants
over the years, and whatever nostalgia he had was
connected to those days of his youth when it was still
possible to dream of streets lined with gold.

Aleksander Sergeiovich Ovyetchkin. The cold wind
drifted across his narrow face and blew a few strands of
thinning gray hair down in front of his hazel eyes, but he
took no notice. Aleksander Sergeiovich Ovyetchkin. His
lips moved as he said the name, his name, silently.

But an American needs an American name, and
what name is more American than Brown?

Of course, Paula Riasanovsky had never cared about
his name. Ovyetchkin or Brown, it made no difference to
her. She had been attracted to his courtliness, his
kindness, and his enthusiasm, and she would have
married him no matter what his name was. She had
allowed his dreams to become hers, and so lovely a
dream it had been. A resort hotel in the mountains of
upstate New York. Four or five children. It would be
hard work, yes, but it would be a good life.

A good life, Alex thought bitterly. A run-down

tavern in a dying town, no children, and a wife cut down in her prime by cancer.

He closed his eyes tightly for a moment, and then smiled at the plaque. "I'm sorry, Paula," he whispered. "My mind, it wanders sometimes. Maybe I get old, eh?"

Alex stood up slowly and with some difficulty. He paused in brief ceremonial reverence before the grave before turning and walking slowly back to the 1959 Ford station wagon that was parked on Bennets Road in front of the small cemetery. He climbed into the car and then drove back to Beckskill's short main street with the ease of a man in no hurry to get there; no hurry to return to the bar he had run for twenty years and that was now sinking deeper and deeper into debt with each passing season; no hurry to return to the room above the bar, the only room in his hotel that was ever occupied, where Alex slept alone each long, lonely night; no hurry to return to the row after row of unused glasses and his pointless, daily ritual of washing them.

As Alex walked from the street to the door of his tavern he paused to look up at the sign. BROWNS' HOTEL. He smiled sadly. Browns', not Brown's. Paula had insisted and he had complied happily.

Always the same thoughts, always the same memories. The past was a beautiful thing. The present is a desert.

Alex tied the apron strings around his waist and filled half of the double sink beneath the bar with warm, soapy water. Sighing softly, he removed a clean glass from the shelf, a glass he had washed the day before but not used, and placed it in the sink. He waved it around mechanically beneath the warm water for a few moments, his eyes and his thoughts elsewhere. Then he removed it, dipped it into the clear water in the other sink, and then dried it inside and out with the towel that hung from the apron. He rubbed his tired eyes, rubbed his arthritic elbow, placed the glass back on the shelf, took hold of another clean glass, and continued the ritual.

Alex looked out the large front window at the ruddy mountains that formed the backdrop for the small valley town of Beckskill, and watched as the wind moved the almost naked branches of the trees that lined the street. A few of the remaining leaves blew off and grazed the window of the general store directly across the street from the bar before drifting down to the sidewalk. It's so lovely here in the fall, he thought. Paula always loved the colors.

As he gazed out at Beckskill's main street, he wondered if the new factory would be enough to save the town, to provide the jobs that would keep the young people from moving to Albany or Kingston. The farmers whose lands surrounded the town were unenthusiastic about a plastics factory on the banks of the Beckskill River, but the desperate merchants and economically strapped townspeople were praying that when the matter came to a vote at the next town meeting, they could muster enough votes to ensure its passage. The negotiations and planning sessions between the town council and the Craigo Corporation had been concluded successfully, and all that was now lacking was the formal permission of the community. The Craigo representatives had chosen Beckskill primarily because the town council had offered to cede the desired land to the corporation free of charge, which was, of course, an attractive inducement. All that was now needed was one final town meeting, and then the papers could be drawn up and construction could begin.

We shouldn't have gone into business here, Paula. It seemed like a good place back in the forties, but with Hunter Mountain so close, who comes to Beckskill to ski? The town was supposed to grow, Paula, that's what the real-estate people told us, and it has been shrinking bit by bit every year.

But maybe now . . . maybe now . . . with the factory . . .

A dilapidated pickup truck pulled to a halt in front of the bar and Alex watched as Old Johann Schilder climbed out and hobbled toward the door. Alex glanced at his watch. Barely six o'clock. Schilder was early. The radio and the old bowling machine were the only diversions in the bar, and Alex kept most of the lights off most of the time so as to save money; but a customer was coming, so he switched on the lights, turned on the radio, plugged in the bowling machine, and smiled his best proprietory smile as Johann Schilder walked into the room.

"Hallo, Alex," the old man said. "I haf an idea, a damn good idea."

Alex laughed as he drew the old man a beer from the tap. "Another idea, Johann? You still think you're my business manager?"

"It is money you vant to make, *ja*? Attract the customers? So, I haf an idea." Schilder had come to America from Germany decades before Alex had come from the Ukraine, but neither man had ever successfully shed his accent.

"All right, Johann, what is the idea?" Alex asked with forced cheerfulness and no enthusiasm.

"You go to a printer, haf him make up signs, *ja*? You hang de signs on de trees on de side of de road. People see de signs and dey come." Schilder smiled proudly, and his wizened face collapsed into a mass of deep wrinkles.

Alex shook his head. "You're getting old, Johann. I tried that five years ago, and I got a ticket from the state troopers." He placed the glass of beer down in front of the old man, who studied the foam for a few moments before taking a sip.

Alex took the fifteen cents from the bar top and put it in the cash box, and returned to washing the glasses. Schilder looked around the room and asked, "Vhere is Reichhardt?"

Alex shrugged. "You're early today. Maybe he don't get here for an hour or so."

Schilder grunted, and then took another small sip. He drank only one glass of beer per hour, never more than six a night, and he had years of practice in making each beer last. After a few moments he said, "Alex, you got to get married."

"Never mind, Schilder. Just drink your beer."

Schilder was armored with the presumptuous insensitivity of old age. "You can't just live out your life vit no family."

"Johann, don't give me no advice, okay? I don't need any."

"Every man needs a vife, somevone to cook and clean."

"So how could I support a wife? On what I make here?" He dismissed the thought with a wave of his hand.

"Vhen I vas your age—"

"I know, Johann, I know. Drink your beer." Alex could be no sterner than this. Schilder, Reichhardt, and the other local families were his only steady customers and he could ill afford to drive them away. Soon, he knew, Fritz Reichhardt would show up and the two old men could keep each other busy. He was correct, for Reichhardt meandered in a half hour later, and Alex's two barroom fixtures stationed themselves on the corner stools where they always sat, nursed their beer, and jabbered away in their Swabian German.

As the sky began to grow gray with the approach of

dusk, Alex turned on the outside light to illuminate the tavern sign. The light was one solitary bulb in a casing once shiny and attractive, now tawdry and dull. As the sun set behind the mountains, Alex stood behind the bar and cleaned the mirror, and dusted the unused bottles of liquor, and wiped the bar top, and washed the glasses, and washed the glasses, and washed the glasses.

"Him, he looks like shit," Reichhardt said, and Alex looked up from the sink and followed the gaze of the two old men who were staring out the window. Clayton Saunders was walking through the door of the general store across the street, carrying two cases of Old Bohemian beer toward the jeep parked at the curb. Saunders's hair cascaded over his shoulders in long, stringy, matted bunches, and he did not appear to have shaved for the past week. His patched old dungarees had been unwashed, and only infrequently removed, since he purchased them a year before, and his long, tattered, ill-fitting Salvation Army vintage coat hung decrepitly upon his tall, lanky frame. Saunders loaded the beer into the back of the jeep and then went back into the general store for the rest of his order, which consisted of a bag of groceries and two more cases of beer.

Old Man Schilder nodded in agreement with Reichhardt's sentiment, and then repeated his words. "He looks like shit."

"*Ja, ja,*" Reichhardt muttered. "It's disgusting. Look at vhat he buys. Him and his sister, dat's all dat lives up dere on de mountain, and look how much he buys to drink." He frowned and shook his head.

"And look how he's dressed. Like a bum, like a dirty bum."

Alex yawned and returned his attention to the sink. He hummed along with Eddie Fisher on the radio as he went mechanically through the motions of washing and drying. Then Schilder turned to Alex and asked, "Alex, dese bums come here to drink. Saunders and his sister and dere no-good friends, dey come in here and get drunk. Vhy you don't trow dem out?"

Alex shrugged. "Their money is as good as anybody's, Johann. I can't afford to drive away paying customers."

He spat. "Ach, you don't need dere money. Maybe if dey didn't hang around here, more people vould come, maybe." He and Reichhardt nodded vigorously, and Alex smiled but did not respond. He knew that his problem stemmed from the lack of customers, not from the nature of the ones he had.

Clayton Saunders heaved the last of the beer into the back of the jeep and then ambled over to Alex's bar. The two old men stared at him malevolently and he grinned at them as he walked by, nodding his head in what he considered a mockery of country charm and saying, "'Mornin', 'mornin'," though it was early evening. He slid onto the stool directly in front of Alex and clapped him on the shoulder with unwelcome familiarity and said, "So, Alex! How 'bout a shot of bourbon and a beer?"

The older man frowned inwardly. Bourbon, beer, vodka, beer, gin, beer . . . The young man seemed to drink more than all his other customers put together. Alex was an experienced tavern keeper, and he certainly did not disapprove of occasional excessive drinking, but the sheer quantity of Saunders's consumption disgusted him. Nonetheless, money was money, so he poured the shot and began to draw the beer from the tap.

"So what's new here in town?" Saunders asked with annoying informality. Alex shrugged in reply, his eyes averted from Saunders's steady and piercing gaze. "You seen my sister around? I was supposed to meet her here about now." Alex shrugged again. "Talkative today, aren't you, Al!" Saunders laughed. He tossed the bourbon down his throat, emptied the beer glass in two swallows, belched loudly, wiped his mouth on his sleeve, and then tossed a five-dollar bill on the bar top. As he walked back toward the door he said, "Do me a favor. If Becky shows up, tell her I went home and she can go fuck herself for all I care."

"Goddamn bum," Schilder muttered.

Saunders turned to him with exaggerated slowness and asked in his best John Wayne accent, "You talkin' ta me, old-timer?"

"*Ja*, I talk to you," Schilder replied hotly. "Vhy you don't get a job?"

Saunders laughed. "Why I don't get a job? I don't get a job 'cause I don't need a job."

"You don't vork. Nobody shouldn't vork. You, you live off udder people."

"No, I don't, old-timer. I live off stock dividends and bank interest and rents." He smiled, knowing that one of the reasons for Schilder's dislike of him was the fact that the old man's son-in-law, Frank Bruno, rented and worked land that Saunders owned and Bruno could not afford to buy.

"Dividends and rents," Schilder echoed angrily. "Interest from de bank. Dat isn't vork! Dat's living on udder people's vork!"

"My God, a socialist!" Saunders responded wondrously. "A commie, right here in Beckskill! I gotta introduce you to my friend Russell. You two could get together and set up some barricades or something."

"I knew your parents," Schilder said, ignoring the remark. "Dey vas good people. Dey turn over in dere graves from you and your sister."

"Yeah, Mom and Dad were okay," Saunders agreed, still smiling. "They sure did okay in this town. They could buy and sell all you guys."

Alex clenched his jaw. So unfair, so unjust. He's only twenty-one, his sister is only nineteen, and their parents left them so much when they died in that plane crash. Thousands of acres of good farmland. Probably hundreds of thousands of dollars in stocks, and hundreds of thousands more in the bank. Must be that much, from the way the people in the bank over in Corinth fall all over them. And insurance, there must have been insurance.

So unfair. So wealthy, so young . . .

"But, hey, money don't mean nothin'," Saunders was saying. "Me 'n Becky, why, we's jus' honest, God-fearin' folk what don't act uppity 'round our neighbors."

His sarcasm was infuriating. "Vhy you don't take a bath?" Schilder demanded. "Vhy you don't get a haircut?"

"Why you don't mind your own business?" Saunders replied good-naturedly as he took out a cigarette.

"You goddamn bum!" Schilder shouted.

Saunders's face still smiled, but there was no humor in his narrow eyes as he said, "Careful, there, old-timer. We don't want our friend Frank to see his rent go up, now do we?" Schilder was seething, but he forced himself to remain silent as Saunders walked out the door, climbed into his jeep, and drove away toward his mountain.

"Piece of trash," Alex muttered. So much time ahead of him . . . so young . . . so much money . . .

The time passed. Alex rubbed his eyes and then looked up at the wall clock. It was almost seven, and soon what passed for the evening rush would begin; the rush of ten, perhaps fifteen people coming to unwind after a hard day in the fields, after the long commute back home from the factories and offices in Albany and Kingston. Alex looked around the room. The nut rack was filled, the outside light was on, the glasses were clean. He was ready.

Soon Schilder's son-in-law, Frank Bruno, came in with his wife Jacqueline for their evening drink with friends and, perhaps more importantly, to make sure Papa got back to his house safely. They sat down at the bar and smiled at Alex as Bruno said, "'Evening, Alex." He sipped the beer that Alex had drawn for him and then asked, "How's business?" The same question, every night.

"Fine, Frank, fine." The same answer.

"Has Pop been behaving himself?" The same humorous small talk.

"Well, he ain't reached his limit yet." Laugh.

Fred and Joanne Wallenstein came in about seven, and the Eggers brothers soon thereafter. Then Walter and Ruth Rihaczeck, the Warshays, old Bill McGee and Mrs. Pullmann, who had been keeping company lately, and a few other townspeople. By eight, business was booming.

"Hey, Alex! 'Smatter, the keg dry?" Laughter, and another sixty cents toward the mortgage.

"You got any beer nuts? Yeah, them there. Gimme three bags."

"Hey, Alex, give us a pitcher and three glasses, will you?" Two dollars for the electric bill.

At around 10:30 Dr. Timothy Ostlich entered the bar and heaved his massive girth onto one of the stools, which seemed to groan beneath it. Ostlich was the town's only physician, and as such had prospered according to the potentials of his trade. His suit was expensive and finely tailored, his fingernails were manicured, his short salt-and-pepper hair was carefully clipped; but any effort he made to be well groomed and dignified was offset by his florid, fleshy face, his multiple chins, and his enormous stomach. He looked around the room and muttered, "Schilder, Rihaczeck, Bruno, Brown . . . Alex, has Imhof been in tonight?"

"No." He shook his head. "I haven't seen him for a few days."

"He's in Syracuse, visiting his son," Bruno said from one of the tables behind Ostlich.

"Well, five out of six . . ." He paused and then said, "Alex, we have a slight problem."

Alex frowned in confusion, and then realized what Ostlich's muttering referred to. Of the six members of the Beckskill town council, five were present in the bar at that moment. Only Mike Imhof was absent. Inasmuch as the town council had only one piece of important business at the moment, Alex surmised the nature of the problem. "The factory? Something has happened?" His voice was suddenly very nervous.

Ostlich turned away from the bar. "Walter, Johann, Frank. Can you come here for a moment?"

"What is it, Doc?" Schilder asked as he drew closer.

"Something about the factory," Alex offered.

"Ach, damn de damn factory," Schilder grumbled, and then went back to sit with Reichhardt. "Vhy don't dey just build de damn ting and stop all dis jabbering."

"Don't pay any attention to him," Alex said quickly. "Tell us what's wrong?"

"Maybe nothing," Ostlich said. "But . . . " He licked his lips. "Alex, might I . . . ?"

"Yes, yes, of course," he said impatiently as he poured the rotund physician a glass of sherry. "So?" he asked.

"Well," Ostlich began to his raptly attentive audience, "you remember that when the people from Craigo came to scout out a location for the plant, they said the best site—"

"Was old Edith's place," Bruno finished for him. "So what's the problem? She died a few years ago, she didn't have any family, and the town can take over the property just by paying the back taxes to the county. We've all known that, ever since—"

"Frank," Ostlich broke in, "we *assumed* that Edith Sweet didn't have any family, and we *assumed* that taxes were owed on the land. But she did have a family—a brother, Vernon. And he's living there in the old house right now!" He mopped his brow. "I just came from trying to talk to him about selling the property to the town. My heart almost stopped when I saw him."

"Vernon Shveet?" Old Man Schilder said from the other end of the bar. He glanced at Reichhardt. "Did I hear dat right? Vernon Shveet has come back?"

"Do you know him, Mr. Schilder?" Ostlich asked.

"I remember vhen he left, back in de tventies," Schilder replied.

"But do you *know* him, so as to talk to him, to be able to persuade him . . ." Ostlich turned to the others. "As far as I can tell, he has no intention of selling the land."

"What!" Alex cried. "He has to! We are all depending—"

"Take it easy, Alex," Bruno said. "This is a problem, but it isn't unsolvable. We can have the county take the land away and give it us by the—what is it?—the eminent-domain thing, isn't it?"

Everyone turned to Walter Rihaczeck, who was a clerk in the legal department of the Sperry Corporation. He was the closest thing the town had to a resident lawyer. He shook his head. "Right of eminent domain. That takes time, Frank, lawyers and court appearances. I don't know if Craigo'll wait."

Ostlich turned back to Schilder. "Can you talk to him about this? If you remember him, maybe he remembers you, and—"

"Did you see him, Doc?" Schilder asked.

Ostlich blanched slightly. "Yes, I saw him. God help me, I saw him."

"*Ja*, so you saw him, so you know vhat he looks like. Vell, let me tell you vhat I remember about Vernon Shveet. His mind is as crazy as his body. He's a mental case, he's stupid, he's simple."

"He's retarded?" Bruno asked.

"Yes, I think he is," Ostlich said. "And he is horribly deformed."

"He vas a monster," Schilder said. "He looked like one of dem tings . . . you know, dem tings on de Cat'lic churches."

"A gargoyle." Ostlich nodded. "Yes, the poor, poor man."

"*Ja*, the poor, poor man," Schilder mimicked sarcastically. "I remember he vas maybe tventy, tventy-five years old, right before he left town vit dat freak show, he vas playing with himself, right in de middle of de dry-goods store. It vas disgusting."

"If he's retarded, he might not . . ." Bruno began, and then paused. "I mean, he wouldn't know that it was wrong."

"You're missing something there," Rihaczeck said. "If he's retarded, really retarded, he probably isn't competent to make decisions about the property." He looked to Ostlich. "How bad off is he? You said you talked to him, right?"

"I said I *tried* to talk to him," Ostlich corrected him. "All Sweet did was . . . well, all he did was coo."

"Coo?"

"Yes, like a pigeon or a baby. He made soft little noises." Ostlich seemed a bit ill at ease.

"Wait a minute, wait a minute," Bruno said. "Let's get this all from the beginning. Doc, how did you find out that this Vernon was living in Edith's house?"

"My daughters found out about it, Lydia and Dorcas. They went up to the old Sweet place a few days ago, and there he was, all cozily moved in."

"Why on earth did they go up there?" Bruno asked.

"I'm sure I have no idea," Ostlich snapped defensively. His tone conveyed his desire that this particular question be left unanswered, and the other members of the town council respected the implication. They all knew that Dorcas was a good girl, but Lydia was another matter. Her reasons for going to a supposedly deserted house off in the woods were matters best left unexplored in a public discussion.

"Okay," Bruno said, "so Dorcas and Lydia told you that someone was living up to the Sweet place, and you went to investigate, right?"

"Precisely."

"And so you spoke with Vernon Sweet, and all he did was coo. So how do you know he won't sell the land?"

"He isn't alone," Ostlich replied. "Apparently he has a . . . well, a companion, I suppose you'd call him."

"Probably his keeper," Schilder muttered.

"He was the one I spoke to," Ostlich went on. "From what I gathered, he and Sweet seem to have quite a bit of money between them. He told me that he's been paying the property taxes for Vernon over the years, and that they had come here to retire and live out the rest of their lives. He was very emphatic about that, by the way."

"Damn it," Alex mumbled.

"That other man," Ostlich began, and then paused as if choosing his words carefully. "He is a, well, dark-complexioned person. . . ."

"A nigger!" Schilder shouted. "A nigger, here in Beckskill? *Gott im Himmel*, first ve haf de hippies, den ve haf dat crazy animal come back, and now ve got us a *gottverdammte nigger!*"

"Come on, Pop," Bruno said. "Don't get so excited."

Schilder ignored him. "Vhat de hell is happening to de vorld? *Gott helf mich, Ich sollt in Regensburg bleiben . . . !*"

The door of the bar slammed shut and a slurry voice boomed out, "Hey hey hey, Al!" All conversation ceased and all heads turned in the direction of the voice.

Rebecca Saunders, her bleary eyes half-closed and her gait less than steady, sauntered up to the bar and grinned at Alex. As she unwrapped her scarf and unbuttoned her coat she said, "Hiya doin', sugar. Gimme a beer." She smiled at the other men at the bar. "Hiya, boys." She took off her coat and tried to drape it over a bar stool, but it slid off and fell to the floor. She did not seem to notice, any more than she noticed the hostile stares from all quarters of the room.

Alex placed the glass of beer in front of her. As she tilted her head back and poured the beer down her throat Alex could not keep himself from gazing at the soft flesh beneath, the tanned skin of her neck growing whiter and whiter until his view was obstructed by her T-shirt. She put the empty glass loudly down upon the bar and asked, "You seen Clay?"

Alex looked away and shook his head, and Rebecca smiled slightly. Alex always acted this way when she spoke with him, avoiding her eyes, trying to disguise the fact that he was fascinated by her body, and Rebecca found this endlessly amusing. She pulled on the bottom of her yellow T-shirt, ostensibly to straighten it, but really so as to tighten it around her breasts and to cause the taut garment to accentuate the outward thrust of her nipples. "He was supposed to meet me here sometime. Like if we was both here at the same time, you know?"

Alex wrenched his eyes away from her chest and pretended to himself that he disapproved of young women not wearing bras. He coughed. "He was here a few hours ago."

"Ah, shit," she muttered. "Where'd he go?"

He shrugged. "How should I know?"

"Yeah, yeah, right right right," she replied. "Gimme 'nother beer." Rebecca appraised him almost affectionately as he drew another glass of beer from the tap. There was no real maliciousness in her playing with him, no intentional cruelty; but she derived a thrill of pleasure from the power she was able to exercise over this middle-aged man. She was both old enough to feel the libidinous pull of sexuality and young enough not to understand the inhumanity of her erotic toying with so lonely, bitter, and frustrated a man as Alex Brown.

She downed the second glass of beer and then inhaled sharply as if in sudden concern. "Oh, wow, man, I just remembered, I don't have any money! Hey, Al, you think I can like owe it to you?"

Alex shook his head. "I don't give no credit."

She pouted impishly. "Aw, c'mon, Al. I'm good for it."

"I don't give no credit," he repeated.

She frowned as if in thought, and then leaned forward and said very softly, "Maybe we can make a trade. Anything I got that you might want?" She smiled and tried to look into his averted eyes. He did not reply, so she added, "I must have something you'd be willing to trade for a couple of beers, Al."

"Young woman," Ostlich said angrily, "I would like to speak with you, outside, if you please!"

"In a minute, Doc. Me and Al are negotiating a trade here."

Alex coughed. "Forget it. On the house." He walked away from her and busied himself refilling the nut rack.

"Now, Miss Saunders!" Ostlich said sternly.

"Yeah, yeah, sure. I gotta go anyway. I was supposed to be in New Paltz two hours ago. Hey, thanks a lot, Al. I'll see you 'round." She picked up her coat and threw her scarf around her neck as she walked toward the door. Alex stared at her lithe form for a moment, until his view of her was obscured by Ostlich as he followed her out into the street.

As Rebecca Saunders buttoned her coat Ostlich asked, "What were you trying to do in there? Have you no sense of right and wrong, young lady?"

She laughed. "Gimme a break, Doc. I was just fuckin' around. It didn't mean anything."

"And I'll thank you to watch your language!"

"Yeah, yeah, sure," she responded casually. "Anything else?"

"Yes." He coughed. "Where are Lydia and Dorcas? Neither of them came home last night."

She shrugged. "Beats me. Why don't you ask Sarah?"

"My youngest daughter does not associate with the riffraff who are trying to ruin Lydia and Dorcas," Ostlich replied haughtily. "She does not approve of her sisters, and they know it. They certainly wouldn't tell her where they were going."

"Yeah, well, they didn't tell me where they were going either. They're probably down on Long Island with Pete and Russ. I think they were going to see Artie playin' at Zoli's. He had a gig last night."

"I do *not* want them staying out all night!" he said angrily.

She shrugged again. "So tell them that."

"I *have* told them. It doesn't do any good."

"So why are you tellin' me?"

"And I don't like those boys, either. I want them to stay away from my daughters."

"So why are you tellin' *me*?" she repeated. "I got

nothin' to do with it." She paused. "Besides, Lydia isn't interested in them. She's stuck on my brother."

"Yes, God help her," Ostlich muttered. "He's the worst of the lot."

Rebecca bridled slightly. "Hey, fuck you, you know?"

He frowned and pursed his lips. "You will not speak to me in that manner, Rebecca! Why, if you were my daughter . . ."

"If I was your daughter?" She laughed derisively. "From what Lydia tells me, if I was your daughter, you'd have your hand down the front of my pants by now." Ostlich's face grew red with rage and embarrassment, but Rebecca pretended not to notice. "Besides, if I really was your daughter, I'd be down on Long Island, gettin' stoned and gettin' laid." She walked away from him and got into her shiny new red Camaro, leaving him to sputter angrily at her. Ostlich took a few moments to compose himself, and then went back into the bar.

He found the other members of the town council nodding their heads in vigorous agreement with something Frank Bruno was saying, and as Ostlich resumed his seat Bruno turned to him. "We've figured out what to do, Doc."

"Good." Ostlich sighed, his mind elsewhere. *What are they doing down there?* he was thinking. *And why on earth were they prowling around the old Sweet place the other day?*

"We have to bring the factory question to a vote anyway, so we've decided to have a town meeting day after tomorrow. If we can't persuade Sweet to sell, we can initiate the eminent-domain proceeding at the same time. At least that way we'll be getting things moving, we'll be showing Craigo that we're serious about this."

"Good, good." Ostlich nodded. "Well, let's announce the meeting, post the notice. Walter, can you find out what exactly we'd have to do if it comes to a court action?"

"Sure," Rihaczeck replied. "I'll ask around tomorrow. . . ."

The conversation drifted off to inconsequentials, and soon thereafter the bar began to empty out. On Friday and Saturday Alex stayed open until early in the morning, sometimes because he had customers, sometimes because he nurtured the hope that some would show up; but this was a weeknight, and by eleven o'clock Alex Brown was standing alone in the large empty room.

He collected the used glasses and placed them all in the sink. Wash 'em tomorrow, he thought as he shut off the radio and unplugged the old bowling machine. He locked the front door and the back door, turned off all the lights, and then walked slowly up the stairs to his bedroom.

The Saunders girl had unnerved him and made him tense, and so Alex took the vodka bottle from the night table and helped himself to a few large swallows before opening the window and drinking in the cold mountain air. The view from the second floor of the Browns' Hotel allowed him to look up at the dark mountain where Clayton and Rebecca Saunders lived, as well as out at the winding Beckskill River and the River Road that ran between it and the forest, the forest that apparently was now owned by Vernon Sweet.

All the money that bum has, he thought morosely. Even that retarded freak and that nigger seem to have money.

He took the bottle to bed with him and lay back upon the pillow, his thoughts drifting to Rebecca Saunders. He tried to tell himself that his feelings for her were paternal. Not her fault, he thought. No parents to raise her. Living with that bum of a brother. Not her fault.

But she's young yet, she can change, straighten out, grow up. Maybe she'll meet a nice boy. . . .

A nice boy . . .

Alex clenched his jaws angrily, for he had met Sean Brenner, Rebecca's boyfriend, on a number of occasions when they had come to drink at his bar, and it was Alex's opinion that Brenner was even more degenerate than Saunders. A drunken junkie, he thought. A goddamn draft dodger. Piece of filth, piece of filth . . .

In his mind, against his will, he pictured Brenner and Rebecca together, she drunk and naked, he running his hands eagerly over her body, his lips floating upon her breasts, his genitals rubbing against hers, her brother sitting nearby, laughing and laughing. . . .

Alex jumped up from the bed and threw the bottle against the wall.

His own action startled him, and he stood staring at the shattered glass for a few moments. Then he went down to the bar to get another bottle. He needed the vodka badly, for he had not been able to sleep sober since the death of his wife.

"I'm tired," he whispered as he sat back down on the edge of the bed. "So tired."

It was nearly dawn before the vodka bottle lay empty upon the floor and Aleksander Sergeiovich Ovyetchkin sank at last into a troubled, restless sleep.

Chapter Two

November 21, 1968

"A car isn't private property, goddamn it!" Russell Phelps insisted. "It's *personal* property, totally unrelated to the means of production!"

Sean Brenner dragged deeply on the joint and then passed it back to Peter Geerson in the rear seat of the old Volkswagen Beetle. He held the intoxicating smoke in for a few moments and then exhaled it loudly. At last he responded, "That's all bullshit, Russell. You keep saying that nobody should own anything, and you own this car. So how can you call yourself a socialist?"

"Jesus Christ, Sean, you are so dense! Didn't you read any of those books I gave you?"

"He started to," Peter said, "but he lost interest when he realized that Harpo didn't write *Das Kapital*."

"Fuck you, Peter," Sean muttered.

"No pictures in it, either," Peter added. He took a small toke on the marijuana cigarette and then gave it to Lydia Ostlich, who was half sitting on his lap. He knew better than to offer it to her sister Dorcas. She sat silently beside them in the cramped backseat, stealing occasional glances at Peter, wishing that she were as bold as her sister, wishing that it were she and not Lydia whose thigh was resting upon his.

"This is great dope, Pete." Lydia coughed. "You get this from Eric?"

"No, it's Sean's," Peter replied. "I've just been holding it for him during his, ah, recent business difficulties."

Sean laughed softly and repeated, "Fuck you, Peter."

"There's an interesting problem for you, Russell," Peter said. "Sean's an entrepreneur. If he hadn't gotten burned trying to sell Meth to a cop, he would have made a bundle. I mean, dealing drugs is private enterprise. Why doesn't that bother you?"

"Don't be obtuse, Peter," Russell responded as he took the joint from Lydia and dragged on it. "Selling dope is a revolutionary act in a bourgeois society like this one. . . ."

"Yeah, and in the workers' paradise it's thirty years to life at hard labor in Siberia," Peter observed.

"Yeah, sure, but only because Stalin beat Trotsky in the power struggle after Lenin died!"

Peter shook his head and laughed softly. "We're exterminating the whales, pouring poison into our air and water, raping the surface of the earth, eating God knows what in our food, and you're upset about Trotsky and Stalin. Russell, you're incredible."

"You know," Sean said, "sometimes I don't know which of you two guys is the bigger pain in the ass, Russell with his fucking Marxist bullshit or you with your goddamn fish."

"Whales aren't fish."

"Whatever."

Russell glowered at him. "You know what your problem is? You're selfish and irresponsible. Why, I don't think you've ever taken a political stand in your whole life."

"I thought I just committed a revolutionary act by selling speed."

"Funny, Sean, very funny."

"I . . . uh . . ." Dorcas began tentatively.

"What, Dorcas?" Peter asked.

"Well, didn't Sean . . . I mean, I saw him burn his draft card at that rally in Poughkeepsie last year."

She did not understand why Peter and Russell began chuckling until Russell explained, "Sean used to let his draft deferment lapse every September. After they'd send him a 1-A draft card, he'd renew the deferment, get his 2-S, and have an extra card to burn at dramatic moments."

"Sean, that's terrible." Lydia laughed. "Why would you do something like that?"

"Impresses the girls," Peter offered.

The Beetle puttered along the New York State Thruway in the fading light of early dusk. Dorcas and Lydia had hitchhiked down to Long Island the day before and had met Peter, Sean, and Russell at Zoli's Bar on Hempstead Avenue in Nassau County. Dorcas had remained straight and relatively sober during and after the musical performance of their friend, Artie Winston, but her sister Lydia had joined the others in the customary indulgences. After an uncomfortable night's sleep on the floor of the small, rattrap apartment that Peter and Russell shared with Artie in Maspeth, Queens, they had cajoled Russell into driving them up to Beckskill.

As they approached the thruway exit that would lead them to the road into town, Sean's thoughts were not on Russell's socialist diatribe. "I don't believe I beat it," he muttered.

"What?" Russell asked.

"I don't believe I beat it," he repeated.

"You haven't heard a word I've said! Damn it, Sean!"

"Come on, Russell," Peter interjected. "If you went through what he just went through, you wouldn't be that interested in the struggle of the workers either."

"I don't believe I beat the rap," Sean mused, stroking his wispy beard absentmindedly. "I was sure I was gonna do some time."

"Well, you were in jail overnight, until Clay bailed you out," Russell reminded him. "And you're on probation for five years. That isn't exactly beating the rap."

"I ain't in prison. That's the important thing."

"And are you surprised?" Russell asked.

"Shit, yes!"

"You shouldn't be, not in this racist hellhole we live in. You're a nice little white boy. Nice little white boys don't go to jail for selling speed. Only blacks do. It all boils down to racism. Why, under a Leninist system—"

"Hey, Russell, give it a rest, will you?" Sean said as they pulled off the thruway exit. They were silent as Russell paid the toll, and Sean did not speak again until they were on Route 32. "Drive faster, will you, Russ?"

"You in a hurry to visit your aristocrat friends?"

"Clay and Becky, aristocrats?" Sean laughed.

"Well, what would you call them? I mean, don't get me wrong, I get a kick out of Clay, but he sure isn't leading a productive life."

"So what's a productive life?" Lydia asked. She fancied herself madly in love with Clayton Saunders, and reacted very defensively when he was criticized. "I mean, if you're gonna like cure a disease or something, I guess that's productive. But other than that, what's a productive life? I mean, he's like doing what you'd be doing if you only had the money."

"Don't try to insult me, Lydia. Your wits aren't sharp enough."

"Hey, like, fuck you, you know?"

Russell's comment had not been intended to wound, and neither had Lydia's response, so he went on, unperturbed. "The whole tune-in, turn-on, drop-out thing bothers the hell out of me to begin with, but to be a *rich* dropout . . . that's just sick."

Sean glanced back at Lydia and smiled, "Sounds good to me." She giggled.

"It really isn't funny," Russell said. "It really isn't. Clay is the worst possible product of the capitalist system. At least Bob and Cathy . . . you know Bob and Cathy Johannson, right?"

"Sure. Their parents own the piano-hammer factory at Redhook."

"Right. At least they work in the goddamn factory, at least they *do* something. Clay and Becky don't do *anything*."

"You don't understand Clay," Sean insisted. "He's like Peter Pan, you know? He has enough money so that he never has to work, and so there's no pressure on him to get anywhere or be anything. Hey, just think about what it was like six months ago, when we were all still in college."

"Right," Peter said wistfully. "Stoned for breakfast, stoned for classes, stoned for dinner, and drunk at night with the girls uptown."

"Exactly. No responsibilities. Four years of doing nothing but fucking around. That's what it's like for Clay, except it isn't just four years. It's the rest of his life."

"It's disgusting," Russell muttered.

"I don't see you out there with Che in the jungles of Bolivia," Sean pointed out.

"I've been a social studies teacher for the past three months. I do the people's work in a different way, by telling the truth to—"

"Truce in the class war," Peter interrupted. "Here we are."

As the Beetle pulled up the long, steeply inclined dirt road Sean asked, "You all coming in?"

"No," Peter replied. "Me and Russell are gonna

head back down to New Paltz. I want to try to see Professor McDonald about my Beckskill report."

"Beckskill report? What are you talking about?" Sean asked.

"Pete's doing an environmental impact study on that plastics factory they want to build around here," Russell answered as he pulled to a stop at the top of the hill.

"What the hell for?"

"To try to stop them from building it," Peter replied. "I may not be able to do anything about strip mining in Pennsylvania, but I might be able to help keep the Beckskill River clean."

Sean shook his head and laughed as he opened the car door. "Lydia, Dorcas, you coming in?"

"I'd love to," Lydia said, "but Dorcas wants to go home and she doesn't want to face Daddy all by herself."

Dorcas nodded. "He's gonna be furious."

"You aren't even gonna come in and say hi?"

"No." Lydia shook her head. "If I do, I'll end up staying all night. I know myself. Tell Clay I'll see him tomorrow."

"Okay. Hey, comrade, thanks for the ride."

"See you, running-dog lackey." Russell smiled and then began to drive back down the dirt road.

Sean Brenner paused for a few moments and surveyed that portion of the Saunders property he could see from where he was standing. A short, narrow dirt path stretched off to his right and led through the woods to the trailer where Clayton and Rebecca lived. A wider and longer path to the left led up to the large Colonial house where their parents had lived before the accident that had left the brother and sister wealthy orphans. Straight ahead loomed the crest of the blunt mountain that Clayton owned, and beyond that, Sean knew, stretched the hundreds of acres of land Clayton rented out to the local farmers.

As he began to walk along the path to the trailer, Sean wondered why Clayton and Rebecca had continued to live there instead of moving back to the house. Their parents had made the mistake of establishing nonrevocable trust funds for their son and daughter, to become theirs at age eighteen; and they were quite upset when Clayton, upon reaching that age, dropped out of college after three months, had a trailer brought up the mountain, moved out of his parents' house, and proceeded to drink and smoke himself into oblivion on a daily basis. His parents bemoaned the fact that he had opted for such a lifestyle instead of continuing college, little knowing that it had been college life that had engendered this life-style in the first place. As Rebecca entered into the commonplace adolescent conflicts with her parents, she began spending more and more time in Clayton's trailer, until eventually she, too, was living in it. And when their parents died three years ago, Clayton and Rebecca just stayed where they were. The big house was in disrepair, and they seemed neither to notice nor care.

The door to the trailer was unlocked as always, and Sean entered to find Clayton sound asleep on the floor in one corner of the small living room and Rebecca sleeping on the tattered old sofa. Though Sean had not been sentenced to prison, his experience in court earlier that day had left him tense and wired, but it relaxed him just to be standing once again in the living room of the trailer. He looked around at the familiar furnishings; the posters of Dylan, the Beatles, Che Guevara, and, Clayton's favorite picture, John Wayne as a cowboy on horseback with a caption bubble saying, "Buy a dachshund"; the incredibly expensive stereo system with speakers five feet high; the piles of records, most of them uncovered, scratched, and dusty; the red and blue bulbs burning in the table lamps; the placards and stickers that had been pasted and tacked on the walls and windows . . . Lee Harvey Oswald, where are you when we need you? . . . Support our boys in Vietnam, bring them home . . . Beautify America, sterilize LBJ . . . Kill a commie for Christ . . . and everywhere, empty beer cans and full ashtrays. It did not bother Sean at all that the trailer reeked of hashish smoke, spilled beer, and stale tobacco. Clayton smelled the same way. So did Rebecca, more often than not.

"Toto, I don't think we're in Kansas anymore," he muttered.

He walked over to where Rebecca lay, and bending over her he kissed her softly on the lips. She awakened slowly and gazed at him for a moment. Then she smiled and returned his kiss with a long one of her own. "Hi," she said.

"Hi," he replied, his tone very casual. Theirs was a comfortable relationship, one born of long acquaintance, dating back to Clayton's brief stay at college where he had roomed with Sean. For a number of years Rebecca had been nothing to Sean but his friend's sister, someone with whom to drink, get stoned, ride motocycles. Over the past year, after Sean managed to graduate from college and then had to face the problem of earning a living, he had altered the relationship. While Peter did graduate work and Russell taught high school, Sean dedicated himself to the pursuit of his own career goal: getting his hands on Rebecca and her money.

It was an easy task, for Sean had been Rebecca's first and only love as she passed from puberty into young womanhood. She had worshiped him long before he had even noticed her, and his amorous attentions were more than welcome. And to be fair, he did find her physically attractive, with her long brown hair and slender figure, her slightly turned-up nose and cheerful smile. But truly loving her was another matter altogether, for Sean Brenner was not a sentimentalist.

As he sat down beside her and pulled off his work boots she said, "I'm glad you're here. I was afraid they were gonna put you away or something."

He laughed. "*You* were afraid! I was shitting in my pants. You don't know what it's like to stand up in a courtroom and face a judge and think to yourself that this guy has the power to ship you off to prison. It was like really scary."

Her brown eyes were closing and she felt herself drifting back off to sleep, so she sat up on the sofa and rubbed her scalp vigorously. "What happened? Did you have to pay a fine or something?"

"Yeah, five grand, and I got a five-year suspended sentence. I gotta go to a probation officer once a week, I gotta live at home, go to work, all that shit."

"That sucks," she said.

"Really. I had to borrow money from my parents to pay the fine, and now they're acting like they got me back under their thumbs or something."

She shrugged. "I'll give you money to pay 'em back. Don't worry about it. You owe the lawyer anything?"

"Yeah, another five grand." He shook his head. "Ten thousand bucks. I only woulda made two thousand if I'd sold all the Meth!"

"Stick to selling pot," she suggested. "It's easier to sell, and the cops don't really care about it." She got up and went into the small kitchen adjoining the living room. Taking two cold beers from the refrigerator, she sat down next to him and said, "I'll go to the bank Monday and get the ten thousand."

"Thanks, Becky. I really appreciate it." He took a long, welcome drink of the beer. "It's living at home and going to work that's gonna be the hardest part of the probation. And the rules I'm supposed to follow are like really terrible. I'm not supposed to go to bars, I'm not supposed to hang around with the wrong kind of people—"

"So the same day you beat the rap you go to Zoli's to hear Artie sing, you get stoned, and you come up here." She grinned. "Real smart, Sean."

"And"—he smiled as he reached into his pocket—"I scored some great hash from Eric." He held up a plastic bag.

Her eyes went wide. "Gold hashish! Holy shit!"

"Great price, too. Twenty-five a quarter."

"Wait a minute, man," she said, shaking her head. "You can't take chances like this. I don't know a whole lot about being on probation, but I know that if you do shit like this and get caught, they'll slap you in jail."

He shrugged. "So I won't get caught."

"That's what you said when you started dealing Meth."

"Hey, give me a break, will you?"

She paused and then smiled. "Okay, I'm sorry. I just don't want to have to do without you for five years, that's all." She watched as he crumbled a small cake of hashish into an ornate little brass pipe. "So like who can't you hang around with, for instance?"

"Like you and Clay, for instance."

"We're the wrong kind of people! I always thought we were kinda nice."

"I had to tell my probation officer about all my friends. Didn't want to lie to her, just in case she double-checked things with my parents."

"She? Your probation officer is a she?"

"Yeah, Mrs. Steyert." He decided to torment her a bit. "She's young, and real cute. A tall, willowy blonde. You know how I've always liked blondes."

"Why, you son of a bitch!" She laughed and

punched him in the chest just a bit too hard to be playful. "You keep your fucking hands off her!"

"All right, all right. Jeez, Becky, that hurt!"

"Good."

"And I almost spilled the hash."

"Gimme the pipe. I'll get it started." She placed the mouthpiece between her front teeth and struck a match. In a moment the heavy aroma of hashish was flooding the room. "So who else can't you hang around with?"

"Russell and Peter and Artie. I told her that all they ever do is sit around and argue about philosophy, but she didn't believe me."

"She's right," Becky said as she passed the pipe to Sean. "They sit around and argue about philosophy and drop acid all the time."

"Yeah, but she couldn't find out about that." He laughed softly. "You know, those guys kill me. They sit around that hole-in-the-wall apartment in Maspeth and yell at each other about revolution and bald eagles."

"The Marxist and the environmentalist." She laughed. "Sounds like a TV show."

"Yeah," he said, drawing the smoke deep into his lungs and then exhaling loudly, "with Artie providing the musical score in the background. Lenin meets the whales."

"Sean, be serious for a minute. Can you get in trouble for being here?"

He shook his head and handed her the pipe. "My parents think I'm at Kenny Schimik's for the weekend. He'll cover for me if they call there. I don't have to start working until next Thursday, so everything's cool until then."

"You know, I really don't want you to risk getting thrown in prison just to come up here. I mean, I can come down to the city just as easy. Easier, in fact, 'cause I have a car."

He sniffed and said softly, "I hate the city. I hate the noise and the dirt and all the assholes running around trying to get ahead." He sighed. "I'll have to stay there for at least a year. I don't know if I'll last a year."

"A year isn't forever."

"It seems like forever." The hashish had gone out, so he took a match and relighted it. As he toked again upon the pipe, he looked again at his surroundings.

I'm in Oz, he thought, I'm over the rainbow, I'm in fucking never-never land. Peter Pan, that's what Clay is. Never has to work, never has to kiss anybody's ass, never has to get a haircut or wear a suit and tie. Twenty-one years old, and he can do whatever the fuck he wants for the rest of his life. Smoke, drink, screw, travel, sleep till noon, anything, anything. He has all the money he'll ever need, all the money in the world.

He looked at Rebecca. All the money in the world.

"I love you," he said.

She smiled warmly at him. "I love you, too."

"Let's mess around."

She glanced over at Clayton, still snoring loudly in the corner, and then put her fingers to her lips. "Shhh," she whispered, and then, taking him by the hand, led him into one of the two bedrooms.

The bedroom was small, of course, but made to seem all the smaller by the huge bed that occupied most of the space. Sean and Rebecca embraced and fell together onto the mattress. He moved his hands slowly beneath her flannel shirt and began to stroke and fondle her unencumbered breasts, pinching and rubbing the hardening nipples. She in turn unbuckled his belt and thrust her hand downward into his pants, her fingers tightly grasping his swelling organ. They explored each other slowly, kissing and licking and stroking as clothing was discarded and skin flushed red.

"Let's do some acid," she whispered. "It's always better with acid."

"It'd take a half hour to get off," he panted. "I can't wait a half hour." He parted her legs with his knee and then rolled over onto her, allowing her to guide him in before beginning his slow, rhythmic thrusts.

She sighed and gasped as he grunted and moaned, holding his muscular body tightly with her arms and legs, running her fingers through his long, thin blond hair, kissing the wispy beard on his hot cheeks. "Oh, Sean, I love you so much. . . ." *It's me you want, it's me you love, no dollar signs in your eyes, it's me, it's me.*

"I love you, Becky," he panted, "I love you. . . ." *You rich piece of ass.*

He began to drive into her more rapidly, his hands almost frantically squeezing her arms and back. She froze for a moment and then lay limp beneath him. "I love you," she repeated dreamily. *You love me, Sean, you love me.*

A cunt with money, and it's all mine. Fantastic, fanfuckingtastic. He grunted and shuddered as he ejaculated and then sank heavily down upon her sweat-drenched body. "I love you, too, Becky."

"I love you both," Clayton shouted from the other room, "and if you two don't get your asses out here, I'm gonna eat this whole bag of hash and then come in and join the fun."

"The fun is over," Sean shouted back.

"Besides, you're not my type," Rebecca added.

"You! Who wants you? It's tight-buns Brenner I want!"

Sean laughed. "Wait till I tell Lydia that she's in love with a faggot."

"Lydia? Lydia? That swine, that whore? Tell the wench whatever you want, by God. Here goes the first piece of hashish. . . ."

"Don't you dare!" Sean cried, and jumped to his feet, withdrawing from Rebecca's body rapidly and without preamble. "Let's get dressed and go out there before he eats the whole damn quarter ounce."

She felt somehow discarded, and she pouted. "Not yet, Sean . . ."

"Come on, we don't want Clay to get lonesome, do we? He began to pull on his dungarees.

"Here goes the second piece," Clayton said.

"Damn it, Saunders . . . !" He rushed from the room, and Rebecca followed reluctantly a few moments later.

Chapter Three

November 21 (continued)

The Volkswagen came to a stop in front of the large refurbished farmhouse where Dr. Timothy Ostlich lived with his three daughters, and the two of them who were in the backseat looked at it with undisguised dislike. For Lydia, the dislike was a function of resentment and rebelliousness, and for Dorcas the dislike mingled with dread.

"He's gonna be so pissed at us," she said nervously.

"Me n' him have been pissed at each other for years," Lydia responded. "Besides, I'm the one who's gonna catch all the shit. He's only gonna yell at you, Dork, so don't worry about it."

"Don't call me that," Dorcas insisted.

"So change your name." Lydia shrugged. "You got a nutty name. It ain't my fault."

Peter glanced at Dorcas's miserable expression and said, "You don't have to use that nickname, Lydia. It isn't very flattering."

"Dork? What's wrong with Dork? Besides, what other nickname can you get from a stupid name like Dorcas?"

"Well . . ." He thought for a moment. "How about Cas, or Cassie?"

Lydia shook her head. "She isn't a Cassie. She's a Dork."

Peter bristled slightly. "Hey, you're real sensitive, Lyd, you know?"

"Peter, it's okay," Dorcas said quickly. "Let's just forget it. Russell, thanks for driving us home."

"My pleasure," Russell said, just a bit impatiently. "We'll see you soon."

"Yeah," Peter added as Lydia and Dorcas got out of the car and he followed after them to get into the front seat. "And be sure and let me know if you can find out when they're gonna have that meeting about the factory."

"Sure will," Dorcas said, smiling at him. "I think it's just like so great that you're getting involved in this whole thing, trying to keep the river clean and stuff."

"Yeah, a knight in fucking shining armor," Lydia said. "Come on, let's go face the monster. See you guys."

As Peter and Russell began to drive back toward the thruway, Lydia walked toward the door of their home with Dorcas following behind, her hands rubbing together nervously. "He's gonna be—" she began.

"Yeah, yeah, so pissed off. So let him. So what."

The door swung open before they reached it, and their younger sister Sarah stood in the doorway, glowering at them. She folded her arms haughtily across her chest and tapped her foot as she said, "Well! Decided to come home, have we?"

Sarah bore a strong family resemblance to Lydia and Dorcas, but the similarity seemed less obvious when all three were together. Lydia and Dorcas were identical twins, and such differences as existed between them were not physical. Both had long, light brown hair, but Lydia's fell freely down upon her back while Dorcas kept hers in braids. Both had soft green eyes, but Lydia's were bloodshot more often than not. Their builds were the same, a bit too heavy but with the weight pleasingly distributed; they carried themselves differently, however, so that Lydia seemed curvaceous and Dorcas merely stocky.

Sarah, on the other hand, at sixteen three years their junior, was thin and rigid, her medium-length dark brown hair combed into a tightly rolled flip with short bangs. All three Ostlich girls had the same full lips, but while Lydia's dropped into an occasional sneer and Dorcas's rose into an occasional, nervous smile, Sarah's seemed pulled long and narrow into a perpetually disapproving grimace. At that moment she was focusing this grimace on her sister.

"What are you, the greeting committee?" Lydia asked as she pushed her way past Sarah into the house. Dorcas avoided looking at Sarah as she followed.

"Lydia! Dorcas! Come here this instant!" their father's voice boomed from the study.

"Now you're gonna get it," Sarah said as she closed the door behind her.

"I got it last night," Lydia muttered, "long, hard, and slow."

"You're nothing but a cheap tramp," Sarah spat. "You're disgusting. You make me sick."

"Aw, shit. No Christmas present from Sarah this year."

"And you, Dorcas," Sarah said. "After what you've been through? Where on earth is your common sense?"

Dorcas fidgeted with the edge of her leather bomber jacket. "I . . . I just wanted to hear Artie—"

"Yes, and see that Peter of yours!"

Lydia chuckled as she walked toward the study. "A dork with a peter. Not bad, Sarah."

"You're disgusting!" Sarah shouted at Lydia, and then turned back to Dorcas. "Do you want to end up back in the psychiatric ward? Is that what you want?"

"I didn't drop any acid," Dorcas replied defensively. "I didn't even smoke any pot."

"Oh, sure. You expect me to believe that, I suppose?"

At age nineteen, Dorcas might have been expected to put her sixteen-year-old sister in her place, but such self-assertion was alien to her nature. "Honest," she insisted. "All I had was one beer—" Her words were interrupted by sounds from the den: Lydia laughing, Dr. Ostlich yelling, and then a crisp, resounding slap. Dorcas blanched. "Oh, Lordie," she whispered, and then went to the study.

She entered to see Lydia's face growing red with rage and then noticed a thin trickle of blood on the corner of her mouth. Tears were welling up in Lydia's eyes, but she seemed determined not to give her father the satisfaction of seeing her weep. "You bastard," she spat, trembling with rage. Ostlich swung his heavy hand at her again, but she stepped back out of his reach. "Too fast for you, Dad. I guess it bothers you that the only time you get to touch me anymore is when you hit me."

He stepped forward and raised his hand to strike at her again. "Daddy, don't, please," Dorcas cried. "We didn't do anything wrong, honest we didn't—"

"That's not what Lydia just told me," Sarah said vindictively. "She just told me she slept with somebody last night."

Lydia's eyes blazed with venom. "I swear, I'm gonna kill you someday, you little bitch."

"Slut," Sarah shot back.

"Stop it, please, all of you." Dorcas pleaded, beginning to weep. "I just can't stand this."

"Sure," Sarah said, "you two cause all the trouble in this family and then you go into your nervous-breakdown act to try to get sympathy."

"Shut the fuck up, Sarah," Lydia said. "Leave Dorcas alone."

"Lydia," her father declared, "Sarah is just concerned about Dorcas. And she's concerned about you as well, just as I am." He tried to lower his agitated voice, and when he spoke, it sounded like an irritating whine. "Don't you understand that your behavior is going to destroy you?"

Lydia closed her eyes and forced herself to calm down. "Look, Dad," she said evenly, "all we did was go down to Long Island to hear Artie Winston play guitar at Zoli's—"

"And stay out overnight without permission!"

"We're nineteen years old. Why the hell should we have to get permission?"

He shook his head, intending to seem understanding but firm. "As long as you're living under my roof, you simply must abide by my rules."

Lydia glowered at him. "Abide by your rules, Daddy dear? Do I understand you right? I have to do whatever you say? Do you think I'm gonna let you start that shit with me again, you son of a bitch?"

"Now, Lydia, stop it!" he commanded. "That's not what I meant, and you know it. That's all in the past. I'm worried about your present, and about your future. Those boys you hang around with are no damned good, Lydia, and—"

"That's the problem, isn't it! You're all pissed off because I get it on with Clay, while you . . . while you . . ." She could not finish the sentence. Instead she glared at him hatefully for a moment and then stormed out of the room.

Sarah put her hand gently on her father's arm. "She's just mean and rotten, Daddy. Don't you let her upset you."

Ostlich gave Sarah a grateful smile, squeezed her hand quickly, and then turned to Dorcas and sighed. "And you! Dorcas, I would have thought that one breakdown would be enough for anyone. Don't you realize that those reprobates and all their drugs and alcohol are what caused your problem in the first place?"

"Daddy," she whined, "all I did was listen to—"

"And what were you doing at the old Sweet house the other day?" he demanded, adding before she could reply, "And don't tell me the same lies you told me before. I don't believe for a minute that you felt lonely for old Edith Sweet and you like to keep her house clean. Why, the woman's been dead for five years!"

"It's true, Daddy," she wept. "Miss Sweet was always so nice to me and always made me feel so welcome when I'd visit her—"

"Dorcas, I want the truth!"

"That *is* the truth, honest to God. I love that old house, and I loved that old woman, and I always felt so . . . so good there, so peaceful and calm . . . and Miss Sweet was like a . . . like a grandmother to me . . . she loved me, Daddy, and I loved her. . . ."

"I see," he said skeptically. "And Lydia, who doesn't even wash her hair half the time, went to help you clean the house?"

"She had nothing better to do that day, that's all. Honest, Daddy, that's the whole truth." She paused for a moment. "In fact, I wouldn't mind helping those two old men keep the house up, if they want me to."

"Oh, that's delightful." Sarah laughed. "Cleaning house for them!"

"Yes indeed," Ostlich agreed. "To your long list of subhuman friends you now want to add a heathen and a deformed simpleton."

"Daddy, I—"

"Go to your room," he ordered. She hurried away without another word, and Ostlich shook his head as Sarah leaned her head against his shoulder. "Thank God for you, Sarah," he muttered, putting his arm around her waist.

"Thank God for *you*, Daddy," she replied.

Dorcas went slowly, mournfully up the stairs to the second floor of the old farmhouse and entered Lydia's room to find her twin sister angrily throwing clothing into a battered old knapsack. Her eyes widened. "Lydia! What are you doing?"

"What's it look like I'm doing?"

"It looks like you're packing."

Lydia laughed humorlessly. "Bull's-eye."

"But we just got home . . . I mean . . . Lydia, what . . . ?"

"Obey his fucking goddamn half-assed rules as long as I'm living under his fucking goddamn half-assed roof," she said. "So I'm getting the hell out of here."

"But . . . but where are you gonna go?"

"To Clayton's," she replied simply.

Dorcas frowned, distressed by the thought of her sister leaving her alone with Sarah and their father. "Clay never asked you to move in with him. I know you're stuck on him, and he seems to like you an awful lot, but . . ."

"So we'll see how much he likes me. At the very least he's gotta let me crash there for a while. I mean, I let him fuck me often enough. At least he owes me a roof!"

Dorcas was once again on the verge of tears. "But you and he aren't . . . I mean, you slept with Artie just last night!"

"Yeah, and Russell too. So what? So I got a weakness for guitarists and radicals." She slammed the suitcase shut and snapped the catch. "What do you think, that I'm the only girl Clay messes around with?"

"But . . . but . . ." Dorcas was trying desperately to find an argument that would keep her sister at home. "But how will you get up the mountain to Clay's?"

"I'll drive my motorcycle," Lydia replied, throwing

the knapsack across her shoulder and bounding down the stairs.

"But the motorcycle doesn't have any brakes!" Dorcas shouted after her.

"So what?" Lydia responded. "The whole drive is uphill." Her words were followed by the slam of the front door and the boom of their father's voice.

Dorcas sat down on the edge of her sister's bed and looked out the window at the dusky sky. I can't stay here if Lydia leaves, she thought miserably. I'll just die if I'm here all alone with Daddy and Sarah. The sound of a motorcycle revving in the garage beside the house reached her, and she sighed loudly. Then she got up from the bed and went downstairs.

"Where does your sister think she's going?" her father demanded as she reached the bottom of the stairs.

"I don't know," she lied. "For a ride, I guess." She headed toward the front door with an overstated air of casualness.

"Dorcas, come back here!"

She turned quickly and said, "I'm just going out for a walk," she said, her voice shaking. "I just want some air, that's all. I'll be back soon, honest. I'm just going for a walk, Daddy."

His eyes bored into her as if to take her measure, and then he said, "Well . . . well, all right, but don't be out after dark."

"Okay, sure, I promise," she said, and then was out the door. Before her feet hit the bottom step, she knew where she was going. She needed to go to the only place where she had ever felt safe and secure and loved.

As Dorcas walked slowly along the roadside toward the river Lydia was barreling up toward the Saunders property. It was not quite true that the motorcycle had no brakes, but they were spongy and only intermittently effective, so she found it necessary to downshift on occasion. At one point she almost flipped the bike over, but managed to pull out of it safely. She reduced her speed after that and fifteen minutes later found herself at the foot of the dirt road that led up the mountain. The bike stalled at that point and refused to start up again, so she went the rest of the way on foot.

She was uncomfortably winded by the time she reached the trailer, and leaned against a tree to catch her breath. She heard voices and laughter coming from the trailer and decided that before entering she had better make sure Clayton was not entertaining another girl. She would be hurt and angry if he were, despite the things she had said to Dorcas a short time before; but she would be mortified if she burst in on them unexpectedly.

She walked to the trailer quietly and peeked in through the window. Clayton, Sean, and Rebecca were sitting on the floor taking turns sucking on the tube of a large, ornate hookah. Sean was smiling, Rebecca was laughing, and Clayton was shouting at Sean.

"That's what happens when you lead a life of crime. Goddamn kids today. You give 'em a good education, you do your best to bring 'em up right, you work hard all your life to give 'em a good home, and what do they do? They flush it all down the goddamn toilet. Bunch of goddamn, good-for-nothing bums." He took a drink from the can of tepid beer that rested on the floor beside him. "And why the hell can't you punks stick to good old-fashioned drugs like beer? Why you gotta mess around with that RSD stuff and that XYZ and that IRS and that marry-chu-honor. Just look at you. Look at you! With that hair you look like a goddamn *girl*, for Christ's sake! An *ugly* girl!"

"Clay," Sean said, laughing softly, "cut it out, will you? One to five on probation ain't funny."

"Goddamn fags, ruining the country," Clayton screamed. "But don't you think we're agonna let it git no further, no sirree. We know who's behind this, all them commie folksingers and them pinko professors and them nigger dope dealers and them goddamn smelly hippies!"

Lydia pushed open the trailer door and smiled at Clayton. "Hiya, Clay."

"Hey, mamma," he yelled. "Show us your bazoombies!"

Lydia glanced at Rebecca. "He's Harry the Hard Hat tonight?"

"Just for the past few minutes," she replied, shifting closer to Sean so that Lydia could sit on the floor next to Clayton. "Before that he was Billy the Bumpkin."

"Pay no attention to the man behind the curtain," Sean muttered.

Lydia laughed, relaxed in the free surroundings and relieved to be away from her father. "Sean, did you memorize the *Wizard of Oz* or something? Thanks," she said as Rebecca handed her the hookah tube and Clayton went into the kitchen.

"Best movie ever made," Sean replied. "I've seen it fifty times."

"He drives me nuts when it's on TV," Rebecca added. "He sits there and recites the whole fucking movie from start to finish, every single word."

Lydia inhaled the hashish smoke, held it in briefly, and then let it out. "Where'd you get this, Becky? This is great hash."

"It's Sean's."

Lydia turned to him. "You had this with you all the way up here and you didn't share it with anybody in the car?"

He smiled at her. "Nope."

"What a rat!"

"Yup."

Clayton sat back down and handed Lydia a beer. "So to what do I owe the pleasure of this visit?" She summarized for him the events that had just transpired in her house, and when she was finished, he shook his head. "Bummer," he said.

"Really," she replied.

"You shouldn't have left Dorcas there all by herself," Rebecca said quietly.

"Hey, if she wants to leave, she can leave. I'm sick and tired of being her keeper, you know?"

"She isn't strong like you, Lyd. You remember how she acted when your mother . . . when she like passed away. . . ."

"You mean when she killed herself?" Lydia asked evenly. "You don't have to be afraid to say it. It don't matter to me." She paused. "I mean, I loved her and I miss her and I wish she hadn't done it, but I'm not ashamed of it or anything. I mean, it was all Dad's fault anyway. Sure as hell wasn't mine."

"Yeah, sure, right," Rebecca said quickly. "But I mean, Dorcas really kinda flipped out when it happened, and then when she took that acid and really went nuts . . ."

"Look, Becky," Lydia said tiredly. "I love Dork. I'm closer to her than I am to anybody in the world, and I care about her and I make sure she gets out and sees people and goes places and all that shit. But I don't need a goddamn shadow, you know? She knows where I am right now. If she wants to come here, too, fine. If not, fuck her."

"I'd love to," Clayton said as he relit the hookah. "It sounds so delightfully incestuous."

Lydia forced herself to laugh, though she did not find this jocular reference to incest at all amusing. "Clay, you're such a pig."

Rebecca saw Lydia's hands shaking slightly. The girls served each other as confidantes, and so she knew why this particular conversation caused Lydia so much pain. "Clay," she said seriously, "cut it out, will you?"

Clay looked at Sean, his eyes twinkling. "They think I'm kidding."

"You better be!" Lydia said in a tone not quite flippant.

"Just think about it," he said, and then inhaled some hashish smoke. "Identical twins. What a threesome it would make! Two identical mouths, four identical legs, four identical tits, two identical—"

"Clayton . . ." Lydia warned. Even though she was pretending to be a good sport, this oft-repeated fantasy of his made her very uncomfortable.

"But to tell you the truth, it's Sarah I'd like to get between the sheets," he mused.

"With that rod she's got stuck up her ass?" Sean asked.

Clayton shrugged. "Might make her tighter."

"Stop it, Clayton," Lydia insisted, punching him in the arm just a bit too hard for it to be playful. "I don't think this is funny, okay?"

He relented. "Okay, okay, just kidding."

"Yeah, I'll bet you are," she muttered.

Rebecca did not find the conversation amusing either, so she changed the subject. "Let's go do something. If we just sit around here smoking hash, we're all gonna be asleep in a half hour."

"Let's go drinking at your boyfriend's place," Sean suggested.

"Huh?"

"Your boyfriend. You know, Alex Sonovbitch."

"Oh, Al." She laughed. "You know, I went into his bar yesterday, looking for Clay, and I swear he almost had a heart attack from having to talk to me."

Sean smiled and shook his head. "You're cruel."

"I am not. He loves it. It's probably the high point of his day."

"You gotta watch weird old men like him, Becky. He might really get mad about you messing with his head."

"Alex? Don't be silly. He's a pussycat."

Sean took his turn with the pipe stem and then asked, "What's his problem, anyway? What's he so bitchy about all the time?"

She shrugged. "Beats me. He isn't getting any, that's for sure, and I think it's driving him nuts. Every time I see him he stares at my boobs like he can't quite figure out what they are."

"So why doesn't he go to the whorehouse in Newburgh and get his horns trimmed, if that's the problem?"

"Alex part with twenty-five bucks!" Clayton exclaimed. "Are you kidding?"

"And just how do you know how much it costs at the whorehouse in Newburgh?" Lydia asked evenly, leveling her eyes at him.

Sean laughed loudly. "Whoops!"

"I've heard tell, I've heard tell, yup, yup," Clayton replied, slipping into his Billy the Bumpkin persona.

"Very funny," Lydia muttered.

"Look, let's go do something," Rebecca repeated. "And I don't want to just go to Al's place. He waters down the beer, there's no jukebox, and I hate that stupid fucking bowling machine of his."

Lydia's eye lit up with a sudden inspiration. "Hey! You guys haven't heard about it!"

"Heard about what?" Rebecca asked.

Clayton passed the pipe stem to Sean. "What are you talking about, Lyd?"

She looked in turn at Clayton, Sean, and Rebecca as she asked, "How would you guys like to see a real live, honest-to-God, genuine, dyed-in-the-wool goblin?"

* * *

The same dream, always the same dream.

Time passes and the details of memory shift their forms, becoming other than they once were. Small things assume centricity in the dream memory and become large and awful, while things great and majestic shrink into nothingness. Seasons merge and blend, events partake of each other, and the past fact drifts far from the present memory, and memory is influenced by dreams, and dreams reflect the imperfection of the aging, fading mind.

What had happened on that strange and terrible day? Had it been as he now dreamed it? Had it been otherwise? Is the waking memory the reality, or is the sleeping dream the reality?

And is there truly such a thing as reality, or are we all walking phantoms from a dream in the mind of Purusha, the slumbering god?

Ashvarinda Patanjali saw himself sitting in the lotus posture within his small living quarters. In his dream as in his daily meditative exercises, he saw the brilliant white light glowing upon his forehead and upon his chest, and by an act of will he caused the glowing energy, the life-giving *prana*, to spread out to every inch of his body, and he drew stength and life and peace from the *prana*, which was the very breath of God.

"Rinda," he heard Vernon calling from a distance.

Not now, Vernon. Not now, my little friend, my poor little outcast. Later I will walk with you through the woods and laugh with you at the birds and the little squirrels and find a cold stream to drink from and wade in. Now I meditate, Vernon. Now I renew all that I am.

"Rinda," Vernon called again.

Oooooommmmm, he chanted in the silence of his meditation, not needing to verbalize the mantra.

"Rinda! *Rinda!*" Vernon screamed.

The laws that govern dreams allow for movement without motion, and Ashvarinda Patanjali stood horrified as he watched the long mottled snake slithering toward the geek cage where Vernon Sweet was cowering, whimpering, trembling.

"*Rinda!*"

His feet were made of lead and he ran through an ocean of quicksand, trying to reach the cage before the snake, hoping that he would be able to unlock it and free his friend.

Slowly, so slowly he moved. So quickly did the snake slither.

"*Rinda!*"

His hearing, awake or asleep, was sensitive, and he heard the voices drifting to him. Dream voices? Real voices? Voices floating up from his sleeping mind or voices floating down upon his sleeping body? He did not know as he ran with agonizing slowness toward the cage.

"Who's he?"

"That's the other guy, the yogi guy."

"Like the Maharishi, that guy with the Beatles?"

"Yeah, I guess so."

"Where's the goblin, Lyd?"

"I don't know. Let's find another window."

"Shhh, shhh, not so loud."

"*Rinda!*"

He was close enough to the cage to see the face of the serpent, to see the cold eyes alive with appetite. He saw the jaws of the reptile open and unhinge, and he screamed as the beast's two long fangs became four and then eight and then grew innumerable as it slipped between the bars of the cage and clamped its jaw shut upon the back of Vernon's head.

"Goddamn it, Sean, will you watch what you're doing? That's my fucking foot!"

"I'm sorry. Jesus, how can I watch what I'm doing when it's so dark?"

"Shhh!"

"*Rinda!* RINDA!"

Vernon Sweet's eyes went wide as his brain was sucked out of his shattered skull and Ashvarinda Patanjali was yards away, unable to help. Then in an instant he was right in front of the cage, watching in speechless horror as the serpent's broad, flat head grew large and round, as short, stubby legs grew out of the long leathery body.

"Rshhhssssss," the snake breathed, staring at him, its rows of fangs still buried in Sweet's skull. The reptilian eyes grew vaguely human, and long, thin arms began to erupt from the scales just below the quivering head. "Rnnnssss," the thing breathed louder. "Rnnnnnn."

Ashvarinda's body shook uncontrollably as the creature dropped Sweet's body onto the floor of the cage and smiled at him. "Rinnnnn," it said. "Rinnnnnnd . . ."

"*Bhagawan Vishnu,* " the yogi whispered, "*meyriy muhdud kuhro. . . .*" Lord Vishnu, help me, help me. . . .

Two Vernon Sweets were in the geek cage. One was lying dead, the other standing and staring at Ashvarinda Patanjali.

"Rinda," it said.

Om, shanti, shanti, shanti . . .

"This sucks, Lydia. Let's go."

"You gotta see this guy, Clay, really. You won't fucking believe it."

"Rinda," Sweet said.

I know what you are. It took me much time, much thought, much prayer, but I know what you are, and I know why Vishnu guided my feet to this land across the water. I alone can guide you and control you and bind

*your memory with psychic chains, that you may not take
human life, that you may remain forever in this form,
that you may forget who you are and what you
are. . . .*

"Rinda, Rinda, wake wake." Sweet was shaking his
arm, and he sat up on the long mat that served as his
bed. "Come see, come see. Friends! Friends for Vernon!"

"What are you saying, Vernon?" he asked, blinking
his eyes to dispel the vestige of sleep that was clouding
them.

"Come see, come see," Sweet repeated eagerly. "Hi
hi hi, hello! Hi hi hi, hello!"

He rushed from the room, pulled open the front
door of the old house, and ran down the steps. "Vernon,
wait!" Ashvarinda called, and then, tightening his white
loincloth, followed him out into the darkness of night.

Sean Brenner was lighting a cigarette as he, Clayton, Rebecca, and Lydia walked through the woods back
to Rebecca's car. "Well, that was a lot of fun, Lyd. Really
great idea."

"Well, shit, we didn't stay around long enough to
see him! I'm not kidding, man, when me and Dork saw
him a couple of days ago, I almost shit in my pants!"

Sean ignored her. "You want to go to Alex's place, or
you want to drive to Charlie's?"

Rebecca shrugged. "Charlie's is a long drive, and
we're all pretty fucked up."

"I don't know," Clayton said. "The air's kinda got me
straight. Charlie's ain't so far away." He turned to Sean.
"Gimme a cigarette, would you?"

Sean complied. "Alex's is a lot closer."

"But the place sucks, Sean."

"Look," Lydia insisted. "Why don't we just go knock
on the front door and act like we're just being neigh-
borly, like welcoming them to town or something?"

"Forget it, Lyd," Rebecca said. "It sounded real exciting and different before, but I feel like a Peeping Tom or something now."

"Hey, Lydia!" Clayton said. "I got an idea. Let's go peek in the windows at your place and see if we can catch Sarah or Dorcas naked."

"Fuck you, Clay," she spat.

"Sean . . ." Rebecca said softly, squinting her eyes and peering into the darkness behind them. "What's that?"

He looked in the direction of her gaze and squinted also. "I . . . I don't know. . . .

Vernon Sweet was running toward them on his short, bandy legs, his arms outstretched, yelling, "Hi hi hi, hello! Hi hi hi, hello!"

"Holy shit!" Clayton muttered. "Is that . . . ?"

"Yeah," Lydia said nervously. "That's Grogo."

Sean took a step backward and Rebecca moved behind him. "Is he . . . I mean, he looks like he's charging at us. . . .

"Hi hi hi, hello! Hi hi hi, hello!"

Rebecca coughed. "I'm getting out of here." She began to run back toward the car, and her companions followed immediately. Their brisk jog became an all-out sprint as the little man drew closer to them.

"Hi hi hi, hello! Hi hi hi, hello!"

Sean tripped on a tree root and tumbled hard down onto his side. He scrambled to rise but his feet slipped on wet leaves and he fell again. By the time he got to his feet, Vernon Sweet had almost reached him. He backed away, yelling, "Get the fuck away from me, you goddamn retard!"

"Hi hi hi, hello!" Sweet repeated, but the hostility in Sean's voice seemed to have awakened long-buried anger in him, and his broad smile grew hard and sardonic as his voice dropped lower. "Hi hi hi, hello!"

"Vernon!" Ashvarinda cried from far back in the woods. "Where are you? Vernon! Come back, Vernon!"

Sean began to run again, just as Sweet's hand raked against the back of his jacket. Clayton, Lydia, and Rebecca had already reached the car and started the engine, and Sean saw the front door waiting open for him as the maddening greeting kept repeating from close behind him, lower and more menacing in tone with each repetition.

"Hi hi hi, hello! Hi hi hi, hello! Hihihi hello! Hihihihellohihihihellohihihihello!"

Sean leaped into the car and Rebecca sped off before he was even able to close the door. "Jesus Christ, did you see that guy!" Rebecca exclaimed.

"Told you." Lydia was grinning, pleased at having her suggestion validated.

"What the hell was wrong with him?" Sean asked, shaking and breathing heavily. "I think he was trying to attack me."

"Like heavy-duty weird," Clayton muttered.

Vernon Sweet watched the red taillights disappear into the distance. "Hi . . . hi . . ." his low, guttural voice rasped. "Hello . . ." He heard a sound off to his right, the sound of footsteps. He turned and smiled hungrily. "Hi," he said.

Dorcas Ostlich emerged from the darkness of the woods and walked toward him.

He stretched out one long arm toward her, his delicate fingers quivering like serpents. "Hi . . . hi . . . hi . . ." he said.

She took his hand and squeezed it warmly. "Hello, Vernon," she said. "Do you remember me from the other day? My name is Dorcas. Remember?"

He stared up at her quizzically for a few moments, and then his face softened. "Dor Dor!" said Vernon Sweet. "Hello!" They walked slowly back toward the house, hand in hand.

Chapter Four

November 22, 1968

Alex Brown gazed out the window of his bar with irritation and distaste. From his vantage point he could see the sheet-and-blanket-swathed heathen walking nimbly toward the general store across the street at the same time that Clayton Saunders parked his jeep unevenly in front of the bar.

What is the world coming to? he wondered glumly. Old Man Schilder is right. We got them hippies up on the mountain, and now a heathen and a circus freak move in. It's disgusting, it's horrible.

"Afternoon, Al," Clayton said merrily as he stomped into the bar. "It is afternoon, isn't it? What time is it, anyway?"

Alex Brown gritted his teeth as he replied, "Two o'clock."

"Ah, good. I was right, then." He slid up onto one of the bar stools. "I'll just take a beer, then. A little too early for a drink."

"So what's a beer?" Alex muttered, but placed a glass beneath the tap nonetheless.

"Mother's milk, Alex, mother's milk." Clayton yawned. Alex placed the beer in front of him and he took a long swallow and then emitted a contented sigh. He saw Alex looking past him toward the window, and he followed the direction of the older man's gaze. "Oh, the Hindu," he said, watching Ashvarinda Patanjali entering the store.

"Should wear clothes," Alex muttered to himself.

Clayton chose to pretend that this was part of a conversation, so he added, "Yeah, and take a bath." He laughed softly as Alex shot a dagger glance at him and then turned his attention back to the sink. Clayton drained the glass and said, "Another, Alex, if you'd be so kind. And . . . oh, what the hell, a shot of bourbon, too. Hair of the dog, as they say."

Two o'clock in the afternoon, Alex thought angrily as he refilled the beer glass and poured the shot.

Clayton nursed the boilermaker and Alex began to wonder what he was doing there. It was Clayton's custom to stop in, have a drink, ridicule whoever else was in the bar, and then be off on his way to whatever he happened to be doing that day; but now he sat and waited, as if Browns' Hotel was in fact his destination. Alex did not ask him about it. The less they said to each other, the better Alex liked it.

Soon thereafter Ashvarinda left the general store, carrying a large brown paper bag from the top of which extended the green stems of assorted vegetables. He stepped off the curb, very carefully looked both ways on the deserted street, and then walked over to Alex's bar.

Let him try to come in here for a drink, Alex thought angrily. Just let him try. I'll kick his black ass into the street, by God, kick him into the gutter where he belongs.

Ashvarinda walked up the few steps to the door and then pushed it open slowly. He walked in, set his grocery bag down upon a table, and then approached the bar. He placed his palms together, brought the tips of his fingers to his lips, and bowed slightly to Alex. "*Namas-tay*," he said softly. I bow to you. He turned his entire body to Clayton and repeated the gesture. "*Namastay.*"

"Nama can stay wherever he wants." Clayton grinned, lifting his shot glass in a gesture of greeting.

"What do you want?" Alex spat.

"The proprietor of the store is unfortunately out of nuts—" Ashvarinda began to explain.

"If you're looking for nuts," Clayton interrupted, "you're in the right town."

Alex glowered at him for a moment and then looked back at the aged yogi. "So? So what?"

"He suggested that I see if you have nuts available for purchase." He paused, looking from Alex to Clayton. "I am what you would call a vegetarian, you see. I do not eat meat, and—"

"I know how that is." Clayton nodded. "I'm on a liquid diet myself."

Ashvarinda glanced at the amber liquor in the shot glass. So much poison in this culture, he thought sadly. "In any event, I have been able to purchase most of the vegetables I seek, but—"

"I ain't got no nuts," Alex muttered, and then thrust another clean glass into the soapy water.

Ashvarinda looked with some perplexity at the row after row of cellophane bags attached to the clips of the nut rack, and Clayton was about to make a quip about Alex's last statement, when the door opened and Russell Phelps walked in. "Hi, Clay," he said. "Artie gave me the message. Why'd you . . . ?" He stopped speaking when he noticed Ashvarinda, and he smiled broadly. "*Namastay,*" he said with a curt, prayerful bow.

"*Namastay,*" Ashvarinda bowed back, repeating the gesture once again, pleased and surprised at the young man's courtesy and knowledge.

"My name is Russell Phelps." He was aware of caste prohibitions, and thus knew better than to attempt to initiate a handshake.

"I am Ashvarinda Patanjali"

"I'm honored to meet you, Pantanjaliji."

Ashvarinda smiled. "You seem to know quite a bit about our culture, young man,"

"I've always been interested in India," Russell explained. "I visited your country two years ago, during the summer, and—"

"The summer!" He laughed. "Summer is not the best time for Americans to visit India!"

Russell returned the laugh. "Yeah, it was kinda hot." He glanced at the table upon which Ashvarinda had placed his grocery bag, and he gestured toward it, saying, "Please, sit down." He saw neither Alex's furious glower nor Clayton's amused smirk as he and Ashvarinda seated themselves. "I'm a great admirer of Jawaharlal Nehru," he said.

Ashvarinda shrugged noncommittally. "The Nehrus are secularists."

"Of course they are"—Russell nodded—"and they have a difficult task ahead of them. India has been drowned in religion, castrated by imperialism—"

Clayton leaned to Alex and said, "That must be why he's looking for nuts." Alex ignored him.

"—pressured by America through our puppet state in Pakistan. India has to deal with a hostile Chinese regime, a terrible population pressure, crippling ethnic diversity. . . ." He shook his head. "Your government has an awesome job to do. At least the Soviet Union is giving some support and assistance."

"Yes, well . . ." Ashvarinda made a motion to stand.

"I've been following Indian policy toward East Pakistan with great interest," Russell went on, and Ashvarinda remained politely seated. "The Bengalis have been second-class citizens in Pakistan for two decades now, and I wouldn't be surprised if the separatist movement—"

"Russ," Clayton broke in.

"What?"

"All the guy is trying to do is buy some nuts. Give us all a break, will you?"

He looked back at Ashvarinda. "Nuts?"

"Yes. As I was explaining, I am a vegetarian."

"Of course you are."

Ashvarinda blinked. "Are you a vegetarian?"

Russell coughed. "Well, no, but I have the greatest respect for the ethical aspect of vegetarianism, and of course I respect the ethnic tradition."

"What a guy!" Clayton chuckled.

"Yes . . . yes, well . . . " Ashvarinda did not quite know how to behave in the midst of what was to him a peculiar social situation, so he attempted to extricate himself from it by saying, "I have been unable to purchase nuts in the general store, and the proprietor of this establishment has informed me that he, too, is lacking a supply of the food."

"Yeah." Clayton nodded earnestly. "Alex ain't got no nuts."

Russell looked over at the bar. "Excuse me, sir, but you have rows of nuts over there."

"They ain't for sale," Alex muttered as he dried a glass.

Russell frowned in confusion and then began to bristle. "Oh, sure. I get it. He isn't wearing a gray flannel suit and his skin's a little too dark for your tastes, right?"

Alex's face grew red with anger. "Who do you think you're talking to? You get the hell out of here!"

"Hold on, hold on," Clayton said calmly. "Let's not all get pissed off. Al, just sell the old man some nuts and be done with it."

"You don't tell me what to do in my place!" Alex shouted.

"I'm not, I'm not," Clayton said soothingly. Jeez, what an asshole! "Look, I'll pay you double for ten bags, okay? You charge a dime for 'em, right? Here's two bucks," and he took the money from his pocket and placed it on the bar top. "Just give him ten bags and he'll be on his way. Okay?" Alex did not respond, and Clayton repeated, "Okay?"

Alex took the money, ripped a few bags of nuts from the rack, and tossed them in Ashvarinda's general direction. He had only taken six bags from the rack, but Clayton did not quibble. "There," the older man muttered. "Now get out."

Ashvarinda took the nuts and dropped them into the grocery bag. He smiled at Clayton. "Thank you for your generosity, young man."

"Skip it," Clayton said. "Hey, Al, another beer, and one for my friend."

Ashvarinda took his groceries and went to the door. "*Namastay,*" he said as he opened it.

"*Namastay,*" Russell said.

"Take Nama with you," Clayton said.

As Ashvarinda left the bar Clayton took the two fresh beers and went over to the table where Russell was still sitting. "Clay, why did you tell Artie to have me meet you here? How come we aren't doing this at your trailer?"

"Because Peter has been there for the past two days rehearsing his fucking speech, and he's driving me crazy." Clayton explained. "If I hear him talking about monomers and polymers one more time, I think I'll scream."

Russell nodded. "Yeah, that makes sense. Okay, now listen. We have to go over some very important procedural points, and you have to pay careful attention.

Remember, if you fuck this up, they won't let Peter speak."

"Have no fear," Clayton responded expansively. "The crystalline waters of the Beckskill River are in safe hands."

Russell grimaced. "Why doesn't that inspire me with confidence?"

"Because I'm a capitalist?" Clayton laughed.

Russell laughed also. "An accident of birth. You couldn't help it."

"Aw, thanks, Russ." Clayton said, simpering.

"Now listen . . ." Russell began explaining the intricacies of parliamentary procedure. To his surprise, Clayton actually listened carefully.

What are those bums talking about? Alex wondered.

Outside on the sidewalk, Ashvarinda was shaking his head sadly as he walked briskly back toward the River Road. So much anger in that poor man; he sighed inwardly. So much hatred. And he does not know that the pain of such feelings is but the bite of the serpent's teeth as it devours its own tail.

He started slightly at the blast of a horn, and he turned to see a car pulling to the curb beside him. He peered in through the window and smiled. "Dorcas!"

"Hello, Mr. Patanjali." She smiled. "This is my sister Sarah."

"*Namastay.*" He bowed. Sarah turned her face away pointedly and did not respond to his greeting, so he looked back to Dorcas. "I have been purchasing food."

"Oh, gee, we're just coming back from doing some grocery shopping over in Haddlyville," Dorcas said. "You should have let me know you needed things. I'd have been happy to pick them up for you."

"Oh, no." He laughed. "I would never trouble you in such a way. And it is not a far walk."

"Well, can I give you a lift back to the path?" she asked.

Before Ashvarinda could respond, Sarah snapped her head in Dorcas's direction and said, "I will *not* sit in the same car with that person!"

"Sarah!" Dorcas said quickly. "Please, you're embarrassing me."

"I don't care," she huffed. "Let him get an ox cart or something."

"Sarah!"

"I'll tell Daddy, I swear I will. You know how he feels about those two weirdos."

Ashvarinda coughed softly. "I enjoy walking, Dorcas. But thank you just the same."

"Well . . . okay. Will I be seeing you tomorrow?"

"Of course." He smiled, and then, bowing again, continued on his way.

Sarah frowned at her sister. "See him tomorrow where?" Dorcas shrugged as she drove away from the curb, and Sarah's eyes widened. "Dorcas, you didn't tell him about the meeting!"

She shrugged again. "They live in the town. It's a public meeting. They have their rights."

"Their rights!" Sarah exclaimed. "What on earth is wrong with you?"

Dorcas sighed. "Come on, Sarah, okay?"

"Well," Sarah said, her voice cattily imperious, "I suppose that this is what comes of spending so much time with those left-wingers. Their rights! He's a foreigner and the other one is retarded, and you want them to have their rights!"

Sarah continued to browbeat her sister all the way back to their house, and Dorcas accepted the assault in silence, thinking of all the things Lydia would be saying in response, if only Lydia were with them. But Lydia was with Clayton, and so Dorcas did not respond as her younger sister began to catalog her faults. She repressed a smile as she recalled something Clayton had once said about her sister Sarah. Some women, he had observed, are born to be mothers. And others are born to be mothers-in-law.

Chapter Five

Peter Geerson sat on one of the numerous wooden benches in the town hall and chewed the nails on his right hand nervously as he waited for the meeting to begin. His left hand was holding a pile of papers and a file folder, and at his feet rested a large plastic athletic bag. Dorcas Ostlich was sitting beside him, gazing at him adoringly, her hands clasping a stiff-bristled whisk broom, a metal dust shovel, and a thick burlap bag. Her expression went unnoticed as Peter turned to his right and asked Russell Phelps, "Where the hell is Clayton?"

"He'll be here, Pete. Don't worry. He knows how much this means to you."

"But it's almost two o'clock! He's the only one who has the right to speak at this meeting, not me. If he doesn't show up . . ."

"He'll show up, he'll show up," Russell insisted. "Calm down, will you? He can tell time, you know. He doesn't want the river fucked up any more than you do." He paused. "That's what he claims, anyway. I don't trust him. And besides, I still think you've got the wrong perspective on this."

"Russell, please." Peter sighed.

"The problem isn't just pollution, it's capitalism. If our economy were centralized and removed from market pressures, and if industry was nationalized—"

"Not now, not today, okay?" Peter heard the sound of more people entering the hall, and he turned to see Rebecca Saunders and Sean Brenner walking toward them. As they sat down beside Russell, Rebecca said, "Hiya, Pete, Russ. Hiya, Dork."

"Where is he?" Peter demanded.

"Billy the Bumpkin?" Sean replied. "He's outside talking to the locals about crop yields and rainfall and how we should all give the president a chance."

"Yeah"—Rebecca laughed—"and how we gotta stop the red menace even if it means bombing Vietnam back into the Stone Age."

"Oh, for Christ's sake," Peter muttered.

"He's just having a little fun," Rebecca said. "Don't get so upset."

Clayton ambled in a moment later and sat down to Peter's right. "Howdy."

"'Bout fucking time," Peter said reprovingly, though obviously relieved. "Where the hell have you been?"

"Pete, you gotta take things less seriously." Clayton grinned. "Ride with the tide and go with the flow, and all that shit."

"I think Peter's just a little nervous about standing up and speaking to all these people," Dorcas said. "I mean, who wouldn't be?"

"I wouldn't be," Clayton replied.

"Me neither," Rebecca and Sean said in unison.

"Clay, you know what you're supposed to do?" Russell asked.

"Sure. It ain't hard."

"Okay, but remember, I've got parliamentary procedure down pat—"

"Great," Clayton interrupted. "I'm glad that your two months of law school didn't go to waste."

Russell closed his eyes and forced himself to be

patient. "If they throw something at you that you can't handle—"

"I'll duck."

"I'm serious, man. If that happens, let me tell you what to say. Don't just shoot your mouth off."

"Me? Shoot my mouth off? Russell, you've cut me to the quick!"

"Listen, Clay, it's very easy for the chairman of the meeting to deny someone the right to speak if they don't follow procedures. This is important to Peter, so don't mess it up."

"All right, all right," Clay replied. "Jeez!"

It seemed as though every landowning family in Beckskill was represented in the room, and the soft conversations of the nearly three hundred people present combined to make the town hall's general meeting room very noisy. But the sounds of voices hushed suddenly and all heads turned toward the door as Vernon Sweet and Ashvarinda Patanjali entered.

By now everyone in Beckskill had heard of the return of the deformed man, but this was the first opportunity most of them had actually had to see him. Ashvarinda had swathed himself in clean white linen, for he had never in all his decades in America purchased Western clothes, and he forced himself to ignore the insults and derogatory observations uttered sotto voice as he led Vernon to one of the benches in the rear. Vernon was wearing a pair of baggy trousers and an ill-fitting workshirt that had been found in an old bureau drawer in his house. Ashvarinda had seen to it that Vernon dressed for the occasion, after Dorcas informed them of the date and time of the meeting.

It had not occurred to Dr. Ostlich that his daughter would transmit this information to Vernon and Ashvarinda, and he had been furious at her when he found out about it, almost as furious as he was at that very moment as he saw Dorcas sitting beside Peter Geerson and so close to Clayton Saunders. Lydia, of course, was nowhere to be seen. She knew her father, as town supervisor, was to chair the meeting, and so she made a point to be elsewhere.

Dr. Timothy Ostlich was the small town's sole physician, and as such was one of the few educated people living in Beckskill. (Clayton Saunders's three months of college attendance four years earlier did not count, of course.) Having been so valuable a community member for nearly a quarter of a century, it seemed only fitting that Ostlich should also be on the town council, and he had, in fact, been town supervisor for the past seven years.

He sat now behind the center of a long table that stood along the rear wall of the meeting room. To his left and right sat the other members of the town council: old Johann Schilder, who was staring angrily at Vernon Sweet's huge round head at the other end of the room; his son-in-law, Frank Bruno, local farmer; Walter Riha-czeck, ad hoc legal expert for the town; Mike Imhof, retired French teacher and Beckskill native who had returned to his hometown after thirty years in Albany; and Alex Brown, self proclaimed restaurateur, whose narrow eyes were fixed on Rebecca Saunders and Sean Brenner. *He's no damn good for her,* he was thinking. *He's going to get that poor child in trouble someday, that bastard, that bum.*

In front of the long table were the twenty rows of permanent benches and the folding chairs that had been fished out of the basement and dusted off for this occasion. Beckskill had town meetings so infrequently that a large turnout was both expected and encouraged. By the time Ostlich pounded his gavel and called the meeting to order, every seat was taken and dozens of people were standing along the wall near the door.

The gavel descended a few times, and the buzz of voices, which had subsided when Sweet and Ashvarinda had entered and then had risen again, settled into attentive silence. "This meeting will come to order," Ostlich intoned. "This is a public meeting of the town council of Beckskill, New York, November the twenty-third, the year of our Lord nineteen hundred and sixty-eight." He turned to Rihaczeck. "Mr. Secretary, I will hear a motion to dispense with the reading of the minutes from the last meeting."

"So moved," Rihaczeck said.

"Seconded," Alex Brown added.

"All in favor?" A multitude of hands were raised in the hall. "Opposed?" None. The gavel descended. "Motion is carried." Michael Imhof raised his hand. "The chair recognizes Mike Imhof."

Imhof cleared his throat. "Mr. Chairman, I want to open discussion on the subject of the Craigo factory."

"Seconded," Alex Brown said again.

"All in favor of opening discussion on the proposed construction of a factory in Beckskill by the Craigo Corporation?" Again the room was filled with raised hands. "All opposed?" Again none. "Motion is carried," Ostlich said. "Mr. Imhof, you may present your report."

Imhof was a husky man with silvery gray hair and a Napoleon III mustache and goatee, a vestigial image of his days as a French teacher. He cleared his throat once again, rose to his feet, and placed his right hand magisterially upon his stomach as he began to address the assembly. He had spent his entire professional life in front of a classroom, talking to groups of people, and he relished the opportunity to do so once again. Addressing the town meeting was all the more pleasurable because, unlike a classroom of teenagers, the people he was to speak to would actually be listening to him.

As Imhof moved from his opening remarks into an

enthusiastic explanation of the benefits that would accrue to the town from the construction of the factory, Peter Geerson turned back to Russell Phelps and whispered, "Isn't there supposed to be a time limit on each speaker?"

"Only if the chairman imposes one at the outset of the meeting," he replied. "Right now a member of council is presenting a report to the community, so technically he isn't a speaker. We have to hope that Ostlich doesn't impose a time limit before you get the chance to speak."

"This isn't a report," Peter said angrily. "This is a goddamn pep talk. He isn't giving any specific information on anything. He sure isn't making any comments on the ecological impact."

"Hey, this is an example of low-level bourgeois democracy. What did you expect?"

Time passed with agonizing slowness as Imhof spoke on and on, at last concluding by saying, "And so, on behalf of the council, I make two recommendations: one, that we as a community vote in favor of the construction of the Craigo plant; and two, that the council be formally empowered to use community funds to acquire the proposed site of the factory for the purpose of ceding the land to the Craigo Corporation. We make these recommendations after much thought and research and discussion, and it is our belief that by doing so we will be ensuring the prosperity and security of ourselves and our children and our children's children as well." A smattering of applause followed as he resumed his seat.

Ostlich smiled and nodded, saying, "Thank you, Mr. Imhof. Now, if there is no more discussion to be held on the matter, I suggest we put it to a vote and then turn our attention to the problem of the location of the plant."

"So moved," Rihaczeck said. Alex Brown opened his mouth to second the motion, but another voice cut him off.

"Point of order, Mr. Chairman," Clayton Saunders said.

Ostlich's expression of surprise turned to an angry glower. He was silent for a few moments as he thought hard, trying to find some procedural excuse not to grant Clayton the floor. There was none, and he knew it, so at last he said, "The chair recognizes Clayton Saunders." His voice was low and obviously displeased.

Clayton rose to his feet. "Friends and neighbors, we've all enjoyed the speech we just heard. But there's a downside to this factory issue, and it's a real downer of a downside."

"Mr. Chairman," Rihaczeck broke in, "if there is to be further discussion on this, I move that we set a time limit."

"Point of order," Clayton said again. "I have not yielded the floor." Russell stood up behind Clayton and whispered in his ear, and Clayton added, "Nor can a time limit be set on a speaker who has already been recognized, as I'm sure the chairman knows."

Ostlich drummed his fingers on the table and then said, "Sorry, Walt. He's right."

"As I was saying," Clayton went on, arching his back and placing his hand on his outthrust stomach in obvious mimicry of Imhof, "the community has the right to have all the facts presented to it before voting." He waved his hand toward Peter with a melodramatic flourish. "I have called upon the services of an expert witness who has been researching the environmental impact of the proposed factory, and I wish to present his findings to the community at this time."

"Point of order, Mr. Chairman," Rihaczeck said.

Thank God, Ostlich thought. "Yes, Mr. Rihaczeck?"

"This person is not entitled to speak in these proceedings. He is not a town resident."

Russell whispered again into Clayton's ear. "Mr. Chairman, *I* am a town resident, and I have the right to present evidence at a town meeting. This is my presentation, made through the agency of my associate Mr. Geerson. As such, the point of order just raised is invalid."

Russell smiled and winked at Peter as Rebecca leaned to him and whispered, "Hey, that sounded pretty good!"

"I spent all day yesterday rehearsing him," Russell whispered back.

She nodded. "I didn't think he could have come up with all that by himself."

Russell looked at the town council as Rihaczeck huddled with Bruno and Ostlich. "I bet I know what they're saying," he whispered to Rebecca. "They're going to try to prevent Peter from talking by refusing to accept him as an expert."

"And what will Clayton say?"

"Just listen." Russell was smiling broadly, enjoying the battle.

"Mr. Saunders," Ostlich said as Bruno and Rihaczeck resumed their seats, " the council sees no reason to accept your description of . . ." He paused and raised his eyebrows quizzically.

You know damned well who he is, Clayton thought. *Your daughter's nuts about him.* "Mr. Peter Geerson," he said helpfully.

"Yes, Mr. Geerson. Your reference to Mr., ah, Geerson as an expert witness cannot be accepted by the council without a full exploration of his credentials."

Peter handed Clayton a file folder and Clayton began to pull documents from it. "A copy of Mr. Geerson's diploma as bachelor of science from the State

University College at New Paltz. A statement verifying his appointment as research assistant in biochemistry at Queens College of the City University of New York. Certified letters of reference from professors of chemistry at Queens College and New Paltz College, testifying to Mr. Geerson's ability to research the ecological impact of the proposed construction."

"We have no way of knowing at this point in time that the documents you have presented are legitimate," Ostlich said.

Russell stood up and whispered to Clayton, "Tell him that the council must accept the legitimacy of the documents in the absence of any evidence to the contrary, subject to later verification."

"The council must accept the legitimacy of the documents in the absence of any evidence to the contrary, subject to later verification," Clayton said, and then, after grinning at Russell, added, "And section 12, paragraph 36, subsection 17 of the Town Incorporation Code of New York State states that refusal to accept such evidence in clear violation of parliamentary procedure serves to invalidate any subsequent actions of the council at that particular council meeting."

Russell rested his elbows on his knees and covered his face with his hands. Rebecca leaned to him and whispered, "What's the matter? Didn't he say it right?"

"He made it up." Russell sighed miserably.

Ostlich leaned over to Rihaczeck and asked, "Is that true?"

"I have no idea," he whispered back.

"Do we have a copy of the Incorporation Code?" Ostlich had never heard of the Incorporation Code.

"Of course not. Why would we, in a town this size?" Rihaczeck had never heard of it either.

Rebecca whispered to Russell, "Maybe Clay got

that stuff from the Town Incorporation Code all by himself."

Russell's face was still covered by his hands as he shook his head. "There's no such thing as a Town Incorporation Code. Only cities are incorporated. This is just a town."

"He's being advised by that fellow sitting behind him," Ostlich whispered to Rihaczeck. "He seems to know what he's doing."

"Yeah, they've prepared themselves for this, damn it. . . ."

"Furthermore," Clayton said loudly, "the matter before the town council today concerns town finances and has an impact on taxes and other revenues. I'm sure I don't have to remind the council of the risk they run of criminal liability in the event of a violation of legal procedures, as spelled out in Section 235c of the New York State Criminal Code."

"Oh, Jesus!" Russell sighed softly.

The drumming of Ostlich's fingers on the table grew louder and more rapid. "Is that supposed to be a threat, Mr. Saunders?"

"Heavens, no!" Clayton replied. "I just don't want to see any of you guys get in trouble."

Ostlich nodded. "Yes, of course you don't." He looked at Rihaczeck, who shrugged, and then said, "Very well. We will listen to Mr., ah, Geerson, and then bring the matter to a vote, if there are no further objections."

Alex Brown jumped to his feet. "Well, I object! We don't have to listen to these bums. I say we just throw them the hell out."

A wave of applause greeted his outburst, and Ostlich pounded the gavel hard. "Order!" he demanded. He turned to Alex and said, "Sit down. We can't afford to have anything happen here which might call the validity of the meeting into question."

"But these bums—"

"Alex, sit down!" Ostlich repeated sternly. Alex sat and placed his clenched fists on the table, his whole frame shaking with anger. His eyes met Rebecca's, and she winked at him. He looked away.

"Thank you, Mr. Chairman," Clayton said, and nodding to Peter, sat back down.

Russell leaned forward and whispered angrily, "What the hell is the matter with you? Was that supposed to be funny or something? What if they had called your bluff? Where would we be then?"

Clayton shook his head with disapproval. "That's the problem with you goddamn commies. No sense of humor."

Peter went to the front of the room and handed each member of the town council a copy of the report he was about to present to the assembled town residents. Then he opened the athletic bag and said, "This bag is made of plastic. And what you are about to see is the residue of the manufacture of plastic, residue which is going to end up in your water." With that he upended the bag and a thick congealed mass fell with a loud spat onto the floor. The smell was sickening, and a chorus of disgusted protests were immediately directed at Peter.

Ostlich brought the gavel down hard on the table and said, "Order, Order!" He turned his furious gaze at Peter and said, "I'll thank you to clean that up immediately, young man! This is an official meeting, and we will not tolerate any cheap theatrics."

Clayton leaned back and whispered to Sean, "I think Doc Ostlich watches too much 'Perry Mason.'"

"Sure, okay," Peter replied to Ostlich's reprimand. "I just wanted everybody to see an example of what I was about to discuss." He glanced at Dorcas Ostlich, who responded to his signal by scurrying forward to scoop up the rancid jelly and dump it into the bag. She tried not to look up at the livid face of her father as she removed the noxious material from the hall.

"The report I've just given to the council explains everything in detail," Peter said to the townspeople, whose hostility was undisguised and whose anger was clearly visible on their faces. He tried to ignore it as he said, "Let me summarize it for you, and explain to you how the plastic is manufactured. This is not a process as simple as pouring metal into molds or welding steel. To make this plastic, you begin with two chemicals called monomers, specifically vinyl chloride and vinyl acetate. To these you then add a solvent and a catalyst. Heat the mixture up in a sealed reaction vessel, and you wind up with a copolymer, which is plastic in its raw form."

Sean leaned to Clayton and whispered, "I wonder if everybody else finds this as fascinating as I do."

Clayton laughed softly, and Dorcas said, "Shhh! This is important!"

"Yeah, right." Sean yawned.

"Once the copolymer has been produced," Peter went on, "it goes through other steps in the manufacturing process. After being washed with another solvent, the copolymer is dried, dyed, and mixed with plasticizing chemicals. The end result is a strong, durable material which can be made into products such as this plastic bag." He made an attempt at a dramatic pause, but this served merely to annoy the already impatient audience. "The only problem," he said at last, "is that this process results in the production of large quantities of vile, carcinogenic waste materials which are going to be dumped into the river and onto the land and will eventually show up in your water. And please, don't think of this waste as harmless, unimportant stuff that you don't have to worry about. Think of it as stuff that you drink when you get a glass of water in the kitchen. Think of it as stuff that is absorbed by your crops when you irrigate your fields. It's the stuff that will be in the water when you boil your spaghetti, when you sterilize your babies' bottles. If you have dairy cows, this stuff will be in their milk. If you raise chickens, this stuff will be in their eggs." He allowed his eyes to drift slowly across the room. "This is poison, ladies and gentlemen, poison. If the plastics factory is built on the banks of the Beckskill River, you're gonna be harvesting poisoned crops, breeding poisoned livestock, drinking poisoned water, and eating poisoned food." Peter let out a deep breath. "That concludes my report. Thank you."

He walked back to his seat, and Dorcas, who had returned to the hall after disposing of the gelatinous waste, grabbed his hand and squeezed it hard. "Peter, I'm so proud of you!" she gushed softly.

"Any other discussion of the matter?" Ostlich asked.

"Yes," said Dave Dolak, a local carpenter. "I move that we ignore this left-wing jackass and bring the matter to a vote."

"All in favor of accepting the council's recommendation?" Ostlich asked.

The hand of every town resident was raised, along with some but not all of the local farmers.

"All opposed?"

A few hands went up, Clayton's and Rebecca's among them.

"Point of order," Rihaczeck said.

"Mr. Secretary?" Ostlich prompted.

"Miss Saunders is under twenty-one."

"Accepted, Mr. Secretary. Miss Saunders, you cannot vote in these proceedings because you are not of legal age in this state."

"Pig!" she shouted, and was drowned out by imprecations.

"A revote is called for," Ostlich said. "All in favor?" A sea of hands waved. "All opposed?" The same few hands went up, except Rebecca's.

"Point of order," Clayton shouted.

Ostlich closed his eyes and bit his lower lip. "The chair recognizes Mr. Saunders."

"The vote is not unanimous. I move that a rollcall vote be taken."

Ostlich stared at him hatefully. "That will take time, Mr. Saunders."

Clayton shrugged. "I got nothing else to do."

Ostlich pounded the gavel to quiet the din that erupted after Clayton's remark, and then said, "A motion has been made for a rollcall vote. Is the motion seconded?"

A few long moments of motionless silence ensued. Ostlich smiled and was about to bring the gavel down again upon the tabletop and declare the motion void. And then, from the corner of his eye, he saw a hand shoot up from the back of the room.

"Hi hi hi," said Vernon Sweet. Ashvarinda Patanjali whispered to him, and then he said, "Second second second. First second third. Second second second. First second third."

The hall erupted into shouts of anger and laughter, and Ostlich's gavel was barely audible over the noise. "Order!" he yelled again and again, cracking the wooden table top with the small hammer. "Order!"

"He can't second a motion," Old Man Schilder yelled from his end of the table. "He only got half a brain! He can't vote in de meeting!"

Ostlich stood up behind the table, hoping that the sight of him standing imperiously before the assembly would quiet them in short order. Sure enough, one person saw him standing as if waiting for the opportunity to speak, and he quieted two others. They in turn urged calm, and in a few minutes some semblance of order had been restored.

"Now, I want everyone in this room to listen to me

very carefully," he began, summoning up every bit of authority his voice could muster. "We are going to deal with the issue, and then we are going to move on to the other issue confronting us today. This vote is important and it must be conducted properly. I want no further outbursts, and no disruptions. Is that clear?" It was, of course. Ostlich cleared his throat. "A motion has been made and seconded for a rollcall vote. I accept Mr. . . . Sweet's second as valid, inasmuch as I have no evidence to indicate that he has been declared mentally defective by a court. So, all in favor of a rollcall vote?" Only Clayton raised his hand. Vernon Sweet was smiling and looking around the room, and Ashvarinda could not get his attention. "All opposed?" The sea of raised hands once again arose.

Ostlich sighed, relieved at having finally dispensed with what should have been a quick and easy procedure. "The motion is defeated. Let the record indicate that the town of Beckskill has chosen to conclude the arrangement with Craigo Corporation, the vote in favor being an absolute majority of the voters present." He picked up the gavel once again and struck the table gently in a different spot. "The rest of this meeting concerns itself with negotiations for the purchase of the property which is the proposed site of construction. Inasmuch as this is a private matter which we are taking up with an individual citizen, the council will now meet in closed session. Mr. Sweet, we had not expected you to attend this meeting today, but since you are here, we request that you remain. And your, ah, friend, of course . . ."

The hundreds of people in the room had but one set of doors through which to exit, so movement from the town hall was slow. Clayton, Rebecca, and Dorcas had been separated from Peter and Russell by the tidal shifting of the crowd, so that the two out-of-towners found themselves surrounded by a sea of unfamiliar faces. Russell patted Peter on the back comfortingly as they shuffled toward the doors, saying, "Sorry, Pete. We did our best. But you didn't really expect to have any sort of impact here, did you?"

"Not really," Peter conceded, "but this is just the first step. The important thing is that my report has been read into the record, and that makes it public information. Now I contact some ecology lobbyists I've heard of, and some newspapers—" His words were cut off abruptly when someone in the tightly packed crowd bumped into him hard. "Watch it," Peter muttered; but then as a second and then a third unfamiliar shoulder jostled him, he realized that it had not been an accident.

"Who the hell asked you to butt into this, anyway?" a heavyset young man with a florid face demanded.

"Yeah, who even wants you in our town?" another stranger agreed, a wiry man whose muscular arms had heaved many a hay bale onto many a flatbed.

Russell and Peter exchanged apprehensive looks and then Peter yelped as a fist landed a short jab into the small of his back. He stumbled forward into the person in front of him, who immediately shoved him backward into someone else, who proceeded to shove him forward again. Russell began to reach out a hand to help steady his friend, but he felt a stabbing pain as an elbow rammed into his ribs and he spun around defensively.

And then they were standing outside the town hall, and the crowd was dispersing calmly in all directions as if nothing had happened. Peter and Russell were both trembling as Clayton, Rebecca, and Dorcas reached them and Dorcas grabbed Peter's arm. "Are you okay?" she asked with concern.

"Y-yeah," he stammered. "What the hell was that all about?"

Clayton frowned. "You goddamn furrinurs a'comin'

heah an' a'buttin in wheah you ain't wanted. Why, we oughta jus' string you up!"

"That wasn't funny, Clay," Russell said, breathing hard as he pushed his long brown hair away from his face. "That could have gotten real ugly real fast."

"Hey, don't take it so seriously." Clayton laughed, slapping Russell on the shoulder. "Nothing ugly ever happens here in Ox Bow, you know that."

"I was afraid they were gonna hurt you," Dorcas said, still clasping Peter's arm. She had grabbed it in a moment of sincere concern, and was now reluctant to let go of it.

"Yeah, so was I," he said, laughing with relief. He looked at Clayton. "Let's get out of here. I need a drink or something."

"Not yet," Clayton replied. "I want to hang around for a little while."

"What for?" Rebecca asked. "There's nothing else we can do here."

He looked back into the town hall's general-meeting room. "I want to say hi to the little guy who seconded my motion. We're neighbors, after all. Should be friends."

"Friends?" Sean asked. "Are you kidding? Friends with that thing?"

"Oh, sure, go ahead, be judgmental." Clayton grinned. "Don't you support the deformed-retard-rights movement?"

"Why should I?" Sean rejoined, laughing. "They have too much power as it is. They already run the government!"

"Look," Rebecca said, "I'm going back up to the trailer, see if Lydia's there. Anybody who wants to go with me, come on." She started to walk toward her car. Peter and Russell followed her wordlessly, each glad to be rid of the town hall.

"I'm gonna stay here with Clay," Sean called to her.

"I'll see you in a little while." He turned to Dorcas. "What about you?"

"I want to say hello to Vernon and Mr. Patanjali," she replied. "And then I guess I'll go home."

"VERnon," Clayton mimicked. "He a buddy of yours now, Dork?"

"He's a very nice little old man," she huffed. "It's not his fault that he has some problems."

"Is that all they are, some problems?" Sean laughed grimly. "He's got problems like a dog's got fleas."

Clayton barked and scratched for a few moments, and then he, Sean, and Dorcas sat down on one of the benches near the Civil War monument to wait for Ashvarinda Patanjali and Vernon Sweet.

Chapter Six

The large stretch of forest which had been owned by the Sweet family for well over a hundred and fifty years rested between the River Road and the foot of Saunders Mountain. Much of it had once been a farm, well back in the early-nineteenth century, but successive generations of Sweets had abandoned farming for trading, seafaring, hunting, fishing, trapping, and general malingering, so that what was once fertile if challenging farmland was now but a sixteen-square-mile expanse of thickly wooded forest.

Eland Sweet, Vernon's father, was a ne'er-do-well whose cheerful disposition endeared him to everyone, and whose sole means of support was the potent moonshine he brewed and sold furtively to other locals. He married Clara Koenig, daughter of a local minister, who promptly disowned her. Eland and Clara lived simply in the old Sweet house, and their income derived largely from Clara's job as a clerk in the dry-goods store in Beckskill. Clara gave birth to two healthy boys, then three healthy girls, and then Vernon. The delivery almost killed her, and the product seemed unworthy of the effort. For obvious reasons, she bore no more children, and proceeded to drink herself to death a few years later.

By the midpoint of the twentieth century, very few Sweets were left. Both older brothers were long since dead, and of the three sisters only Edith Sweet had remained in Beckskill, living on her modest schoolteacher pension and sinking deeper with each passing year into a cranky old spinsterhood. She disliked everyone except little Dorcas Ostlich, to whom she taught sewing and knitting and cooking and a dozen other domestic skills. With her death in 1963, the Sweet line, it was generally assumed, had come to an end. And then Vernon returned to Beckskill and took up residence in the old family house.

The house itself was typical of post-Colonial rural architecture. The basic, central structure was the log cabin built by Harrison Sweet, Vernon's great-great-grandfather, who had settled along the banks of the Beckskill, fought the Iroquois, cleared the land, and established a claim in the last years of colonial New York. Great-grandfather Calvin had faced the logs with stucco and Grandfather Lucius had overlaid them with planks. The rest of the house followed the same type of pattern, with each generation making additions and alterations, until what was once the large unbroken interior of a one-room cabin was now the large central room of a house. Lucius had torn off half the roof and had added two upstairs rooms; at Clara's insistence, Eland had built on a kitchen and a porch, and had even indulged her in the extravagance of electricity. Someone, possibly Edith or one of her brothers or sisters, had installed a refrigerator and a gas-canister stove. But other than these two appliances and the power wire that ran under the ground from the utility pole on the River Road to the base of the house, no other modern conveniences were in evidence. The sole source of heat was the wood-burning fireplace, and a broken-down outhouse served other natural needs.

It might have been a picture of pristine rusticity, but the house was in serious need of repair. The porch steps bent and creaked beneath the feet of those who mounted them; the upstairs windows were cracked and boarded over; and decades of freezes and thaws had caused sections of the siding to split and fall off, uncovering in places Calvin's stucco and Harrison's ancient colonial logs.

Near the house stood an old barn, unused for the past seventy years, and used only for storage for a half century before that. It was a dry, brittle, colorless structure that seemed forever on the verge of collapsing. The barn, like the house, bespoke long years of inattention, for Edith had grown uninterested in such things during her long decline, and even Dorcas Ostlich's periodic cleaning binges did little to alleviate the general atmosphere of squalor and decay.

The house and barn stood in a clearing at almost the exact center of the property, two miles east of the River Road, two miles west of the foot of Saunders Mountain, two miles north of Beckskill proper, and two miles south of the farmland that Clayton rented to the local farmers. The property had once reached to the banks of the Beckskill River. It had been when the county decided to build the River Road back when Eland Sweet was a boy, and when his widowed mother had refused to sell her land along the bank, that the Sweets had first heard the phrase which even now was causing Ashvarinda Patanjali such confusion and concern: the right of eminent domain.

The elderly Hindu was frowning at the words in the dictionary. "Can they really do such a thing?" he asked.

Dorcas Ostlich nodded sympathetically. "I think so, Mr. Patanjali. They can, can't they, Clay?"

They were sitting on the floor of the large central room of the old Sweet farmhouse in the fading light of

dusk. Clayton had agreed to drive Vernon and Ashvarinda back home after they left the town hall, and he
now sat cross-legged and passed the third joint of the
afternoon over to Sean Brenner, who was trying very
hard not to look across at Vernon Sweet.

It was an odd little company. Dorcas to Ashvarinda's
right, watching the worried old man with concern
written on her face; Vernon Sweet sitting to the old
yogi's left, smiling at Sean with blank, empty, reptilian
eyes; Sean, his back partly turned from the little man,
giving Clayton little looks and head nods indicating his
desire to leave; Clayton happily drifting into a cannabis
stupor; and Ashvarinda gazing down at the words in the
crumbling old dictionary Dorcas had found in the
kitchen when she was cleaning the house the day before.

"Eminent domain," Ashvarinda muttered, reading
aloud the subsection definition of the word "eminent."
He shook his head. "I have lived in America for fifty
years, and never have I heard of such a thing."

"I don't think they do it too often," Dorcas said.
"Only like when they're gonna build a highway or
something."

He looked up. "So they can take our home away
from us."

"Gotta pay you for it," Clayton said, billows of
greenish smoke pouring from his mouth as he spoke.

"Tomatoes," Vernon said, staring at Sean.

Sean clenched his teeth and tried to ignore the
deformed man as Ashvarinda said, "We have just cleared
out an area near the house to plant a garden when spring
comes. Vernon loves to watch plants grow."

"Looks carnivorous to me," Sean muttered. "Hey,
Clay, let's go up to the trailer, okay?"

"Yeah, yeah, in a minute." Clayton yawned. He
smiled at Vernon and said, "So you were in the circus."

His smile was not a friendly one. It was perfunctory and somehow vaguely acerbic.

"Mean face." Vernon nodded.

Clayton's eyebrows rose. "Oh, really! You looked in the mirror lately?"

"Clayton!" Dorcas said.

Ashvarinda laughed. "No, no, mean face is the phrase Vernon uses to refer to the people who came to see him in the freak show. You must remember that the audiences were not friendly, not kind."

Clayton nodded. "Yeah, I guess not." He took another joint from his jacket pocket and lighted it, ignoring both Sean's pained look and Ashvarinda's unspoken disapproval. The aged Hindu came from a part of the world where opium and hashish were commonplace indulgences, and he knew full well what evil could come of them. Still, Clayton's karma was Clayton's karma, and Ashvarinda did not voice his thoughts. "So you're a yogi," Clayton said conversationally as he dragged on the joint and then handed it to Sean.

"I seek union with the Absolute through the discipline of hatha yoga," Ashvarinda replied.

"That means yes, right?" Clayton waited for Sean to hand back the joint, toked on it, and then asked, "What do you think of this Maharishi guy, the guy the Beatles are hanging around with?"

"Do you mean the Maharishi Mahesh Yogi? I know little of him," Ashvarinda said. "But as I understand it, he is seeking to introduce meditation to your people. If this is true, then his dharma is royal and his karma must be a well of goodness."

"Huh?"

"Hey, you got anything to drink?" Sean asked.

"We have tea," Ashvarinda replied. "Would you like some?"

He sighed. "Never mind."

"Drink? Drink? Medicine!" Vernon chirped. "Papa medicine! Drink drank drunk. Drink drank drunk."

Sean forced himself to look over at him. "What are you talking about, Grogo?" He used the pseudonym sarcastically and with undisguised contempt.

"Papa medicine," Vernon repeated, jumping to his feet. "Come see, come see! Drink drank drunk!"

No one made a move to rise and Vernon just stood waiting as Dorcas said, "I don't know much about Hinduism, Mr. Patanjali, except what we learn in school, about castes and stuff. I don't think anybody around here knows much about it. That's one reason why people seem so unfriendly to you. That, and this whole factory thing."

"The stranger is rarely welcome in the village short of rice," he said nodding.

"General store's got a shitload of rice," Clayton said, yawning once again.

"Oh, Clay, you know what he means," Dorcas said, and then turned back to the old yogi. "Do you, like, worship all sorts of gods and stuff like that?"

He shrugged. "We believe that all which exists is but a manifestation of the Absolute, and that the Absolute takes many forms as gods and men and animals. But there is only one God, as you would say it. And that one God is all that truly exists." He paused. "One of our ancient writings expresses it poetically, saying that the god Purusha fell asleep and dreamed the universe. Thus we are all shadows in Purusha'a dream, and life is an illusion."

Clayton nodded. "I always kind of suspected that this fucking town didn't really exist."

"Clay, come on, huh?" Dorcas said. "I'm interested in this."

"Yeah, you would be. They don't call you Dork for nothing." He paid no attention to the hurt look on her face as he said to Sean, "I'm dying of thirst. Let's go get some beer."

"Papa medicine, Papa medicine," Vernon repeated urgently. "Drink drank drunk. Come see, come see!"

Clayton's laughter was that of cruel amusement. "Come on, let's see what Grogo's getting all excited about." As he rose to his feet Vernon scurried from the room and ran from the house.

"Like talking to Lassie," Sean muttered. "Like you know he's trying to tell you something."

"Timmy, Timmy," Clayton cried, "the barn's on fire, the barn's on fire! Woof! Woof!"

Dorcas watched them follow Vernon out of the house and then said, "I'm sorry about them, Mr. Patanjali. They aren't very nice sometimes."

He shrugged again. "That is their karma, not yours, Dorcas."

"Their what?" she asked, and he began to explain.

Outside, Clayton and Sean watched with amusement and impatience respectively as Vernon began digging into the ground with his bare hands. The little man had run over to a large old oak tree that stood some fifty feet from the porch, and he was now burrowing frantically into the hard, cold earth, saying, "Papa medicine, Papa medicine, drink drank drunk," over and over.

Clayton's brow furrowed as a thought occurred to him. "Hey," he said slowly, "you know . . ."

"You know what?"

He thought for a few more moments and then turned to Sean. "I read somewhere that moonshiners, like in Kentucky and places that like, bottle the shit and then bury it. Like to let it ferment or age or something, or maybe to hide it from the revenuers, you know?"

Sean emitted a curt laugh. "You think old Grogo's daddy was a moonshiner?"

"Could be. A lot of the old men around here make their own booze, like wine and beer and stuff like that. I don't know when Grogo's parents died, but he looks to be like seventy or something, so it must be a long time ago. Twenty-five years, maybe."

"Moonshine buried in the ground for twenty-five years? And you'd drink it? That's disgusting!"

Clayton shook his head as he watched Vernon scratch at the hard earth. "What's better, Sean, beer made last week or beer made last year? Wine made last year or wine made five years ago? Bourbon made five years ago or bourbon made ten years ago?"

Sean considered this for a moment and then nodded at Clayton. "You got a point there."

They smiled at each other and then jumped down on their hands and knees and joined Vernon in throwing handfuls of dirt in all directions.

They dug for a few minutes, and their fingers were raw and sore by the time Sean touched the neck of the earthenware jug that protruded from the three-foot-deep hole. Another few seconds, and he and Clayton pulled the jug out.

"Holy shit!" Clayton exclaimed.

"Drink drank drunk." Vernon chortled.

"Yeah, I'll bet!" Clayton laughed. He struggled to pull out the cork, but it would not budge. "Hey, Grogo, you got a corkscrew in there someplace?"

"Drink drank drunk," Vernon repeated.

"Yeah, yeah, right, sounds great to me, too," Clayton said with strained tolerance. "Get me a corkscrew, or a knife. You understand, knife?"

"Knife," Vernon echoed, and then scurried back toward the house.

"And a cup," Clayton called after him. "Get us a cup."

"Cup!" Vernon cried happily as he ran up the stairs.

"What do you want a cup for?" Sean asked. "I don't think I've ever seen you drink out of anything except a bottle, except in bars."

"You ever drink moonshine?"

"No."

"Well, I have. And if this shit does to me what I think it's gonna do to me, I'll drop the jug if I drink from it."

Sean licked his lips. "Sounding better and better."

"There is a triad, not a trinity in the Christian sense," Ashvarinda was saying to Dorcas as Vernon rushed past them into the kitchen. "We believe that the Absolute manifests Itself in the form of three great gods, each of which represents one of the aspects of existence."

"But it's not like Father, Son, and Holy Spirit," Dorcas said, trying to show him that she was following what he was saying.

"No," Ashvarinda went on. "We speak of Brahma the Creator, Vishnu the Preserver, and Shiva the Destroyer."

"Cup! Cup!" Vernon sang as he ran past them again and bounded down the steps. He had taken a weathered old dipper from a nail on the kitchen wall and now handed it to Clayton proudly. "Cup!" he repeated.

Sean looked at the dirty, rusty ladle and said, "Real inviting, Grogo."

"Don't worry about it," Clayton said. "The moonshine'll strip it clean. Grogo, where's the knife?"

"Cup!"

"No, no, knife, knife."

"Cup!" Vernon insisted.

"This is *harder* than talking to Lassie," Sean muttered.

"Listen, Grogo," Clayton said. "We can't drink the medicine if we can't get the cork out. Understand? Cork must come out." He started laughing softly. "Naughty, naughty cork. Make bad cork go 'way."

"Cork!" Vernon agreed, nodding.

"Clay, let's just split, okay?" As Sean was speaking Vernon grabbed the jug from Clayton's hands and, placing it on the ground, bent over it and pressed his mouth to the cork. Sean was looking at Clayton and Clayton had turned to him and was about to reply, but a low gnawing sound, almost a very brief buzz, caused them both to turn to Vernon. The little man had apparently bitten through the entire neck of the jug, and he smiled at Clayton as he spat the piece of neatly sawed pottery out onto the ground. "Cork go 'way," he said happily.

"Way to go, Grogo!" Clayton laughed. "How the hell'd you do that?"

Sean stared at him. "Smile again, Grogo," he demanded.

Grogo smiled and Clayton asked, "Why'd you want him to smile."

Sean shrugged, still staring at Vernon. "His teeth looked . . . I don't know, funny for a minute, I thought. But I guess not."

Clayton studied the small, yellow, broken, and crooked teeth in the smiling, malformed mouth. "You guess not? Are you kidding?"

"No, no, I thought . . . I mean, for an instant I thought his teeth . . . " He sniffed. "Forget it."

Clayton already had. He had taken the jug and cradled it in his right arm, tipping it so that the contents could pour into the dipper he held in his left hand. The liquid had a slightly yellowish tinge and looked almost like brackish water, but the powerful smell that drifted up from the dipper made Clayton's eyes water. "Holy moley," he said. "I think we could put this shit in the gas tank of the jeep."

"You gonna drink it?" Sean asked.

"Drink drank drunk," Vernon said.

"Yeah, that's how it usually works, Grogo old boy," Clayton said, and placed the ladle to his lips. He took a very small sip, swallowed, waited for a moment, and then his face grew red as a beet and tears began pouring from his eyes. His trembling hands dropped the ladle and he fell to the ground, whining, shaking his head, clutching at his chest and stomach.

Sean dropped to one knee beside him. "Clay! Are you okay? Clayton!"

Clayton took a deep breath as some of the redness faded from his face. "Sean . . ." he gasped. "Sean . . ."

"You want a doctor? You want to go to the hospital?"

"Sean . . ." he gasped again, "that shit . . . that shit is fucking incredible! It's fucking *great!*"

"Yeah?" Sean asked, apprehension mingling with curiosity as he looked at the ladle that lay on the ground. "Maybe I'll try just a little . . . just a sip. . . ."

"Drink drank drunk. Drink drank drunk."

"Shut the fuck up, will you, Grogo?" Sean muttered. He poured a small amount of the fiery liquor and sipped it cautiously. A moment later he was sitting on the ground beside Clayton, and when he was able to speak again, he said, "Oh my God!"

"They don't call it white lightning for nothing." Clayton giggled.

"Clay, I think this shit could probably kill you."

"Oh, yeah, definitely. You gotta go slow with it."

Sean smiled stupidly. "Gives you a nice little buzz, though." He reached for the ladle and looked at it with distaste. "Grogo, you got something less disgusting than this? Like something that doesn't look like it's been used to clean up dog shit?"

"Cup!"

"Yeah, another cup. You got another cup?"

"Cup!" he sang, and then ran back to the house. He entered to find Ashvarinda and Dorcas deep in conversation, which he interrupted by saying, "Friends for Vernon!"

Ashvarinda smiled at him. "Yes, Vernon, it is good to make new friends."

"Cup!" He ran into the kitchen and began searching through the cabinets.

"And who is Krishna?" Dorcas asked, prompting the elderly man to resume the explanation of his religion. "You know, like with the Hare Krishna people in the airports?"

"Well"—he thought for a moment—"in your religion you believe that God took the form of a man, correct?"

"Yes, Christ."

"In our religion, we believe that Vishnu the Preserver does the same thing, frequently. We call these incarnations of Vishnu his avatars, and Krishna is his most famous avatar, though there have been many others."

"And what about that other god, Sh . . . what was his name?"

"Shiva," he repeated patiently. "Shiva the Destroyer."

"Yeah, Shiva. Does Shiva have avatars, too?"

"Cup!" Vernon cried as he ran past them and out again down the steps.

Ashvarinda Patanjali watched Vernon go and his lips barely moved as he said softly, "Yes. Shiva has avatars."

"That's more like it," Sean said, taking the cloudy glass from Vernon's hands. "It's dirty, but at least it ain't rusty." He poured some moonshine into the glass and took another sip. He and Clayton were still sitting on the ground, having reasoned that no purpose would be served by standing up before having another drink.

"Whoa!" Sean cried, falling backward to lie out flat on the cold ground.

"Agghhh," Clayton gasped a moment later. Sean took another sip, Clayton took another sip, then each took another, and another.

Soon they were both lying motionless on their backs, and Sean mumbled. "Hey, Clay?"

"Yeah?"

"I can't feel my feet or hands."

"Huh?"

"I can't feel my feet or hands."

"Weren't you paying attention in there? You don't have any. They're all an illusion. So are you and me."

"Yeah?" Sean laughed. "Well, this illusion's drunk on his ass already."

Clayton began to laugh uproariously. The quip was not particularly funny, but Clayton found it absolutely hysterical, and he rolled onto his side and doubled over. At last Clayton was able to say, "We better get going. If I drink much more of this, they'll have to bury me in that hole. I mean, this stuff is like unbelievable."

"Great fucking shit," Sean said as he struggled to get up onto his hands and knees.

"Great fucking shit," Clayton agreed, staggering to his feet.

"Great fucking shit," Vernon echoed happily. Those words coming from Vernon Sweet seemed so incongruous and absurd that Sean and Clayton collapsed back onto the ground in laughter, and a few minutes passed before they once again made the effort to stand up.

"I feel like I just drank a quart of bourbon." Clayton smiled.

"Grogo," Sean said, "tell Dorcas we're leaving,

okay? You know, Dorcas? Say bye-bye for us to Dorcas. You understand?"

"Bye-bye. Bye-bye."

"Yeah, hang loose, Grogo," Clayton said, and began stumbling toward the woods.

"Bye-bye. Bye-bye." Vernon watched them walk off into the forest and then turned and scurried back to the old cabin.

"That little freak drives me nuts," Sean muttered as he followed Clayton into the woods.

It was after dark by the time Dorcas returned to her father's house. Fascinating stuff, she thought as she opened the front door. I guess everybody wonders what's real and what isn't. I have, anyway. But maybe it's just that bad acid trip I had that makes me think about that kind of thing.

She closed the door loudly behind her and then went into the living room. She tossed her parka on the floor and then sat down on the sofa to pull off her boots. It had been snowing lightly as she trudged back through the woods from Vernon's house, and the snow on her hair had melted as soon as she was in the warm house. She considered leaving her braids intact to dry so that her hair would be all ripply when she undid them later, but they were so wet that they were dripping down her back and making her extremely uncomfortable. Better dry my hair, she thought as she rose from the sofa and walked up to her bedroom. I feel kind of chilly anyway. Don't want to get sick.

She unwrapped her braids and plugged in her hair dryer, and then stood motionless in front of the mirror, staring at herself. She smiled sadly. I look just like Lydia with my hair like this.

Dorcas flipped the "on" switch and began running a brush through her hair as she bombarded it with the stream of hot hair. Thank God, I'm *not* Lydia, she thought. I don't think I could live with myself, doing what I did. I think I'd hate myself so much that I'd . . . well, I'd try to do what she tried to do, slitting her wrists like that. It's all so crazy. It wasn't her fault . . . she was just a kid . . . and Daddy was a grown man. It's his fault, all his fault, Mom's suicide, Karen's breakdown. . . .

Karen's breakdown?

She paused. What on earth am I thinking? Lydia never tried to kill herself. She's too strong for that, too resilient, too self-assured. She sighed. It's the acid. Must be the acid. When I flipped out that time, everything just got all jumbled up in my head, all my memories just got all screwed up. It was after that bad trip that *I* tried to kill myself, not Lydia. And I don't even *know* a girl named Karen.

She emitted a grim laugh. "Good point, Mr. Patanjali," she whispered. "What is reality, anyway?"

"Lydia!" Her father's voice attacked her from the doorway. "Where's Sarah?"

Dorcas turned to him, "Daddy, I'm not—"

"I asked you a question, young lady," he said, grabbing her roughly by the arms. "Where is your sister?"

"I . . . I don't—"

"Don't lie to me, Lydia!" he shouted, shaking her. "I sent her out to find you and Dorcas this afternoon, and she never came back. Where is she?"

He shook her harder and she started screaming. "Let go of me. Get away from me!"

"Damn it, Lydia!" he bellowed. "Where's Sarah?"

"I'm not Lydia!" she cried. "I'm Dorcas!"

He released her abruptly and stepped back. He stared at her for a moment and then said more calmly, "Have you seen Sarah?"

"No," she replied, weeping.

"She should have been back hours ago, even if she didn't find you or that sister of yours." He worked his fingers together nervously, thinking hard. "You stay here, right here, do you understand? Don't you leave this house." He turned and walked to the bedroom door, muttering, "I'd better call the police."

It was only then that Dorcas understood the gravity of the situation and the depth of her father's concern. Sarah was missing.

Chapter Seven

November 25, 1968

Alex Brown relished the atmosphere of community, the feeling of belonging, as he stood in the large crowd of neighbors who were milling about in front of the town hall, speaking with each other in hushed tones. He hoped that everything would turn out all right, of course. They all hoped that everything would turn out all right. Sarah Ostlich was a good girl, not the type to run away from home or stay somewhere for even one night, not to say two, without discussing it first with her father. Perhaps she had injured herself and was unable to move. Perhaps she had tripped over a root somewhere in the woods and had knocked herself out. Perhaps she had stepped into a bear trap.

Perhaps she was dead.

No one uttered these words, but they were in the minds of everyone as they waited for Dr. Ostlich and Mike Imhof to speak. Desultory conversations about weather and politics passed the time, and only occasionally did anyone make reference to the reason for the hastily assembled search party. "Last thing we know is that her dad sent her out to try to find her sister. . . ." Alex heard someone say. "Probably went up toward where them damn hippies live. . . ." another voice commented from another conversation elsewhere in the crowd. Alex smiled grimly when a third voice reached him, saying, "Ought to check out the woods around the Saunders place, if you ask me."

Goddamn bums, he thought.

As if in response to the comments and the thoughts, Clayton and Rebecca Saunders pulled up to the curb near the town hall. She turned off the engine in her blue Camaro and then she and her brother walked quickly toward the crowd.

Rebecca had overheard a conversation about the planned search party while she was in the head shop in Rosendale buying a new hash pipe and some black light posters. When she told her brother about it, he had decided with an uncharacteristic firmness of purpose to take part in the search. He had been less enthusiastic about her insistence on joining him, but Clayton never attempted to play any sort of domineering-older-brother role with Rebecca, and today was no exception to the pattern. Nevertheless, when they reached the crowd, she was a bit relieved to see that she was not the only female who had turned out to join the search.

But commonality of gender or residence meant little to the people of Beckskill as far as Clayton and Rebecca were concerned. They were met with hostile looks and dark mutterings as they made their way through the people and approached Dr. Ostlich. "'Mornin'," Clayton said casually.

Ostlich's eyes were reddened by lack of sleep, and the worry that suffused his face was not dispelled by the antagonism his voice expressed. "What do you think you're doing here?" he demanded.

Clayton chose his words carefully. "Look, Doc," he began slowly, "I know you don't like me and I'm not crazy about you either, but that's not important. Lydia and Dorcas are friends of mine. . . ." He put up his hand to cut off the words he knew Ostlich was about to say. "I know you don't like that either, but that's also beside the point. They're my friends, and they're both worried sick about Sarah. If I can help out somehow, then I want to help."

"They're worried sick, are they?" he said bitterly. "I suppose that's why Dorcas left me a note saying that she was going back down to Long Island with Lydia? They're worried sick and they aren't even here to help?"

"You know what Dorcas is like, how high-strung and skittish she is," Clayton replied. "All the tension and worry are just too much for her. She had to get away, that's all, so Lydia took her to visit her friends on the Island."

"Yes, she's high-strung, but she wasn't high-strung until you started giving her drugs."

This was not true, but Clayton decided simply to counter one falsehood with another. "She never got any drugs from me. 'Cept beer, maybe."

Ostlich looked at him hard. "I have to be honest with you, Saunders. If something has happened to Sarah, you're the first one I'll think of blaming."

Clayton's eyes narrowed angrily. "That's your right, Doc. If you want to start looking for her on my property, you go right ahead. Just take Rebecca with you to kind of keep an eye on things. And once everybody's satisfied that whatever has happened has nothing to do with me or Becky, then we can get down to some serious searching. Okay?"

Ostlich pursed his lips. Maybe the boy is being sincere, he thought. I suppose every man has some element of goodness in him, even if you have to dig very deep. On the other hand, one might have to dig far deeper than this with Saunders. At last he said, "Very well." He did not thank him for his offer of assistance as he turned to Imhof, who was speaking to Rihaczeck. "Let's get things moving."

Imhof walked up to the top step of the town-hall entranceway and called out, "Can everyone quiet down, please? Everyone, please." He waited for a few moments as the conversations ceased and all eyes turned to him, and then he continued. "Let's review the facts here. The last anyone saw of Sarah was when her father sent her out to try to find her sister Dorcas. That was about four in the afternoon, day before yesterday. We know she went to the general store, but beyond that there's nothing."

A hum of voices arose briefly and Clayton's name was mentioned a few times, but he acted as if he had not heard it. Rebecca looked around nervously as Imhof continued, "Now, the state police tell us that forty-eight hours have to pass before they can start a missing-person investigation, and it'll be forty-eight hours about six hours from now, but we don't want to wait another six hours." Nods of agreement came from all sides. "We're going to split up into five search parties. . . ." He paused and leaned down as Ostlich whispered to him. "Six search parties. I stand corrected. Each group leader should see to it that the emergency-supply kits we've assembled are brought along. First aid in case the girl is wounded, a radio to summon help if needed, rope in case logs have to be moved or climbing has to be done, and so forth."

Rebecca leaned to her brother and whispered, "Why does he have to sound so pessimistic? We don't even know if Sarah got hurt. She may just have like split, you know?"

Clayton laughed humorlessly. "Sarah, run away from home? Are you kidding?"

"Lydia did, remember? Right after her mother died?"

"Lydia had a reason."

Rebecca looked at Ostlich with disgust and whispered, "Maybe Sarah has the same reason. . . ."

"Clayton Saunders has offered to allow us to search his land," Imhof was saying, "so Dave Dolak will lead one group to the fields and Bill McGee will lead the other group to the mountain. Joe Eggers will take the third group down the road to Bennetsville. Norm Brust's group will take Jenkins's orchards, and we of the town council will take two groups to search the forest along the River Road. That's a big stretch of woods, so we'll need two groups to cover it thoroughly. Mrs. Rihaczeck will stay here by the phone. . . ."

The division of the crowd into six groups of roughly equal size was accomplished without much difficulty, and a scant ten minutes after Imhof had given the instructions each group was on its way to its respective destination. Much against her wishes, Rebecca returned to the area around the trailer with one of the search parties. She refused at first to do so, until her brother reminded her quietly that they had left their drug-packed trailer unlocked. More out of a fear of losing the dope than of getting in trouble, Rebecca went back to her home with the two dozen townspeople.

Some three hundred people thus proceeded to spread out over the rural environs of Beckskill in search of the missing girl. Progress was slow, for while the area to be covered was limited and circumscribed, it also consisted largely of forest. This not only slowed down the pace of the searchers, it also gave them cause to stop and examine every fallen log and half-covered gully, just to be certain the girl was not somewhere hidden from sight.

Two hours later, Alex Brown had finished exploring yet another suspiciously high pile of leaves, again discovering no trace of Sarah Ostlich. He was part of the search party assigned to the woods between the River

Road and Saunders Mountain, and despite the gravity and potential tragedy of the situation, he was enjoying the community effort. Neighbors, he was thinking as he proceeded to trudge on through the woods with the others. That's what this is all about. Neighbors helping out in time of need, just like you see on the television, in the western movies.

He frowned slightly when his least favorite neighbor called out, "Hey, Alex! Over here. I found something."

He looked to his left, where Clayton Saunders was gazing down at something on the ground. Alex scurried over, and was almost immediately joined by old Johann Schilder and a half-dozen other men who had heard the call. "What?" Alex asked breathlessly.

"Look here," Clayton said, picking up two pieces of broken pottery.

"A broken bottle," Alex said with irritation. "So what?"

"So smell it," he said, handing Alex a shard. "I think there was gas in this or something. Here, Mr. Schilder," he said, handing the second piece to the old man and then picking up two others. "Doesn't it smell like gas?" Schilder sniffed at the shard, and his aged brow furrowed.

Alex tossed the shard away. "What the hell's the matter with you? This isn't important!"

"You see a road through here?" Clayton demanded. "You see someplace somebody would run out of gas and take a bottle of it out of his trunk to fill his tank? You see a motorboat around here anywhere? I mean, isn't it like suspicious?"

"Dis pot shmells like moonshine," Schilder said with certainty.

"What?" Clayton asked.

"*Ja*, dere vass moonshine in dis, vhite lightnink," Schilder said, nodding. "I know dis shmell anyvhere."

"Moonshine!" Clayton exclaimed. "There are still moonshiners around here? I knew that Vernon Sweet's old man used to make this stuff, but I thought—"

"Nah, ain't been no moonshiners around here for a long time," Schilder interrupted. "But you're right, Eland Shveet vas de last moonshiner I heard about in dis neck of de voods, and he died vhen I vas a young man, maybe fifty, sixty years ago." He looked at Clayton. "How do you know about Eland Shveet?"

"Vernon told me about him," Clayton replied simply.

That seemed to satisfy the old man and he sniffed again at the shard. "*Ja*, back den, 'round de turn of de century, lotta people made moonshine in dis neck of . . ." He paused and frowned as he looked off in the general direction of the old Sweet house. "Vait a minute, dat's right! Eland Shveet, dat *gottverdammte* gargoyle's fadder, he made moonshine. Used to bury it in de voods."

Whatever comments Schilder's words might have elicited were cut short by a sudden cry from a few hundred yards away, followed by a scream, and they all dropped the shards and ran in the direction of the sounds. Clayton stepped on three of the larger pieces of broken pottery that were still on the ground as he ran after the others of the search party.

He arrived at the circle of men to see Dr. Ostlich leaning against a tree, clutching his chest and weeping with low, frantic gasps. Clayton did not push his way through the circle, but as people moved about from side to side he caught brief glimpses of Sarah Ostlich's corpse, of the blackening face and the leaf-filled open mouth and the staring eyes and the dessicating flesh that had already provided a feast for the rodents and insects of the forest. He felt his knees beginning to buckle as he saw the body of the dead girl. He leaned back against a tree and muttered, "Shit!" This is like really gross, Clayton thought.

"Sarah," Ostlich wept as his knees gave out and he sank down beside the tree. "Oh God, oh God!"

"Her . . . her, uh . . ." Alex Brown stammered. "Her clothes are . . . it looks like she's been . . ."

"Oh, sweet Jesus," Ostlich moaned, "sweet Jesus . . ."

"De moonshine," Schilder said, his voice shaking as he turned to Alex. "I told you dat simpleton, he used to play vit himself all de time." A chorus of voices demanded that Schilder repeat, explain, enhance. "Dat Vernon dere in de old Shveet house. He vas a pervert, right from de beginning. I remember him as a child, long time ago, playing vit himself in public!"

The words sank into the minds of everyone present, everyone other than Ostlich, who was too deeply in shock to hear them. Common assumptions constructed an identical scenario in each imagination. The twisted mind of that twisted sideshow freak had been twisted even more when he found an old jug of moonshine. He had drunk it, thus raising his perverse, animalistic longings to the level of violent, uncontrollable lust. Sarah Ostlich, innocently searching for her sister, had wandered into the woods, or had been walking along the River Road, or had possibly even gone to the Sweet house, and that drunken monster had attacked her, violated her, murdered her. . . .

Not a word was spoken at first, after the groans of sorrow and disgust had been exhausted; but then, as pair of infuriated, vengeful eyes met pair of infuriated, vengeful eyes and communicated a common thought, the men began to move in the direction of the Sweet house.

Seventy men walked quickly and then began to run through the woods, occasional mutters and expletives of anger rising to furious cries of rage. Alex Brown's eyes were filled with tears of bitterness and anger as he shouted, "That goddamn bastard! That godddamn perverted bastard!"

"Gonna kill that son of a bitch!" Walter Rihaczeck cried.

Frank Bruno was shaking his fist as he ran. "We ain't gonna let no goddamn judge set him loose, by God!"

"We have a rope!" Michael Imhof shouted. "We know what we have to do!"

"String that goddamn freak up by his goddamn neck!"

"And that goddamn heathen with him!"

When Ashvarinda Patanjali was a child in what was then British India, his Hindu village was set upon by Moslem marauders in retaliation for the sacking of a Moslem village by Hindu marauders two days earlier. Now, eighty years later, he could still remember the sound of the frenzied, screaming, hateful voices as they rose softly in the distance and then grew louder and louder until at last they were a deafening cacophony of madness enveloping his little village.

He had not thought of that childhood experience for over half a century. He thought of it now as he heard the same tones reaching out toward him from the woods surrounding Vernon's house.

He frowned, confused rather than frightened, and rose from his meditation mat to go out onto the porch and see if he could discover the source and cause of the painful cries. He passed Vernon in the sitting room, where the little man was happily playing with an old baseball he had found in the attic, and went to the front door. The screams had become extremely loud, and he heard the sound of feet stomping up the old wooden steps as he turned the doorknob and pulled.

The two actions were virtually simultaneous: he stepped through the portal and was wrenched forward by a half-dozen hands, which grabbed him roughly by the arms and hair and beard. He found himself being lifted from his feet and thrown through the air, to land on his face upon the hard dirt ground.

"Where's that little bastard, you goddamn heathen?" Alex Brown demanded.

"Wh . . ." he stammered, "what . . . what do you want here?"

"You know vhy ve're here!" Schilder bellowed, feeling half his age in his fury. "Dat murdering freak! Vhere iss he?"

"Vernon?" Ashvarinda asked, trying to rise to his feet before a hard kick to his side sent him crashing down again. "What do you mean? Vernon hasn't . . ." And then he paused. Appleby! They must have found out about Appleby, and Florence Jackson and Bernie Sherman. "No . . ." he said quickly, "no . . . you do not understand . . . he did not mean to . . . he could not help himself. . . ."

"It was him!" Alex screamed, almost triumphantly. "The heathen just admitted it! It was that freak that killed the girl!"

The girl? Ashvarinda wondered frantically. Do they mean Florence?

"Vass you dere?" Old Man Schilder demanded. "Vass you part of dis ting? You tell de trut', or by Gott we string you up along vit' him!"

"I . . ." Ashvarinda began, weighing his danger against the bad karma of lying, and choosing the future benefit over the present peril. "The bodies . . ." he whispered. "I had to dispose of the bodies. . . ."

"Bodies!" Alex shouted. "There's more than one? You bastard!" He grabbed Ashvarinda by the back of the head and began pounding his face against the hard earth.

"*Ja*, it's just like ve figgered." Schilder nodded as Clayton came up behind the others. "Dat *gottverdammte* monster got drunk on de moonshine, ant he raped and killed the Ostlich girl!"

Blood was pouring from Ashvarinda's mouth as his voice gurgled, "Ostlich . . . Ostlich girl . . . no, no, wait, I thought you meant . . . wait, you are making a mistake. . . ."

But a blow to his head sent him spinning down into unconsciousness just as the door opened again and Vernon Sweet came out onto the porch. "Hi hi hi, hello," he said cheerfully. His look of childish trust shifted to one of utter dismay when he saw his friend lying motionless on the ground. "Rinda!" he cried and attempted to run forward.

He was grabbed on all sides and dragged from the porch toward the oak tree near which he had dug up the moonshine two days earlier. "Rinda!" he cried again, and then his frightened eyes grew hard and fiery as his voice sank to a guttural snarl. "Rrrrrindaaa," he said again, and then began to claw at the hands of his captors with unexpected strength.

The men were shouting so loud that they had not heard the change in his voice, but there was no mistaking the strength of his arms as he flung them away from him; and as four and then eight and then twelve members of the mob attacked him, he began snapping at them with the long, almost horizontal teeth that seemed to have sprung from his champing jaws. His bulbous head whipped left and right as his teeth snapped shut on empty air, unable to find the soft flesh it was seeking as the men avoided his jaws, tied the rope around his long thin neck, threw one end over the branch of the tree, and hoisted him upward.

"Grab his arms!" someone shouted. "Don't let him get his hands on the rope!"

Two men ran forward, each one grabbing an arm, and Vernon swung them back and forth in an attempt to dislodge them. For a moment it seemed that either the branch or the rope would break, but both held firm, and soon Vernon's desperate motions grew spasmodic and intermittent, and then they ceased.

Silence.

The onetime search party, onetime lynch mob resumed its previous character. Seventy individuals stood and watched as the body of the man they had just hanged swung slowly at the end of the rope. The creaking of hemp against wood whispered horribly in the profound quiet.

"What should we do now?" Bruno asked after a few long moments.

No one answered at first, and then Alex Brown said, "We put their bodies over there, in the barn, and we burn it down." No one responded to his suggestion, so he repeated it forcefully. "I say we put them in the barn and then we burn it down."

Mutters of agreement dropped like lead from the mouths of the others, and they wordlessly set about lowering the body of Vernon Sweet from the impromptu gallows. They carried him into the old barn that stood some fifty yards from the house, and then placed Ashvarinda beside him. It took a few minutes to find enough loose dry wood to ensure a raging blaze, and then fires were set in the barn and along the exterior parameter.

They stood and watched as the flames billowed up, and then Old Man Schilder barked, "Let's get out of here. Ve wait avhile, den ve call de fireman, before de whole forest burns." They all moved quickly back into the woods, back toward the body of Sarah Ostlich and the shocked, grieving father who was kneeling beside her. Alex grabbed Clayton by the collar of his jacket and said, "You're part of this, too. You keep your mouth shut."

"Sure, Al, sure," he replied softly. Alex released him and went off after the others. Clayton watched the fire for a few moments and then emitted a long breath. "Holy shit," he muttered. Then he walked back into the woods.

No one remained to see the flames licking up from the walls of the old barn to the roof and thence up into the bleak autumn sky. No one remained to see the timbers crash into the inferno as the barn collapsed into itself.

And no one remained to see the dark shape moving through the flames.

II

Freak Show

I am he whose gaze destroyeth hope
as soon as hope doth bloom.
I am he by none beloved,
and cursed by all that live.

—Mikhail Lermontov, *The Demon*

Chapter Eight

November 26, 1968

It was almost five o'clock. Sean Brenner's appointment with his probation officer was supposed to have been at four, and she had not yet arrived. He sniffed in annoyance, lighted another cigarette, and slumped down in the uncomfortable plastic chair in the anteroom of the probation office. He glanced up at the clock. "Fuckin' bitch," he muttered. Does she think I got nothing better to do than sit around waiting for her to show up?

He looked up as his probation officer came striding briskly down the hallway. Deborah Steyert was a woman who deliberately understated her attractiveness, perhaps as a means of counteracting the male tendency not to take attractive women seriously. She was dressed simply, almost austerely, and her long blond hair was pinned up tightly in a chignon. During his first meeting with her, Sean passed the time fantasizing about what she would be like under other, less official, more intimate circumstances. Today he was too tense to do anything other than act annoyed.

She nodded at him as she unlocked the door to her office. "Come in, Brenner," she said.

As he seated himself in front of her desk, he said, "You know, Mrs. Steyert, I've been sitting here since three forty-five. . . ."

Steyert sat down at her desk and took some papers from her briefcase. Without even looking at Sean, she said, "Well, if you hadn't been selling Methedrine, you wouldn't be sitting here at all, now would you?" Sean did not reply, and Steyert looked up at him. "Would you?"

He coughed. "No, I guess not."

"No, I guess not, too," she said, leaning back in her chair. "As it happens, one of my juveniles was almost killed by her father this afternoon, and I've been at the hospital with her. I hope that's a good enough excuse for you."

"Yeah, yeah, sure," he muttered, taking out a cigarette.

"Do not smoke in here, please," she said crisply. He put the cigarette away. "What have you been doing since we last met?"

"Nothing much," he replied. "I started work today."

"I know. I called. What about before that?"

"Nothing much." he repeated. "Hung out with my friend Artie. Drank a little beer, watched some TV. Went to the movies."

"Uh-huh. What movie did you see?"

He paused. What film that he had already seen was playing locally? "Ah . . . *Yellow Submarine.*"

"Uh-huh. Go to any bars?"

"No."

"Any pool halls?"

He laughed. "No."

"Smoke any pot?"

"Of course not. I don't want to screw up my probation, Mrs. Steyert. I'm not stupid, you know."

"You aren't unintelligent," she conceded, leaving Sean to mull over the difference. She stared at him for a long while, tapping the tip of her pen on the desktop with maddening regularity. At last she said, "You know,

Brenner, I can't for the life of me understand why they gave you probation."

He sighed. "Come on, ma'am, it was a first offense. . . ."

"Yes, but not a first offense for smoking marijuana or shoplifting. A first offense for selling a dangerous, addictive, potentially deadly drug is a little bit different. Methedrine is not marijuana, you know."

Sean smiled despite himself. "I know."

Steyert frowned. "Yes, I'm sure you do." She leaned forward and stared him in the eye. "Brenner, you're not fooling me. You know that with our limited budget we can't keep an eye on you twenty-four hours a day, seven days a week. You or any other of the degenerates the courts have decided to turn loose. But let me warn you, my friend. One slipup, just one, and I'll see that they slap you into the penitentiary so fast you won't know what hit you."

"Look, ma'am, you're not being fair," he whined. "I'm doing what I'm supposed to be doing, ain't I? I don't know why you're so down on me."

"Because you don't fool me a bit," she repeated. "All you're interested in is getting off probation so that you can go right back to being what you've always been, a lazy, self-indulgent, parasitic child."

He bristled. "What is this, some weird new sort of pep talk?"

"Don't be flippant," she said evenly. "I deal with probationary cases all day long, but they aren't kids like you. They've started life with two strikes against them, and sometimes when they fight back, they break the law. I don't approve, mind you. I'm not one of these people who believes that poverty excuses crime. But it does explain it. I can understand and even sympathize with people who are born in the middle of crime and violence and then struggle and claw to survive. But you!"

"Look, Mrs. Steyert—"

"You're nothing but a spoiled brat, Brenner, you and a million kids like you, always looking for the easy way, always avoiding responsibility, treating everything like a joke."

"You see me laughing?" he demanded. "You see me acting like I think it's funny being here?"

She appraised him coolly. "Not at the moment, no. Let's just hope you understand that a good lawyer kept you from getting the punishment you deserve. You might not be so lucky next time, so there had better not *be* a next time. You understand?"

"I'm hip," he muttered. "Can I go now?"

"Go where?"

None of your fucking business, he thought, but instead answered, "I'm tired. I been working all day. I want to go home and go to sleep."

A low, sarcastic laugh accompanied her response. "Yes, I'm sure. Okay, Brenner. Be here at four next Thursday. And keep your nose clean."

Sean rose to leave. "Yes, ma'am." The moment he walked through the door of her office he was filled with an intense, if temporary, euphoria. From early childhood Sean had been a rebellious, disobedient, insolent boy, and it was only now in the wake of arrest and trial and probation that he found himself having to be at least marginally courteous to people in positions of authority. He had no practical experience in being anything other than snide to them. Thus it was as if a weight had been lifted from him as he walked down the stairs from her office and out onto the cold street.

He left the Kew Gardens judicial complex and went to the nearest bus stop on Queens Boulevard. He lighted yet another cigarette and let it dangle from his chapped lips as he thrust his hands into the pockets of his short leather jacket and jumped up and down a few times in an attempt to keep warm in the early cold of late November. He squinted up the broad street in the direction of Jamaica and saw his bus approaching from the distance.

It was a forty-minute bus ride down Queens Boulevard to Grand Avenue in the slowly moving rush-hour traffic, and then a half-hour walk up through Maspeth to the aging apartment building where Russell Phelps, Peter Geerson, and their friend Artie Winston shared two small rooms with each other, with a plethora of urban insects, and with whatever it was that they occasionally heard scratching behind the walls. I suppose you get what you pay for, Sean reflected as he pressed the downstairs buzzer. Russell, Peter, and Artie were paying seventy-five dollars a month.

He unwrapped his long scarf and pressed the buzzer twice more. At last the responding buzzer sounded, admitting him into the dirty, decrepit lobby. He walked quickly up the three flights of stairs and knocked on the door.

"So, Sean!" Russell said as he opened the door. "Come on in and do a doob."

Sean entered to find Artie Winston sitting on the floor, a well-polished and obviously cherished Gibson acoustic guitar lying to his right, a bowl of dust-fine marijuana to his left. "Hiya, Artie," he said, sitting down beside him and pulling off his boots.

"How is our redoubtable felon?" Artie asked as he carefully rolled a generous line of pot in the cigarette paper.

"Funny," Sean muttered. "Real funny."

Artie ran his tongue along the length of the joint, lighted it, and handed it to Sean. "So how was the dragon lady tonight?"

"She don't like me, that's for sure."

"You blame her?" Russell asked, sitting down on the

floor with them. "Most of the people who know you don't like you." He laughed.

Sean shrugged as he toked on the joint. "So most of the people I know don't have any taste." He passed the joint to Russell and then turned to Artie. "Where's Peter?"

"Over at the lab at school," Artie replied, taking off his thick round glasses and attempting to clean them on his grimy shirt. "He should be back here by now. We have to leave for Zoli's."

"You playing there again tonight?"

"Yup."

Sean nodded. "That's great, really great. I always figured you'd be able to get something going with your music if you set your mind to it. I never could understand why you were wasting your time with college. You're too good a musician."

"Thanks," Artie replied, "but I don't have any illusions about it. I'm good, I know that, good on the guitar and I sing good, too."

"And you're modest," Russell observed.

Artie ignored him. "But there are probably a hundred thousand guys just as good as me, and ten thousand who are better, and of those ten thousand there are probably no more than a few hundred who are making a living."

"Making a living!" Sean exclaimed. "Who's talking about making a living? You got a place to crash, you're never short of dope and acid, and you could get laid every fucking night if you weren't so shy around girls."

"I'm not shy," Artie responded defensively. "I'm just selective. And anyway, that may be all I need now, at twenty-one. What about when I'm forty-one?"

Sean frowned and waved away the objection. "By the time you're forty-one, you'll be rich and retired."

"Just like you, if you marry Becky," Russell observed.

"Cut it out," Sean said.

"I can just see it," Russell went on. "You and Clay and Becky living your laborless fantasy just as our society finally comes to its senses and abolishes private property."

"That'd be nice." Artie nodded. "I'd hate to have to get a regular job."

"Tell me about it." Sean sighed. "You know what I have to do all day? I stuff junk mail into envelopes. Eight hours a day, stuffing junk mail into envelopes. Jesus!" He turned to Russell. "Doesn't it get to you, getting up every morning and going into that high school to teach?"

Russell did not reply, and Artie chuckled. "Russell is, as they say, between positions at the moment."

Sean looked over at his friend. "You got fired?"

Russell sighed. "Yeah."

"What for?"

"Oh, I tried to organize an open forum on the Gulf of Tonkin incident, and I got into an argument with my chairman and the principal."

"Let me guess," Sean said, taking the joint. "You got all upset and flew off the handle and started yelling at them, right?"

"Basically."

"What did you say? Did you insult them?"

He shrugged. "I suppose so."

"'Whoremongers of the capitalist vampires' was the operative phrase, I think," Artie offered.

Sean smiled. "Good move." He felt himself relaxing, a combination of the marijuana and the comfortable company of his old friends. "Want me to get you a job?"

"Packaging junk mail? Forget it. I'll just go on unemployment."

"I'd love to do that, but my probation officer won't let me."

The door opened and Peter Geerson walked in. "Hiya, guys," he said cheerfully.

"'Bout time," Artie said. "We gotta leave in a few minutes."

"So roll some joints and let's go," he replied. "Just let me wash the monkey shit off my hands."

"Cleaning the animal cages again?" Artie asked as he began to roll the joints.

"Yeah," Peter said as he disappeared into the bathroom. "Grad assistants get all the glamorous jobs."

Russell decided to be merciless. "You know, Pete, I think that short hair really looks good on you."

"Fuck you, asshole," Peter called out from the bathroom.

"Been thinking about getting mine cut real short, too."

"Fuck you, asshole," Peter repeated.

Sean tossed the burned-out roach into a nearby ashtray. "Did he have to get his hair cut off for this graduate-assistant thing?"

"Hell, no." Artie laughed. "Pete's a sailor."

"A sailor! What are you talking about?"

"Well," Artie said as he licked another joint along its seam, "he had his draft physical last week down at Fort Hamilton in Brooklyn, and the poor son of a bitch passed it."

"Pete's 1-A?" Sean was astounded.

"Yeah, but because he can still claim to be a full-time student . . . you know, the master's-degree program and the graduate-assistantship and all that shit . . . he was able to join the navy reserve. That gives him a breather while he pays off a shrink to say that he's . . ." He paused, and then shouted, "Hey, Pete. What's your shrink saying's wrong with you again?"

"Chronic immaturity," Peter replied over the loudly running water that was splashing into the sink.

"Yeah, right," Artie went on. "But he's still got to go to the navy-reserve meetings every week, and he had to get his hair cut."

"That's really a bitch," Sean muttered, shaking his head. "Why didn't he do what you and Russell did, take some speed before his physical so his blood pressure was high?"

"I was gonna do that," Peter said as he walked out of the bathroom, wiping his hands on his shirt, "but my Meth dealer got busted."

Sean laughed softly. "Sorry 'bout that."

"Helped one of us, anyway. With a felony conviction on your record, you don't have to worry about getting drafted."

"I'd rather not have the record," Sean said. "It'd be easier just to get fucked up for the physical."

"It's funny, isn't it?" Artie mused as he unfolded another rolling paper and began deftly to pour marijuana into it. "Of all the people we know, only Mario couldn't beat the draft. I mean, me and Russell did the Meth thing, Buzzy and Tom convinced the draft board that they're allergic to milk, Doug convinced them that he had like terminal hemorrhoids, and when Clay went in for his physical, he wandered around Fort Hamilton all day jerking off until they threw him out."

"Yeah." Sean nodded. "They classified him 4-Y."

"What's that mean?"

"According to Clay, it means that if we're ever in a declared war and the enemy has already conquered twenty-six states and there's nobody left to draft except him and fourteen-year-old kids, the fourteen-year-olds get drafted first."

Artie nodded. "Sounds pretty safe."

"And you know, Mario didn't really try to beat the

draft," Sean said. "He's from Cuba, and he told me once that Castro killed a lot of people in his family and all that shit. I think he wanted a chance to kill some communists, so he let himself get drafted and get sent over to Vietnam."

"But he knows I'm a communist," Russell pointed out, "and he's always been friendly to me."

"Yeah, but he doesn't take you seriously."

"Great," Russell mumbled. "I wish my principal didn't take me seriously."

"I'm ready," Peter said. "Let's hit the road."

In the parlance of the era, Zoli's Bar on Hempstead Turnpike in Nassau County was a head bar, as opposed to a hitter bar or a jock bar; its clientele consisted largely of "freaks," a term commonly used to refer to long-haired, denim-clad, drug-oriented middle-class white kids. They were members of an unusually affluent generation, and the affluence was so common and unexceptional that it went largely unnoticed by them. They did not think of themselves as wealthy, of course, despite the fact that very few of them were ever strapped for cash, thanks largely to vast sums of money borrowed as college loans from banks or made available by indulgent parents; and a good deal of this money was, by nine o'clock, finding its way into the cash register at Zoli's, exchanged for pitcher after pitcher of beer.

As Sean, Russell, and Peter sat at a table with Dorcas Ostlich, her sister Lydia, and their friends Deirdre Duell and Nancy O'Hara, Artie Winston sat on a small dais near the far wall of the bar, playing his guitar and harmonica, singing one of his own compositions.

> *"Well, I've heard tell that Jefferson said*
> *Revolution keeps a country free,*

And I've heard tell that Andrew Johnson
    Drank, but it's news to me,
And that Warren Harding kept a personal whore,
And that Polk up and started the Mexican War.
Well, I never heard such things before,
So you're gonna have to prove it to me."

"She's all right, don't you think?" Dorcas asked Lydia. "I mean, it's just not like her to take off like this."

Lydia drained her beer glass and then replied, "Look, Sarah's probably off somewhere communing with the Holy Ghost or something. Don't worry about her."

"I mean, I know we don't get along. . . ."

"Dork, cut it out, will you?" her sister snapped. "Sarah's gonna turn up."

"Sure she is," Deirdre Duell offered. "She'll probably be home when you get back to Beckskill tomorrow." She was an exquisitely beautiful girl, madly in love with Artie Winston, who was too shy to talk to her.

"Of course she will," Nancy O'Hara agreed, sniffing with irritation at Dorcas's concern. "Everybody splits from home sometimes. It's nothing to worry about."

"I hope not," Dorcas muttered. "I just couldn't stand it if anything happened to her." She turned to Peter, who was sitting beside her. "Sarah's okay, right, Pete, don't you think?"

"Sure she is, Dorcas," Peter said supportively. "Maybe she's more, I don't know, adventurous than anybody realizes. Maybe she just took off for a few days, or met some guy or something."

She shook her head. "That doesn't sound like Sarah." She looked across the table at Sean. "But she's probably okay, right?"

"Yeah, sure," Sean replied, not looking at her. "She's fine."

* * *

"Well, I've heard tell that marijuana
 Ain't the same as LSD.
And I've heard tell that whiskey's the worst,
 You can get addicted and OD.
Well, I've heard tell that grass don't kill
 And there's suicide in the backyard still.
Well, brother, you can think whatever you will,
 But you're gonna have to prove it to me.
Yup, I'm from Missouri and I'm damn proud to say
That our thoughts ain't changed since Grandpa's day,
And we never let evidence get in the way.
 So you're gonna have to prove it to me."

"Hey, Sean," Russell said, taking his hands off Nancy O'Hara and turning to his friend, "I scored some great acid from one of the kids in my class. You want to do a hit?"

Sean considered it. "You gonna?"

"As long as I'm not the only one, sure. I hate to trip alone."

"Yeah, me too." Sean thought for a few moments. "No, I don't feel like it. Not tonight."

Russell looked beyond him. "What about you, Peter?"

"Count me out," he replied. "I've been bumming out a lot lately. I doubt I'll be doing acid anymore."

"Everybody gets into a bad head now and then," Sean said. "It'll pass." He drank some beer and then asked, "What kind of bummers you been having?"

"You know, I hear voices, shit like that."

"You're just hearing your own thoughts, that's all," Lydia said. "Happens to me sometimes. The acid does weird shit to your brain, so you hear what you're thinking."

"Yeah?" Peter asked. "You too? You ever hold conversations with yourself?"

She shrugged. "Sometimes."

"I mean like for real, not just like saying your thoughts out loud. Like you're sitting there and somebody who looks like you is sitting next to you, and you talk to them and they talk back. You ever do that?"

"Sometimes," she repeated. "It's no big deal."

Peter laughed. "I wish I could deal with it that easily. It scares the hell out of me."

"Just think about happy stuff when you bum out," Lydia suggested. "Me, I like dogs, so if I'm starting to bum out, I just start thinking about dogs, and it kinda gets me out of it."

"She's got a point there," Sean said. "I do the same thing. If I start to have a bad trip, I just start to think about—"

"*The Wizard of Oz,*" everyone at the table finished for him in unison.

"Hey, fuck you guys, you know?" he muttered.

> "Well, I've heard tell them blacks want jobs
>   And financial security,
> And I've heard tell them Chicano boys
>   Just want to get a decent fee,
> And that Indians want to be left to do
>   Whatever they want, like me and you,
> And I've heard tell that Christ was a Jew,
>   But you're gonna have to prove it to me.
> Yup, I'm from Missouri. . . ."

Dorcas's face was a study in fear and worry, and Peter took her hand gently, saying, "Listen, Dorcas, you want to get out of here, go somewhere else, somewhere quieter?"

"No, Pete, thanks." She sighed. "I guess I feel a little guilty about leaving home yesterday morning, not staying there while this is all going on."

"So what could you do at home?" he asked. "All

you'd end up doing would be sitting around your house, all alone, worrying."

She shrugged. "I'm sitting here worrying."

"Yeah"—he smiled—"but you're not alone."

She returned the smile and waited for him to lean forward to kiss her. He picked up his beer instead.

> *"Well, I've heard tell not all longhairs*
>> *Are guilty of sodomy,*
> *And I've heard tell a hard day's work*
>> *Ain't all life was meant to be.*
> *But I ain't the only one to sing this song,*
>> *Been just like my neighbors all along,*
> *And they're all right, so I can't be wrong,*
>> *And you're gonna have to prove it to me. . . ."*

Dorcas turned to Lydia and said, "You don't think that Daddy has . . . I mean, you remember when you ran away?"

"Yeah, I remember," Lydia replied, discomfort evident in her tone.

"Well, is it possible that . . . well, do you think Daddy's been . . . I mean—"

Lydia found Dorcas's tactful approach annoying, so she cut her off. "Has Dad been molesting her like he used to molest me?"

Dorcas lowered her eyes. "It might explain what happened. If she ran away, I mean."

Lydia shook her head. "I don't think it's been happening, and even if it is, it wouldn't make her run away." She took a drink of beer. "She'd probably enjoy it, anyway."

"Lydia!" Dorcas exclaimed. "That's a terrible thing to say!"

Lydia sighed. "Yeah, yeah, I know. I'm sorry. I didn't mean it." She turned to her sister and said, "Look,

Dork, Dad went to the same shrink you and I did. He doesn't do that kind of stuff anymore, not to me, not to Sarah."

Dorcas nodded. "He was a good psychiatrist."

"He was an asshole," Lydia countered. "Telling me that I shouldn't hate myself and shouldn't blame myself because it wasn't my fault and I was just a kid and all that shit. Christ, I knew that! I didn't need him to tell me."

Dorcas mustered up the courage to disagree. "He seems to have helped Daddy."

Lydia shrugged, dismissing the statement. "Dad is still a bastard, I still hate his fucking guts, and I'll never forgive him. I think I'll hate him till the day I die. But none of that stuff has anything to do with Sarah."

Dorcas seemed on the verge of crying. "Then where is she, Lydia?" Her sister did not reply.

Artie ended the song with a riff on the harmonica that was suspended in front of his face in a wire holder, and a smattering of applause followed from those people in the bar who had been listening. The bartender went to the dais and whispered in Artie's ear, after which Artie said into the microphone, "Lydia . . . hey, Lydia. You got a phone call."

Lydia's friends watched as she went to the bar and picked up the phone. They saw her smile as her lips formed a greeting he could not hear; then her face went white. A few moments later she walked unsteadily back to the table and sat down heavily beside her sister.

"Lydia?" Dorcas asked. "Lydia? What is it? Is it . . . is it Sarah?"

"That was Becky," Lydia said with trembling voice. "They've . . . been trying to . . . to find us since yesterday afternoon."

Dorcas put her hands to her mouth, knowing from her sister's behavior that something was horribly wrong. "Lydia," she asked, "what about Sarah?"

"Sarah's dead," Lydia whispered, tears beginning to run down her cheeks. "They found her body in the woods. She was murdered."

Dorcas began to cry and everone else's eyes went wide with shock. "Do they have any idea who did it?" Sean asked.

"Yeah, they know exactly who did it," Lydia said, her weak voice growing suddenly firm with outrage. "It was that goddamn fucking freak, Grogo!"

Chapter Nine

November 28, 1968

The people of Beckskill thought it quite appropriate for it to have rained on Thanksgiving, for there seemed little out of the ordinary about which to be thankful. It is easy to say that one should be thankful for life and health and a full stomach and a strong roof, but this is an aphorism, a proverb more honored in the breach than the observance. For the people of Beckskill, Thanksgiving of 1968 brought them a murdered girl, a jeopardized economic future, and a collective crime on the minds of all and on the lips of none.

The sky was still overcast on the afternoon following Thanksgiving as a large group of people stood in a silent assembly around the freshly dug grave of Sarah Ostlich. A slight drizzle fell upon the solemn faces, mingling with the tears of some and running in rivulets through the furrowed brows of others, and the clouds moved with sullen deliberation through the gray sky.

Nearest the grave, beside Pastor Benke of St. Hugh's Church in neighboring Rosendale, stood Dr. Timothy Ostlich, his desolation accentuated by the fact that he stood alone. His two remaining children stood apart, not quite in the crowd but nonetheless distant from their father. Dorcas was dressed in a dark flowered dress with padded shoulders, 1940's vintage, obtained in

165

a thrift shop down in New Paltz. Beside her was Peter Geerson, who had returned with her from Long Island two days before and who had conducted himself as the soul of propriety in these dire circumstances, even to the extent of being kind and sympathetic to her father, with whom he shared a mutual dislike. Lydia, dressed in a black leotard gathered at the breast by an antique brooch, and a skirt sewn together from a multitude of dark paisley-print scarves, stood next to Clayton Saunders, who had attended the ceremony only because his sister had cajoled him into it. Rebecca Saunders stood next to her brother, her face almost as tearstained as those of the Ostlich family. She did not weep for Sarah, whom she heartily disliked. Her tears were for Lydia and Dorcas.

"O God, our God," Benke was saying, "who marketh for each man his little time in this world, we commit into your keeping the soul of our sister, Sarah Olivia Ostlich. . . ."

Clayton was very uneasy. Funerals always bothered him anyway, and his mind was filled with depressing images. The decaying body of Sarah Ostlich, the blood pouring from the head of the old yogi, Vernon being hoisted up by his neck, the billowing flames in the old barn . . . What a drag, he thought. I wish they'd hurry up so I can go home and do a pipe.

"I am the resurrection and the life, saith the Lord. Whosoever believeth in Me, though he were dead, yet shall he live; and whosoever liveth and believeth in Me shall never die. . . ."

Alex Brown stood with his friends and neighbors, his eyes moving from Dr. Ostlich to Clayton Saunders. For his fellow council member he felt crushing sorrow. To lose a child, he thought, that must be the greatest heartache, especially a child as upright and innocent as Sarah. And look what he has left. That little slut who is always with the bum, doing God knows what, and that other one, the crazy one, the one they had to put away last year. Poor man, poor man.

His emotions ran from sympathy as he looked at Ostlich to hostility tinged with fear as he looked at Clayton. Goddamn good-for-nothing bastard. Flaunting his money like he does, never done a day's work in his life. Trying to mess up the factory deal, trying to hurt the town, trying to hurt me.

And he was there, he saw, he knows what we did. Me and Schilder, we were the ones who stirred up the others, and that bum knows, that bum saw. He was there, standing back, watching, not taking part, keeping out of it, that bum, that bastard.

He tried not to look at Rebecca, but he could not keep from thinking about her. She must get away from that brother of hers. She must be given the chance to grow up right.

". . . ashes to ashes, dust to dust . . ."

Similar thoughts drifted through the minds of the townspeople as the damp clumps of earth thudded upon the coffin lid. What about the factory, the jobs, the future of the town? What about the Sweet land? What do we do now?

". . . in the sure and certain hope of the resurrection of the body and the life everlasting. Amen."

The people in the crowd began slowly to disperse after stopping to mutter condolences to Ostlich, and only now did Lydia and Dorcas walk over to stand with him. Peter, Clayton, and Rebecca walked away a few yards and then stopped by the cemetery gate, waiting at a discreet distance as the twin sisters stood beside their father, ignored by the people who stopped to speak to him. Dorcas looked over at Peter, who smiled at her, and Lydia glanced at Clayton, who winked. They were all understandably somber, but the story Clayton had shared with them about the lynching of Vernon and Ashvarinda, and about which he had sworn them to secrecy, made the events of the past few days seem even more terrible than they had at first imagined. Dorcas's first reaction to the tale was to declare her intention to go to the police, but Clayton made her understand that if she did, he would be in as much trouble as everyone else present in the clearing that day. It was with a heavy heart that she agreed to keep the matter to herself, and so she stood now mourning not only Sarah, but also a kindly old Hindu and a pathetic little man who, she was certain, could not possibly have killed her sister.

"This is heavy." Peter sighed.

"Yeah, a real bummer," Clayton agreed. "You think Lydia wants to come back with us?"

Rebecca shrugged. "I don't know. You'd think she'd go home with her father, but . . ." She shrugged again. They fell silent as the other mourners began to depart.

At last no one was left beside the open grave except the members of the immediate family, and Dr. Ostlich put his hand gently on Dorcas's shoulder. "Let's go home now, honey." He looked at Lydia. "Let's all go home. I think we should have a talk."

"Yeah, sure, Dad," Lydia said gently. "I'll go tell Clay that we're—"

"No, Lydia, please," Ostlich said softly, his voice strained and roughened from weeping and prayer. "You two are all I have left in the world. I don't want you to destroy yourselves, and that's what I'm afraid will happen if you keep seeing that boy."

Lydia shut her eyes tightly for a moment. "Dad, I don't think this is the right time. . . ."

"And you, sweetheart," he said, cutting Lydia off as he turned to Dorcas. "You mean so much to me, so much. It would kill me if anything ever happened to you. Please, *please* stay away from that drunken rabble."

She glanced at Peter, who was still waiting near the entrance of the cemetery. "But Daddy," she whined, "Peter isn't—"

"Listen to me, both of you," he said. "Don't you see that you are partly to blame for this? If I hadn't sent Sarah to try to find at least one of my wayward children, she would be alive today, she wouldn't have—"

"I don't fucking believe this!" Lydia exclaimed. "You blame *us* for what happened to Sarah? Are you kidding?"

"Lydia," he said, his voice breaking, "I didn't mean that. But you must realize that your behavior—"

"Daddy, Lydia," Dorcas said quickly, "Let's just go home, okay?"

"Oh, shut up, Dork," Lydia said angrily. "Look, Dad, I'm real sorry about Sarah. I mean, it's just eating me up inside, you know? But to try to blame it on us . . ."

"Face the facts, honey. If you had been at home where you belonged, and if you"—he looked at Dorcas— "hadn't been out God knows where doing God knows what—"

"And if it wasn't such hell living with you," Lydia interrupted, "we probably would both have been home! Why the hell'd you send Sarah out looking for Dork, anyway? She's a big girl. If she wants to go out somewhere and see some people or something, why is that any of your fucking business?"

"Stop it!" Dorcas begged. "Stop it, please! I just can't stand it, not here, not now!"

Her father's face mirrored his internal struggle between grief, love, guilt, and anger. "Why Sarah?" he asked at last, beginning to weep. "Of the three of you, why her?"

"What are you . . . ?" Lydia began to ask, and then understood her father's words. Her face grew red as she spat, "You son of a bitch!"

"*Stop it!*" Dorcas's breath was coming in short gasps, and her body was trembling from head to foot.

Tears rolled down Ostlich's face. "Thank God your mother isn't alive to see this."

"Yeah, sure," Lydia shouted back. "Thank God she isn't alive to have to go on living with *you*, looking at you every day and knowing what you are! That's why she killed herself, Dad. She killed herself because of what you did to me!"

"*Stop it!*" her sister cried.

"That's the truth, and you know it, you bastard!"

Dorcas pressed her fists against her temples and screamed. Then she ran, away from her battling family, past her friends, and out onto Bennets Road. Peter stood dumbly and watched as she ran by him, and he looked from her disappearing figure to her sister and father and then back again. "Dorcas?" he said, and then called louder, "Dorcas! Wait a minute. Where are you going?"

Ostlich glared at him angrily through his tears. "You keep away from her!"

"But where is she going?" Peter asked. "What just happened?" He walked past Ostlich and began to follow Dorcas, but her father stopped him by grabbing his arm. "Hey! Get your hands off me!"

"I don't want her to have anything to do with you!"

Peter threw the hand firmly away. "I care a lot about her, in case you haven't noticed!"

"Let's go, Clay," Lydia muttered as she walked briskly by them. "I gotta get away from him."

"Yeah, sure," Clayton responded. "What about Dork?"

"She'll calm down and either go home or meet us at the trailer." She sighed. "Come on. Let's get out of here."

"Lydia!" her father pleaded. "Come back here!"

"Fuck you," she spat, and continued to walk away.

Clayton followed her, and Rebecca followed him. Peter remained for a moment and then said, "I'll meet you guys later. I'm gonna go after Dorcas."

"Suit yourself," Clayton called back as he climbed into his jeep and started the engine. Lydia and Rebecca entered the vehicle and they then began to drive up toward the mountain. Peter began to trot in the direction Dorcas had been running, leaving Ostlich alone in the cemetery.

Clayton pursed his lips, thinking as he drove. "Hey, Lyd, you think Dork's gonna go home?"

"Beats me," Lydia replied.

"What about you? You gonna go home?"

"Only if you throw me out. Why?" Her heart skipped a beat as she began to worry that Clayton was about to begin distancing himself from her.

"I just wanted . . . " He stopped and thought for a few more moments. "Look, the town still wants that land, right?"

She shrugged. "I guess so. So what?"

"So I think I know how they're gonna try to get it. And if they're gonna do what I think they're gonna do . . . well, then there's something *I'm* gonna do."

They waited for an explanation, and when none was forthcoming, Rebecca asked, "You want to let us in on this, Clay?"

"Yeah, yeah, sure," he said distractedly, still sunk in thought. "Look, you can't pay taxes if you're dead, right? And what happens if you don't pay your taxes on your land?"

"I don't know," Lydia replied. "The bank takes it, I guess."

"Only if you got a mortgage. I mean, what happens if you own it, no mortgage or nothing, and you don't pay your taxes?"

She shrugged. "I have no idea."

"It gets auctioned off by the county," he said. "You gotta pay taxes to the county, and if you don't, the county auctions it off."

"Okay. So?"

Rebecca laughed softly. "Clayton, you wouldn't!"

He grinned. "Why not?"

"Hey, come on." Lydia frowned. "Get to the point, will you? I don't feel like guessing what you're talking about. I mean, this hasn't been a really good day for me, you know?"

"The town council is gonna bid on the land," Clayton explained. "I mean, I think they have to, for this whole factory thing. The deal was that the town would donate the land to Craigo, and they'd build—"

"Yeah, yeah, I know all that," Lydia said impatiently. "What's that got to do with me going home?"

"Your father is on the council. He'll know when and where the auction'll be, and I'll bet they'll manage to speed up the whole thing, have it sooner than they're supposed to."

"So?"

"So I want to know when and where, too."

"Why?"

He smiled. "So I can bid against the town and buy the Sweet property."

Lydia digested this and then began laughing loudly. "Clay, that's hysterical! That is just so fucking funny."

"Peter's gonna be happy as a pig in shit," Rebecca added.

"They bid a hundred grand, I bid a hundred and fifty," Clayton went on. "They bid a hundred and fifty, I bid two. The land's only worth fifty, sixty grand anyway. The town's gonna have to sell bonds or something to raise the money, and they're gonna have to do it before the auction. They won't be expecting anybody else to bid, not up to the level they're willing to pay, so I doubt they'll raise more than a hundred grand, tops." He started laughing. "Can you imagine the look on old Alex's face? He's gonna shit in his pants."

He was still laughing a few minutes later as he pulled the jeep to a halt near the path to his trailer. "I could use a cold beer and a hot pipe."

"You and me both," Lydia said. "Jesus, what a week!"

Soon thereafter they were all sitting on the floor of the trailer's living room, taking turns with the small brass hashish pipe. "You think Dork's okay?" Rebecca asked.

"Sure," Clayton replied.

"I mean, after what happened to Sarah . . ."

"That was because of that fucking nut Grogo," Clayton said quickly, shaking his head. "Nothing bad ever happens around here. I mean, he's dead, so there's nothing to worry about."

Lydia toked on the pipe and then handed it to Rebecca. "I just can't believe he would do something like that. I mean, there's no doubt he was screwy, but he just, I don't know, just didn't seem the type."

Clayton shrugged. "So who's the type? Pay no attention to the man behind the curtain, you know? Besides, maybe it was an accident. Maybe he didn't mean to do it."

"Yeah, sure, right," Rebecca said sarcastically. "He raped and murdered her by accident. Guilty with an explanation."

"Well," he said, shrugging again and not really wanting to discuss it further, "whatever. It's all over."

"I don't see how it can be all over," Lydia objected. "I mean, don't get me wrong, I'm not upset that you guys killed the nut who murdered my sister, but—"

"Hey, include me out, man!" Clayton objected. "I just watched. I had nothing to do with it."

"Okay, but I mean, you can't just hang somebody. I mean, it's against the law!"

"You gonna call the cops?"

She hesitated for a moment. "Well, no . . ."

"Me neither."

"But won't he be missed?"

"By who?" he asked. "As far as we can tell, nobody knew he was here except the people who live here."

She nodded. "Yeah, I guess so. But what about the other guy, Asher-what's-his-name? He didn't do anything wrong."

"He said he helped hide the body," Clayton replied. "I heard him say that myself."

"Yeah." She nodded. "But he didn't deserve to die."

Clayton nodded in agreement. "Yeah. Bummer."

She sighed and then nodded in turn. "Bummer."

Rebecca tapped the pipe onto the top of an empty beer can. "This is played," she said.

"Play!" Clayton shouted, grabbing Lydia's hand and pulling her to her feet. "An excellent idea! Come, wench, let us play!" She was not at all in the mood, but inasmuch as she always made a point of giving Clayton what he wanted when he wanted it, she feigned laughter as he dragged her into the bedroom.

Rebecca reloaded the pipe. I wish Sean were here, she thought as she smoked in solitude and listened to the laughs and moans and the pounding bedsprings, clearly audible through the thin walls a few feet away. He said he's going to try to get up here tomorrow, but that goddamn probation officer is on his ass every minute, checking up on him, calling up the people who are covering for him. She's not making it easy for him to get away. God, I miss him. I miss him so much. She heard Lydia cry out and then moan softly as Clayton grunted and the bedsprings ceased creaking. Well, that didn't take long, she thought. You're some lover, Clay.

The phone rang in the small kitchen, and she

jumped to her feet and ran over to answer it, hoping it was Sean. "Hello?" she said eagerly.

"Hiya, Becky."

"Oh, Peter." She sighed. "It's only you."

"Hey, thanks a lot." He was making an effort to be humorous, but his voice was tense.

"What's up? Where are you calling from?" She opened the refrigerator and took out a beer as she spoke.

"I'm over in Redhook, at the hospital with Dorcas."

She was suddenly very attentive. "Dorcas is in the hospital?"

"What?" Lydia asked from the bedroom. "What'd you say?"

"Hold on," she said to Peter, and then called out, "Pete's on the phone. He says Dorcas is in the hospital in Redhook."

Lydia was off the bed in an instant, still wrapping a sheet around herself as she ran to the phone. She grabbed the receiver from Rebecca's hand and said breathlessly, "Peter, this is Lydia. What happened? Is she hurt? Is she okay?"

"She isn't hurt," he replied. "But she . . . well, I think she's flipping out again."

"What do you mean?" she demanded. "She didn't . . . hey, you didn't give her any acid. . . ."

"Oh, don't be ridiculous!" he said angrily. "Of course I didn't give her any acid. What do you think I am, stupid?"

"Well, what the hell happened?!"

"I was trying to follow her," he explained, "but I didn't really know where she went. She got out of sight pretty quick."

"Yeah, yeah, I know, go on, go on."

"I was down near the River Road, and I saw her just as a state trooper was picking her up, so I ran over to them and—"

"Goddamn it, Peter, I don't give a shit what you were doing!" Lydia shouted. "What happened to my sister?"

"She was hallucinating, like maybe she was having a flashback from the acid or something. She was screaming, 'He's after me, he's after me,' and shit like that."

"Who? Who'd she think was after her?"

He sighed. "Grogo the Goblin. She said he was trying to drag her into the woods."

Chapter Ten

January 3, 1969

The year 1968 had ended very much the way it had begun, with unrest at home and a seemingly endless war abroad. One president was coming to the end of his tragic tenure as another was preparing to take control of the nation's destinies in a few short weeks. Long-smoldering discontent erupted into sporadic violence in black ghettos, young whites marched and chanted and shook their fists on a thousand college campuses, and everywhere authority and tradition and convention were being challenged, attacked, rejected. It was as if all the old certitudes and assumptions had melted away, and the nation seemed to be either at the dawn of a new and better age, or on the edge of a precipice.

Such things held the attention of most of the country; but the little town of Beckskill had other concerns, more urgent, more pressing, more immediate.

At four o'clock in the afternoon of the day Clayton Saunders purchased the Sweet property for $250,000, an emergency meeting was held of the Beckskill town council. Alex Brown and Dr. Timothy Ostlich waited nervously for the others to arrive, and by 4:15 everyone was present except old Johann Schilder. Ostlich drummed his fingers nervously upon the desktop and said at last, "We can't wait for him any longer. We have to come to a decision about this, and I'm sure that Schilder will agree with whatever we decide on."

"It's better to have a unanimous council vote if we're going to persuade the voters," Imhof pointed out.

"We'll have a unanimous vote, I'm sure," Ostlich said. "We're all agreed in principle already. All that remains is for Walter here to lay out the details."

Walter Rihaczeck cleared his throat. "Well, I'm sure we've all discussed this situation privately amongst ourselves by now. . . ."

"Yeah, we discussed it," Alex shouted, "and I vote we take that son of a bitch out and shoot him!"

"Calm down, Alex." Ostlich sighed wearily. Were the truth to be known, his enthusiasm for town politics had diminished greatly since he had buried his youngest daughter six weeks before, and his continued participation in meetings and planning sessions was little more than habit. It also served to distract him at least temporarily from the open wound of his loss. "What's done is done. We couldn't have anticipated it. What we have to do now is try to salvage the situation."

Alex was not to be diverted. "Ever since that goddamn bum was in high school, he's been a problem in this town. We should have known, we should have *known* he would do something like this!"

"Come on, Al," Bruno said. "We thought we had taken care of everything. We knew that when December first came and went without the semiannual taxes being paid on the Sweet property, it would be put into county receivership, and we managed to get that part of the plan done quicker than any of us thought possible. We persuaded the tax assessor to reduce the waiting period before the auction from sixty days to thirty. We floated a bond issue for two hundred thousand dollars, much more than the property is worth on the open market. We did everything we logically could have thought of doing. Who would have thought the boy would pull this stunt?"

"It isn't a stunt," Imhof said pensively. "It's a very shrewd business move. He knows that nobody wants the land but us, and he knows that we're desperate to have it. He's got us over a barrel, and I'll be surprised if he doesn't bleed us for every cent we can raise."

"Every cent we can raise!" Alex exclaimed. "What the hell's wrong with you, Mike? He doesn't want to sell us the land. Him and his goddamn communist friends want to keep the forest and the river for the goddamn squirrels and the goddamn fish! He ain't going to sell us the land, not for any price."

Imhof shook his head. "I can't believe that, Alex. We're talking about big money here. If Saunders has to weigh some wildlife against, say, a profit of a hundred thousand dollars . . ."

"A hundred thousand dollars!" screamed Alex, for whom last month's seventy-five-dollar utility bill had been hard to meet, who still owed the bank twelve thousand on the mortgage, who was one month in arrears with the beer distributor. "A hundred thousand dollars! We're supposed to give that goddamn son of a bitch a hundred thousand dollars?"

"If we have to," Bruno said calmly. "And more than that, if we have to. Listen, Alex, Mike is right. Saunders has us over a barrel, and—"

"What about the eminent-domain thing?" he asked, turning to Ostlich. "We were going to do that with Sweet. Why can't we do it with Saunders?"

"Because," Ostlich replied, sighing again, "we don't have the time. Moving through an eminent-domain petition against a retarded freak and an uneducated Indian is one thing. It would be something quite different against Saunders. He may be lowlife, but he isn't stupid. And anyone with that kind of money must have lawyers."

Alex was fuming. "It ain't right, goddamn it, it ain't right. That bastard has too much money now. Look how he behaves, look at how his sister behaves, that poor little girl, so young, so pretty, and she drinks the booze and she takes the drugs and she has sex with that bum she goes with, that lousy bum, he uses her like a whore, I know he does, that bastard, and she should be with someone nice who'll take care of her, and she could have his children and make a home for him. . . ." He stopped, realizing what he was saying, seeing the embarrassed looks on the faces of the others present. He lapsed into silence.

"No one here likes Saunders," Ostlich said uneasily. "But we have to face facts. He doesn't need the land, and we do. We don't have the land, and he does."

"And that's the basis of business," Rihaczeck said, trying to bring the conversation back to his outline of the course of action to be pursued. "I figure that he bought a piece of land worth about seventy thousand for almost four times its value. If he can see a profit of say twenty percent, he'll think his investment a success. That means we'll have to be prepared to offer him three hundred thousand. But, as I said, we may have to go as high as three hundred and fifty."

"And where are we gonna get another hundred and fifty thousand dollars?" Alex demanded. "It was a close vote for the two hundred thousand."

Rihaczeck shrugged. "We have to push for another bond issue. We don't have any choice. Now, the way I see it, we're going to have to make a—"

"So we offer him three hundred fifty thousand," Alex shouted, "and he asks four. So we do another bond? And then he raises it to four fifty?"

"Alex . . ." Ostlich began gently.

"No," he said firmly. "We don't pay that son of a bitch one goddamn cent. We take him to court, we sue him, by God, we sue him!"

"Sue him for what?" Bruno asked. "For outbidding us at a public auction?"

"Alex," Ostlich began again, "we don't have any choice. Let's make this a unanimous vote, for the sake of the voters, for the sake of the community."

"No!"

Ostlich sighed. "It'll be five to one if you insist on it, but the proposal will still have passed the council."

"And I don't get asked nutting about dis?" old Johann Schilder asked angrily as he hobbled into the room. "Vhat is dis, you votink for me and I ain't efen here?"

"Johann," Imhof said, "we weren't leaving you out. You're just a bit late, that's all, and we wanted—"

"Ach, *ja*, I'm late." He nodded, fury in his aged eyes. "So ven you are my age, ve see how fast you valk, eh, Imhof? Ve see how qvick you get places, *ja*?"

An outburst of octogenarian pique is the last thing we need at the moment, Ostlich thought. "We apologize, Johann. We just all knew how you feel about this, and we knew how you'd vote, so we—"

"*Ja*, you know how I vote, *ja*?" he spat. "So here is my vote. Ve don't sell no more bonds, ve don't buy dat land, ve don't build no factory, and ve keep de river for de fishes."

The five men stared at him, speechless. At last Imhof said, "Johann, what are you talking about? You've been in favor of the factory from the beginning."

"*Ja*, so I change my mind, okay? I start to tink maybe dat young fella is right, dat ve shouldn't dump all dat garbage in de river, okay? So I vote ve don't buy nutting from dat *gottverdammte* hippie bum. Ve leave de whole place just like it is, ve don't touch nutting. Ve leave it for de animals."

Bruno jumped to his feet and gaped at his father-in-law. "Dad, what's gotten into you? You know as well as I do that this town needs that factory!"

"De hell vit de town, and de hell vit de factory," Schilder barked, and then turned to Alex. "So I hear vhen I come in dat you don't vant to buy from dat bum, too. So good. Four votes to two."

Ostlich's face was growing flushed. "The proposal still passes, Johann."

"*Ja*, you pass de proposal," he grumbled, turning to walk back out the door he had just entered. "You pass it, and me and Alex, ve tell de people not to vote for it." He stormed from the room.

Bruno ran after him and called out, "Dad! Where are you going?"

"None of your *verdammte* business!" he shouted, and walked on.

Ostlich looked at Alex. "Well? Is this what you want? A four-to-two vote, when we need at least a firm majority if we intend to sell this idea to the public?"

Alex wiped his brow with his palm and stammered, "W-well, n-no, I—I want the factory as much as you do. I just . . . I just don't want to see that son of a bitch make a profit from this."

"We can't afford to think in those terms," Bruno said, walking back from the door. "We have to do what we have to do."

"Yes, yes, of course," Alex said softly. He was shaken by the vehemence of Schilder's words and frightened by the sudden realization that his own obstinacy might prove fatal to his own prospects. "I, ah, I'm changing my mind. I'll vote for the new bond issue. . . ." And I'll help make that goddamn good-for-nothing bastard a hundred thousand dollars richer.

A hundred thousand dollars! Goddamn him to hell!

"Very well," Ostlich said, his voice now sinking back into a weary, lifeless monotone. "This is how I think we should approach getting the idea across to the community, especially to the farmers. . . ."

As Dr. Timothy Ostlich was beginning to discuss strategy with four of the other five members of the council, his daughter Dorcas was walking slowly along the River Road, her hand tightly held in Peter Geerson's. Neither of them spoke, but Peter glanced at her face periodically. When they came to the slight break in the wood line that had once been the entrance to the path, she paused for a moment and then turned to enter. Only then did he say, "Dorcas, are you sure you want to do this?"

She nodded. "I have to see the spot."

He sighed and allowed himself to be pulled gently forward into the snowy forest. This is not a good idea, he thought. She's only been out of the hospital for a week and a half. The last thing she needs is to see the place where her sister was killed. And why in God's name does she want to visit Grogo's house?

"Dorcas . . ." he began again gently.

"Peter, I know you're worried about me, and I appreciate it," she said, "But I'm okay, really. It was all just such a shock, that's all." She breathed deeply, and the bitter winter air stung her nostrils. "What's done is done. Nothing will bring Sarah back, and I have to learn to live with it, that's all. Seeing where it happened will . . . I don't know, make it easier."

How the hell will that make it easier? he wondered as they went deeper into the woods. The density of the forest, even with the branches now denuded of foliage, made it difficult to walk side by side, so she released her grip on his hand and preceded him. Dorcas knew the way to the old Sweet place by heart, but to Peter, who had never been there, it seemed that they were walking aimlessly through the woods. Dorcas knew where the path had once been, where the path still was for those who had eyes to see it. Peter was beginning to fear that she had gotten them lost. "We don't even know for certain where it happened," he said. "Hey, do you know where we are? I mean, it's getting dark already. . . ."

Melancholy warmth was in her smile as she said, "Peter, I know these woods like the back of my hand. I could find my way in and out blindfolded."

"That's good to know," he muttered as he followed her. "But we still don't know where it happened."

"Daddy told me that Vernon broke a jug of moonshine nearby. He got drunk and then attacked Sarah, they say. I don't believe it."

"Had to have been somebody."

"Yes, somebody else."

"How can you be so sure?"

"I just am."

Okay, he thought. No logic problem here. "It isn't gonna be easy finding a broken jug in a forest at night, Dorcas."

"If it's still here, I'll find it," she replied with conviction.

They walked on through the darkening woods for a half hour, and then Dorcas said, "There it is, I think."

"There?" he asked. "Where? I can't see a fucking thing!"

"Right there." She sighed, walking forward a few yards and then stopping to look down at the shards. "So it must have happened here, or right near here."

He stood quietly to one side as she gazed down at

the supposed signature of the crime. "I don't believe it," she repeated. "It couldn't have been Vernon."

"Yeah, maybe not." He coughed, all his urban fears of the wilderness being brought to the fore by the increasingly hazy light of the forest dusk. "You want to go back now?"

"No," she said. "I want to go to his house."

"Dorcas . . ."

"Please, Peter? Please?"

His face wore an exasperated look as he sighed and said, "Okay, okay. But let's not waste time. I mean, let's not just hang around there, okay?"

"Okay." She smiled. "Thanks, Peter. You're awful considerate."

He grinned. "Yeah, one of my many fine qualities." She held out her hand and he took it and squeezed it gently. She released it as they began again to walk single file deeper into the woods, and Peter's smile faded immediately. The chirping of the crickets and the croaking of the frogs unnerved him, and he jumped, startled, at the hoot of a nearby owl. *Shoulda stayed in Queens,* he thought, and then grinned sheepishly. *A fine environmentalist I am, scared of the woods.*

When at last they drew close to the old Sweet place, Dorcas stopped abruptly and peered ahead of her. "What's the matter?" Peter asked.

"Lights," she whispered. "Somebody's there."

He cleared his throat. "Uh, look, Dorcas, I think maybe we should like go back now, you know?"

"Who could it be?" she mused, not listening to his suggestion. "Nobody's supposed to be here, nobody I can think of anyway. . . ."

Peter released a soft laugh of relief when he heard the distant voices of Clayton Saunders and Sean Brenner crying. "All right!" in unison. "Clay and Sean," he said smiling.

"What are they doing here?" she wondered aloud, a hint of annoyance in her voice.

Peter shrugged. "Clay bought the place this morning. It's his now, isn't it?"

She shrugged as she began again to walk toward the house. "I suppose," she muttered. "I can't help but think of it as still belonging to Miss Edith."

"Miss . . . ? Oh, Grogo's sister?"

"Vernon's sister," she corrected him.

"Yeah, right." Grogo, Vernon, tomato, tomahto . . .

Sean saw them as they approached, and he waved and called out. "Hey, Pete, Dork! Come and look what we've found!"

"What are you doing out here?" Peter called back, and then saw Lydia sitting on the steps of the porch and Rebecca standing in the doorway. Rebecca seemed cheerful and excited. Lydia looked bored to tears. "Hiya, Becky, Lyd. What's going on?"

Rebecca waited until they were closer before replying, "I found all this neat shit in the house! Come on in. You gotta see this stuff!"

Peter nodded, but turned to Clayton instead, looking quizzically at the bright glowing Coleman lanterns, the numerous holes in the ground, and the shovels he and Sean were holding. "What are you guys doing?"

"Digging for buried treasure," Clayton cackled, "and we've found some. Look!" He pointed down into one of the holes and Peter peered into it. "Old Man Schilder said that Grogo's father was a moonshiner, and he buried jugs of this shit all over the place. We've been digging around in front of the trees near the house all day, and we found one. Fucking forty-year-old moonshine!"

"Wow," Peter whispered. "How'd you know to dig by the trees?"

Sean coughed. "That's where Grogo found the other one, the one we drank from that day before he . . . well, you know." He shook his head. "If we'd have taken that moonshine back with us instead of leaving it with Grogo, things would have turned out a lot different."

"Yeah, probably." Pete looked over at Becky. "What's in the house?"

"C'mere, both of you," she replied, and then went back inside. Peter and Dorcas followed her up the stairs and into the large central room of the house. A single bare bulb of low wattage burned in the ceiling socket, and Peter squinted his eyes as his nostrils flared against the dusty, musty air in the house. Rebecca walked over to a pile of books, pictures, and papers that were strewn on the floor beside an empty duffel bag and said, "Look at all this stuff!"

Dorcas picked up one of the pamphlets and read the title aloud. "'Life History of Grogo "The Goblin," Written by Himself.'" She opened it and perused it quickly. "Vernon didn't write this. He couldn't have written this. He couldn't even write."

"Yeah, I know. He could barely even think," Rebecca agreed. "But look at this other stuff, all these old pictures and stuff."

Peter walked over to Rebecca and began examining the rest of her discovery. There were old photographs of Vernon and his family, pictures of him as a child and in the sideshow, etchings of Hindu gods on thick parchment, and books printed in a peculiar cursive script that Peter did not recognize.

As he and Rebecca sat on the floor and went through the plunder, Dorcas began to read the pamphlet. It was four pages in length, printed on cheap, yellowing paper, and bore the price notation "5 cents" prominently beneath the title.

A SHORT LIFE STORY OF VERNON L. SWEET, KNOWN AS "GROGO, THE GOBLIN BOY"

For those who are interested, this is a true story of my life, and summed up with a few notes of the famous story of Rip Van Winkle, as written by Washington Irving. The identical spot as mentioned in this legend is just ten miles from the place in the heart of the Catskill Mountains where I was born and spent a very eventful life.

Beginning my story with the day of my birth on February 1st, 1895, in the town of Jewett, Greene County, New York State, the people of that vicinity were witnessing a severe snowstorm; the snow already four feet deep on the level was overhauled by a gale on the day of my birth and rapidly drifting into banks making it impossible to go forth for any reason whatsoever. I was an unusually large baby, weighing fifteen and a half pounds when first born. During the first part of my life I didn't see many well days, owing to the fact that at birth the back of my head was crushed, also my jaw was dislocated, and my collarbones misplaced. The doctors of that vicinity did not know my trouble or it might have been adjusted right when I was young. But it was not until I was eighteen years of age that I learned the cause of my unnatural and retarded development, and it was too late by then to do anything to improve my difficulties. But old Mother Nature had worked her wonders and I had become practically well at the age of fourteen years. Surely there is nothing can beat God's plan if we give it a chance.

"I wonder how much of this is true?" Dorcas muttered.

"Huh?" Rebecca asked as she rummaged through more of her unexpected bounty.

"This biography of Vernon. I wonder how much of it is true? I mean, it says here he weighed over fifteen pounds when he was born—"

"Talk about an argument for legalizing abortion!" Rebecca laughed. Dorcas frowned slightly and then returned her attention to the pamphlet. Rebecca Saunders was not at all intrigued by the subject of Vernon Sweet's life story, so she decided not to make any effort to share it with her.

> During the winter months I earned a small sum from hunting and trapping the furbearing animals until I became eighteen years of age when I had the misfortune to fall upon some ice and badly fracture my hip joints. This has never healed properly and has deprived me of that freedom and pleasure of getting about as in previous days. It was when consulting a specialist in regards to the fractured joint that I learned the cause of my unnatural growth, also learned that my joint would never be much good anymore.

She noticed Peter reading over her shoulder, and she moved the pages to make it easier to him to see. "Do you think it's true?"

"Sure, I guess so." He shrugged. "But he couldn't write this. I mean, I hardly knew the guy, but he sure seemed retarded to me."

"Yes." She nodded. "But look at what he says in here. He used to carve little animals out of wood and sell them to tourists—"

"I bet Patanjali wrote this," Peter interrupted. He was reading intently, and she sensed that he did not want her to read any sections of the pamphlet to him. She fell silent and read on.

> I was the third child of six, having two brothers and three sisters; the sisters have all acquired diplomas for teaching school, and each taught a few terms of school. My father still lives, but I lost my dear mother in January of 1923, and our family is scattered since then to different places, excepting one sister and myself, when I came this season with the circus of Ringling Bros. and Barnum and Bailey's.

"He was with Ringling Brothers?" Peter asked skeptically.

"I used to go to that circus when I was a little kid," Dorcas said. "I don't remember a freak show."

"Probably did away with it," Peter mused. "Upgraded their show and put the little guy out of work."

"And sent him out to some freak-show circuit or something. That's terrible."

Peter shrugged. "Progress, I guess."

"Right, progress. Like dumping waste into rivers?"

He smiled, "Touché." They finished reading the old pamphlet.

> They have entitled me "Grogo, the Goblin" from the fact that I came from within ten miles of the spot where the story was written of Rip Van Winkle as previously mentioned. I recall how it stated that old Rip was driven from home one terrible stormy night by his enraged wife, and he took refuge in the Catskill Mountains. While there, he met with a colony of little people called the Goblins, who took pity on old Rip and gave

him a drink of their own brew, which put Rip to sleep, and he slept for twenty years.

Peter shook his head. "Weird shit."

"What is?" Lydia asked as she entered the room. She had been sitting and watching Clayton and Sean dig holes for hours, and was restless and irritable.

"This," he said, handing her the pamphlet. "It's a biography of Grogo from back when he was in the circus, or the sideshow, or whatever. I wonder how much of it is true?"

"Hmm," Lydia grunted, not the slightest bit interested. She looked down at her sister and said, "You know, Dork, I don't think being here is the best thing in the world for you."

"I'm okay, Lydia," Dorcas said softly as she gently, almost lovingly touched a leather-bound book. "Really I am."

Lydia took the book from her sister's hands. "What's this thing?"

"I'm not sure," Dorcas replied. "It isn't printed in English. Looks like some kind of Bible or something. Probably some holy book from Mr. Patanjali's religion."

"Yeah, probably," Lydia said, tossing the book back to her, not the slightest bit interested in this either. "Hey, Becky, can you drive a car with like a clutch?"

"Yeah, sure," she replied. "Why?"

"'Cause those two assholes out there are barely gonna be able to get into the jeep, let alone drive the fucking thing. They're drinking that disgusting shit they dug up."

Rebecca's eyes locked with Lydia's for a moment, and they shared a common thought: two drunken boy-friends make for a particularly unamorous evening. "Son of a bitch," Rebecca muttered, and then preceded Lydia out the door.

Peter watched Dorcas fondle the old book, and he asked, "You gonna take that with you? I'm sure Clay doesn't care."

"No," she replied. "No, I don't think so. I don't know." She shook her head. "This isn't right, Peter. I feel like a burglar or something. I mean, I know they're dead and all this stuff belongs to Clay now, but still . . ."

"I understand." He nodded. "Look, let's go, okay? We can go back to the trailer for a while and hang out, and then I'll take you home if you want." He grinned. "If I can get Russell's car started."

Whatever reply Dorcas would have made was cut short by angered shouts from outside the house, and she and Peter went quickly to the door. They found old Johann Schilder confronting Clayton and Sean, shaking his fist at them and screaming, "You bums got no respect for udder people's property!"

"This is *my* property, old man," Clayton shouted back, slurring his words.

"People lived in dis house, made dere lives here!" Schilder said angrily. "You treat it like it vas nutting, like you can do vhatever you vant here, digging tings up, getting drunk on somebody else's likker!"

"You ain't listening, Pops," Sean said, his voice even less distinct than Clayton's. "This is his liquor, and this is his house, and this is his land, and so why don't you like get the fuck outta here, you know?"

"That's right, by God!" Clayton shouted, laughing. "You're trusspessing. I'm gonna put a big sign up, gonna say trusspessers will be persecuted."

Sean tried to snap his fingers. "That's from Firesign Theater."

Clayton shook his head. "I never reveal my sources."

"You lousy bums," Schilder muttered, and then he saw Dorcas and Peter standing in the doorway. "You, young fella. I tink maybe you're right about de river. I vote against de factory. Ve save de river for de fishes."

Peter blinked in surprise, and then smiled broadly. "Hey, that's great, that's great! Thanks a lot!"

"I don't do it for you," Schilder responded, refusing to be amicable. "I do it for de fishes."

"It don't matter what you do," Clayton said. He was sitting on the ground with his arms and legs wrapped around the big old jug he and Sean had discovered. "I own this place, not you or the fucking town." He started to giggle idiotically, singing, "This land is my land, and it sure ain't your land. . . ."

Schilder glowered at him and then turned to Dorcas. "Child, come here. I gotta talk to you."

Dorcas walked down the four porch steps. "What is it, Mr. Schilder?"

"Not here, not vit dese drunken bums," he muttered. "Follow me. I gotta show you someting."

Dorcas had known Johann Schilder all her life, and while he had always been a generally curmudgeonly gadfly, he had never been other than kind to her, as kind as was possible for him, at least. She followed him a few yards away and then asked again, "What is it?"

He looked over at the five other young people as if to make certain they were out of earshot, and then he said quietly, "I know vhat happened to you a few veeks ago. I know you tink you saw dat *gottverdammte* freak in de voods." He paused. "I tink maybe you did."

She stared at him wordlessly for a few moments. "What are you talking about? I know that Vernon is dead. I know what happened here. I know that you people murdered him and Mr. Pantanjali." Her voice was reproachful, but Schilder didn't react to it, so she went on, "I don't understand what you're trying to say."

"Listen to me, child," he said. "Maybe ve vas wrong about dat gargoyle. I don't know. Maybe ve vas right.

Maybe ve should've called de cops, but dat don't matter. Vhat's done is done."

"But . . ."

"Nobody stayed behind aftervard," he went on. "Ve all just figgered dey vas dead, and dat vas dat. But I tink maybe dey didn't die." He paused and sighed. "I know for a fact dat de heathen didn't die, and I tink maybe de freak didn't die eidder."

"Mr. Pantajali is alive!" she exclaimed, and then, with rising excitement, "You mean I *did* see Vernon? I *wasn't* going crazy?"

"I don't know about dat," he said. "Ve hung him pretty good, and he vasn't moving vhen we took him down. But de heathen I find in a cave, over by de foot of de mountain. I find him yesterday vhen I vas hunting deer. He's sick, he's hurt, I tink maybe he dies soon. He tells me he vants to see you, vhat for, I dunno."

She felt her legs twitching with the urge to begin running into the forest. "Where? Where is he?"

"Vait a minute, vait a minute," he said irritably. "Now you listen to me. A lot of good people vas here dat day, and maybe ve make a mistake. I don't vant nobody getting in no trouble about dat whole ting, you hear me? I tink maybe ve all just forget about de hanging, forget about de factory, forget about de whole ting vit dese voods. Too many good people maybe get hurt, too many good husbands and fadders."

She forced herself to be patient. "Mr. Schilder, you're right, what's done is done. I don't want to stir up anything, and I don't want anyone else to get hurt. But if Mr. Patanjali is alive and hurt, we have to help him, now, quickly! Peter and Becky and Lydia can help carry him to—"

"No, you vait vun minute," he barked. "I tell all dis to you because he asks me to, but I don't trust dem bums over dere, not even your sister. You don't tell nobody about dis, or I don't take you to him."

"Okay, okay," she said quickly, thinking that once she knew where Ashvarinda was hiding she could get help, no matter what Schilder said. "But let's go to him, please!"

"All right, all right," he grumbled. "Come on." He started to hobble off into the woods.

Dorcas turned and called out, "Peter, I'm going somewhere with Mr. Schilder. I'll meet you at the trailer later." She followed after Schilder without waiting for a response.

Peter made a motion to follow her, and then stopped. I guess she's okay with him, he thought. Harmless old man. She's known him all her life, and he seems to care about her. She might just want to talk to him about her problems. He might be a grandfather figure or something, maybe. . . . He smiled slightly. And what the hell, he cares about the fish!

As they walked deep into the dark woods Schilder took a flashlight from the pocket of his red hunting coat and switched it on, moving it back and forth in front of him. "I didn't know there were caves around here," Dorcas said.

"Me neidder," Schilder replied, "but I vas tracking dis buck and I took a shot at him . . . missed . . . my eyes, dey ain't so good no more . . ."

"Yes?" she said, "And?"

"And I guess de heathen, he hears de shot and he calls out for help. I follow de voice, and dere is dis cave, right in de mountain, de mouth all covered vit brush."

"How badly is he hurt?"

"Bad, he's hurt bad," Schilder said. "He got hit hard in de head, and den he got burned. It's a miracle he lived at all, and he's been in dere for six veeks, hanging on to life. He got some constitution, dat old heathen."

I have to get him to a hospital, Dorcas thought as they walked onward into the darkness. I don't care who gets in trouble, I don't care who goes to jail, I don't care what happens. . . .

"Here," Schilder said, breathing heavily from the exertion of the walk. "Dis is de cave. I go in first. Maybe dere's bats or something. Gotta be careful in caves." He entered carefully, stepping over a pile of branches and swinging his flashlight around and examining the interior. The mouth of the cave was just high enough for them to enter without stooping over, but jagged outcrops of rock on the sides made it impossible to walk straight ahead, and Dorcas found herself weaving right and left, scraping her arms on the sides of the narrow passageway.

A faint light glimmered from around a sharp turn in the passage, and she followed Schilder into what seemed almost like an oval room, a bubble of space in a narrow pathway into the interior of the mountain. Beyond the oval space the passageway again became narrow and wound its irregular way off into the darkness.

Ashvarinda Patanjali lay upon the cold stone floor of the cave. Beside him burned an old lantern, and a small bucket of water stood beside it. His once-nut-brown skin was a pale gray in those places that were not covered with festering scabs, and his breathing was loud and labored. His eyes were open, but they seemed milky and confused as he turned and looked at Dorcas. It was cold in the cave, not as cold as it was outside in the winter woods, but the temperature well below freezing, and the aged yogi was naked. "You . . . have . . . come . . ." he rasped.

"My God!" she said, dropping to her knees beside him. "Oh, Jesus!"

"Listen to me . . ." he said, straining with the

effort to speak. "*Ey raakshus . . . ey raakshus . . .*
a . . . a demon . . .*"

"Mr. Patanjali, I'm gonna get you to the hospital.
Just try to relax, don't try to talk." She almost tore her
jacket from her body and placed it gently over him.
"You're gonna be okay, honest, just try to hang on for a
little while longer." Over a month, she thought, filled
with rage at the people who had done this to the
harmless old man, he's been lying here like this for over
a month, living on nothing but water. . . .

She frowned. He can't even move. Where has he
been getting the water? And the lantern, where . . . ?
Her eyes went wide. "Vernon," she said. "Where's
Vernon? Is he alive?"

"Yes . . ." Ashvarinda whispered. "He . . . is alive
. . . he pulled me . . . from the . . . the fire."

"*Ja*, dat's vat I figgered." Schilder nodded. "Now,
hurry up vit vhatever you vant to tell de child. Ve got to
get away from here."

"And leave him here like this?" Dorcas shouted.
"Leave him here to die like this? What the hell's the
matter with you?"

"Listen to me. . . ." Ashvarinda said slowly and
with great difficulty. "The Blessed Lord Vishnu has . . .
kept me alive just . . . just long enough . . . just
long enough . . . to tell . . . to tell . . . not enough
time . . . for final meditation . . . final trance . . .
final oblivion."

"Please, Mr. Patanjali, don't try to talk."

Ashvarinda reached over with one weak, bony hand
and grabbed her wrist. "*Listen . . . to . . . me*," he
said urgently. "I formed . . . a link, a link . . . with
my mind . . . my mind to his mind . . . when I die,
the link . . . the link will break . . . he will know . . .
he will know—"

"Shhh, Mr. Patanjali, please . . ."

"No time . . . no time . . ." he whispered.

"Dying . . . dying . . . no time . . . you must say . . . prayer . . . you must pray, each sunrise and each sunset . . . you must pray . . . listen . . . repeat my words."

"I have to get help—"

He seemed almost about to weep as he said, "No, no . . . you must repeat my words . . . you must remember them . . . each sunrise and each sunset . . . for the rest of your life."

"Okay, okay, I'll repeat whatever you say, but then I have to go and get help."

"You hurry up," Schilder grumbled. "I don't like dis place. I feel like maybe de mountain collapses on me or someting."

She shot him an angry, almost hateful glance and then turned back to Ashvarinda. "Go on. What do you want me to remember?"

"Repeat . . . repeat . . ."

"I will. Hurry, please."

He took a deep, rattling breath. "*Mujey suno bhagawan Vishnu*. Repeat . . . repeat it. . . ."

"*Mujey suno* . . . what?" Dorcas shook her head. "Mr. Patanjali, I can't just memorize sounds like this. I don't even know what I'm saying. Listen, why don't we get to a hospital, and then, after you're feeling better, we can take our time and—"

"*No!*" he said with a firmness seeming to belie his broken state. "There is no time . . . no time." Ashvarinda fought back the urge to weep. "Dorcas, child, you must try . . . you must try . . . I will . . . explain the prayer . . . you must memorize it . . . make it a singsong . . . yes, yes, that will help, a singsong . . . a singsong. . . ."

She sighed. "Okay, okay. I'll try again."

"Listen . . ." he said once again, weakly and with

trembling voice. "*Mujey suno bhagawan Vishnu.* Hear me, Lord Vishnu. . . ."

"*Mujey suno bhagawan Vishnu,*" she said, trying to imitate his sound and intonation.

He nodded, and then proceeded with his strange prayer, sentence by sentence, supplication by supplication. Dorcas repeated them as best she could, singing them to the melody of "I Want to Hold Your Hand" as an aid to memorization, much as a child learns to sing the ABC's. She had been raised in an environment at least nominally Christian, and she felt uneasy repeating a prayer to a Hindu god; but she forced herself to do it, forced herself to attempt to remember the words. Ashvarinda whispered on and on, and Dorcas sang.

Mujey suno bhagawan Vishnu. . . .

Hear me, Lord Vishnu. . . .

Meyriy muhduhd kuhro, bhagawan Vishnu. . . .

Help me, Lord Vishnu. . . .

Meyrey sarey achey kurum, mey aphey upiyog key liyey sumpurn kurthiy hu. . . .

All my good karma I surrender to you, Lord Vishnu, I surrender it to you for your use. . . .

Bhagawan, is jan wur ko nirbul buna kur iskiy undr kiy ak ko phor do. . . .

Lord, weaken the beast and blind his inner eye. . . .

Sub jiyvit pranyo kiy or sey thumbariy ruksha key liyey vinthiy kurthi hu. . . .

On behalf of all living things, I beg you to preserve, preserve, preserve.. . . .

A half hour passed as Ashvarinda forced Dorcas to sing the prayer repeatedly. She sang and sang and sang, burning the alien sounds into her mind, and he seemed at last to relax slightly. His body sank down into the cold uneven rock upon which he lay as he whispered, "Every sunrise . . . every sunset . . . never forget . . . always, always. . . ."

"Yes, Mr. Patanjali, I'll do it, don't worry." I'll say anything to get you to calm down and rest while I go and get help.

"He will . . . understand . . . when I die . . . if you don't . . . if you don't . . . say the prayer . . . but . . . control . . . trap him . . . trap him . . . make him forget . . . blind him . . . *maya* . . . *maya* . . . net of illusion. . . ."

He's delirious, she thought. "I'm going to go now and get help. Try to rest, try to sleep. Mr. Patanjali? Mr. Patanjali?" His eyes had closed and he was motionless. She feared for a moment that he had died, but then she saw his chest rising and falling almost imperceptibly. She got to her feet and turned viciously on Schilder. "What kind of person are you? How could you just leave him here like this? Why in God's name didn't you call a doctor, get him to a hospital, something, anything?"

"Dat's vhy," he said, pointing behind her into the narrow darkness of the passageway that stretched out beyond the oval room. She looked where he was pointing and then walked forward to the spot where the rock walls came abruptly closer to each other. She squinted into the passage and saw what looked like a body lying on the rocky ground in the darkness. She looked closer.

It was old Johann Schilder, the back of his head seemingly sheared away, resting in a thick pool of blood.

She spun around just as the old man who had led her to the cave shrank and twisted into a misshapen, monstrous caricature of the human form.

"Hi hi hi," said Grogo the Goblin. "Hello!"

Dorcas began to scream.

Chapter Eleven

January 3, 1969 (continued)

When by ten o'clock that evening Dorcas had not shown up at the trailer, Peter and Lydia had gone off in search of her after agreeing to meet the others at around midnight at Alex Brown's bar. They thus left Rebecca to take care of Clayton and Sean, who had shared a bottle of vodka while waiting and were by now in that intermediate state between dead drunk and terribly hung over. Rebecca was neither so subtle nor so kind as to compel them merely to take cold, sobering showers. She preferred more direct action. She took her brother and her boyfriend by the hair, dragged then out of the trailer to the small pond in the clearing out back, and, after tossing a rock through the thin layer of ice to make certain it would shatter under their weight, pushed them in.

They were not amused, but they were a bit more sober for the experience. Sean's sobriety, if not his sense of well-being, was involuntarily advanced when he climbed out of the freezing pond, fell to his knees, and vomited so violently that for a moment he thought his stomach would rupture. He crawled forward on the ground, trying to rise to his feet on his rubbery legs. He did not notice that he had crawled beneath a low-hanging branch, and when he finally summoned up the

will to stand, he slammed his head into it. It took a scant
fifteen minutes for Rebecca to revive him and help him
change his clothes. After Clayton had done the same,
they left for Alex's bar.

The drive took them just under thirty minutes. It
should have taken them less than half that time, but
Clayton drove very slowly, which was his customary
gesture to highway safety when he was driving drunk.
He had been exercising this responsible caution ever
since his friend Marc Rosenblatt killed himself and a
family of five while driving under the influence. It was
when Clayton watched the police peeling what was left
of Marc from the exterior of the other car that Clayton
resolved, as a simple matter of self-protection and
civic-mindedness, to drive very slowly if he were drinking heavily. He did indeed stray occasionally onto the
shoulder or into the left-hand lane of the two-lane
mountain road, but he and his passengers were fortunate
enough to encounter neither any other motorists nor any
trees on the drive from Saunders Mountain down into
Beckskill.

"Becky, I hate your fucking guts," Clayton muttered
as he parked down the street from Alex's bar at just after
eleven.

"I don't feel good," Sean added woefully.

"Serves you both right." Rebecca grinned, delighting in their discomfort. "You guys had a lot of nerve
getting all fucked up like that so early. I mean, what
were me and Lyd supposed to do when you fell asleep?"

"Contemplate the joys of lesbianism," Clayton suggested, yawning and shaking his head to clear it.

"Good one, Clay," his sister said. "Real funny."

He took a deep breath and then screamed,
"WHOOOOP!"

Sean jumped. "What the hell are you trying to do,
scare me to death?!"

"Not at all, my boy, not at all," he replied as Rebecca began to laugh. "Just waking myself up." He reached into the backseat and slapped Sean in the face. "Wake up, youngster! The night is still young, and there's a bottle of bourbon in yon tavern with your name on it."

"Hey, like, fuck you, you know?" Sean muttered, trying to slap him back and missing his face.

"Hold on, Clay," Rebecca said. "I didn't get him sobered up just so he could get comatose again."

"Oh, shit, Becky, just look at him, will you? His only hope of survival rests in an immediate alcohol transfusion." As if to illustrate Clayton's point, Sean belched loudly. A stale smell of incipient nausea immediately filled the small interior of the jeep.

"Oh, Jesus," Rebecca muttered. "Let's get inside, quick, I'm gonna have to get disgustingly drunk myself just to be able to kiss this animal without throwing up."

"That's the beauty of it," Clayton said. "Even if you do throw up, who's gonna care?"

Sean peered out the window through bleary eyes. "Where the hell are we?"

"Don't you know where you are?" Clayton asked, feigning concern. "I think you need a drink to steady yourself."

"Are we going to Alex's?" Sean muttered. "What the hell for? It's more fun back at the trailer."

"No," Rebecca said. "We have to meet Pete and Lydia here, remember? We'll just hang out and have a few drinks while we wait for them."

"Have a few drinks!" Sean whined. "Are you kidding? I just puked my guts up and almost killed myself."

"I know, I know," Clayton said, frowning and nodding sympathetically. "Terrible experience, terrible. I think you could use a good stiff drink."

"Hey, forget it, man. I'm going back to the trailer."

Clayton reached into his pocket and took out the keys to the jeep. He dangled them in front of Sean and asked, "You gonna walk?"

Sean sighed. "Ah, shit," he muttered, and slowly followed Clayton and Rebecca as they climbed out of the jeep.

"It'll be fun," Rebecca said, taking his arm. "We can listen to Patti Page on the radio, play that old bowling machine of his, drink some nice watery beer. . . . "

"Ah, shit," he repeated.

"Gesundheit!" Clayton replied.

"Come on, Tarzan," Rebecca said, holding him up as one of his legs buckled. "Let's go get you some of the hair of that dog."

"Stupid expression," Sean mumbled. "Hair of the dog that bit you. What the hell does that mean, anyway."

Clayton and Rebecca were laughing at Sean's misery as they opened the door and almost fell into the room. The few townspeople who were still nursing their last beers of the evening looked at them in disgust, but not Alex Brown. He smiled broadly and held his hands out in a bizarre and totally uncharacteristic gesture of welcome, saying, "Hello, come in, come in!"

Sean was immediately suspicious. He leaned to Clayton and whispered, "What's with him?"

"Don't be stupid," Clayton whispered back. "He wants me to sell the Sweet property to the town."

"Oh." Sean nodded. "Real subtle."

Clayton preceded his friends over to the bar and said somberly, "Good evening, Alex. You're looking well."

"What would you like?" Alex asked, the smile remaining plastered on his face. Clayton had been only partially correct in his assessment of Alex's good cheer. The middle-aged bartender saw that Clayton had been drinking heavily, and that presented him with the opportunity of both overcharging and shortchanging him; and Alex had been having a few beers with the locals, as was his custom on weekend nights. He was, as they say, feeling no pain.

"I'd like a Mercedes Benz," Rebecca said as she and Sean sat down on bar stools, thus forcing him to acknowledge her presence by repeating the question to her.

"What will it be?" he asked Rebecca. "A black Russian?"

"Oh, Al, how sweet!" She grinned. "You remembered my favorite drink. Yeah, a black Russian, and a pitcher of beer."

"What about my favorite drink?" Clayton pouted.

Alex snapped his fingers. "Bloody Mary, right?"

"Oh, Al, how sweet," he simpered. "You remembered!" He turned to Sean. "More vodka, buddy?"

Sean looked over at him slowly, tasting the recently relieved nausea still lurking in his throat and mouth. After a long pause he said, "Just beer."

Clayton shook his head. "That's not the hair of the dog, Sean old man."

"Hair of the dog," Sean muttered as Alex drew him a beer and then began to mix the other drinks. "You know, that reminds me. What does that stupid poster mean, that John Wayne poster? I just like don't get the joke."

"What poster?" Clayton asked.

"The one on the wall in the trailer, the one where he's saying 'Buy a dachshund.' I don't get it."

"It's a cowboy saying buy a dachshund," Clayton replied, as if that explained it.

Rebecca sauntered over to the bowling machine and dropped three dimes into the slot. The bowling machine was one of those devices of entertainment so common in modest taverns. It consisted of an alley two yards in length, resolving itself into a series of prongs that rose a quarter of an inch from the surface. Ten small plastic bowling pins hung directly above the prongs, arranged in the customary triangular pattern. The player would slide a metal puck down the sawdust-covered alley, and the number of pins removed from play and electrically scored would be determined by the number and inter-connected sequence of prongs depressed by the puck. It was a simple diversion in may bars. It was the sole diversion in Alex's.

"Hey, Sean," Rebecca said. "C'mon, we're gonna bowl."

He looked over wearily. "I'm sorry, but I can't."

"Why not?"

"If I have to stand up, I'll fall down. I can't see too good, anyway. Just let me sit here and drink my beer."

Rebecca sniffed. "Boy, you're a lot of fun." She turned to Alex, who was busy filling their order. "You wanna bowl with us, Al?"

Alex frequently played the bowling machine with his customers, as a way of encouraging them to spend more money. "Yeah, sure. Wait a minute."

Rebecca took her turn, scoring three on her first shot. The second time she slid the puck down the alley she missed completely. Drunker than I thought, she mused as she tossed the puck to her brother. Clayton rolled up his sleeves, spat on his hands, rubbed them together, and then slid the puck down the playing board so forcefully that it rebounded off the back and slid forward into his hands.

"Steee-rike!" he yelled.

Rebecca was sitting next to Sean at the bar, draped over his shoulder and nibbling his ear, and as Clayton turned to call Alex to take his turn at the machine he noticed that the older man was staring intently at them. He laughed softly and said, "Hey, Al. You go."

Alex snapped his eyes away from Sean and Rebecca

as if Clayton had startled him. He went from behind the bar over to the bowling machine, and Rebecca followed him. Sean remained seated, sighing and gently exploring the lump on his head.

Alex knew the bowling machine as well as if he had built it himself. He had played the machine almost every night for decades, and he was able to score a strike whenever he wished to. He used this ability to boost receipts by challenging his customers to decidedly one-sided games of chance, so Clayton and Rebecca knew what he was about to suggest when he said, "Hey, I have an idea."

"Whatever could it be?" Clayton asked with concern.

"Why don't we make this game a little more interesting? How about maybe a little wager?"

Clayton pursed his lips. "I don't know, Al. I don't think that's legal."

"Come on," Alex urged, oblivious to the sarcasm, "just a friendly little wager. Won't hurt nobody. If I win, you gotta buy a round for the house. If you win, I gotta buy a round for the house."

Clayton pretended to think hard about the proposition and then he nodded. "Well, okay. But what if there's a tie?"

"Then nobody buys for nobody."

"Well, okay," he repeated. "Me and Becky already went, so you go."

Alex smiled and took his shot. It was a strike. Clayton looked at him menacingly and said, "Hey! What's goin' on here? You hustling me or something?" Rebecca then took her second turn and ran up a score of six for her next two shots. Clayton followed, knocking down nine pins.

The games went on for the next hour, interrupted only by Alex excusing himself occasionally to refill the empty glasses of his customers, whose number diminished as the night wore on. Alex's meager income depended upon weekend evenings such as this, for the local farmers stayed until well after midnight, and Clayton and Rebecca stayed even later, if they came to his bar at all. One by one the locals departed, until in the last dark hours before dawn only Clayton, Rebecca, and Sean remained, the latter having slept for a while with his head down on the bar as his girlfriend drank black Russian after black Russian.

Clayton grew bored with the bowling machine, and as he rubbed his eyes and yawned he said, "Let's play something else."

"What else?" Alex laughed. "We got no pinballs here." He was swaying slightly, for the rounds of drinks Clayton had been buying after each game he inevitably lost had caused Alex to drink more than was his wont during working hours.

"Yeah, no balls and no nuts." Clayton nodded. "Why don't we flip coins for drinks?"

Alex shook his head. "No, no, I don't gamble like that. I play the bowling game, but that's different."

"Sure," Sean mumbled from the bar. "Other people got a chance when you flip coins."

Alex glared at him. "What did you say?"

At that moment Rebecca felt the room beginning to spin and she stumbled away from the bowling machine and fell heavily into Alex. She would have slipped down to the floor, but he grabbed her around the waist and steadied her. "Whoa," she said, "that kinda snuck up on me." Alex still had his hands on her waist, and he kept them there a moment or two longer than necessary. Rebecca noticed this, and she smiled at him, her sultry, foggy eyes half-open. He pulled his hands away sharply and looked very uncomfortable as Rebecca continued to smile and Sean chuckled softly.

Alex spun around and approached Sean menacingly. "What you laugh?" he demanded, his generally good English falling victim to the alcohol, the late hour, and his embarrassment.

His tone surprised Sean. "Hey, man, I wasn't laughing at you."

"You don't call me man."

Clayton intervened. "Come on, Al, he didn't mean nothing. Hey, I got an idea. Let's flip coins for shots of tequila."

Alex shook his head sullenly. "I told you, I don't flip coins."

"Come on, be a sport. I tell you what: if I lose, I buy us all a round of tequila, and you can charge me triple for it. How's that?"

He examined this idea, looking for a trick, and not finding one. "Okay, okay, but I do the flipping. We use my coins, three coins."

"Okey-dokey," Clayton said, not expecting to win, and not caring if he lost. These games of chance served merely to introduce an element of diversion into the evening's major goal, which was to drink as much as possible. "I got heads, you got tails."

"No," Alex insisted, "I got heads, you got tails."

"Sure, fine, whatever. Go ahead. But get a lemon and some salt and a knife."

"A lemon? Oh, for the tequila. Sure, sure." Alex scurried away into the kitchen behind the bar.

Clayton and Rebecca sat down on either side of Sean, who was resting his elbows on the bar top and leaning his chin on his hands. "You know he's probably got trick coins, right?"

Clayton nodded. "Of course."

Sean nodded in turn. "Just checking."

Alex returned with two lemons, three quarters, and a long carving knife. "Okay, we start." He tossed the coins one at a time onto the bar, and they came up two heads and one tail. "I win!" he said, and turned to get the bottle of tequila, not noticing as Clayton took two quarters from his pocket and deftly switched them with two from the bar top. He winked at Rebecca, who giggled stupidly.

Clayton lifted the filled shot glass and said, "Okay, a toast to . . . to, ah . . . to President-elect Nixon."

Alex lifted his glass earnestly. "*Da*, I voted for him. I drink to him."

"*Da*?" Rebecca asked.

"*Da*. Is Ukrainian. Means yes."

"Oh. Okay, *da da da*! To Dicky!" She, Clayton, and Alex drained their glasses. Sean merely sipped from his.

"Okay, let's go again," Clayton said. "I feel my luck's about to change."

Alex tossed the coins a second time, and two of them came up tails. He frowned, perplexed, but said nothing as he poured four shots of tequila and began to slice one of the lemons. Sean belched and then groaned, and Rebecca said quickly, "Sean, you are *not* punking out of this. You drink your tequila!"

He shook his head. "Becky, I feel like death warmed over. I swear I'll puke again if I have to drink anything else."

"So you just find yourself another branch to slam against your head," Clayton said. "So what? C'mon, Brenner, don't be such a downer. Finish your tequila. Remember, children in Mexico are sober."

Sean gazed dismally at the four shots of cactus whiskey that Alex set out before them, and he sighed. "Oh, well, what the hell." He licked the arc formed by his thumb and his forefinger, poured salt on it, and then took hold of one of the shot glasses. He licked off the salt, threw the liquor down his throat, and frantically rammed a slice of lemon into his mouth.

"Atta boy," Clayton said happily, and then he, Rebecca, and Alex repeated Sean's gestures. Rebecca and Clayton sighed and smiled as the fiery whiskey burned its way down into their stomachs. Alex shuddered and began to perspire.

"One more time," Clayton said, pushing the three coins toward Alex. The tosses were made, and Alex found himself once again disgruntledly pouring shots of tequila. He blinked his eyes a few times in rapid succession as his vision began to blur.

"Hey, you remember Caroline?" Sean asked.

Clayton laughed. "Yeah. Space cadet."

"Who was Caroline?" Rebecca asked.

"This chick we met in that commune in Idaho two years ago," Sean explained, feeling rather chipper from the tequila, contrary to his expectations. "She said that if you drank enough tequila, you'd trip."

"Yeah"—Clayton laughed—"'cause it's made from the same cactus they make mescaline from."

"Is that true?" Rebecca asked.

"Sure it is," Sean said, "but before you could drink enough of it to start tripping, you'd probably be dead."

"Really." She laughed. "I wish I'd gone with you guys that summer. I'd love to see what it's like to live on a commune."

"It's great," Clayton said. "You sit around all day drinking and getting stoned while you watch all the assholes playing back to nature."

"Some of them were okay," Sean commented.

"Sure, some of them were. Caroline was, anyway. Chick could give a blow job that'd put a vacuum cleaner to shame."

Rebecca laughed louder. "Clay, you're terrible."

"So was being on that fucking commune," he said, licking a few drops of tequila from the bottom of the shot glass. "All these people talking about land and rain and sunshine and plants and loving the universe and all that shit. And then most of them got bored with it and split anyway. Caroline, too. Last I heard from her she was back in college. Swahili major or something."

Alex attempted to sound casual and only slightly interested. "What is this you say, this mescaline?"

"What?" Clayton asked.

"This mescaline you talked about. What is it?"

Clayton washed the tequila taste from his mouth with a swig of beer. "It's like tequila, only it grows like naturally. Does a number on your head, let me tell you."

Alex's eyes narrowed. "This is a drug?"

"Sure," Sean said, "just like alcohol's a drug."

"No, no, you know what I mean. This mescaline, it is a drug?"

"No, I don't know what you mean," Sean insisted. "What's the difference between drugs and booze? They both get you high."

The hostility that Alex felt toward Sean, which he had been repressing all night, began to surface. "How you know about this? You use drugs?"

"Everybody uses some kind of drugs."

"I don't use no drugs!"

Sean laughed. "Give me a break, Alex! You're so drunk right now you can hardly stand up."

"Alcohol has been for thousands of years, all over the world!" Alex said angrily. He looked at Rebecca. "You use drugs? He gives you drugs?"

Rebecca's voice was patient and infuriatingly condescending. "Al, some people use one drug, other people use another drug. You just gotta let people use whatever drug feeds their head, you know?"

"I don't use no drugs!" he shouted.

"For Christ's sake, Alex," Sean shouted back, "you drink, don't you? What do you think alcohol is, ginger ale or something?"

"Is legal, alcohol. Drugs, they ain't legal. The doctors and the government, they both say—"

"Doctors," Sean spat. "They're all full of shit, just like the government is. They all lie through their teeth."

"Ah, you know better than doctors and senators, Mr. Genius, Mr. Wiseguy college kid?"

Clayton disliked the tenor of the conversation, so he interrupted it by saying, "Enough of this drivel, and enough of tossing coins. Al, set up some more tequila. I'll buy." Alex was staring at Sean with blazing, furious eyes, so Clayton tapped him gently and amicably on the arm. "Come on, Al, another round. Hey, let's drink to your homeland. What is it, Bulgaria or something? Yugoslavia?"

"Ukraine," he muttered, taking the tequila bottle and pouring four more shots.

"Oh, yeah, the Ukraine." Clayton nodded. "What's it like in the Ukraine? Is it like around here?"

"Who gives a . . . ?" Sean began to mutter until Clayton's elbow rammed hard into his ribs.

"No, no, is no mountains where I come from," Alex said. "I come from Kivertsy, near Poland. All flat. Farms and cows, though, like around here. Lotta cows. When I was a child, we had lotta cows. Pigs too."

"Moooo," Sean said softly. "Oink oink."

Alex's attention was once again riveted on Sean. "You think it's funny, farming? You think working on your land from sunrise to sunset is funny? You think hard work is funny?"

"Hey, I didn't . . ."

"You think you're better than people who work, maybe, 'cause you don't work? You try working sometime, you see it ain't so funny."

"What are you talking about, man? I didn't say nothing about farmers."

Clayton sighed. The asshole brigade is out in full

force tonight, he thought. "He didn't mean nothing, Al. Come on, finish pouring the shots and we'll drink to the Ukraine." He looked around. "Nobody's left but us, so why don't we take the bottle and all go sit at a table. You don't have to wait on anybody else, so you don't have to stand up." He laughed heartily. "Besides, I don't think you *can* stand up!"

Alex found Clayton's laughter infectious, and he grinned slightly. "Yeah, maybe I'm a little tipsy."

"Maybe, just a little," Clayton said. "Come on, let's go sit at a table."

It was no easy task for them to manage to convey themselves, the shot glasses, and the bottle of tequila the seven feet from the bar to the table, but it was accomplished with a minimum of spillage and no serious injuries. "Here's to the Ukraine," Clayton slurred, and tossed back another shot of tequila.

Alex did the same, muttering something in his native tongue. Rebecca sat motionless beside the drunken bartender, staring off into space with dull, vacant eyes, and Sean swayed in small, slow circles upon the chair. Alex took out a handkerchief and mopped his brow, saying, "It got awful hot in here."

"Yeah," Clayton agreed, not having been at all uncomfortable a moment ago. Now he decided that he was sweltering, so he removed his leather vest and tossed it over to lie on the floor near his jacket, which he had dropped there hours before.

Rebecca watched her brother for a moment, and then mumbled, "Wow, yeah. I'm drenched with sweat. Turn down the heat, will you, Al?" She slowly pulled off her sweater and let it fall to the floor. Alex struggled to bring his surroundings into focus, and his attention was immediately riveted upon Rebecca's chest. She was braless beneath a white tank top, and the dampness of her own perspiration caused the thin cloth to cling to her breasts. Alex gazed at them obsessively, but then, realizing what he was doing and fearing to invite ridicule, he pulled his eyes away and looked around the room.

How long has it been, Aleksander? he thought. How long since you have caressed a warmth, touched a softness, held a woman? How long can you go on this way? He shifted his weight uncomfortably, intimidated by the proximity of youth, by the unconscious brazenness of the half-exposed breasts that moved as she breathed and quivered when she coughed. His eyes moved back to the girl and he looked with longing at the white, unblemished throat framed by long, jet-black tresses.

His gaze drifted over to Sean. How can she like a thing like this? he wondered as he looked at the long blond hair, matted and dirty, and the unshaven face. How in God's name can she like a thing like this?

"Why you have hair like that?" he asked, only half realizing that he had spoken his thoughts aloud.

Sean stared dully at him for a moment. "Huh?"

"Why you have hair like that? You look like a bum. Why you don't get it cut?"

Sean laughed. "Are you serious?"

"Why you want to look disgusting like this? Why you don't want to look like decent people?"

"I want to look like a degenerate, just like all my friends do," Sean replied sarcastically.

"That kid who loves the birds and the fishes, he don't got long hair," Alex spat. "He got short hair, like man."

"Like a man! Are you for real?"

"Yeah, he got hair like a man, not like you!"

"Only till his shrink gets him out of the navy reserve," Sean replied. "He couldn't beat the draft like the rest of us did, so he—"

"Who gonna hire you for a job looking like that?" Alex demanded. "You look like a bum. Who gonna hire you for a job?"

Sean shrugged. "Who wants a job? I got one now I don't want. I'll do like Russell says, just hang around and wait for the revolution. Then nobody'll have to work. We can just hang out all the time, getting stoned." Rebecca started to laugh, but then saw the concerned look on her brother's face and realized that the conversation was becoming volatile.

"You think you make a revolution?" Alex shouted. "You and your kind, you bums, you little shits?"

"Hey, we got twenty million people in this country who smoke dope, five million who do acid. We're gonna be the majority pretty soon."

"Yeah, you counted them all, Mr. Big Shot?"

"Don't be like obtuse, man," Sean replied, his voice dripping with condescension. "I mean, how many communists were there in Russia in 1917, you know?"

"You're a communist, too, you bum?"

"Russell's a communist. I'm an anarchist."

"You think you can make everybody like you, you little bastard, use drugs all the time and kill yourself with liquor?"

"Oh, right, Mr. Sobriety over here!"

"The children, they are good children. They don't use no drugs."

"Don't kid yourself, man. There's as much dope in high school as there is in college."

Clayton shook Sean's arm roughly. "Sean, cut it out. Let's go home."

"Yeah," Rebecca echoed, "let's go home."

Alex was fuming. "The children don't use drugs, not here they don't."

"Bullshit." Sean grinned. "There's grass growing on the roadside along Route 42."

"You think the children should use drugs? You think it's good the children use drugs?"

"I don't think it's any of your fucking business what I think."

"Sean, goddamn it!" Clayton said. "This is nuts! Stop arguing with him, and let's just split."

"You know what I think, you goddamn hippie?" Alex yelled. "You don't work for a living, you don't want to work for a living, you're disgusting! I think you're too damn lazy and selfish and stupid to overthrow anything, you goddamn dirty, stinking piece of shit!"

Sean rolled his eyes heavenward. "Oh, yeah, sure. Go ahead, be judgmental!"

"You take everything this country gives you and you waste it. You and your kind, you don't build up nothing, you just tear down."

"Yeah, great fucking country," Sean shouted back, "so long as you're white. The Vietnamese don't think it's such a great fucking country, neither do the Indians or the blacks—"

"You don't know shit about this country!"

"You don't know shit about nothing. You sound like my parents, for Christ's sake."

"Your parents, they know what a lousy bum you are? You know you break your mother's heart?"

"That's her problem. She got her life, I got mine."

"You goddamn kids, you got everything on earth just handed to you, you don't gotta struggle, you don't gotta suffer, you just waste money and live like filth."

Sean laughed. "Give me a break!"

"Yeah, yeah, I give you a break, I give you a break in your goddamn head, you bum!"

Clayton grabbed Sean by the arm and pulled him to his feet. "That does it. Come on, we're leaving."

Sean pulled his arm free of Clayton's grasp and shouted at Alex, "Who the fuck do you think you are, you old asshole? What makes you think you're so fucking great?"

"You don't talk to me like that!"

"I'll talk to you any way I fucking want to talk to you, you horny old bastard. You're just jealous, that's all. You're too old to do what I'm doing, and it eats you up inside."

Alex slammed his fists down on the table and screamed, "You shut up!"

Sean saw the sensitivity, and he attacked it with the grim determination of a boxer who has just seen a cut open on his opponent's eye. "You're getting old, man, too old to get the girls, to old to have any fun. You've been working so long that you've forgotten how to live. You ain't pissed at me because of what I'm doing, you're pissed at life because you ain't doing it, too."

"You filthy bum!" Alex screamed, tears welling up in his eyes. "You goddamn filthy bum!"

Clayton shouted in Sean's ear, "Jesus Christ, Brenner, what the hell's the matter with you? Let's go, goddamn it!"

"Work, work, work, Alex." Sean smiled cruelly. "Your whole fucking life, all you ever did was work. You sit here in this broken-down old bar in this little crack-in-the-plaster town and you make believe you're a businessman, but you're nothing but a failure, a fraud."

"*Shut up!*"

"You're old and you're useless, Alex, and you're on the way out. Life has passed you right by, old man. Look!" and he made a quick sweeping gesture with his hand. "There it goes!"

Alex grabbed Sean by the hair and drew back his fist, screaming, "I break you in half, you bastard!"

Sean knocked Alex's hand away and Clayton began to drag him toward the door. "Becky," he said curtly. "Go start the jeep."

She ran outside without stopping to gather any of the clothes that were strewn about the floor. As Clayton dragged him from the room, Sean was yelling, "Hey, hey, old man, fuck you, old man, hey, fuck you, old man!"

Alex screamed unintelligibly and grabbed the knife he had been using to slice the lemons. He ran toward the door, crying, "You filthy bastard! I cut you in half, you goddamn bum, I kill you!"

Clayton pushed Sean outside and then shut the door, holding tightly onto the knob to keep Alex from pulling it open. "Get in the back of the jeep," he ordered Sean, "and tell Becky to get out of the driver's seat." Sean hesitated, and Clayton shouted, "Goddamn it, Brenner, do what I say or I'll beat the shit out of you myself!" As Sean complied Clayton pushed the door open, knocking Alex to the floor inside, and then ran for the jeep. He jumped into the driver's seat and began to drive wildly up the road.

Chapter Twelve

January 4, 1969

Her eyes felt heavy, much heavier than they should have upon awakening from a night's sleep. She stretched and yawned, reaching up behind her to where the brass bedstead should have been. She felt only roughly hewn wood. Realizing that something was odd, she opened her eyes and saw that she was not in her bedroom. She sat up in bed and gasped.

Dorcas looked around frantically, not knowing at first where she was, and then recognizing the bedroom where she had visited with elderly, ailing Edith Sweet so often during her childhood. *I'm in the old Sweet house. What on earth am I doing in . . . ?*

Then she remembered, and she shrieked.

No sound answered her cry, no footsteps hurried toward the door in response. The only movements were the shadows made by the old curtains as the cold sun of winter dawn streamed in through the windows, and the only sound she heard was the whistle of the wind as it blew through the naked branches of the trees.

"What happened?" she wondered aloud. "I was in the cave . . . I saw Mr. Schilder . . . Vernon . . ." She shuddered at the memory and threw the blanket from her as she jumped out of the bed. She was still dressed as she had been the previous day, and she found her jacket hanging on a hook beside the bedroom door. She donned it hurriedly and ran from the house.

She was just about to run into the woods and make her way back toward the River Road when she stopped abruptly and stared into the cumulative thickness of the trees in front of her. *What if he's waiting for me in there?*

That's stupid, she argued with herself. *Vernon doesn't mean you any harm. He could have killed you last night in the cave if he wanted to.* She looked back at the house. *He must have carried me here and put me to bed, took my jacket off, and covered me with a blanket.*

Did Vernon do it or did Mr. Schilder do it? Did I really see what I thought I saw? Did I see Mr. Schilder lying dead in the cave? Did I see Vernon . . . did I see him . . . change?

What in God's name is going on?

"The cave," she whispered. "Mr. Patanjali . . ."

Without further consideration or hesitation she turned around and ran in the opposite direction, back into the woods behind the house, toward the foot of Clayton Saunders's mountain.

It took her a half hour to find the mouth of the cave. It seemed to be covered with brush much thicker than it had been last evening, though she admitted that it had not been easy to see in the gloom of the forest dusk. She cleared away enough of the brush to allow her to enter, and then, taking a deep breath, walked into the cave.

It was empty. No dead body, no dying yogi, no lantern, no goblin. She began to tremble. *It didn't happen. I imagined it, I hallucinated it. I'm losing my grip again. They're gonna put me away again, lock me up, give me those injections again. . . .*

And then the dim sunlight that managed to make its way into the cave glinted on the floor. She knelt down and touched the glimmer. It was blood. It might have been Schilder's, it might have been Ashvarinda's, there was no way for her to know. But it was most definitely blood.

"It was real," she whispered. "It was all real. They were here. I saw it all, just like I remember it."

She was torn between ecstasy at having her sanity reaffirmed and confused fear at the nature of the memory that had just been validated. "I don't understand this," she said to the empty rock walls. "What the *hell* is going on?"

A distant voice cried, "Dorcas!" and she froze and listened. Again she heard "Dorcas!" followed by another voice crying, "Dork! Where are you?"

She ran out of the cave and called out, "Peter! Lydia! Here I am! Here I am!"

She saw Peter Geerson descending the steep incline of the mountainside awkwardly, skidding his right foot to slow his movement. Her sister Lydia was behind him, her years of life in the country affording her enough experience with this type of terrain to allow her a more graceful descent. "Dorcas!" Peter said when he reached her. "What the hell happened to you?" She had not even had the chance to respond before he grabbed her and hugged her tightly, and then kissed her on the mouth.

She felt short of breath. "Peter, what a nice hello!"

He was slightly embarrassed at his own impetuosity, and he cleared his throat before saying, "I was so worried about you."

"Where'd you go, Dork?" Lydia asked as she came up beside them, the concern in her face slowly changing to annoyance now that her sister had been found. "We've been looking for you the whole damn night!"

"It's a long story," she replied, not wanting Peter to take his arms away. Over and above the attraction she felt for this boy, she needed very badly to be held just then.

But he unwrapped his arms and took her by the

hand. "You can tell us on the way back to the car, which I hope is still parked on the roadside, or Russell's gonna kill me." He began to lead her into the woods, but then, remembering that he would never be able to find the road, stepped aside so that the two girls could precede him.

"So what happened to you?" Lydia asked. "The last we saw of you, you were going off with Old Man Schilder."

"That wasn't Old Man Schilder," Dorcas said. "It was Vernon Sweet."

Both Peter and Lydia laughed as Peter said, "Look, Dorcas, Schilder and Grogo don't exactly look alike, you know? I mean, I think I would have noticed if he was wearing an Old Man Schilder mask or something."

"You won't believe me," Dorcas said, "but this is what happened. . . ."

They listened in silence as Dorcas told them her story, omitting no detail and sharing with them her reactions upon awakening. By the time they were in Russell's Beetle, both Peter and Lydia were urging Dorcas to go and speak with the psychiatrist who had worked with her while she was in the hospital, and by the time they were driving down Beckskill's main street, Dorcas was in tears.

Lydia stopped browbeating her sister long enough to say, "Peter, look there, parked in front of Joanne's."

Peter slowed down and saw Clayton Saunder's jeep among the few other cars in front of Beckskill's small restaurant, Joanne's Ham and Eggery. "Good," he said, turning the car into the parking lot. "Maybe Becky can talk some sense into you."

He stopped the car and they entered the old-fashioned family restaurant to find Clayton, Sean, and Rebecca sitting in a booth, drinking coffee. Sean was hanging his head sullenly as Clayton, laughing softly, reminded him in great detail of his antics of a few hours before. Rebecca looked up and saw them approaching, and she smiled weakly. "Hey, look who's here! Sorry we weren't at Alex's to meet you guys, but—"

"We never went to Alex's," Peter interrupted. "We only found Dorcas a little while ago."

"Hi, Dork," Rebecca said. "Where the hell'd you go, anyway?"

Lydia slid into the seat next to Clayton and Peter gently led Dorcas to sit beside her. He seated himself opposite with Sean and Rebecca and said, "She doesn't want to go home, and she won't go back to the hospital. I don't know what to do with her."

"I'm not crazy, Peter," Dorcas said. Her voice was subdued and even, but her lips were quivering and her eyes were red with tears.

"Like, what's happening?" Sean asked, hoping that attention would now be diverted from him.

Clayton refused to allow it. "You know what this asshole did last night? He nearly got us killed by old Alex Sonovbitch."

Peter grinned. "How'd he do that?"

"He and Alex got into the stupidest argument I've ever heard. The old guy chased us out with a fucking machete!"

"He started it," Sean muttered. "And it wasn't a machete. It was just a kitchen knife."

"Oh, that' okay then." Clayton nodded. "The way I remembered it, it was something dangerous. But just an ordinary old kitchen knife . . . well!"

"Fuck you, Clay," Sean muttered.

"Forget these two idiots," Rebecca said. "Dork, what happened to you? Where'd you go?"

Peter sighed. "Dorcas, tell them what you told us."

She recited her tale once again and concluded by saying, "And I guess I fainted after a while. The last thing I remember is just screaming and screaming, and the next thing I knew I was lying in bed in the Sweet house. My jacket was hung on a hook, and there wasn't anybody else there. I went back into the cave, and all I found was blood on the ground." She looked at Peter. "I'm not nuts, Peter. I know what I saw. And last time, last month, when everybody thought I was having another nervous breakdown, I wasn't. I really did see Vernon. He isn't dead. Mr. Patanjali isn't dead." She reached over and took a sip of Rebecca's beer. "But Vernon must have moved him. He must have moved everything, even poor Mr. Schilder." Tears began to well up in her eyes and to roll down her cheeks. "Nobody's gonna believe me. Daddy's gonna put me away again. . . ."

"Dork"—Clayton yawned—"let me get this straight. You're saying that Grogo ate Old Man Schilder's brain and then turned into Old Man Schilder, just so he could trick you into following him into a cave so a half-dead yogi could teach you a prayer. Is that about the size of it?"

His incredulity angered her, and she glowered at him through her tears. "That's right."

Clayton nodded earnestly. "Well, it certainly makes sense to me!"

"Shut up, Clay," Rebecca said, and then reached out to take Dorcas's hand. "Look, Dork, you gotta know deep down inside that none of this happened. Grogo—"

"Vernon," she said softly.

"—killed your sister, and so he's like some sort of a nightmare for you and you keep hallucinating about him. That's all this is, honest."

"Of course, Dork" Sean muttered. "That fucking little freak is dead. It'd take one hell of a séance for him to tell anybody anything."

"A séance!" Clayton shouted, his eyes widening

with sudden interest. "What a far-out idea! We could have a séance! We can get everybody together, I mean like everybody, from New Paltz, from Long Island, from the City, I mean like everybody we know. We all drop acid and then go to Grogo's house and have a fucking séance. It'd be so far fucking out!"

"Damn it, Clay," Peter repeated, "this is serious, okay?"

"You think I'm kidding? A goblin's ghost, a séance, and LSD. It's great!"

Neither Dorcas nor anyone else paid any attention to him. "You saw Mr. Schilder take me into the woods," she pointed out. "You all saw it."

"Yeah, sure," Rebecca countered, "and so he probably took you aside and told you not to hang around with us—"

"Goddamn hippie bums," Sean agreed.

"—and then he went on his way, and you wandered off and had, I don't know, a seizure or something." She squeezed her hand harder. "Dork, think about what you've just told us. I mean, it's like ridiculous, you know?"

"Makes sense to me," Clayton repeated, and then belched. "And I think having a séance is a great idea. We can have Eric get some of that dynamite acid he gets from Steve Wolzer, and—"

"Clay, shut the fuck up, will you?" Peter snapped. "This isn't funny."

"That's the thanks I get for keeping your river nice and clean," he said, feigning offended dignity.

"Oh!" Dorcas exclaimed. "Get me a paper and pencil, quick. Quick!"

"What for?" Lydia asked.

"Just get it, *quick!*" Lydia went over to the counter to ask the waitress for writing materials and returned a few moments later with a pen and a paper napkin.

Dorcas grabbed them from her hands and began scribbling furiously.

"What are you doing?" Sean asked.

"Writing down the prayer before I forget it," she muttered.

Peter sighed. "Oh, Jesus."

Rebecca sipped her coffee and then said, "Listen, Dork, you need to rest, I mean like really, really rest, you know? Why don't you go home and—"

"No," she snapped, still writing on the napkin.

"Maybe you should go to a doctor, just to talk. . . ."

"No," she snapped again, and then added as an afterthought, "Besides, my father's a doctor, and I sure don't want to talk to him. Not now. Not after last night."

"You know what I think?" Clayton said firmly. "I think the solution to this problem is for you and Peter to get falling-down drunk, and then go home and fuck your brains out."

Dorcas and Peter both blushed as Lydia punched Clayton hard in the side. "You asshole! This is serious. Stop making jokes."

"Who's making jokes?" he asked, snaking his arm around her waist and stroking the underside of her breasts. "Doesn't getting drunk and fucking sound good to you?"

"Later, okay?" Lydia said sharply, pushing his hand away. "Can't you see how upset Dorcas is?"

"And haven't we gotten drunk enough for one twenty-four-hour period?" Rebecca asked.

Sean moaned and laid his head down on the table. "I'm never gonna drink again."

"Of course you won't." Clayton nodded. "I believe that. Yup."

"I'm not upset," Dorcas insisted quietly. "I'm scared, and I'm stunned, and I'm relieved to still be alive, but I'm not upset. You guys are the ones who are upset."

"I'm not upset," Sean and Clayton said in unison.

"Why don't we all just go back to the trailer and kind of unwind?" Peter suggested, looking angrily at his two friends. "Watch some TV, listen to some music."

"That's a good idea." Lydia nodded. "Let's just go back and relax, all of us."

"Dorcas, is that okay with you?" Rebecca asked. "Go to the trailer, watch some TV or something?"

Dorcas sighed with exasperation. "You guys just don't get it, do you! Mr. Patanjali is someplace in those woods, hurt and dying, and we have to get him help. And there's been a murder, for Pete's sake! We have to go to the cops and tell them Old Mr. Schilder has been killed."

"What's that?" Walter Rihaczeck asked from the door of the diner. "What are you talking about, Dorcas?"

Dorcas bit her lip as the town councilman entered the diner and walked over to their table. "What did you say about Johann? That he's been killed?" His tone was serious, but a smile was on his lips.

She forced herself to smile back as she shook her head. "It was nothing, Mr. Rihaczeck. Just a little game I was playing."

"Well, I'm sure Johann'll be happy to hear that." He laughed. "I just saw him not ten minutes ago taking his morning walk."

"You . . . you saw him?" she asked.

"Sure. I leave for work pretty early, you know, and I see him most days. He takes a walk every morning. You can practically set your clock by old Johann Schilder."

Dorcas frowned, perplexed. Vernon acted like Mr. Schilder to get me to go with him to the cave. But he already got me there, so why would he still be . . . I don't know, still be impersonating him? And why would he be following all of Mr. Schilder's personal habits, things that no one would notice even if he didn't follow them? If he didn't take a walk this morning, Mr. Rihaczeck wouldn't have noticed, so why would he take a walk? And how would Vernon know that Mr. Schilder took a walk every morning in the first place? This doesn't make sense, it doesn't make sense.

Unless none of it happened.

Maybe I did imagine it. Maybe there wasn't even blood on the floor of the cave. Maybe it was just rock slime or something, or bat shit, or something else disgusting. I couldn't see very well in there. I might have been wrong this morning. I might have been wrong last night. Maybe Becky's right. The whole thing with Sarah . . . maybe . . . maybe . . . Her head snapped up when she heard her name. "I beg your pardon?"

"I said I hoped your dad was feeling better," Rihaczeck repeated. "The shock about your sister and all. You know."

"Oh, yes, yes," she replied. "We're all doing fine, thank you."

Rihaczeck nodded and then turned to Clayton. "Actually, Clay," he said, radiating friendliness, "I came in here on my way to work because I saw your jeep out front." He grinned broadly. "It's kind of a distinctive car. All those bumper stickers, I mean. No doubt in my mind whose it was."

"I strive to be different," Clayton said, returning the grin.

"Could I, ah, speak to you for a moment? Privately?"

Clayton sighed and motioned for Lydia to let him out of the booth. As he and Rihaczeck went off into the corner to speak, Sean turned to Rebecca and said,

"Funny how popular Clay is now that he owns the Sweet place."

"Yeah." She nodded. "Last month that guy wouldn't give us the time of day, and now he's sweet as sugar."

"You think he's trying to get Clay to sell the land for the factory?" Peter asked anxiously.

"Of course," Sean replied.

Peter began biting his left thumbnail. "Clay wouldn't go along with it, would he?"

"Of course not," Sean said, and then finished his cup of coffee. "Hey, I'm dead on my feet. Let's split."

Clayton walked back to the booth and said, "I heard that, Brenner. Busting up another good time, are you?"

"Give me a break, Clay." He sighed. "It's been a long night."

"What do you say, Dork?" Rebecca asked. "Back to our trailer? TV and music and then just fall out for the rest of the day?"

"Sure," Dorcas said quietly, folding the paper napkin and sticking it into her pocket. "Anything. I don't care. I don't know what to think and I don't know what to do. I just don't care." Her sister watched her carefully, knowing that the cool, emotionless exterior was covering a mass of fears and troubles. Lydia and Dorcas left as Rebecca went to the counter to pay the check.

Sean turned to Clayton and said, "That is like one really fucked-up chick, you know?"

"Like, really!" Clayton nodded.

"She's been through a lot," Peter said. "Don't give her a hard time, okay?"

"Sure, sure," Clayton said. "Don't worry about it. I'll behave."

As they walked to the door of the diner Peter asked, "Did Rihaczeck make you an offer for the Sweet property?"

"Not yet. He wants me to go to a council meeting

tomorrow. Closed session, very hush-hush." He laughed.

"But they'll probably make you an offer, right?"

"Of course they will. Three hundred grand, I figure." He saw Peter's eyes grow tense, and before he could protest Clayton's even talking to them, he said quickly. "Don't worry about it, Pete. I'm just gonna fuck around with them. They'll keep offering me more and more, and I'll just keep saying it isn't enough."

Peter relaxed visibly. "Yeah, of course, I know. Of course you won't sell them the land. If they think you will, they've got a surprise coming."

Not as big as the surprise you've got coming, Peter, m'boy, Clayton thought as they left the diner.

The jeep and the Volkswagen Beetle began driving west toward the mountain and the trailer as Walter Rihaczeck drove east in the direction of Route 42, which would take him to his job in Kingston. Rihaczeck glanced into the rearview mirror to make certain that Clayton and the others were well out of sight, and then he turned his old Buick around and headed down Main Street toward the River Road. He drove along the road for two miles and then pulled his car to a stop along the wood line.

Rihaczeck looked around to make certain he was not being observed and then walked into the woods. He walked for over an hour, past the spot where Sarah Ostlich's body had been discovered, past the old Sweet house and the charred ruins of the old barn, deeper and deeper into the forest until he came to the upslope of Saunders Mountain. He walked along the base of the incline, past the brush-covered mouth of the cave that Dorcas had inspected a few hours before, and stopped when he reached another pile of brush that covered the mouth of another cave. He moved some of the brush aside and entered. He walked deep into the cleft in the base of the mountain until he came to a large open space.

Ashvarinda Patanjali was lying motionless in the center of the natural room, his eyes shut, his breathing even more labored that it had been the previous evening. A canteen was lying beside him, and Rihaczeck picked it up and poured a thin trickle of water onto the parched, brittle lips, paying no attention to the two corpses that lay a few feet away, the dead bodies of Johann Schilder and Walter Rihaczeck.

"Rinda," he said softly. "It's me, Vernon. Can you hear me?"

Give my body the strength to live, Vishnu, Vishnu . . . keep my mind alive to do your work, to contain the beast, Vishnu, Vishnu. . . .

"I know you don't like it when I play the trick with people, Rinda," the Rihaczeck-thing said sadly as he sat down on the cold stone floor next to his comatose friend. "But I just had to. You know that when I'm Vernon, I don't think very well, I don't understand things. I had to make sure the girl didn't tell anyone about us. At least I had to make sure that no one believed her about old Johann."

Ashvarinda's lips moved spasmodically. "*Mujey raakshus ko kaabu ruhkney . . . key liyey jiyna hiy hoga*. . . . I must live . . . I must live . . . to control . . . the beast. . . .

The Rihaczeck-thing sighed. "I just don't want to lose the house, Rinda. I grew up there. It's my home. I can't think, I can't understand or act when I'm just Vernon, so I have to do these things. You understand, don't you? I had to go to the council meeting yesterday and say that I . . . I mean, that Schilder wouldn't vote for their plan to buy the land from Saunders. I had to, Rinda, I didn't know what else to do."

Bhagawan Vishnu, meyriy muhduhd kuhro. . . .
Lord Vishnu, help me. . . .

"And just now, I had to tell the boy to come to the meeting . . . that was what Rihaczeck was going to do today, it was in his mind when I killed him . . . but what will I do now? I'm scared, Rinda, so scared."

Bhagawan Vishnu, mujey suno. . . .

Lord Vishnu, hear me. . . .

"You've always taken care of me, but now . . ." He started to weep. "Now you can't. And I don't know what to do to take care of you. I can't get a doctor or take you to a hospital, you understand that. But I don't want you to die, Rinda. I love you too much. I don't know what to do, I don't know what to do. . . ." His weeping became loud and bitter in his misery, and as if the overpowering emotion had robbed him of his self-control, he lost his Rihaczeck form and dwindled down once again into the shape of a malformed dwarf.

"Not go 'way, Rinda," Grogo wept. "Not go 'way. . . ."

He stoked Ashvarinda's cold forehead gently, bathing the aged yogi's face in his tears. When his body had reverted to its own form, his mind had followed suit, and he was no longer able to comprehend what was happening to him. He no longer understood why the mean faces had done what they had done, no longer understood why he and his dying friend were hiding in this cold cave.

And his mind was much, much too simple for him to understand that adding to his unhappiness and his fear was the slowly emerging suspicion that he was not really Vernon Sweet.

III

The Dance of Shiva

*And he said, But my face
shalt thou not see;
for no man shall see my face
and live.*

—Exodus 33, xx

Chapter Thirteen

January 10, 1969

> ### COME TO THE SÉANCE! JANUARY 11!
> ### R.S.V.P.
>
> *You are cordially invited to attend a séance as a guest of the late Grogo the Goblin on this coming January 11th, at the Saunders estate in scenic Beckskill, NY. Drink and dope will be provided, but it would be cool to make a contribution to the common pot (Get it? Ha-ha!)*
>
> ### ONLY TWO WEEKS LEFT TO IMPEACH LBJ!
> ### VERNON SWEET FOR PRESIDENT!
> ### R.S.V.P.

Alex Brown was standing in the cemetery, his weary eyes pressed tightly shut. He came here to visit his wife's grave whenever things began to seem too much for him to bear, as if to seek some vestige of the peace and contentment he had once known. The pressure has been getting too much for me, he thought. If only I could afford a vacation. I wouldn't have gotten so upset the other night if I'd had some rest, if my nerves weren't so frayed. He gritted his teeth at the memory. His anger at Sean Brenner had not abated, but it was balanced by the fear that he had lost Clayton and Rebecca Saunders as customers. They spent enough money when they came to his bar to make them worth the aggravation they caused him. And Rebecca, her eyes, her lips, the way she walked, the almost unconsciously provocative way she dressed, the lilt in her laugh . . .

Alex held the collar of his coat closed against the chill, bitter wind. He gazed at Paula's name as he always did and sighed as he always sighed, wondering when, if ever, the pain of his loss would finally leave him. The memories arose unbidden as he gazed down at the simple burial marker.

"We have to get out of the City, Aleshka," Paula was saying as she brushed her thick, dark blond hair. *"I do not want my children to grow up in the City. It is not healthy here, not for them, not for us."*

"Yes," he was replying, *"of course, of course. . . ."* He was twenty-seven, five years older than his bride of three months, and his hair was dark and full.

"It's a good business," the real-estate agent was saying. *"Isn't far from the main road, Route 42. Only bar for a few miles. Building's in good shape, too."*

"But the governor says—"

"Don't worry about Tom Dewey's pipe dream. The state legislature will never fund construction of a thruway. Route 42 is the main road, and it's gonna stay the main road."

"This is a pretty little town, Aleshka."

"Beckskill's on its way up, Mrs. Brown. Why, in five years' time vacationers'll be paying top dollar for rooms near those ski slopes."

"The roof needs mending," Aleksander Ovyetchkin said. *"And the bar top is in bad condition."*

"Well, I'm not saying it doesn't need some work, but my client is willing to take that into consideration when discussing the price."

"We could be happy here, Aleshka. . . ."

He was standing in the large barroom for the first time. Such room, he was thinking, room to dance, to eat, to celebrate. His imagination showed him crowds of spectral merrymakers dancing polkas, lifting glasses of beer to their thirsty lips, laughing, singing. . . .

"We could be happy here, Aleshka. . . ."

"Glad to have you joining our little community," Dr. Timothy Ostlich was saying, shaking his hand.

"We're sort of the unofficial welcome wagon." Mrs. Doris Ostlich smiled, handing a warm casserole to Paula. Her soft brown eyes were somehow sad and weary.

"Why, thank you," Paula said, returning the smile.

"Goddamn governor," Walter Rihaczeck was saying, "goddamn spineless assembly . . ."

"Is it true? They're going to build a thruway?"

"We could be happy here, Aleshka. . . ."

"Come away, Alex," Dr. Ostlich said softly. "There's nothing you can do now. She is at peace."

"Paula . . ." he wept. "Paula . . ."

"It's better this way, Alex . . . she was in so much pain . . . it's better this way."

"Paula . . . Paula . . ."

"We could be happy here, Aleshka. . . ."

He knelt down to brush the snow off the marker when Rebecca Saunders came up behind him and said, "Real nice, Al. She'll like it a lot better now."

He turned when he heard her voice and then rose to his feet. Alex swallowed hard and asked, "What are you doing here?"

She sniffed. "I saw your car, so I figured I'd stop and give you a piece of my mind. I mean, you're probably sober now, and I don't think you're armed, so I'm probably safe." She paused, as if she expected her sarcastic criticism to elicit a response from him, but his only reply was to turn away and begin to walk back toward his car. "Hold on, Al baby. . . ."

"Go away."

"You had a lot of goddamn nerve acting the way you did, starting a fight like that. Who the hell gave you the right to be so—"

"Leave me alone," he snapped, and then added, "And don't use that kind of language. It isn't ladylike."

"Ladylike!" she laughed. Holy shit!"

"I told you—"

"Yeah, yeah, I heard what you said. Did you hear what I said? I think you owe us an apology."

Alex reached his car and opened the door, but before he could get in Rebecca interposed herself between him and the seat. "Go away!" he repeated more forcefully, and then grabbed her by the shoulders to push her out of the way.

But he felt the soft give in her arm beneath the fur and denim of her jacket and the cold breeze carried a breath of perfume to his nostrils, and he could not bring himself to push her away. He looked into her eyes, and she seemed to be gazing back into his. He saw her lips part slightly and the tip of her tongue ran pink and moist against her bottom lip. He brought his mouth closer to hers and he could feel her breath on his face as she said softly, "Al?"

"Yes?" he whispered.

"What the *fuck* do you think you're doing?" she shouted, accentuating the expletive with a hard punch to his stomach.

He staggered back, embarrassed and resentful, and he shouted, "Why don't you leave me alone? What the hell do you want from me?"

"I sure as hell don't want to make out with you!" she spat. "Maybe Clay is right. Maybe you really should go to the whorehouse in Newburgh, you horny old bastard!"

"You should be ashamed," he said, trembling, his fists clenched at his side. "If your mother . . . if your mother . . ."

"Ahhh, *your* mother," she muttered, and then walked back to her car. He heard her say, "Stupid old fuck," as she got in and started the engine.

Alex got into his car and leaned his head against the steering wheel. If only Paula had lived. I wouldn't care about the debt and the worry. If only I had her to hold each night, to share the struggle with, even to share the failure with. If only Paula had lived.

We could be happy here, Aleshka. . . .

COME TO THE SÉANCE! JANUARY 11!
R.S.V.P.

You are cordially invited to attend a séance as a guest of the late Grogo the Goblin on this coming January 11th, at the Saunders estate in scenic Beckskill, NY. Drink and dope will be provided, but it would be cool to make a contribution to the common pot (Get it? Ha-ha!)

ONLY TWO WEEKS LEFT TO IMPEACH LBJ!
VERNON SWEET FOR PRESIDENT!
R.S.V.P.

"Sean, this is nuts!" Artie Winston was screaming into his ear from the back of the motorcycle.

"What?" Sean Brenner screamed back.

"I said this is nuts! We should have taken a bus or something!"

"What?"

"Pull over, pull over!"

"What?"

"I said *pull over*, goddamn it!"

Sean slowed down and drove the motorcycle onto the shoulder of the thruway. He kept the motor revving as he turned behind him and said, "Hey, you know, Artie, we're never gonna get up there if you keep making me stop every fifteen minutes."

"I don't think we're ever gonna get up there at all," Artie responded sullenly. "I'm scared to death."

Sean was growing exasperated. "What the hell's the matter with you? You've been on motorcycles before."

"Yeah, but not in the middle of fucking winter on an icy road with a guitar strapped to my back." As he spoke he fussed with the makeshift harness Sean had concocted from a few belts and a long piece of rope. Artie's guitar was tied to his back, the neck extending upward behind his head and the box resting against his spine.

"Ice!" Sean exclaimed. "There isn't any ice on the road. It's so clear it might as well be July! And besides, you should have left the fucking guitar at home."

"I don't go anywhere without my ax."

"Okay, so what's the problem? Jesus, Artie, it's almost one o'clock. We left Queens two fucking hours ago, we aren't even halfway there, and it's only supposed to be a three-hour drive."

"I keep feeling the wind pushing the guitar, like it's gonna be like a sail or something, like I'm gonna get blown off the bike. You know, like in that Arlo song?"

"I'm gonna blow you off the bike if you don't stop this shit. If riding on the bike bothers you so much, why the hell didn't you ride up with Peter and Russell?"

"You know damn well that you can't fit those two guys and Deirdre and Nancy and their bags and me in that Beetle, not with my guitar."

"So why the hell do you need the guitar? Christ, Clay has a guitar. Why don't you just play his?"

"That piece of junk? That old broken-down Guild? Are you kidding? I wouldn't be caught dead playing something like that."

Sean reached into his pocket and pulled out a plastic prescription bottle. "Do you know what's in here, Artie?"

"Yes." Artie sighed. "You've told me ten times already."

"Well, here's the eleventh. In here we have twenty-five tabs of absolutely the purest, most potent LSD-25 you can buy."

"I know, Sean." Artie sighed again.

"I got this acid from Steve Wolzman himself before he got busted last week."

"I know, Sean."

"Do you know what's gonna happen when you and me and everybody else takes this acid?"

"Yes, Sean."

"Yes, Sean," he mimicked. "Well, one of the things it's gonna do is get everybody so fucked up that it won't make a goddamn bit of difference if you play a Guild or a Gibson or a fucking cigar box with rubber bands on it, so . . ." Sean stopped in midsentence and whipped his arm downward, tossing the pill bottle underhand behind him into the snow along the shoulder of the road.

"What the hell'd you do that for?" Artie asked.

Sean motioned with his head. "Cops. Hey, you aren't holding, are you?"

"Just a few joints in the harmonica compartment in my guitar case."

"Shit," he muttered. "That'd be enough to screw me royally with my probation officer."

"You holding?"

He looked over at the hole in the snow made by the plastic bottle. "Not anymore."

They sat motionless and breathless on the motorcycle as a police car pulled onto the shoulder behind them and a solitary state trooper emerged. He walked over to them and smiled. "Afternoon, boys."

"Good afternoon, Officer." Artie nodded deferentially. Sean said nothing as the blood began to drain from his face.

"What's the problem?"

"Problem?"

"Yes, I saw you pulled over here and I thought there might be something wrong."

He was looking at the driver, awaiting a response, and after a moment Sean said, "No, no problems. It's just kinda hard driving a bike this time of year. I just pulled off to rest my eyes for a minute."

"You know, you shouldn't be driving a motorcycle at all during the winter months. It isn't a safe vehicle under the best of conditions."

"Yeah, well," Sean muttered.

The trooper appraised him closely. "Mind if I see your license and registration?"

"No, no, not at all," Sean said just a bit too eagerly as he fumbled with his wallet, praying that he had not stuck a joint in, which would come dropping out.

The trooper went back to his car to call in the name and numbers, and Sean turned to Artie. "Please be cool, man. I can't afford any trouble with this pig. It could mean the state pen for me."

"Who do you think I am—Russell? You think I'm gonna start telling him he's a lackey of the military-industrial complex or something? Come on, Sean, give me some credit, will you?" He paused. "And calm down, for Christ's sake. This is just a routine check. The way you're acting, he's gonna think you're a fucking bomb thrower."

Sean looked at his friend angrily. "Look who's talking! Who was it last summer when the cops pulled Becky over for running a red light, got out of the backseat, put his hands on the hood, and spread his feet apart?"

"I was real stoned," Artie muttered. "I just assumed we were getting busted."

"All the cop did was tell Becky to give him her license, and there you are, waiting to be fucking frisked!" Sean began to laugh at the memory.

Artie laughed in turn. "It was kinda funny, I guess."

"Yeah, in retrospect." Sean nodded. "It wasn't so funny at the moment, not with a half a pound of pot in the trunk." He stopped speaking as the trooper walked back over to them and handed Sean his cards.

"Just checking, boys." He smiled. "Now, listen, the road is pretty clear up to Albany, but it gets a little slick after that, and you can never tell when you're going to hit ice. So drive carefully."

Sean nodded. "We will, Officer." He waited until the patrol car had pulled back onto the thruway before letting out the breath he had been holding. "God, that was scary." He hopped of the motorcycle and retrieved the bottle of LSD.

"You heard what he said," Artie reminded him. "Drive slow, okay?"

"Okay, okay."

A few minutes later Sean was once again barreling up the road, and Artie was screaming, "Slow down!"

"What?"

"I said slow down, damn it!"

"What?"

"For Christ's sake, Sean, you're gonna get us killed! Will you slow down!"

"What?"

* * *

COME TO THE SÉANCE! JANUARY 11!
R.S.V.P.

You are cordially invited to attend a séance as a guest of the late Grogo the Goblin on this coming January 11th, at the Saunders estate in scenic Beckskill, NY. Drink and dope will be provided, but it would be cool to make a contribution to the common pot (Get it? Ha-ha!)

ONLY TWO WEEKS LEFT TO IMPEACH LBJ!
VERNON SWEET FOR PRESIDENT!
R.S.V.P.

"I don't trust him," Russell was saying as he steered his Volkswagen Beetle off the thruway exit.

"Don't be ridiculous," Peter replied from behind him. "Clay's got all the money he needs, and he loves nature as much as we do."

"I don't love nature," Nancy O'Hara said. "I think nature is boring. Dorcas made me go out and look at the stars with her once." She shrugged. "It was okay, I guess."

"How can you be so unromantic?" Deirdre Duell asked. "I mean, think about all the poetry about nature, all the art work, all the writing. Didn't you ever read Thoreau?"

"Yeah, sure," Nancy said. "He was that guy who crawled off to live in the woods and stare at a lake or something."

"Incredible," Peter muttered.

"This has nothing to do with nature," Russell insisted. "Clay's a lot of fun most of the time, and I get a kick out of going up to hang out with him and Becky, but I don't have any illusions about him. Someone as self-destructive as he is wouldn't worry about fucking up a river."

"That's the word for him," Nancy agreed. " He's the most self-destructive person I've ever met."

"Look who's talking!" Peter exclaimed. "You still snorting heroin, Nance?"

"I never got into that too deep," she replied defensively. "I was just experimenting a little."

"Yeah, but experimenting with heroin isn't like trying out some new pot," he reminded her. "And you, Russsell. Clay drinks, and so do you. Clay gets stoned, and so do you. Clay drops acid, and so do you."

"I drop acid maybe once a month," Russell replied. "I go drinking on weekends. I smoke maybe one or two joints a day. Clay drinks and smokes from the minute he wakes up to the minute he passes out."

"That's not the point. . . ."

"It is the point. Okay, we're going up to Beckskill and we're gonna drink and smoke and trip all weekend. But come Sunday, we'll all be coming home. And on Monday you'll be going back to work at the college. I have a job interview with that parochial school in Maspeth, Nancy's gonna go back to her nursing practicum and Deirdre's gonna be back hitting the pavement with her paintings, going from gallery to gallery. But Clay's gonna spend Sunday and Monday the same way he spent Friday and Saturday."

"So what?" Deirdre asked. "So he doesn't have to work like the rest of us do. So what?"

"It doesn't have anything to do with work," Russell insisted. "You've read Freud, Peter. You know what Thanatos is."

"Come on, Russ. He doesn't have a death wish."

"So why does he always talk about Kerouac in such glowing terms, a self-centered hedonist who did nothing for the cause of social justice, a fucking good-for-nothing who drank himself to death on purpose?"

"Kerouac was an artist," Peter said testily. "And don't change the subject. Clay bought that land so the town couldn't give it to some big corporation, and that's that. He'll never sell it to them. You don't give him enough credit."

"I hope you're right," Russell said, "but I still don't trust him. He's a rich man, and no matter how much they like to pretend that they're like the rest of us, they aren't. The more money he has, the less risk he runs of ever having to do anything for a living."

"But the river . . ."

"So if the river gets polluted, he'll go buy another mountain near another river someplace else."

"You're not being fair," Peter insisted.

"And you're not being realistic," Russell responded.

"And you're both getting like really boring, you know?" Nancy broke in.

"Really," Deirdre said. "Hey, who else is gonna be up here this weekend? Is Artie going?"

"Sure," Peter replied. "I think he's going up with Sean."

"Oh, great. I love listening to him sing."

"Give up, man," Nancy said. "He'll never try to get together with you. He's too scared of girls."

"That's why he always carries his guitar around with him," Russell agreed. "When he sings, he doesn't have to talk."

"He's just shy and sensitive," Deirdre said. "And I think he's cute."

"And I don't think Clay would ever sell that land." Peter insisted. Both girls sighed and resigned themselves to having to listen to the same endless argument for the rest of the way up to Beckskill.

* * *
COME TO THE SÉANCE! JANUARY 11!
R.S.V.P.

You are cordially invited to attend a séance as a guest of the late Grogo the Goblin on this coming January 11th, at the Saunders estate in scenic Beckskill, NY. Drink and dope will be provided, but it would be cool to make a contribution to the common pot (Get it? Ha-ha!)

ONLY TWO WEEKS LEFT TO IMPEACH LBJ!
VERNON SWEET FOR PRESIDENT!
R.S.V.P.

Maybe he did and maybe he didn't. Maybe he was and maybe he wasn't. Maybe I'm nuts and maybe I'm not.

Dorcas was sitting on the floor of her bedroom, and as she lifted the bottle of sherry to her lips and drank long and deep, she inadvertently knocked her head against the wall. She seemed not to notice the pain as she covered her mouth and burped softly.

What is reality? If we think we know things, how do we know that we know them? When I see the color blue, how do I know that I see the same thing somebody else sees who sees the color blue? How do I know that anything exists outside the room I'm in right now? Why is it you can go for months and months without ever stubbing your toe, but then when you finally do, you stub the same toe the next day? Why does Venus rhyme with penis? Are cats aloof, or are they just stupid? How much wood could a woodchuck chuck if a woodchuck could chuck wood? And are there answers to these eternal questions?

She giggled and took another swig of sherry.

Maybe I really am nuts. Maybe I never saw Mr. Schilder change into Vernon. Maybe I never spoke with

Mr. Patanjali in that cave. Maybe I made up that prayer in my own imagination. It's all just sounds, anyway. Maybe I cooked the whole thing up in my messed-up brain.

But on the other hand, maybe I saw everything just as I thought I saw it. Maybe it's all true, all real.

On the other hand, it all might be a flashback from that horrible acid trip I took last year.

But on the other hand, it certainly seemed real enough, I think. It didn't feel like an acid trip. But then how accurate can your memory be of an acid trip?

"Maybe it's all an illusion, just like Mr. Patanjali said," she whispered. "Maybe none of it's real, not even me." Isn't that a funny thought? What if I don't exist? What if Lydia's imagining me, or maybe I'm imagining her, or maybe Karen is imagining both of us.

Karen. She frowned. Who's Karen? She looked at the bottle of sherry. Potent stuff. I don't even know what I'm thinking. And that's the whole point, isn't it? If you can't trust your own thoughts, how can you know what is real?

Mr. Rihaczeck saw Mr. Schilder, so what I thought I saw couldn't have been real. On the other hand, Vernon fooled me, so why couldn't he fool Mr. Rihaczeck? But why would he bother to fool Mr. Rihaczeck? On the other hand, why not?

"I don't know anything," she sang, "I never did know anything, but now I know that I don't know, all on a Christmas morning. . . ." She finished the bottle of sherry and let it drop loudly onto the floor of her bedroom. "Pay no attention to the man behind the curtain," she whispered.

"Hey, Dork!" Lydia called out from downstairs. "Becky's outside. Come on."

Dorcas pulled herself to her feet and stumbled out into the hallway. She almost fell as she descended the stairs, and her sister said, "Whatcha been doing? You drunk?"

"Just a little mellow." Dorcas giggled, and then fell flat on her face in the foyer.

"Ah, shit, Dork," Lydia muttered as she helped her sister stand up. "The party hasn't even started yet, you know?"

"Where do you think you're going?" Dr. Ostlich asked angrily as he entered from the study. He frowned when he saw Dorcas. "Have you been drinking, Dorcas? Answer me!"

"Well," she sang, "I've been a moonshiner for many a year, and spent all my money on whiskey and beer . . ."

"Get outside and get into the car," Lydia ordered, pushing Dorcas out the front door and hoping that she could manage to get to Rebecca's car. She turned to her father. "We're going to a party. We'll see you probably Sunday."

"I absolutely forbid it," he bellowed, "for you and in particular for Dorcas!"

She shook her head. "You really don't understand, do you? You ain't in a position to forbid anything, man."

She turned to follow Dorcas, but her father grabbed her by the arm and said, "You wait just one—"

"Get your fucking hands off me!" Lydia shouted, pulling her arm free. "I told you years ago I never wanted you to touch me again, not ever, not after . . ."

She did not finish her sentence, and he did not respond to it. They both knew the events to which she was referring, those many nights of her early puberty when he would creep into her room and touch her and make her touch him, until that night when Lydia's mother saw them, that night before the morning she took the shotgun and placed the barrel into her mouth and . . .

"We'll be up at Clay's," Lydia said evenly. "We'll see

you Sunday. Maybe Monday." She slammed the door behind her, leaving her father alone in the foyer of the large, empty house.

COME TO THE SÉANCE! JANUARY 11!
R.S.V.P.

You are cordially invited to attend a séance as a guest of the late Grogo the Goblin on this coming January 11th, at the Saunders estate in scenic Beckskill, NY. Drink and dope will be provided, but it would be cool to make a contribution to the common pot (Get it? Ha-ha!)

ONLY TWO WEEKS LEFT TO IMPEACH LBJ!
VERNON SWEET FOR PRESIDENT!
R.S.V.P.

Clayton Saunders had all but depleted the small general store of its supply of beer, and as he heaved the last case into the back of the jeep he thought, Gonna be a great weekend. Haven't thrown a mammoth party in almost a year. Gonna be great, great. Lotta dope, lotta chicks, lotta liquor. Ain't life grand? He looked across the street at the Browns' Hotel. If we want to go out drinking someplace, we'll probably be too fucked up to drive any distance. Wouldn't wanna go someplace unfamiliar, not with so many people tripping. Al probably won't even notice, and even if he does, all Beck'll have to do is wiggle her tits at him and he'll go hide somewhere. Yeah, it's gotta be Al's place, or nowhere. Guess I better go make nice to old Alex.

Alex Brown was standing behind the bar washing the glasses as Clayton walked through the door and sat down on a bar stool. "'Mornin', Al. How's it going?"

Alex wiped his mouth with the back of his hand. "Listen, last weekend . . ."

The older man's eyes were somehow odd, lacking the usual combination of resentful disapproval and money-grubbing obsequiousness, and Clayton noticed the difference. He noticed his hands shaking slightly as he wiped the glasses, and he noticed the feverish cast on his face. "You feeling okay, Al? You look a little under the weather."

"Yeah, yeah, I'm fine," he muttered. "Look, that night last weekend . . ."

"Yeah, you were pretty obnoxious. What about it?"

Clayton was not making it any easier for him, and Alex struggled to keep the hatred from showing in his face. This bum has money, money I need, money I depend on. What have I come to, that I have to be polite to scum like this? "Well," he said haltingly, as if each word were causing him physical pain, "we were all pretty drunk. . . ."

"What do you mean 'we'?" Clayton laughed. "Yeah, we'd had a few, but you were like totally out of your mind, you know? Don't try to spread the blame. You started a fight with Sean all on your lonesome." Though he had entered with the intention of mending relations, Alex's apparent eagerness to do the same thing made it seem less urgent, and Clayton was delighting in his discomfort.

"Maybe I got a little out of hand," Alex conceded at last. "I just want to say I'm sorry it all happened."

"Yeah. What you mean is you need our business and you hope we'll keep coming in here to drink." He smiled broadly. "Well, here I am! Gimme a Bloody Mary. I didn't get my juice this morning, and I, ah"—and he winked at Alex—"after what happened last time I was here, I don't think I should have a Tequila Sunrise, if you know what I mean." He enjoyed seeing Alex clench his jaw as he began to mix the drink. "As for my friend Sean, you're gonna have to apologize to him in person. I mean, it was him you tried to rough up."

Alex shrugged in an effort to seem unconcerned. "You bring him in, I'll apologize. It wasn't right for me to get drunk like that." He paused. "Not that it was all my fault. He went out of his way to get me mad."

"Get off it, Al," Clayton said. "You were in a shitty mood and you took it out on us."

Alex began to grow red in the face. "Listen!"

Clayton patted him gently on the shoulder. "Take it easy, take it easy. Okay, let's just forget it." Alex placed the Bloody Mary down in front of him, and Clayton lifted it to his lips and downed it. He sighed contentedly. "Having a big party this weekend. Got to go home and get my shit together. We all might stop by tonight or tomorrow and give you some business." He stood up and walked to the door. "See you 'round, Al."

Alex breathed deeply, relieved at having discharged so unpleasant an obligation as repairing relations with his most free-spending customer. "Bastard!" he muttered, and then returned his attention to the glasses in the sink.

COME TO THE SÉANCE! JANUARY 11!
R.S.V.P.

You are cordially invited to attend a séance as a guest of the late Grogo the Goblin on this coming January 11th, at the Saunders estate in scenic Beckskill, NY. Drink and dope will be provided, but it would be cool to make a contribution to the common pot (Get it? Ha-ha!)

ONLY TWO WEEKS LEFT TO IMPEACH LBJ!
VERNON SWEET FOR PRESIDENT!
R.S.V.P.

Sean collapsed into a flurry of snow, much to the amusement of the horde of inebriates who felled him with scores of snowballs. Rebecca was laughing along with the rest of them as she ran up and jumped on him before he could get to his feet. Others soon followed her example until Sean lay beneath a mountain of people halfway down the snowdrift beside the trailer. A stray dog who had been halfheartedly adopted by Rebecca, and who had been christened Heineken by general acclamation a few weeks earlier, ran over to the mound of people and began barking furiously. The human pile immediately disassembled and began to pelt the dog with snowballs, which sent the animal howling and snarling to the other side of the trailer. A few awkwardly positioned floodlights were the sole sources of illumination in the dark winter night, and this fact combined with the general state of intoxication to allow the animal to escape unscathed.

In the confusion attending the mass assault, Sean had managed to maneuver Rebecca to a position beneath him, and when the others rose and ran off to torment the dog, he quite pointedly made no attempt to move. He grabbed her wrists and pinned them back behind her head, smiling. "Well, this is cozy."

"Yeah, real romantic." She laughed. "I'm freezing my ass off."

"Want me to warm it up for you?"

"I'll start screaming rape," she warned her, eyes twinkling. Sean was about to attempt a witty reply when Heineken bounded over them, knocking into Sean and throwing him onto his side. Rebecca jumped to her feet and ran away, laughing.

The afternoon and early evening had been passed in an atmosphere of general merriment and abandon, and now, at nine o'clock at night, everyone was fast approaching the point at which a decision had to be made: either summon up the energy to go out drinking or settle in for a brief if relaxing evening of beer, pot, and Artie

Winston's singing. Inasmuch as Alex's was the only local watering hole, the decision was easily made, if grudgingly accepted.

By eleven o'clock, two dozen people were lounging about the floor and furniture of Clayton's trailer, an assembly of friends from college, from the City, from Long Island, and from Beckskill itself. They sat in almost pensive silence as the resident minstrel of the group blended his mellow voice with the gently finger-picked guitar and soft harmonica.

> *"Well, I know right well that I am city-born,*
> *But even so I know that I'm a mountain man.*
> *My branches grow out in the city where I dwell,*
> *But I got roots that reach way deep into the land.*
> *Because the forests and the fields and the streams*
> *Are where the living is the best for them like me.*
> *And I got to follow trails in my dreams*
> *And live upon the land or die upon it free. . . ."*

Clayton, Rebecca, Lydia, and Dorcas were the only ones present who had not spent the previous week in some gainful pursuit. Thus three of them were also the only ones present whose eyes were not shutting with the pent-up weariness of Friday night. The fourth, Dorcas, had consumed so much sherry before coming to the trailer, and had indulged in so much beer and marijuana since then, that her head was lolling from side to side and her eyes kept closing against her will. She sat beside Peter and forced herself to gaze in front of her blankly, struggling to fight off the alcohol-and-drug-induced slumber that was gaining on her with each passing minute.

Rebecca had taken Sean's suggestive remarks of a few hours ago at face value and was beginning to feel a little miffed at his rather mellow weariness. He had been working a steady job, day after day, and he was unaccustomed to it. As her erotic inclinations grew, his seemed to diminish, and she was growing annoyed. Lydia was likewise unable to elicit any sort of response from Clayton, but unlike Rebecca she had no explanation for the inattention. Clayton was wide-awake and cheerful, but was ignoring her completely. She did not notice, or chose to ignore, the way he was looking at Dorcas as the pipes were passed around.

"I got so much soot a'lying in my lungs
That I get stoned each time I breathe the mountain air.
I got a life expectancy of forty-one,
But dying don't seem quite so scary way up there.
Both of my feet are flat from walking on cement,
I rarely see more than a dozen stars at night,
My ten-foot room costs a hundred dollars rent.
I'm waging war where it isn't worth the fight.
So I'm leaving you, my darling, leaving you today,
Leaving you unto your world of windowsills,
Of cold cement and streets and great big steel homes,
And I believe I'll be a'heading for the hills. . . ."

Peter and Dorcas were sitting together on the floor near one of the silent stereo speakers, her limp hand held in his, both of them as oblivious to Clayton's leering eyes as was Lydia. Deirdre sat beside them, staring at Artie as she swayed slowly to and fro with the rhythm of the song. Her friend Nancy sat beside her, very obviously bored to tears.

The people in the room represented both different stages of Clayton's life as well as the different locations of his residence. From his early high-school years, when Beckskill was a weekend retreat for his parents and Long Island their permanent home, were his old friend Buzzy

Van Der Donk, Danny Douglas, Eric Franklin, and Gary Mercier, in addition, of course, to Deirdre and Nancy. From his brief stint in college, Sean, Peter, Russell, Artie, and a girl named Suzie Kosloski, whose inclusion in the group was a function of a promiscuity extraordinary in its extent and absolutely mind-boggling in its lack of discrimination. Dorcas and Lydia were, of course, from Beckskill, and from nearby Haddlyville had come Bill Scott and Teddy Metzger, whose devotion to the rock group the Grateful Dead had caused them to be nicknamed the Doo-dahs. Six other people had been dragged along by Clayton's invited guests. He did not know them well . . . indeed, three of them he did not know at all . . . but they had brought wine and marijuana with them, so they were welcome.

"When God made Adam, or so the stories say,
He made his body from the green and grassy ground,
And then he put him in a garden right away,
Not in Chicago, in L.A. or New York Town.
So fare thee well, my love, I hope someday you'll go
To where the people make their lives upon the land.
And even though each one of them is city-born,
Deep down inside each one of them's a mountain man.
So I'm leaving you, my darling, leaving you today,
Leaving you unto your world of windowsills,
Of cold cement and streets and great big steel homes,
And I believe I'll be a'heading for the hills. . . ."

As the closing harmonica riff wound to its end, Peter nodded and said, "That's beautiful, Artie. And it's just so true, you know? We should all live up here in the country. Right, Dorcas?" He turned to her as he spoke, and found that her chin was resting on her breast and she was snoring softly.

"Well, *that's* a comment on your singing if I ever saw one, Artie!" Clayton snickered.

"She just had too much to drink," Lydia said. "And what's your excuse?"

He chose to ignore her as he said perfunctorily, "Great song, Artie, great song."

Artie smiled and nodded as the others muttered words of agreement, and a few other heads began to nod. "You wanna hear another one?" he asked hopefully.

No one answered at first, and then Deirdre said, "Oh, I do! Play that song about the guy . . . you know, the guy who's at the end of his rope . . . you know . . ."

"'Sam McDougal's Blues?'" he asked.

"Yeah," she said, "that's it." She looked around for support of her request and saw more closing eyes. She looked back at Artie and said softly, "I think everybody's about to fall out."

"Yeah," he said glumly. "Looks that way."

"Why don't we go next door, like to the bedroom? You can serenade me."

Clayton suppressed his laughter as Artie and Deirdre left the room. They're like little kids, he thought, making a big deal out of getting laid. If Artie ever makes a move, that is.

"Great," Lydia muttered. "There's only two beds in this fucking place, and one of them just got taken."

"Lyd, my dear"—Clayton smiled—"you seem out of sorts."

"Fuck you," she spat.

"And that's the problem, I suppose."

Nancy yawned loudly. "Clay, I think we better liven this group up a little. This is starting to feel like an old folks' home."

"She's right," Rebecca said. "It's too early to fall out. Let's go to Alex's for a little while." A series of moans arose from the company, and she added quickly, "Look, it's either Alex's or Charlie's, and Clay and Sean can't go to Charlie's."

"Neither can you," Sean pointed out. A year before, after a particularly riotous drunken spree, the three of them had been permanently expelled from the only other bar within easy driving distance.

She waved his objection away impatiently. "I could get in, no sweat. Charlie was just pissed at me because I was with you two."

"So go to Charlie's" Sean shrugged. "You wanna party and I just wanna go to sleep."

"Yeah," Clayton agreed. "Everybody who wants to go out drinking, go with Becky. Everybody who wants to fall out, stay here."

Rebecca, Lydia, and Nancy managed to arouse some degree of enthusiasm from most of the small company, and they began to vacate the trailer and head for the numerous vehicles that were parked at the foot of the path. Artie and Deirdre remained in the bedroom, and Peter looked at Dorcas with concern and said, "I don't know if I should leave her here like this . . ."

"She had too much to drink," Clayton said. "Who hasn't, sometime or another? Stuff a pillow under her head and don't worry about her, Pete. She'll wake up feeling like shit, is all."

"Yeah." He nodded uncertainly, then walked to the door and called out, "What do you think, Lyd? Okay to leave Dorcas passed out like this?"

"I think you treat her like she's made of glass or something," Lydia called back as she climbed into Russell's Volkswagen. "Come on, let's go, okay?"

Peter did as Clayton had suggested and then followed the others out into the cold darkness. From the bedroom came the soft sound of Artie's guitar. Sean rolled one final joint, and as he lighted it he looked at Clayton and asked, "Hey, what's with you, man?"

"What do you mean?"

"You look like really uptight."

Clayton shook his head. "Just waiting."

"Waiting for what?"

Clayton did not reply. Instead he listened as the engines of the automobiles rose and then faded into the distance. Then he sidled over to where Dorcas was lying and begun to unbutton her flannel shirt. Sean watched with disbelief. "Clay, what the hell are you doing?"

He chuckled. "Fulfilling a long-standing fantasy."

"Cut it out, damn it! You know what happened last—"

"Sean, shut up, will you? You'll wake her up." He frowned. "Shit. She's wearing a bra. This is gonna be tricky." Dorcas was lying on her side, and he was able to slide his hand beneath her shirt to her back and unhook her bra without awakening her. Then he gently rolled her over onto her back and pulled the bra up over her breasts. "Holy shit! Her and Lydia, their tits are like identical!"

"Clay, for Christ's sake!"

"Both starting to get those lines on the top, you know what I mean? I hate that. Always happens to girls with big tits, I guess."

"Clay, cut it out!" Sean was clearly concerned about the ramifications of what his friend was doing.

"Just relax," Clayton said. "Hey, you can have sloppy seconds, if you want." He pulled Dorcas's belt open, unbuttoned and unzipped her dungarees, and then began to pull them down.

At this point the girl's eyes fluttered and an inarticulate sound escaped her lips. Clayton pulled off his own pants and then began to massage her vulva and explore her interior with his grimy fingers. Her eyes opened wider. "What . . . what . . . ?"

"You've seduced me, you little fox," Clayton whispered, and he moved on top of her and inserted himself into her.

Dorcas awakened to find herself in Clayton's embrace as he plunged repeatedly into her. "What are you . . . Clay, what . . . ?"

"Don't try to pretend you don't remember." He smiled down at her. "As soon everybody else left to go drinking you came on to me like crazy."

"I . . . I did?" she asked. Worry and confusion were written on her face as she lay unresisting beneath him. *I wouldn't do something like that . . . like this . . . would I?*

"You sure did." Clayton panted as he approached climax. "It was like you were in heat or something. Don't you remember?"

"I . . . I guess so . . ." Dorcas had no experience upon which to base a reaction. She knew that she did not want to have intercourse with Clayton, but she clearly was doing so. She did not remember initiating it, but he said she had, so it must have happened that way. She had only one sexual experience in her background, and that was brief, unpleasant, and two years earlier with a boy she never even saw anymore; and yet here she was, having sex with her sister's boyfriend while her best friend's boyfriend sat and watched.

She whimpered softly as Clayton squeezed her breasts and thrust himself into her, grunting, "Tight as a drum, tight as a drum . . ."

She frowned. *How could I have said something like that? How could I be doing something like this?*

And did I see Mr. Schilder?

And did he turn into Vernon?

And was Mr. Patanjali in the cave?

She sighed as a tear rolled from the side of her eye. *I don't know what I'm doing anymore, what I'm saying,* what I'm thinking. I don't know, I just don't know. She closed her eyes and tried to think about something else, anything else, as minutes crept by like hours and Clayton pounded into her.

At last he emptied himself into her and then rolled off onto his side. "That was great, Dork, just great. Hey, don't say nothing to Lyd, okay? She'd be really pissed at you."

"No, I won't," she said quietly, her voice tremulous with repressed weeping. "I won't tell anybody."

"Atta girl." Clayton grinned. "It's been a long day and we got a lot to do tomorrow, so let's get some sleep, okay?"

Dorcas's fingers seemed to move spasmodically as she dressed herself and then lay back down on the floor, huddling onto her side.

After a few minutes Sean asked, "Hey, Clay?"

"Hmmm?"

"What does that thing mean?"

"Hmmm?"

"That poster of John Wayne saying 'Buy a dachshund.' What the fuck does it mean?"

"It's a cowboy saying 'Buy a dachshund,'" Clayton muttered.

"I know that. But what is it supposed to mean?"

"Buy a dachshund," he slurred dreamily. "Get a long little doggie."

Sean considered this. "That's really stupid, Clay." Clayton did not respond, and a moment later he began to snore.

Soon thereafter Sean began to snore also. Artie's guitar ceased its melody as he and Deirdre lay sleeping, chastely clothed, in each other's arms. And Dorcas lay in the darkness, weeping softly, her head throbbing and her heart racing as a hangover began to exacerbate her misery and her shame.

Chapter Fourteen

January 11, 1969

"The time has come," Clayton said, "to talk of other things. . . . "

"Of goblin ghosts and haunted woods," Rebecca continued, "and bats with furry wings."

It was all very, very camp.

Timothy Leary, the self-proclaimed high priest of lysergic acid, once noted that the setting of an acid trip was the prime factor in determining whether the trip would be a good one or a bad one. He recommended surroundings with soft, muted colors, music pleasing to the tastes of the tripper, an atmosphere of security, and the company of close, trusted friends and lovers. As the two dozen young people walked through the woods toward the old Sweet house in the early dusk of January 11, 1969, Peter Geerson wondered what Dr. Leary would make of this rather bizarre beginning to the night's acid trip; and he was also very, very worried about the effect the drug might have upon Dorcas Ostlich.

The revelers had made it back to Clayton's trailer soon after the bars had shut down at four o'clock that morning. They were without exception dog tired and dead drunk, and the winter sun's brilliant afternoon rays brought them both unwelcome wakefulness and throbbing headaches. The breakfast of six warmed-over pepperoni pizzas added heartburn to their physical woes, and the afternoon barbecue of chili dogs and onion burgers did not serve to improve their conditions.

Of course, indigestion that would put a fifty-year-old in the hospital or an eighty-year-old in the grave was but an inconvenience to people whose ages ranged from nineteen to twenty-two. It did not, however, serve to engender a general mood of high spirits. Only Artie Winston and Deirdre Duell seemed generally content on that cold winter morning, for their previous evening had ended early, undramatically, and with a minimum of self-sedation. Dorcas Ostlich was severely hung over, and her usually melancholy personality had been rendered even more morose and withdrawn for reasons to which most of the others were not privy. Her sister Lydia was tired and still angry at Clayton, and Russell and Peter each felt as if a week of rest would be welcome. Most of the others were no better. Buzzy and Gary, Nancy and Suzie, Danny and Eric and the others were, in the parlance of the age, wiped out.

But not Clayton, who the previous evening had, as it were, exercised and then retired early. And not Rebecca, with her incredible capacity for merrymaking.

And the destination of the straggling band as they stumbled wearily through the woods was itself not conducive to a good trip. Here, known to them all, was the forest where the body of Sarah Ostlich had been found a month before; here was where Dorcas had twice been confronted by Grogo the Goblin (or was I? she wondered); here was where Clayton had witnessed the lynching and the arson that had bound so many of the townspeople in a conspiracy of criminal silence; here were the woods bounding the river to whose protection Peter Geerson had dedicated himself, the woods which, unknown to any of them, Clayton Saunders had agreed to sell to the town two days earlier.

For various reasons known to all, the old house of Grogo the Goblin was not the ideal site for a communal acid trip; and it was to this old house that they were making their way as the sun began to set behind the Catskills.

"Come on, stragglers," Clayton called out to those behind him. "Don't get lost, or Grogo'll getcha!"

It was twenty minutes after five as they drew nigh the old Sweet house. Almost everyone had dropped acid at 4:30, figuring that they would be safe in allowing an hour and a half for the drug to take effect. Peter, the victim of numerous recent bad trips, had not taken any LSD; neither had Danny Douglas, who had gallantly volunteered to remain straight so that he could ferry others about in his van. Peter would drive Russell's car, and Clayton would manage his jeep as best he could. He had a good deal of experience driving while under the influence of intoxicants and hallucinogens, and he was confident that he would be able to drive adequately, as long as the road remained free of dinosaurs.

It had been assumed that Dorcas would adhere to her resolve never to take LSD again, not after that one very bad trip a year ago had landed her in a psychiatric hospital; but to the surprise of all and to the concern of Lydia and Peter, she took half a tablet. Lydia had been worried about the marked changes in Dorcas's behavior in recent days, the heavy drinking, the peculiar comments, and the dull, emotionless cast of her face and voice. She knew about her sister's recent hallucinations and generally unstable personality, and as they approached the Sweet house she said, "Just remember, Dork, you only did a half a tab, so it won't be like a real heavy trip." Lydia gasped softly as she saw a tree shift from brown to orange.

"I know, Lyd," Dorcas said impassively.

"I still don't know why you wanted to take even that much," Lydia went on, and then added quickly, "I mean, nothing's gonna go wrong, you know? Everything's cool. But still . . ."

"It's an experiment," Dorcas said softly.

"An experiment. What are you talking about? What kind of experiment?"

Dorcas did not answer immediately. She was looking at the gently shifting waves of soft color that were drifting over the forest floor, a sure sign that the drug was beginning to take effect, that she was, as it was said, "getting off" on the LSD. At last she said, "What is reality, Lydia?"

"Huh?"

"Do we really exist? Can we be like really sure that anything exists?" She stopped walking and took her sister's hand earnestly. "Think about it, Lydia. What if all that stuff Mr. Patanjali told me that time is true? What if you and I don't exist?"

"Dork, you gotta cut this shit out. This is . . ." Lydia paused. She had almost said, "This is nuts," but then thought the better of it in light of her sister's psychiatric past. "You've been talking about stuff like this too much lately."

Dorcas released her hand as they resumed walking. "I thought I saw some pretty strange stuff, and for the life of me I don't know if I really saw it. And it seems like I've been . . . well, doing things I don't remember doing." Her mind flashed back to the previous night, and she shuddered. "What I mean is that I don't know if stuff is happening that I can't explain or if I'm just going nuts."

"So you took some acid to make sure you are?" Peter asked as he came up beside her, his worry on her behalf masked by the acerbic tone of his voice.

"Come on, Pete"—she sighed—"don't, please. I just know that taking acid brings out all your, I don't know, your inner thoughts, makes you like see them. If I start hallucinating Vernon, then I'll know that it was all in my mind all along, that I never saw him or Mr. Patanjali in that cave."

"Great, just great," he said. "And I suppose that if you *don't* hallucinate Grogo, that'll mean that you really saw him and he really killed that old man and ate his brain and all that shit? For Christ's sake, Dorcas!"

Dorcas did not wish to argue with him, so she quickened her pace to pull ahead of them as her sister jabbed Peter hard in the side. "Peter, cut it out," Lydia said quietly. "What's done is done. She dropped the acid and she's gonna trip. You know as well as I do that we have to make her feel as good as we can, not give her a hard time about it."

"I know, I know," he muttered. "But it was a damn stupid thing for her to do."

"Wasn't as stupid as what you did last summer, dropping acid and then sitting around watching *Dr. Jekyll and Mr. Hyde* on TV while you waited to get off. Real smart, real smart. A movie about a guy who takes a drug that turns him into a monster."

Peter laughed softly at the memory of his own foolish bravado and the subsequent bad trip. "Yeah, I guess that wasn't well advised."

"I guess not," Lydia snapped. "And look at what Buzzy did, dropping acid and then spraining his ankle before he even started to get off."

"Oh, come on," he said. "He didn't sprain his ankle on purpose!"

"That's not the point. Dork already did the drug, so we have to keep her in a good mood, that's all. She sure as hell doesn't need you hassling her about it."

A few yards ahead of them, Sean Brenner was

grinning as he waved his hand back and forth in front of his face, watching as successive transparent images of his hands were left briefly in the wake of the motion. "Gettin' off," he said, and then tripped over a root and fell on his face.

"Yeah, I guess so." Rebecca laughed as she helped him to his feet. "This is great acid. It doesn't give you that jumpy feeling, like that shitty acid Artie copped from Rod Silverio last summer."

"That shit was cut with speed," Clayton said over his shoulder from in front of them. "Made the hallucinations real good, but it kept me awake for two days."

"No speed in this stuff," Sean said. "It's pure. It's even on a Vitamin C pill, so it's actually good for you to take it."

"Yeah, you're such a health freak," Rebecca said.

Clayton moved out of the woods and into the clearing. "Here we are, boys and girls," he called out. "Welcome to the home of Grogo the Goblin."

The clearing had never before looked as it did at that moment, for it had never been viewed through the crystal spectacles of LSD. The charred ruins of the barn were alive with amorphous creepy-crawlies that swirled about slowly upon the blackened wood. A long, thick beam that had somehow escaped total immolation was now writhing rhythmically upon the ground, and an old willow that stood nearby was reaching out toward the ruins as if to embrace them.

The house itself, at most times a plain and rather ramshackle structure, now loomed over the young people as they drew closer. The house had grown considerably since the time they had dropped the acid, and its growth continued as they approached it. "Must be a thousand feet high," Sean muttered.

"Huh?" Lydia asked distractedly. She was staring up

at the moon, wondering why it had begun to sizzle and steam.

"The house," he said. "Thousand feet."

She looked down at the house and said, "Wow" softly, for the house did indeed have a thousand feet. The house wiggled it toes.

"It was the long walk," Clayton said breathlessly. He turned to the others, who were walking unsteadily toward him in groups of twos and threes. "We're getting off like really strong 'cause of the walk. I mean, I'm like getting off, you know? Everybody else getting off?" A few people nodded their heads. Most of them just stared at him. "Yeah, right. All the exercise. I mean, all the exercise, you know? Like the blood pumping and shit, you know?" He seemed to believe that he had communicated his thoughts adequately, so he turned and walked up the steps to the door. The wood was soft and squooshy beneath his feet, and he worried briefly that he would sink down into it before he could grab hold of the doorknob. It was close, but he managed to jump over the final quicksand step and fall against the door before the wood sucked him down into its depths. He grinned at his sister. "C-close call," he stammered.

"Huh? Yeah. Huh?"

Clayton took hold of the knob and then hesitated. He turned and called out, "Hey, Peter, Danny. C'mere."

The only two people present who had not taken any of the drug came up to him, and Peter asked, "What's the matter, Clay?"

"You, ah, go first. You go go in first." He began laughing. "You grogo in first. Fou yogo in girst."

Peter laughed. "You're in great shape."

"This is like dynamite shit, you know?"

"Yeah, it looks it. Why do you want me to go in first?"

Rebecca was nearby, staring at him through grossly

dilated pupils, and Clayton pulled Peter and Danny aside to whisper conspiratorially, "It's the house. I don't think it likes acid heads."

Peter and Danny Douglas exchanged amused looks. "The house doesn't like acid heads?" Danny asked.

"No," Clayton replied seriously. "It just tried to eat me. The steps did, I mean. They like tried to eat me."

"I don't know what you're worried about," Peter observed. "One taste and it would have spit you out anyway."

"Huh?"

"Nothing, nothing." Pete laughed. "Okay, we'll go in first." He pushed open the unlocked door and felt around on the wall for the light switch. "I hope you've been paying the electric bill."

"Huh?"

"Nothing." He knew that Clayton had attended to the essentials, for the bare 40-watt bulb in the ceiling fixture glowed as he flipped the switch. The dim light was barely able to illuminate the large room.

"My God, I'm blind!" Sean screamed, throwing his hands over his eyes.

"Sean, you're still out on the porch," Peter pointed out, "and that bulb isn't bright enough to blind a mole."

"I can't see," Sean wept. "I can't see."

Lydia stumbled up the steps, followed by Russell, Dorcas, and Buzzy. "What's the matter?" she asked.

"I'm blind, I'm blind!"

"Sean's blind!" Deirdre shouted to the others.

"Yeah?" Artie responded. "Wow. Just like Mr. Spock was when McCoy put him in that light chamber."

"Wh-what?" Sean blubbered.

"Yeah, Spock was blind for a while. But he like got his sight back, you know?"

"Yeah?" Sean took his hands from his eyes and looked at Artie. "He really did?"

"Yeah. Can you see me? I mean, you're like looking at me."

Sean's face erupted into a glow of ecstasy. "I can see! I can see!" He paused. "But everything is paisley!"

"Another crisis surmounted," Peter muttered as he sat down against the wall. "Danny, remind me never to stay straight when everybody else trips, okay?"

"You and me both," was the reply.

The others meandered into the large room in a long straggling line and eventually seated themselves in a tightly huddled circle in the center of the room. Russell sighed. "This is great. This is like wonderful."

"We haven't done anything yet," Rebecca said, smiling at the dozens of tiny human beings who were plowing minuscule fields on the floor at her feet. "We gotta have a séance."

"Yeah, yeah, right right right," Eric muttered. "What?"

"A séance," Rebecca repeated. "Remember? We're gonna like have like, you know, I mean like we're gonna . . . I mean . . ." She frowned, having forgotten what she was saying.

"Where's the volume control?" Sean asked. "I can't hear nothing."

"The what?" Clayton responded. "Where's the what?"

"The volume control for the TV," Sean said, staring at the wall. "*The Wizard of Oz* is on, but I can't hear nothing."

Peter and Danny started laughing softly. "You, ah, you watching television there, Sean?"

"Yeah," he breathed, his eyes glued to the wall.

"That's real nice." Danny chuckled. "*The Wizard of Oz,* eh?"

"Yeah . . ."

"What scene are you watching?"

"Dorothy's just meeting all the uh, the, uh, the Munchkins." He sniffed as if he were about to weep. "But I can't hear nothing."

Peter repressed his laughter and he and Danny began singing one of the songs from the movie.

"Oh, wow." Sean smiled. "This is great, this is great. Here comes the lollipop guild!"

Danny glanced at his watch and then turned to Peter. "They're getting off at 5:30. How long you figure before they start to come down?"

Peter shrugged. "It's supposed to be good acid."

"Did he cop it from Steve?"

"Yeah."

Danny sighed. "Shit. That means it *is* good acid."

"Six hours, probably, for the hallucinations to die down. They won't really be straight until the morning."

"So we gotta hang around here and baby-sit until probably midnight."

"Yeah, or until Clay decides to leave. He's the Pied Piper, not us."

"Ah, well." Danny sighed. "I wish I'd taken some acid."

"Thanks." Peter laughed. "You'd want me to be the only straight person here?"

Danny laughed also. "Hey, then it would've been your problem, and I would've been having a good time."

Peter blew into his cupped hands. "Jesus, it's cold in here. Hey, Clayton. Did you pay the coal bill, too?"

"Huh?"

"Is there a furnace or anything in this place?"

"Huh?"

"Never mind." Peter sighed as he went to the fireplace and squinted up the chimney. "This looks usable. Danny, see if there's any firewood outside, like maybe alongside the house." Danny returned a few minutes later with wood and kindling, and Peter searched through the house until he found a pile of old newspapers. Soon thereafter a blazing fire was providing some warmth in the cold room, though Sean complained that it was interfering with television reception.

The hours passed with all memories of the planned séance forgotten. Sean watched *The Wizard of Oz* twice on the wall, and then, at about eight o'clock, he and Rebecca had sex in the middle of the room. No one other than Peter and Danny seemed to notice, and they watched with amused and envious interest.

At 9:30 Gary Mercier, who was in the middle of his senior year at college, solemnly informed Peter that he intended to drop out of school and do acid for the rest of his life. Gary also corrected Russell, who exclaimed that the colors were very intense. "No," Gary said. "It's heavy, but there aren't any colors."

At a quarter after ten Buzzy Van Der Donk went into the kitchen adjoining the large central room to try to find some beer, which was, of course, not to be found; but he noticed that the light from the central room streamed through the kitchen doorway and created a starkly delineated shadow on the kitchen floor. It's like on the moon, he thought. Freezing cold in the shade and blistering heat in the light. He was standing in the light, and felt himself suddenly beginning to broil. He jumped desperately into the shadow, and began to freeze. He hopped back and forth from light to shade, and then began to spin around on the border between them, trying to maintain a stable body temperature. Then he forgot what he was doing and why he was doing it, and wandered back to the others, all notions of beer and the moon forgotten.

At eleven o'clock Russell Phelps discovered that he could fly and begged Peter to take him up to the roof. "I wouldn't jump off, honest!" he swore. "But if I did, I wouldn't get hurt. I would just like float, you know?" Peter did not take him up to the roof.

At 11:30 Artie Winston unbuttoned Deirdre Duell's shirt and, placing his hands on the undersides of her large breasts, began to move them slowly from left to right. Audible light streamed from each nipple with every motion and bathed the entire room with waves of liquidy pink. She was not seeing what he was seeing. She was watching her breasts grow larger and larger, heavier and heavier, dragging her down toward the floor. She fell forward from her seated position and strove to keep herself from plummeting downward through the floorboards. With great effort she pushed herself back up and did not fall through the earth to China.

At 11:45 Dorcas Ostlich rose unsteadily to her feet and announced that she had to take a leak.

"Hold on, Dorcas," Peter said as he stood up. "I go with you."

She looked at the scales that were growing all over his skin and frowned as he began to molt. "I'm okay, Pete. I don't need company."

"You sure?"

"Yeah. I'm just going over behind the palm tree out front."

He smiled. "The palm tree, Dorcas? How's the acid doing? The hallucinations letting up yet?"

"I guess so," she replied, ignoring the melting rubber mountains that were clearly visible through the window. "I'll be right back."

"Dorcas, you really shouldn't go outside alone. I mean, it's not just you. Nobody should be alone when they trip."

"I'll go with her," Lydia said.

"You're in no better shape than she is!"

"I feel like I'm coming down a little," Lydia insisted

as she stood up. "I'm hardly hallucinating at all right now."

Peter shook his head. "I'll go with her."

"Hey, man, what's wrong with you? You get some kind of kick out of watching girls pee or something?"

The question stunned him into an offended silence and he made no further effort to accompany them. Dorcas and Lydia put on their jackets and then went out into the darkness. The murkiness made Lydia uncomfortable, so she left the front door open to give them a little light. Dorcas went behind the nearest tree and attended to her need, steadying herself with one hand on a low-lying stump as Lydia sat and waited on the steps.

"Dor Dor." She looked up to see Grogo the Goblin running toward her from the woods. "Dor Dor. You come, you come. Rinda sick."

"Oh, Lord." she sighed. "I'm doing it again." She stood up and readjusted her clothing as the geek reached her, and she shook her head, saying, "You aren't real. You aren't here. This is all in my imagination." She looked around her at the vibrating, shifting forest. "All my imagination," she whispered.

"Rinda sick, Rinda sick," the little man insisted, tugging urgently on her sleeve. "You come!"

Lydia stood up on the steps and blinked her eyes at what she was seeing a few yards away. "Holy shit!" she muttered.

"I'm not really seeing you," Dorcas told him, pulling her sleeve away from his long, delicate fingers. "It's the drug, that's all. You don't exist. I don't exist. Go away, Vernon." She started walking back to the house.

"Dor Dor," he whined. "Dor Dor!" He watched her mount the steps and then he spun around and ran back into the woods.

Dorcas walked past Lydia without saying a word,

oblivious to her sister's openmouted astonishment. She went into the house and sat down in front of the fire, thinking, So now I know the truth. I'm going crazy.

Lydia closed the door behind her and sat down next to Sean and Rebecca. "Hey, uh, you know what?"

"What?" they asked in unison.

"I just like saw Dorcas talking to Grogo the Goblin."

"No shit?" Sean shook his head. "That's one hell of a hallucination. This is incredible acid."

Lydia sighed and nodded. "Like really!" She looked over at her sister. "I wonder if she saw him, too?"

"Maybe," Sean replied. "Same batch of acid." His reasoning was void of any logic whatsoever, but at that moment his comment made perfect sense to Lydia and Rebecca.

Dorcas allowed her eyes to drift from face to face, forcing herself to remember that the shapeshifting she was seeing was all a result of the drug. She looked at Lydia and shuddered as her sister's hair began to squirm and writhe like the serpents that grew from the head of Medusa. The serpents twisted around each other, forming first eight long braids, then merging to four, then coming to rest as two. That's neat, Dorcas thought. I wish I could make my hair do that. It'd save a lot of time. . . .

She gasped. Instead of her twin sister Lydia, she found that she was gazing at herself. That isn't just a hallucination, that's really me over there, it's really *me*, it's *me*!

The apparition looked at her, and she saw the image of herself gasp with shock, just as she herself had done a moment before. Their locked eyes seemed to become magnets that dragged them toward each other, and as they came together they blended and merged, becoming one. She found herself floating near the ceiling, looking down at everyone; but Dorcas was not there, and Lydia was not there. They're gone, she thought, both gone. I'm the only one left, just me, just Karen.

She shut her eyes for a moment, and when she opened them, she was again sitting before the fire and Lydia was again sitting next to Sean a few yards away.

I'm losing it, she thought desperately. I can't control my thoughts, I can't control anything, out of control, out of control, out of control. . . .

Dorcas turned to stare into the flames that danced in the fireplace. Some of the flames were red, some were yellow, some had stripes, and some intermittently took the form of little tiny Vernon Sweets. Why has all this happened to me? she asked herself. Why is it that everybody else is happy, everybody else is normal, everybody else is sane, and I'm the only one who's never in control of myself or of anything else? Why did my own father have to do those terrible, terrible things to me. Didn't he realize what . . . ?

But no, no, that wasn't me, it was Lydia, it was Lydia. . . .

She felt a pinch of pain and realized that she had been biting her lip so hard that she had pierced the skin with her teeth. She wiped off a drop of blood as she felt her body beginning to shake uncontrollably. Waves of anger and terror began to wash over her, and she hugged her knees tightly to her chest. Why can't I just be normal, like everybody else? Why did I take that goddamn drug? Why did I take that goddamn drug?

"Why did I take that goddamn *DRUG!*" she shrieked.

Everyone else in the room stared at her in silence, until at last Danny turned to Peter and sighed. "Party's over. . . ."

Chapter Fifteen

January 12, 1969

One o'clock in the morning. The few local farmers had already left the bar, and the vacationing couple who stopped in for some coffee at twelve were about to resume their long drive to Montreal. As soon as they leave, Alex thought, I can shut down for the night. Been a slow night anyway, for a Saturday. It'll be good to end it early.

He finished wiping a glass and he placed it onto the shelf. Time was I'd stay open to three or four on a Saturday night, but not lately, not for years. Nobody but the farmers and those goddamn hippies come here anymore. Haven't seen old Schilder and Walt Rihaczeck for over a week, nobody has. I'm worried about them, sure, but it's not just that they were old friends of mine, they were regular customers, too. I cant' afford to lose regular customers. Probably went to, I don't know, Albany or New York City for a long holiday, something like that. Sure miss their business. I'm hurting, I'm hurting. But maybe when they build the factory . . . when they build the factory . . .

"'Night, now," the vacationer said as his wife waved and they left the room. Alex smiled back at them, and his smile vanished the instant they were out the door. Now that Doc Ostlich has the land problem solved, we'll have the factory. Jobs for my neighbors, maybe jobs that will bring people here to live. Maybe then my business . . .

He sighed. I'm old and alone, factory or no factory, successful or bankrupt; and even though there's only five years left on the mortgage, I don't think I can make it. The bank will throw me out, and then what will I have, what will I be? "Why did you leave me, Paula?" he whispered.

He jumped back, startled, as the door swung briskly open and crashed against the wall. "Whoops," Clayton said. "Sorry 'bout that, Al."

Alex frowned as Clayton walked in, and his frown grew deeper as two dozen others followed. Drunk again, all of them, he thought as he observed the unsteady gaits and the peculiar facial expressions. "I was just about to close up." he said pointedly as the group began to disperse to several of the tables.

"Oh, damn it." Clayton grinned, pulling a wad of twenty-dollar bills from his back pocket. "Guess I gotta go spend my money somewhere else."

"No, no, that's okay," Alex said quickly, and then gazed at Clayton's face intently. The younger man's eyes had an oddness to them that Alex had never seen before, but that he was certain was not a result of drinking. "You on something, Saunders?" he demanded.

"Well, I'm on Earth." Clayton nodded.

"Don't you get funny with me, boy, or I'll punch your face in!" Alex said darkly. "You on something?"

"Drugs! You mean drugs?" Clayton was deeply insulted by the question. "That's a hell of a thing to ask! Of course I'm not!"

"You better not be, or I call the cops."

"Calm down, Al." He smiled, slapping him on the shoulder. "We just came in for a few drinks and a little good cheer."

Alex remained suspicious, but he nodded and said, "Okay. You want beer?"

"Yeah, ten pitchers and a couple of bottles of bourbon," Clayton said, taking off his coat and tossing it into the corner. He tossed five twenties down onto the bar top. "Let me know when that runs out."

Alex stared at his back with undisguised animosity as Clayton ambled over to the table where Lydia and Peter were sitting on either side of Dorcas, each holding one of her hands. Rebecca, Sean, and Russell were seated opposite them, and Clayton pulled a chair up to the end of the table and sat down. "So how's the bummer going, Dork?"

"That isn't very funny," Lydia snapped.

He laughed. "Take it easy. Everybody has bad trips once in a while. It's no big deal."

"I think we should take her to the hospital," Peter said. "This idea of getting out of a bummer by drinking yourself into a stupor—"

"Is the only way to do it," Sean interrupted. "Look, if we take her to a hospital, all they'll do is shoot her up with barbiturates, like just space her out until she comes down from the acid. So what's the difference between that and getting drunk? I mean like numb is numb, you know?"

"You aren't a doctor," Peter insisted. "She may need . . . well, more than bourbon and beer."

Why are they all talking about me like I'm not even here? I can hear them, I can see them, so why aren't they talking to me? Why are they all just talking *about* me?

"Don't be stupid," Clayton said. "We take her to a hospital while she's bumming out and not only will she end up staying there like last time, we'll have to talk to cops and doctors and all that shit. Let it be, man. Booze'll do the trick."

"I hope you're right," Peter muttered.

Alex carried over a tray with a pitcher of beer and seven glasses and then returned to the bar to get the bourbon. He kept glancing at Dorcas, wondering what was wrong with her. The girl's face was ashen and her unblinking eyes did not move from the point in space at which they stared. When he brought the bottle over to them he asked, "Dorcas, what is the matter with you?"

Lydia squeezed her sister's hand and thought, Answer him, damn it. He's just enough of a pain in the ass to call the cops or something. Answer him, Dork.

"N-nothing," Dorcas muttered and then jumped slightly, startled by the sound of her own voice.

"Hey, Al," Clayton said quickly, "we're discussing something kind of personal here, so get lost, will you?"

"This is my place," Alex snapped. "You don't tell me what to do in my place."

"Yeah, yeah, sure. Hey, that hundred bucks used up yet?"

Alex glowered at him, but at last he went back to the bar and began filling more beer pitchers. Clayton shook his head. "What an asshole."

"He's awful nasty to you," Peter observed. "I thought everybody around here was being nice to you since you bought the Sweet place."

Clayton shrugged instead of replying.

Russell reached across the table and touched Dorcas on the shoulder. "You feeling better, Dork?"

"How can she be?" Clayton asked. "She hasn't started drinking yet." He poured her a beer and a shot of bourbon. "Down the hatch, Dork." He laughed, adding, "Better this hatch than the happy hatch."

"Clayton, cut it out, damn it!" Lydia spat.

Dorcas sipped the bourbon and then coughed mightily. "This tastes like iodine." Are they making me drink iodine? Are they trying to poison me?

"All whiskey tastes like iodine," Peter said. "Take a swallow of beer. It'll kill the taste." She looked at him and willed herself to believe him, though she still felt threatened and endangered.

"Let's play a game," Clayton suggested. "Let's see how many different ways we can think of to say insane asylum."

"Clayton . . ." Lydia said threateningly.

He chuckled. "All right, all right."

"That's one thing I've never liked about you," she went on. "Sometimes you just act so fucking mean."

"I'm not mean. I just don't coddle people."

"You don't know the difference."

"No? You want to see the difference?" His customary callousness had been hardened beyond measure by the drugs and alcohol of the evening, and he was grinning cruelly as he turned to Peter and said, "Peter, old man, I got some news for you."

"Yeah? What?"

"The town council offered me a half million for the Sweet property."

Peter laughed softly. "What did you tell them?"

"I told them it sounded good to me."

The smile was frozen on Peter's face, but his eyes expressed confusion. "But . . . if you agreed . . . I mean, isn't that like a verbal contract or something?"

"Yup."

"I knew it," Russell said quietly.

"But then . . . but then how are you gonna get out of it? I mean . . ."

"I guess I can't get out of it." Clayton shrugged.

"But . . . but they'll build that factory!"

"Guess so."

"They'll pollute the river!"

"Looks that way."

Peter stared at him, dumbfounded. "But . . . but why?"

"A quarter-of-a-million profit in two months," Clayton said. "A quarter of a million bucks buys a lot of beer."

Peter continued to gape at him. "But what about the river?"

Clayton laughed. "Fuck the river."

"What do you mean, fuck the river!" Peter shouted, startling everyone but Dorcas into uneasy attentiveness. Alex looked up from behind the bar when he heard the raised voices, and he turned down the radio so he could hear as Peter went on, "Do you realize what you've done?"

"Sure I do," Clayton said, lighting a cigarette. "I've just made a quarter of a million dollars."

"I don't understand," Peter moaned. "I just don't understand this! How the hell could you do something like this?"

"Something like what?" he asked innocently. "I'm just making an honest buck, Pete. That's as American as apple pie."

"Clayton, don't you understand that there's a . . . a change going on in this country, a change for the better? Our generation of people don't do things like this! We're a new wave, a new society."

"Oh, really!" Clayton laughed.

"Goddamn it, Clay, this isn't funny! Don't you read the papers? Don't you listen to the music? Don't you watch the news? Where the hell have you *been* for the past six years?"

"Peter, Peter," he said patiently, "you're so fucking naive. Of course I know what's going on in the country. *You're* the one who doesn't."

"I do so!"

"Yeah, sure you do. You know what I see when I watch the news, Pete? I see hundreds of thousands of guys who don't want to get drafted marching in antiwar protests. I see college kids starting all these riots and shit just so they can take over their schools and party like crazy. It's all hypocrisy, Peter."

"Jesus Christ!" Peter shouted. "Are you listening to yourself?"

"Sure I am, and I also listen to the Beatles and Dylan and the Stones, and I wish I had one tenth the money those guys have," he went on. "Businessmen, that's all they are, businessmen who've made it to the top of their industry. They know what kind of music gullible people like you want to hear, so that's what they grind out."

"Clayton, you're crazy!"

"Oh yeah?" Clayton grinned. "Let's see how much people our age give a shit about Vietnam if Nixon ends the draft. I mean, when I beat the draft, Vietnam stopped being all that important to me, you know? There isn't an antiwar movement, Peter, there's only an antidraft movement. And all this civil-rights stuff! Let's see how much whites care about blacks when it starts to cost money. Let's see how much blacks care about equality when they realize it means like sink or swim on your own, you know?"

"For Christ's sake, Clay, there were hundreds and thousands of people of all races marching with Martin Luther King! There are millions of people working against racism and injustice and the war! How can you—"

"Peter, wake up, man!" Clayton shouted. "Everybody's afraid of the draft but nobody really gives a shit about the war. And people go to demonstrations to get laid and buy dope. It's like a social event."

"Clayton, you are out of your fucking mind!"

"Am I? Am I really? What happened to the SDS chapter at New Paltz? Didn't it disband from lack of interest? You got any black friends, Pete? I know I don't."

"You ain't gonna have any white ones either, at this rate," Rebecca muttered.

Clayton ignored her. "Face it, Peter. The newspapers have cooked up a, I don't know, a mythology about all the shit going on in the country right now, and you've swallowed it whole, but none of it's true. Guys don't want to get drafted, everybody does drugs, rock singers are making millions, the black man wants the white man's money, and all the girls spread like cream cheese." He laughed. "And you think it's the fucking Age of Aquarius!"

Peter grabbed his coat from the floor and stood up. "I'm not gonna sit here and listen to this."

"Come on, Pete, wake up," Clayton said calmly. "There's a handful of people like you and Russell who take all this shit seriously. Everybody else is just fucking around."

"That's bullshit!"

"You know what the bullshit is, Pete? It's people like you two guys thinking that the sixties are any different from the fifties. You think that just because all the guys have long hair and all the girls fuck and everybody wears dungarees and smokes pot and listens to the Jefferson Airplane, we all really give a shit about social revolution and racial equality and the fucking whales and the goddamn fucking rivers."

"Fuck you!"

"Ah, a stinging retort!"

"Just look around you, man. Look at everybody's faces. You think they all think this is as funny as you do? Look at them, Clay. Look at them, damn it!"

Clayton looked at his sister. "Quarter of a mill, Becky. And half of it is yours." He turned to Lydia. "I got a lot more money now. That bother you?" He grinned at

Sean. "Anything to say, buddy?" Sean smiled sheepishly, knowing full well that any choice between ethics and ease would be an easy one for him to make. Clayton turned back to Peter. "Yeah, right. Look at 'em, Pete. And while you're at it, grow up, will you?"

Peter looked at the others, and what he saw did not comfort him. On Russell's face he saw sympathy, tinged with an element of rueful vindication; but when he looked at Rebecca, Sean, and Lydia, he saw hesitation, neither approval nor disapproval, but merely hesitation, and that was enough to shatter him. He flung open the door of the bar and stumbled out into the cold winter darkness.

Clayton turned and smiled at a dumbfounded Lydia. "See? Now *that* was mean."

Rebecca turned on her brother angrily. "Clayton, that was just a terrible thing to do."

"What, selling the land? Don't you want your quarter of a million?"

"That's not the point," she huffed. "Why'd you have to tell him about it like that, I mean like the way you did? You knew how much it all meant to him."

"I'm just helping him grow up, that's all," Clayton responded. "Hey, come on, let's not kid ourselves, okay? I mean, who cares about the fucking river besides him?"

"I do," Russell shouted.

"Yeah, sure you do"—Clayton laughed—"but only because some capitalists are gonna build it. And how's Mao Tse-tung's environmentalist movement doing, by the way?"

Russell shook his head. "I'm not surprised by this. I'm a little disappointed, but I'm not surprised." He turned to Rebecca. "I'm gonna go after Pete, maybe take him to Charlie's."

"What?" Clayton asked. "And give up this great atmosphere?"

Artie Winston walked over from a table on the other side of the room and said in a quiet but urgent voice, "Look, you guys, will you stop shouting? I don't know if you've noticed it, but the bartender has been staring at you."

Clayton shrugged. "Fuck 'im."

At that moment the door opened and Peter walked back into the bar. He was shaking with repressed rage as he resumed his seat beside Dorcas and said, "I'm not gonna leave you alone, Dorcas. And you, Clayton, this is all one big fucking joke to you, but you're too fucked up on drugs right now for me to reason with you."

Alex narrowed his eyes in their direction. Drugs? *Drugs?*

"Peter, shut up, will you?" Artie said.

"Yeah," Sean added. "Don't start any trouble, okay? I almost screwed myself out of my probation once in this fucking place. I don't need a repeat performance."

"Yeah, yeah, okay," Peter grumbled, and then looked at Clayton angrily. "But tomorrow morning, you and me are gonna have a long talk."

Clayton raised his glass as if in a toast. "I await it breathlessly."

Peter knew that if he made any response to the sarcasm it would lead to more arguing, so he turned angrily from Clayton and asked Dorcas, "Are you feeling any better? Is the bourbon helping?" He saw that Dorcas had closed her eyes and that a slight smile was on her lips. "Dorcas?"

She opened her eyes. "Huh?"

"Wow." He laughed. "I thought you were drifting away for a minute. The acid seems to be wearing off on everybody else. What about you? Are you still hallucinating?"

She did not answer him, for she had reached that stage of an acid trip when garish, outlandish hallucinations cease and are replaced by distortions more subtle, and thus more insidious. At that moment, as Peter and the others awaited a reply, Dorcas was gazing at Peter's face and contemplating the issue of mortality. His flesh seemed transparent to the bone, and she could almost see the individual cells in the process of birth and dissolution. She saw the blood running through the veins just below the surface of the skin and watched the strands of muscle and sinew stretch and contract as Peter's head and lips moved.

"Dorcas?" he asked, and his voice echoed in her ears as if they were spoken in a sound chamber.

Dorcasdorcasdorcasdorcasdorcasdorcas . . .

As she watched the blood flowing she became aware of her own heartbeat, and the pounding in her chest grew almost immediately deafening. My heart, she thought. It feels like it's going to explode. It must be tired, it must be, it's been beating ever since I was born, since before I was born, never stopping, never resting, *thud thump, thud thump, thud thump*, minutes after minute, year after year. It must be wearing out. It must be wearing out.

Dorcas shuddered. "I'm going to die," she whined.

Lydia coughed nervously. "Well, we're all gonna die, Dork, right? I mean, it's nothing to like be scared of right now."

"Yeah, that's right," Clayton said. Lydia smiled at him, grateful for his support, but her smile faded as he went on, "We're all gonna die. I'm gonna die, you're gonna die, we're all gonna die."

"Clayton," Rebecca said softly, "don't start fucking around, okay? I don't think she's in any shape to handle it, okay?"

"We're all dying right now," he said cheerfully. "You start to die the minute you're born, 'cause every minute you live brings you one minute closer to death. You've been dying your whole life."

Her mouth fell open in wonder. "I have?"

"Sure."

"Clayton, go sit at another table," Lydia snapped. "Now! I mean it!"

"You are absolutely indecent," Russell said. "There's no other word for you."

"Come on, Clay," Sean said, rising from his seat. "Let's go play the bowling machine, okay?"

"Sure. You wanna ask Alex to play, too? Maybe drink some tequila?"

"Real funny," Sean muttered. "Come on." He and Clayton left the table and went toward the old bowling machine, and Sean rubbed his eyes, thinking, Acid's almost gone. Heavy shit, though.

"Thank God Sean got him away from us." Rebecca sighed. "Dorcas, listen to me. Everything's okay. You're doing fine, and you'll be over the trip real soon now."

"No doubt about it." Russell nodded in agreement. "You're handling it fine. Everything, like everything is great."

"I'm really sorry," Dorcas said, looking from Rebecca to Lydia.

"Oh, Dork, don't be silly." Lydia laughed. "Everybody bums out now and then, even without taking acid. It's no big deal."

"No. I mean about last night. I'm sorry I seduced Clayton. I didn't mean to, really."

The smiles on the faces of the other two girls faded into narrow grimaces. "You did what?" Rebecca asked.

"I don't even really remember doing it," she said, starting to weep softly. "But I sort of came to when Clayton . . . I mean when he was . . . I mean like he said that I . . . ." Her tears began to flow in rivers. "I didn't mean to. I didn't even *want* to. . . . "

There was no need for Dorcas to finish her sentence, for her few oblique comments had communicated everything. Peter jumped to his feet and ran over to the bowling machine where Clayton was preparing to slide the puck down the alley. He grabbed him by the shoulder and spun him around to face him. "You son of a bitch!" he shouted. "Getting her drunk and stoned and then raping her! You son of a *bitch!*"

Clayton smiled and shrugged and glanced with amusement at Sean. That one instant of inattention prevented him from seeing Peter's closed fist swing around to thud loudly on his jaw.

"Hey, you!" Alex shouted. "You stop that. I don't have no fights in my bar." He dropped the empty tray he had been carrying and rushed over to stand between Peter and Clayton; but then Peter's words sank in, and he looked down at Clayton, who was sitting dazed on the barroom floor. "What did he mean by that? You gave a girl drugs and you raped her? Is that what he . . ." Alex snapped his head over to look at Dorcas, whose tears were still running down her cheeks. "That's the girl?" He turned to Peter. "Is that the girl he did this to, Dorcas Ostlich?"

The recent conversation had removed Clayton from the roster of Peter's friends, and he did not hesitate as he said, "Yeah, that's her."

Alex grabbed Clayton by the collar and dragged him to his feet. "After everything that poor family has had to go through, you could do a thing like that? You animal! You get the hell out of here, all of you, you goddamn bums, get the . . ." He paused, and his eyes widened. "You were the one found that moonshine jug! You knew where it was all the time! By God, it wasn't that old freak killed that girl, it was you!"

Clayton threw Alex's hand away. "Get the fuck away from me, Alex. Who do you think you're talking to?"

"You talk to the cops, by God!" Alex ran behind the bar and began to phone the police.

Clayton repressed the urge to punch Peter back. "Good work, asshole. Now he's calling the cops."

Peter glowered at him. "Maybe he should call the cops. Maybe he's right." He looked over at Sean and saw the color draining from his face and his hands beginning to tremble. Peter's face registered the shock he was feeling, the refusal to accept the conclusion that Alex had just drawn. "Holy shit," he whispered. "You two guys . . . you two guys did that?"

"No!" Sean cried. "No, just him!"

"Brenner, will you shut the fuck up!" Clayton shouted.

"All I did was help him move the body, that's all I did," Sean whimpered.

Clayton shoved Sean back against the bar. "Shut up, goddamn it!"

Peter stared at Clayton for a moment as if he were a total stranger, and then rushed back to the table. "Lyd, Russ, we've got to get Dorcas out of here before the cops show up, or she'll end up back in the asylum. Come on." No one moved. "Come on, damn it!"

Russell pulled Dorcas to her feet and followed Peter to the door, but Lydia, who had heard everything that had just been said, practically flew at Clayton and began to slash at his face with her nails as she kicked at him and screamed incoherent curses.

"Goddamn it, Lydia, cut it out!" Clayton shouted. "It was an accident. I didn't mean to do it."

"I'll kill you!" she shrieked, her hands flailing.

"*Will you listen to me, for Christ's sake?* She was mad at me because of something, I don't even know what, maybe because you had just split from your old man's house, and she attacked me, and I pushed her away, and she fell down and hit her head on a rock. It was a fucking *accident*, Lydia!" He turned to Sean. "Isn't that how it happened?"

"Oh, yeah," he said, nodding his head vigorously, "that's exactly what happened."

Lydia calmed down slightly, but hatred was in her eyes as she snapped, "They say she was raped."

"We made it look that way," Clayton responded, "messed up her clothes and shit like that."

"What the hell for?"

"To make it look like some sort of regular crime. Look," he said, cutting her off as she began to object to his reasoning. "Sean had just gotten probation for the drug bust and he wasn't supposed to be up here at all. We *had* to make it look like that, like some fucking sex maniac killed her, or else they might have traced the whole thing back to me and him and he'd've ended up in the fucking state pen."

"That's crazy," Lydia insisted. "That doesn't even make sense."

"Okay, so we were stupid, all right? We were drunk and we weren't thinking clear. But that's what happened, okay? Honest to God, Lydia! I'd never hurt anyone in your family, you know that, don't you?"

She felt herself beginning to believe him. "But what about what Dork just said? About last night?"

"Yeah, right," he replied sarcastically. "I seduced her. Sure!"

"Sounds like rape to me," she spat.

"And two months ago she met Grogo the Goblin in the woods a couple of days after he died. And two weeks ago he took her to a cave where that maharishi guy taught her how to pray." He snorted a laugh. "Come on, Lyd. Be serious."

She wanted to believe him, but at that moment the ever-present current of grief was struggling with her infatuation. "My sister is dead," she said, starting to weep.

"I know," he said gently. "And I'm sorry, Lydia. I'm so sorry. But it wasn't my fault, you know?"

"What about Grogo? And that old Hindu guy. What about them?"

"Hey," he said earnestly, "it was them or us. I didn't plan it that way, but that's what it came down to, them or us."

"They were innocent."

He shrugged. "So were we, really." He glanced over at Alex, who was heatedly jabbering into the telephone. "Peter's right. We got to get out of here, all of us."

"*I don't want to die!*" Dorcas screamed. "*I don't want to die! I don't want to go to hell!*" The various confrontations in the barroom during the past few minutes had caused the others to forget that Dorcas was in the throes of a bad acid trip, until she began screaming.

"Wonderful," Clayton muttered. "Just what we need."

Alex slammed down the receiver of the phone and shouted, "I'll see you in prison, Saunders. When the police put the handcuffs on you, I'll laugh so hard it'll make you deaf!"

Clayton ignored him. "Let's get out of here," he said, and then left the bar. Outside on the street he huddled with a terrified Sean, an angry Peter and Russell, a weeping Lydia, and a very confused Rebecca. "Sean, you straight enough yet to drive?"

"Y-Yeah."

"Good. Take Dorcas and like drive around for an hour or so. Cops should have come and gone by then."

"I'll take care of her," Peter said.

"You'll get the fuck out of here and never come back," Clayton snapped. "Go on, beat it!"

"Don't you tell me what to do. . . ."

"Pete," Russell said, "come on, let's go. I don't want

to be here anymore. It's all too disgusting. Let's just drive down to New Paltz."

Peter looked at Dorcas, who was standing nearby, staring at a tree. "I can't leave her alone."

"Pete," Lydia said, "Dork and me live here, you know?"

"Right," Russell agreed. "Come on, Pete. Let's split."

"Peter," Lydia insisted. "Go. She'll be okay. I think the acid's wearing off everybody." He seemed hesitant to leave, so she added, "Look, we don't know what the police will do, and the fewer people there are around to be questioned, the easier it'll be."

Peter's voice was cold as he asked Clayton, "What are you planning to do?"

Clayton sniffed. "What the fuck do you care?"

A few minutes later the street was empty of people. They all went back to Clayton's trailer to pick up their things, and then most of them left hurriedly. Peter, Artie, Deirdre, and Nancy squeezed into Russell's Volkswagen Beetle, Gary and Buzzy appropriated Sean's motorcycle, and most of the others packed themselves into Danny's van. Sean took Dorcas with him in Clayton's jeep, leaving Clayton, Rebecca, and Lydia at the trailer to await the coming of the police.

Chapter Sixteen

It was all so stupid, Clayton thought as he paced nervously back and forth in front of the trailer. Never should have happened, never should have happened. It was really all Grogo's fault, anyway, him and his fucking moonshine. If me 'n Sean hadn't gotten so drunk on that shit, that whole scene with Sarah wouldn't have gone down like it did. He deserved to get lynched for getting me drunk like that, that stupid fucking freak.

Clayton looked out at the road to see if he could see the police coming, but the road appeared dark and deserted. He glanced at the door of the trailer, wondering what was keeping Rebecca and Lydia, and then resumed his pacing. "Sarah's fault, too, the stupid little bitch," he muttered. If she hadn't been such an uptight little pansy-ass, she'd still be alive. "Wasn't my fault," he said aloud, remembering what had happened. "A victim of circumstances, that's all I am."

"That little freak drives me nuts," Sean had said that afternoon three months earlier as he and Clayton were weaving their drunken way through the woods from the old Sweet place. Sean had taken the moonshine jug with him and was gripping it tightly as they stumbled along, walking into trees and tripping over their own feet as they tried to find their way back to the side of the River

Road where Clayton had left his jeep. During the five years since the death of Edith Sweet, the forest had all but obliterated the narrow dirt path that had once led for two winding miles from the road to the house, for in all that time only Dorcas Ostlich had trod it in her weekly cleaning visit. In the absence of a real pathway, Sean and Clayton were following a general direction rather than a route back to the road. The combination of marijuana and moonshine caused them to walk with a staggering, meandering gait that made it less than likely that they would emerge from the woods anywhere near the jeep.

"Don't look gift jugs in the mouth." Clayton belched, his voice slurring. "Jugs. That reminds me. I wonder if Lydia's back at the trailer?"

This might have been the funniest joke ever made, for all the ensuing laughter. They stumbled on through the woods, giggling intermittently at nothing in particular, taking turns carrying the jug, stopping every few yards and wondering where they were. Sean strained his eyes to peer off into the darkening woods, and he said, "Hey, somebody's coming."

"Do they have any more moonshine?" Clayton asked, sputtering a laugh.

"I think it's . . . it looks like a chick."

"Well, then, we know she's got jugs, anyway."

They fell to the ground, again laughing uproariously, and in the process they dropped the earthenware jug and it cracked apart on the protruding root of a large elm tree. "Oh, shit," Sean said as the moonshine spilled out and sank into the earth.

"Guess we gotta go back to Grogo's bar and grill and get some more." Clayton giggled.

This was funny also, and they were sitting on the mossy ground wiping tears of mirth from their eyes when they heard the crunch of feet upon twigs and they looked up.

"Well, well," Clayton said. "Sarah Sarah quite contrarah."

Sean was again struck by a thunderbolt of merriment. "Sarah Sarah quite contrarah!" he cried, short of breath from laughter.

Sarah Ostlich placed her balled fists upon her hips and glowered down at them. "Dead drunk and sitting in the dirt. How appropriate!"

"Yeah, 'sgreat down here." Clayton nodded. "Pull up some leaves and join us." He gazed at the chest beneath the loose sweater and thought, Smaller tits than Lydia's, but I bet they don't flop around so much when she's on her back.

"You're disgusting," she spat.

Sean laughed. "We try."

"I'm looking for my sister," Sarah said in a schoolmarmish tone vaguely reminiscent of her father. "Is she visiting with those two . . . persons?" Had the last word been a dire imprecation, it could not have been more disparagingly said.

"Yeah, she's there," Sean said. "One of your sisters is, anyway. I can't tell which one. They look alike." More laughter.

She turned to go on, but then spun around and demanded, "Just what did you think you were trying to do at the town meeting today? Was that supposed to be some sort of big joke, causing all that trouble? And how dare you bring those radicals with you and force Daddy to let them disrupt everything like that?"

Clayton got to his feet. "Careful, careful. Your sister is stuck on Peter, in case you haven't noticed."

"My sister is an idiot. They both are. Neither of them has enough sense to avoid men like you."

She looks real athletic, he thought, grinning at her. Bet she could bump and buck for hours. "Yeah? And what do you know about men like me? Or about any men at all, for that matter?"

She harrumphed. "Enough to know a good-for-nothing bum when I see one."

"You're so mean, Sarah." He chuckled. "Hasn't Lydia told you anything good about me? Don't you know that I'm great in bed?" *Bet that little cunt of hers is tight as a drum.*

"You're disgusting," she repeated. "And stop trying to change the subject. That factory is important to this town, and—"

She was not expecting his sudden lunge. It took her a few moments to realize what was happening before she began to kick at him, but by that time he had already pulled the sweater up over her head and had torn open her blouse.

Sean was watching them stupidly, as if the scene unfolding before him were on a movie screen, unreal and staged. "Uh . . . Clay?"

Sarah screamed as he bore her down with him onto the cold forest floor, and he put all his weight into the forearm with which he pressed her wrists down into the dirt as his free hand pulled up her bra. He squeezed one of her breasts roughly and then shoved his hand between her legs.

Sean blinked. "Uh . . . hey, uh . . . Clay . . ."

Sarah's screams were shrill and piercing, but they did not carry far through the thickly wooded forest. Her face displayed a rapid succession of emotion, from shock to rage to fear, as Clayton's hand worked its way between her thrashing thighs, tore off her underpants, and then thrust upward into her vagina. She kicked and bit and tried to roll away from him, managing at last to free her hands and begin to sit up, but Clayton shoved her roughly back onto the ground. He did not see the jagged tip of the small rock that protruded from the mossy forest floor, nor did he hear the dull thud as the back of her head struck it.

All he knew in his intoxicated, libidinous frenzy was that she had suddenly stopped struggling. He opened his fly to pull out his engorged member, hopped on top of her, and pushing her legs apart, worked his way into her motionless body and began pounding into her mercilessly. "Like . . . a . . . fucking . . . *drum* . . ." he cried.

Sean felt a sudden, terrified sobriety as he jumped to his feet and shouted, "Clay! What the hell are you doing?"

He cackled. "I'm fuckin' me another Ostlich sister."

Sean's hands twitched as if his mind were commanding them to move without telling them what to do, and then he saw the red pool spreading out upon the leaves beneath Sarah's head. "Clay . . . Jesus Christ, *Clay!*" He grabbed Clayton by the shoulders and pulled him off the girl, causing him to fall roughly back onto the ground, and then stared down at her, stared at the motionless chest, stared into the open, lifeless eyes. "I think . . . I think you killed her!"

Clayton had scraped his penis on the teeth of his zipper as he fell backward, and he was examining the bruise with concern. "What?"

"She's dead!" Sean's eyes went wide with horror. "Holy shit, man, she's dead! You killed her! Goddamn it, Clayton, she's dead!"

Clayton stumbled forward and looked down at the body. He wiped his forehead with a shaking, sweaty palm, and muttered, "Oh, shit."

"Oh, no," Sean whimpered. "Oh, no, no! I'm on one-to-five probation! I can't get mixed up in something like this!"

"You!" Clayton screamed. "You! What about me?"

"Well, fuck you anyway!" Sean screamed back.

"Why the hell did you *do* this? What the fuck's the matter with you?"

"Wait a minute, wait a minute, lemme think, lemme think." Clayton pressed his hand to his mouth and shut his eyes. Sober up, damn it, he ordered himself, sober up, straighten out. At last he said, "Look, nobody saw us. Let's just take the body and hide it off in the woods—"

"We *are* off in the woods, you asshole!"

"Okay, okay, so we move her someplace else and like cover her up with leaves. There's nothing to connect us with this."

"What if somebody heard her?"

"Nobody heard her. Dorcas is still back with those crazy old men, and that's gotta be a mile back. There ain't nobody else around here, not for miles."

"But people'll miss her. They'll know something's wrong."

"So what? Who cares? As long as they can't connect this to us, what difference does it make?"

Sean tried to think. "Okay. Okay. Let's do it." He took her arms and Clayton took her legs and they carried her for a few minutes before Sean said, "Hey, man, I don't even know where we are. Let's just dump her, okay? Let's just get out of here, okay?"

"Yeah, yeah, yeah, start collecting leaves."

As they piled the dead foliage upon the dead body Sean started to cry. "Oh, Jesus, Jesus."

"Will you shut up?" Clayton yelled. "Listen to me. This is important. We're gonna go back to the trailer—"

"Take me to the thruway. I'm hitching home. I ain't staying around here." He was throwing the wet leaves madly at the corpse.

"All right, all right, goddamn it, I'll take you to the thruway. All we did was take Dorcas and those freaks back to the Sweet place, hung out for a few minutes, and then we left."

"But that means we would have met her in the woods!"

"For Christ's sake, will you shut up and listen? We didn't meet anybody, we didn't see anybody. We just went back to car, I took you to the thruway, and then I went back to the trailer. You got that?"

"But—"

"Damn it, Sean, you got that?"

"Yeah, yeah, okay."

"Okay." He stood back and looked at the oblong pile of leaves. "Now let's get out of here. . . ."

Clayton's unpleasant reminiscence was broken by Rebecca. She emerged from the trailer and walked over to him, asking softly, "Clay? Did you and Sean really do it? I mean, honest? You killed Sarah?"

"Goddamn it, Becky," he said almost angrily, "it was a fucking *accident*, for Christ's sake." It could have happened to anybody. It wasn't my fault, honest to God!"

She nodded slowly, desperately wanting to believe the best of her brother. "But what about Grogo and that old yogi? How could you let them get—"

"What the fuck was I supposed to do?" he spat. "Tell everybody the truth and get lynched myself? Would you want Sean to get sent up the river to Attica?" He paused for a moment. "There wasn't anything I could do."

"You kind of led them right to her, though, didn't you?"

"I had to," he said defensively. "Look, the next day when I sobered up I realized that we left that broken moonshine jug right near where we hid Sarah's body. Our fingerprints were all over it. I *had* to make sure that a whole lot of people saw me find the jug, saw me pick up the pieces. Don't you get it? I had to be able to explain what my fingerprints were doing on the jug, just in case, you know?" He rubbed his eyes with his thumb and forefinger. "It never occurred to me that they'd connect her body to Grogo. The whole thing . . ." He sighed. "The whole fucking thing just got out of hand."

They lapsed into silence and then Clayton said, "Look, I better go hide our dope, just in case the cops have a search warrant or something."

"Good idea," Rebecca muttered. How could you, Clay? How could you?

Fifteen minutes later Rebecca was standing atop the roof of the trailer, peering off into the darkness of early morning. "Here they come," she called out.

"The police?"Clayton asked.

"Yeah, Al and company," she replied, climbing down the ladder. "Good timing. You finish hiding the dope?"

"Yeah, I think I got all of it. I put it in a plastic bag and ditched it in the woods."

"Good. Hey, Lydia," she shouted. "You ready?"

"Yeah, I'm ready," Lydia replied as she walked out from the trailer. She had twisted her long hair into impromptu braids and had wiped her face clean of makeup. This, coupled with a conscious effort at poor posture, made her the spitting image of her twin sister.

Clayton nodded. "Okay, let's not fuck up here. This is for keeps." They walked down the path from the trailer, each with a beer bottle in hand, and waited as the police car pulled up. Alex was a short distance behind in his old Buick.

Two state troopers emerged from the car, and one of them smiled disarmingly as he approached Clayton and asked, "You folks waiting for us?"

Clayton returned his smile. "No, sir. Just taking in the stars and having a friendly beer." He extended the bottle to the trooper. "Want a slug?"

"No, thanks. On duty." The trooper laughed softly. "It's pretty cold to be out taking in the stars, isn't it?"

Clayton shrugged. "My grandfather was Norwegian."

The trooper smiled again. "Mind if we have a look around?"

Again Clayton returned the smile. "Got a warrant?"

"Arrest him, arrest him!" Alex was shouting as he got out of his car and ran toward him. "They're using drugs, all of them. Take Dorcas to the hospital, test her blood, you'll see, you'll see. And he's a murderer, he murdered Sarah Ostlich!"

The second trooper's face wore no smile as he said to Clayton, "Mr. Brown has made some very serious accusations against you, boy."

Clayton tried not to appear visibly affected. "Indeed."

The trooper nodded. "Indeed."

"Let me tell you what happened." Clayton sighed. "We were sitting in his bar having a few drinks, and out of the blue he started yelling at me for having long hair and not being in the army and stuff like that."

"You goddamn liar!" Alex screamed, and ran at Clay. Both troopers grabbed him and held him back.

"You see?" Clayton said casually. "He's violent, and very excitable."

"He also says he heard you confess to the murder of Sarah Ostlich, the young woman who was killed around here a few months ago."

"He better calm down and watch what he says," Clayton replied, looking at Alex. "We don't want a lynching, because lynching is murder, and murderers spend the rest of their lives behind bars."

The first trooper frowned. "Nobody's talking about lynching anyone, son." He did not understand the oblique communication that had just taken place as

Clayton reminded Alex that any renewed investigation of the incident in the woods would bring everything to light and would land Alex and many other townspeople in the prisoner's dock. Alex swallowed hard and bit his tongue. He had been so eager to destroy Clayton that he had forgotten the ramifications of his actions. He was silent as the trooper asked, "What about it? Did you say something along those lines?"

"Of course not." Clayton laughed. "That's Sarah's sister Dorcas over there. Ask her if I said anything about killing her sister."

Lydia tried her best to act like Dorcas as she stammered, "Mr. Brown must have imagined that, Officer. I've been with Clayton all night, and he never said anything like that."

One of the troopers walked over to her. "We've met, twice I think."

"We have?"

"Yes, when your mother . . . when she died a few years ago, and when your father filed the missing person's report on your sister."

On both occasions Lydia had absented herself from the Ostlich home and Dorcas had been with her father. "Oh, yes, of course," she said. "I remember you now."

"Mr. Brown says you were having some sort of drug problem in his bar."

"I had too much to drink, I guess," she said. "I don't drink very often, and, well, I like don't know my limit, you know?"

He nodded. "May I speak to you in private?"

"Sure." She shrugged nervously.

As he led Lydia off to the police car he said to his partner, "Keep those two away from each other."

"Don't worry about me, Officer," Clayton said amiably. "Just keep an eye on old Ivan here." He grinned at Alex, who glowered back at him.

The policeman spoke to Lydia in quiet tones, and her replies were equally soft. When they walked back to the others a few minutes later, she was smiling broadly and winked at Rebecca. The trooper had wanted to see if she was in fact overdosing or having a reaction to a drug, and despite the alcohol and residual LSD in her system, she had comported herself well; indeed, the stale smell of beer on her breath lent credibility to her story. The trooper had come to believe that the entire incident resolved itself down to the natural animosity between a young hippie and a middle-aged redneck, exacerbated by Saturday-night drinking. He motioned for Alex to follow him back to the cars.

"There's nothing we can do here, Mr. Brown," he said. "No laws seem to have been broken, and we can't just arrest them without cause."

Alex exploded at him. "Goddamn it! I know what I see and hear!"

"I know, I know," he replied soothingly, "but I think you should just try to forget whatever it was that happened in your bar tonight, whatever you thought you heard. Just go home, Mr. Brown, and forget the whole thing. And keep them out of your bar from now on, if you want to." The two policemen entered their car. "Good night, now." They started the car and drove away.

Alex looked at Clayton's smiling face. "I guess I won the game, Al," Clayton called out. "Drinks are on you." Alex did not reply. He spun around to walk quickly back to his own car and then began to drive back toward the town.

"Okay, Clayton," Lydia said as he rejoined her, "I helped you and Sean get your asses out of the sling, though God knows why I bothered."

"You wanted to keep Dork from being locked up in the happy home, that's why," he replied.

"Maybe so," she conceded. "But I want to know

exactly what happened to Sarah. And don't try to bullshit me."

"Give me a break, will you?" he replied. "I already told you it was an accident. She fell down, hit her head on a rock. I tried to cover it up because I just didn't want Sean to get in trouble."

"You coulda told somebody," she insisted as she unwound her braids. "For Christ's sake, Clay!"

"I'm sorry, honest I am," he said, his voice soft and sincere. "I know we made a mistake, trying to keep out of trouble like we did, but we were both afraid that Sean would end up in prison. Look, we didn't really do anything, you know? The whole thing was one long, screwy, terrible coincidence. Can't you try to understand?" He turned to his sister for support.

Rebecca nodded and then sighed. "Yeah, I guess I understand, Clay. You guys were like victims of circumstances." She and Clayton looked at Lydia, expecting her to agree with Rebecca's assessment. It was obvious from the expression on her face that her faith in his word was less than solid.

They turned at the sound of an approaching car, and Clayton waved as Sean and Dorcas drove up and got out of the jeep. "Cops just left."

"Yeah, I know," Sean said. "I drove around for a while like you told us, but I've been waiting down near the road, watching to see if the cops were gonna stay or leave."

"Everything's okay," Rebecca said, and then turned to Dorcas. "How are you feeling?"

"I'm all right." She sighed. "I guess I really made a mess of things."

"No harm done," Clayton said cheerfully. "Everybody else got away okay?"

"Saw Doug's van heading for the thruway," Sean replied. He tried to light a cigarette, but his hands were trembling like leaves. "Saw Russell's VW, too, off on the roadside. He got a flat tire."

"You stop to help him?" Rebecca asked.

"No. Why should I? Fuck 'em all. It was Peter and Russell who started all the trouble, remember, them and that goddamn fucking son of a bitch Alex."

"Hey, calm down." Clayton laughed. "You're acting like you're gonna have a stroke or something."

"I almost did," he spat. "That stupid bastard. I feel like breaking his fucking neck. Do you realize what he almost did to me?"

"Yeah, yeah," Clayton said. "We've heard the probation-officer-state-pen rap before." He yawned. "This has been a hell of a day. I think I'll fall out."

"I want to go home," Dorcas said quietly.

"Wait until tomorrow, Dork," Lydia suggested. "Let's all just go inside and have a few beers, maybe smoke some grass. . . ."

"I want to go home," Dorcas repeated firmly.

"Okay, I'll drive you home," Rebecca offered. "No sweat."

Lydia and Clayton began to walk toward the trailer, and Clayton called out, "Hey, Sean, you coming?"

Sean did not reply. He was staring down at the road that led from Saunders Mountain to the center of Beckskill. "Son of a bitch," he muttered.

"What?"

"Son of a *bitch*!" He jumped back into the driver's seat of the jeep and gunned the engine.

"Hey!" Clayton yelled. "Where do you think you're going?"

"I'm gonna get that son of a bitch, that's where," he yelled back.

"Damn it, Sean, we've had enough trouble for one night, okay? And you're still too fucked up on the acid to know what . . ." It was too late. Sean was driving down the long dirt driveway toward the road. "Hey! Come back here with my car!"

Sean pushed his foot down on the accelerator and the jeep sped down the bumpy dirt road. He was not as familiar with the terrain as Clayton was, and thus did not avoid the holes and gullies that abounded all the way down to the paved highway. He bounced up and down in the seat, hitting his head on the roof a few times and almost slamming his mouth into the steering wheel, but he managed to reach Route 42 in one piece.

He saw traces of red taillights ahead of him and he increased his speed even more. He was not certain that the car ahead of him was Alex's . . . indeed, it might have been the police . . . but he wanted to get close enough to see and, if it was his quarry, to overtake him and stop him. He saw the snowdrifts along the roadside being illuminated by the headlights of the other car, and in a moment he was able to identify it. "Son of a bitch," he muttered again, and floored the accelerator. He overtook Alex, moved to run alongside him, and then swerved to the right and ran him off the road.

Alex slammed his foot against the brake pedal, steered clear of a tree, and plowed into a snowdrift. He jumped out of his car, shouting, "What's the matter with you? You crazy?" He did not immediately recognize the jeep or its driver, and as he ran over to the side of the other vehicle Sean threw open the door and struck Alex with it. Alex fell to the ground, stunned, and Sean was on him in an instant, kicking him viciously and pummeling him with his fists. When Alex realized who his assailant was, his fury overcame his pain and fear, and he managed to land a kick in Sean's face. As the younger man staggered back and tried to regain his balance Alex lunged forward with his fist and struck him in the face again. Sean reeled back into a snowdrift and Alex came after him, his eyes blazing with murderous fury. Sean was able to collect himself enough to duck the poorly aimed punch that Alex threw at him. Alex drew back to throw another, but before he could, Sean kicked him in the stomach and then brought his fist up into Alex's down-turned face. As the impact of the blow caused him to straighten up, Sean punched him again in the mouth and sent him flying back onto the ground. The snow began to grow red with blood.

Sean stood above the crumpled form, breathing hard as he wiped blood and mucus from his nose and mouth. "You listen to me, old man," he said angrily. "You ever try to screw us like you tried to tonight, I'll slit your goddamn fucking throat, you hear me?"

"You bastard," Alex said weakly.

"You shut the fuck up. I'm sick and tired of you, Alex. You mind your own fucking business or I'll kill you, you hear me? I ain't kidding, man. I'll kill you, I swear to God!" He kicked the older man hard in the side and Alex felt a rib crack. He screamed in pain as Sean went back to the jeep and drove away.

Alex lay in the snow for awhile, trying to muster up the energy to rise. One of his eyes was closed by swelling flesh and the other stared vacantly off into space. He rolled over onto his hands and knees and then stood up slowly, gasping at the stabbing pain in his side. He stumbled over to his car, crawled into the front seat, and then sat motionless for a few moments. Blood was pouring from his mouth, his clothing was ripped and wet, and the flesh of his face was growing purple from the beating.

"I kill you, you scum," he muttered.

He started the car and began to drive back to his bar, where he intended to clean and bandage his wounds, and then load his shotgun.

The sound of his engine was loud in the cold winter darkness as he drove back to Beckskill, as loud as the engine of the jeep as Sean drove back to the trailer. It was for this reason that neither of them heard the maniacal laughter echoing through the woods from the mouth of the distant cave.

Chapter Seventeen

January 12, 1969 (continued)

At just before three o'clock in the morning, the battered old body of the yogi Ashvarinda Patanjali breathed its last breath; but the psychic link that he had forged with such effort and maintained with such vigilance for so many years had already snapped, and the dying man's eyes had gazed up with sorrow and dread at the malevolent face that loomed over him. The small eyes of Vernon Sweet had begun to burn with an unearthly intelligence, and the long fingers had stroked the dying man's forehead almost lovingly as soft words in the ancient Sanskrit language of India had issued forth from the twisted, grinning mouth; and the last thing the old Hindu heard as he sank into the cold darkness of death was a cry of triumphant, hateful joy.

Grogo the Goblin now laughed as he stared down at the lifeless body of Ashvarinda Patanjali. "Oh, child of Vishnu, how clever you were, how clever you were!"

All those years you bound me and you deceived me and you blinded me to my own being. But now you have died, and now the chains are broken and the veil is lifted, and now again I know, I know.

He walked out of the cave and stared up at the stars that twinkled in the dark vault of the sky. "The veil is lifted," he whispered aloud.

I am death, the destroyer of worlds.

For how many *kalpas* did I dance the *tandava* in the ether of eternity? How many years, thousands of years, yes, millions of years, yes, for how many eons did my bloodstained hands whip through the emptiness of non-existence? Had I consciousness then? Had I form and substance, or was my being but a thought in the great long dream of the god Purusha? And is the universe itself but Purusha's dream?

Purusha's dream. Illusion, yes, illusion. *Maya, maya.* All is illusion, and reality is but a stirring in the great sleep of Purusha, a ripple in the endless river of eternal nothingness. There is no reality. Only I am real, only death is real. Life is the shadow of a dream. Only I, of all beings, truly live, for I am death, the destroyer of worlds.

I am the eternal carnivore, devouring all, for all is food. I am misery and pain and sorrow. I am grief and rage and terror. I am Shiva, I am Shiva, yes, the great cosmic glutton, yes, Shiva, Shiva.

Brahma the Creator, Vishnu the Preserver, Shiva the Destroyer. Thus do they call upon the powers in the land of the Ganges. But all which is created is created to die. All which is preserved is preserved only to suffer death. I am all, I am all, Shiva, Shiva, yes.

He walked forward into the forest and smiled as he approached a snow-laden evergreen tree. Then he reached out and touched it with his long, delicate fingers. The green needles grew brown on the instant, the tree withered and rotted and collapsed onto the forest floor. He laughed and walked on.

I become that which I consume, as all things become that which they consume. The aged priests of the Ganges, they knew not what they had brought into being by their prayers to me, by their prayers to Shiva, for I became flesh and dwelt among them, even as

Vishnu took flesh as Krishna, yes. They fled from me, the old priests, they fled from me when first I appeared in their midst, for I am hideous to behold, yes, I am awesome in my monstrous, inhuman ugliness, yes, Shiva, Shiva. I killed the old priest Ramamurti, I consumed him, I burrowed into his skull with my great fangs and devoured his brain, and then my shape changed, my form shifted, and I became Ramamurti, I *was* Ramamurti, I *was* the old priest, down to the last tiny wrinkle on his ancient face, down to the last thought in his wise old mind, down to the last memory of his long life, I was he, and yet I was Shiva, still Shiva, always Shiva.

And I prowled the temples from the Ganges to the Indus, from the warm waters of the Tamil Island to the roof of the world, and I killed and I consumed and I was worshiped for the majesty of my terrible, impassive brutality. And the centuries rolled on in unending joy for me and in unending terror for those men who were given the honor of being my victims.

And when Alexander came with his proud, foolish armies, I devoured solider after soldier, brain after brain, and became each soldier, yes, I took each form and each memory and each mind, and became each man whose life I consumed, for I am Shiva, and I followed the proud Hellenes back from the Indus, through Persia and Phrygia, into Hellas, and there I consumed lives and took the forms of many people, and still I was Shiva, yes, ever Shiva, always Shiva.

And when the northern barbarians with their dragon ships did make war upon the Romans in Constantinopolis, then did I drink Norse lives and eat Norse brains and walk as a Norseman among the unwashed barbarians, and still I was Shiva.

And when the Norsemen did sail from Nor-Way to Ice-Land, I was there. And when Erik called the Red did sail from Ice-Land to Green-Land, I was there. And when Leif Eric's-son did sail from Green-Land to Vin-Land the Good, I was there. I was Ruolf and Lars and Jan. I was Karl and Fjorni and Sigurd. I was always there, devouring brains, consuming lives, shapeshifting, shapechanging, still Shiva, always Shiva.

I am death, the destroyer of worlds.

And I left the dragon ship and dwelt among the Skrellings in the great green forests of Vin-Land the Good, and I stayed long after the Norsemen departed. The Mohawks did I know, and the Cayuga, and the Onondaga, and the Seneca, and I led them to the massacre of the Huron, yes, to the great war of extermination, to the blood and the wails of pain and misery and the death, and the death, the death.

His eyes burned with demonic glee and his small mouth twisted into a terrible smile as he walked out of the woods onto the River Road. He looked left and right, and then began walking aimlessly, reveling in the sensation of self-knowledge, rejoicing in the newly awakened awareness of power.

And then the white man came, yes, the white man, as the Skrellings called him. And the white man's weapons were loud and fierce, and his stockades were high, and the Skrellings fled from him, and I followed the Skrellings and stayed with the men of the green forests. And soon I abandoned the habitations of men, for three thousand years of shapeshifting had made me weak and tired, though yet I was Shiva, still Shiva, always Shiva.

And I waited, yes, I waited. I dwelt in the forests, in the mountains. I consumed the brains of animals, and I became animals, the rat and the hawk, the serpent and the deer, and I waited. I waited because I was weary of drifting from form to form, from flesh to flesh. I waited for a final home, for a shape which would be my dwelling place for all time and until the end of time.

I waited for the body whose shape would cry out to me, saying, Lord Shiva, Lord Shiva, behold a fitting habitation for your inexpressible, horrible majesty. I waited for the body whose ugliness would engender hatred and fear, and I bided my time, and I waited patiently and hastened not, for I am death, and being death, I am the only true immortal.

And the years passed, and the centuries passed, and I was in the form of a serpent when I saw him, the twisted little man sitting in the cage, and though my serpent mind saw only food, my divine spirit cried out, Yes, yes, this is he, this is he! This is the form I will take, this the shape I will always resume, for such ugliness is a fitting form for one such as I. And I slithered forward and I consumed his brain, I burrowed into the skull of Vernon Sweet, and I became Vernon Sweet, and I remain Vernon Sweet, and I wept for joy at the awareness of my own hideous ugliness.

As he walked along the River Road he spied a doe and her fawn that had quickly and cautiously bounded across the pavement to the river to drink. Chuckling darkly, he crept toward them silently, for death creeps upon life always unexpected and unseen until that instant when the grave looms large and the taste of dust is in the mouth. He leaped upon the doe and tore through the back of her head with his burrowing fangs, and the fawn bolted and ran. He laughed again as his hands and feet grew long and narrow, as his fingers melted together into hooves and his skin became lustrous and furry. The doe-thing ran along the roadside, leaving the shuddering body of the deer to pour its blood out onto the snow. He ran for miles, through the empty main street of the town of Beckskill, and when he was once again away from human habitation, he shapeshifted and dwindled down into the twisted form of the side-show geek.

This I have decreed, he thought, this did I decide on that day when I first saw Vernon Sweet. This body, this form, shall be my eternal dwelling place. I shall drift from shape to shape as I devour life after life, but always shall I return to Grogo the Goblin.

He walked on, muttering and laughing softly, until he came to another road. He wandered up it aimlessly, rejoicing in the power so long dormant, in the knowledge so long hidden, in the inhuman vindictiveness so long asleep.

And all would have been well, he thought, were it not for you, child of Vishnu, my oldest friend and my most dire enemy. Was it Vishnu's working, then? Did my brother from the eternal void arrange for you to be there, Ashvarinda Patanjali? Was it happenstance that I found my desired home in the presence of one who could understand what I was, who could devise the prayers to trap me and make me forget, whose mental disciplines were powerful enough to control me through all those years?

"So clever you were," he whispered. "So wise and powerful, Ashvarinda."

But now I am free! Now I am again what I have always been, and I know, and I know!

I am death, the destroyer of worlds.

He stopped walking and looked across the road to his left, and he smiled at what he saw.

The cemetery.

My children, he thought, my sons and daughters, my best beloved ones.

Grogo the Goblin walked slowly forward, thrusting the cemetery gates open with a flick of his finger, and then stood in the middle of the abode of the dead, in the midst of those who had already felt the fatal brush of the cold lips of death upon their own.

And I shall play a great trick upon you, my brothers Brahma and Vishnu? You create, Brahma, and you, Vishnu, you preserve, but is it just that I, Shiva, can but destroy? No, my brothers, for what I have taken away I can return, that which I have clutched to my bosom I can restore. "Shiva the Creator," he cried laughing. "Shiva the Preserver!" Do you find the idea amusing, my brothers? Do not laugh too loudly, lest you awaken Purusha the sleeping god, and we all dissolve into nothingness, we and all else, the phantoms in his eternal dream.

"Sleep on, Purusha," he whispered. "The cosmic game goes on."

He moved his gaze from right to left, smiling at the graves, at the graves of Paula Riasanovsky Brown and Doris Ostlich and her daughter Sarah, at the graves of Michael Imhof's father and Frank Bruno's mother, grave after grave after grave after grave. . . .

He held his arms wide apart as if inviting an embrace, and his voice was high and shrill in the darkness. "I am death," he cried out. "I am your father, my children. I am death, the destroyer of worlds! Come forth to me, my best beloved ones, that I may give to you my blessing! Come forth, all my dead children, come forth! And receive the kiss of life from the lips of death itself!"

There was a long silence in the small rural cemetery.

And then the ground began to tremble, and the tombstones began to move.

Chapter Eighteen

January 12, 1969 (continued)

"I'm cold, Artie." Deirdre Duell blew into her cupped hands and shivered in the backseat of the Volkswagen Beetle. "Can't we turn on the heat?"

Artie Winston shook his head. "No, it isn't safe. You can't turn on the heat without turning on the car, and I don't trust Russell's muffler. Thing looks like a tomato can."

"I don't understand."

"I'm afraid that if we turn on the car and just sit here, we'll die from the carbon monoxide."

"But I'm freezing to death now!"

He wrapped his arms more tightly around her. "Does that help?"

"Don't help me worth shit," Nancy O'Hara grumbled in the front seat. "Where the hell are those guys, anyway?"

"They'll be back soon, I'm sure of it," Artie replied. "Peter said the gas station was only two miles away, and—"

"So how long can it take to walk two miles there and two miles back, for Christ's sake? They've been gone almost three hours."

"Takes a while when you're rolling a tire along with you," Deirdre pointed out.

"Stupid asshole," Nancy muttered.

"I beg your pardon!"

"Not you, Deirdre. Russell. How could he be stupid enough to make a long drive like this without even checking to see if his spare tire had any air in it?"

"He isn't the most well-organized person in the world, that's for sure," Artie agreed.

"Hey," Deirdre said, squinting out the front window. "Is that them?"

Artie and Nancy followed her gaze. It was not quite sunrise, but the light of the impending dawn was sufficient for them to be able to identify the approaching figures. Artie said, "Thank God" as he pushed the driver's seat forward, opened the driver's-side door, and climbed out into the cold dawn. "Was the station open?" he called out.

"No," Russell called back, "but the air pump was. Tire's full now."

"Yeah, and heavy," Peter complained. He was walking stooped over as he rolled the tire along the icy road beside him. "My back is never gonna get over this."

They reached the car and Peter allowed the tire to roll off into a snowbank as he straightened up painfully. "Oh, Jesus, what an ache!"

"Stop complaining," Russell said as he opened the hood and took out the jack. "I rolled it there, you rolled it back. Fair's fair."

"That doesn't help my back."

"Yeah, life's a bitch," Russell snapped. He prepared to slip the brace of the jack under the rear of the car frame, but paused to say impatiently, "You girls want to get out of the car?"

"Oh, yeah," Nancy said. "Sorry." She and Deirdre stepped out into the cold wind and then stood with Peter and Artie, watching as Russell jacked up the car and removed the flat tire. "Check your spare next time, will you?" Nancy offered needlessly. "I mean, this has been like one fucked-up end to one fucked-up weekend, you know?"

"Tires shouldn't blow out like this," Russell said as he pushed the flat away and rolled the freshly filled spare over to the car. "I read someplace that they've invented a tire which can't go flat, but Goodyear bought the patent just so it would never be manufactured and cut into their profits. General Electric did the same thing with long-burning light bulbs. The whole problem is capitalism." The others did not feel like arguing with him, instead contenting themselves with exchanging tired glances.

Peter coughed and asked, "Did anyone slip me any acid when I wasn't looking?"

"No," Nancy replied. "Why would you ask something like that?"

"Well, if I'm not hallucinating, then you'd better hurry up, Russ."

"What are you talking about?" Russell asked as he began tightening the lug nuts.

"Look." Peter pointed up the road behind them. They all looked in the direction he was indicating. "Is that who I think it is?"

"Can't be," Russell said softly. "He's dead, right?"

"My point precisely," Peter replied. "He's dead. And unless there are two of him, that's one pretty lively dead goblin walking our way."

"Shit," Russell muttered, and began working faster.

"Dork? You okay?" Lydia tapped lightly on the door of her sister's bedroom. She waited a few moments and listened to the sounds of rustling sheets within. The door opened and her sister's tired face appeared before her. God, she looks like shit, Lydia thought. "I just wanted to see if you were feeling okay," she explained.

Dorcas yawned. "I thought you were with Clayton."

"I was, and I'm going right back. I borrowed Becky's car. I was like worried about you."

Dorcas smiled. "I'm okay, Lyd. I feel terrible, but I'm not . . . well, I'm not seeing things."

"Good." She paused. "You wanna come back with me?"

"No. I don't think I want to see Clayton again for the rest of my life."

Lydia appraised her cautiously. "Did you really . . . I mean, what you said about Clay . . . "

"That's what he said I did," Dorcas replied. "All I know for sure is that when I came to, he was doing it to me."

Lydia sniffed. "I can't picture you seducing anybody."

Dorcas laughed sadly. "Thanks."

"No, no, that's not what I mean. I just . . . well . . . " She frowned and shook her head. "I just don't trust him anymore."

"Why did you ever?" Dorcas asked. "I don't think he's a very nice boy, Lydia."

Lydia began to respond when she heard the door of her father's bedroom open. "Oh, wonderful," she muttered.

"Well." Dr. Ostlich sighed wearily as he stepped out into the hallway, tying his robe. "Thank God you're alive."

"Dad, not now." Lydia sighed. "It's been a bad night."

"I'm sure it was," he replied. "Though it wasn't any too good for me either, not being able to sleep all night, wondering if the two of your were lying dead somewhere, like Sarah." He saw Dorcas start to close the door of her room. "Wait, honey, please. I have to talk to you, to both of you. We can't go on this way. Things simply have to change." He frowned when he heard a knock at the front door. "See who that is. And then come right back up here." As Dorcas glumly complied with her father's request he turned back to Lydia and shook his head sadly. "I have just about had it with you, Lydia."

"You haven't had it with me since Mom killed herself," she spat.

He closed his eyes for a moment. "That was all in the past, Lydia. I was wrong, I was . . . ill, and I've gotten help. We have to try to put it behind us."

She laughed bitterly. "Yeah, I'll bet you'd just *love* to put it behind me."

He seemed about to weep. "Lydia, please. You simply must forgive me."

"Forgive you!" She laughed. "Why the hell should I?"

"Oh, honey, you have to believe that I'm—" Whatever he was about to say was cut off by a horrendous shriek from below. "Dorcas?" he called out. "Dorcas! What's the matter?" Lydia was already halfway down the stairs before he reached the staircase, and he heard his other daughter scream also before he reached the main floor of the house. He rushed into the living room and then stood in mute shock, staring at the bizarre scene before him.

Lydia and Dorcas were huddled together in the corner, their arms wrapped around each other, screaming at the top of their lungs. The front door was open wide, and standing motionless in the doorway was a skeleton, the rotting burial dress hanging loosely upon its frame and half its skull missing: the half that the shotgun had blasted away when the woman committed suicide five years earlier.

Ostlich was paralyzed. His feet would not move, and his heart was beating so rapidly that he thought his chest would burst. "What . . . what's the meaning of this?" he asked, his mind denying what his eyes were seeing. "Is this some sort of joke? Lydia, are you responsible for this?"

It was as if the skeleton had been waiting to hear the sound of his voice, for it now began to shuffle forward into the room. Ostlich jumped back, and Dorcas and Lydia continued to scream.

One bony hand reached over to the china cabinet beside the door and opened the drawer where Ostlich always kept a loaded revolver. It took out the gun, turned in Ostlich's direction, and began walking toward him.

Ostlich turned to run, but before he reached the door of his study, he heard the explosion of a gunshot an instant before he felt the burning piece of metal slam into his back. He fell forward onto his face, shuddering from the pain, and rolled over to see the remains of his dead wife standing over him. He tried to speak, but blood came from his mouth, and then the skeleton pointed the gun at his face and emptied it into him.

The specter turned and walked back to the two terrified girls in the corner. Dorcas's shock and fear were so great that she had not thought to run from the house. Lydia had been thinking of nothing else, but she could not manage to get her feet to move. The creature came close to them and then stopped; and when it lifted its hand to their faces, both girls closed their eyes and waited to die.

The creature stroked Lydia's hair, touched Dorcas's cheek affectionately, and then walked out of the house.

They stood motionless in each other's embrace for a long while, until at last Dorcas whimpered, "Did you see that, too?"

"Yeah," Lydia said, her voice trembling.

"I'm not going crazy?"

"Not unless I am, too."

"Lyd, that wasn't . . . that couldn't have been . . ."

"That was Mom," Lydia whispered. "What the hell is going on here?"

"But Mom . . . Mom is dead. . . ."

"No shit!"

"I don't understand this, Lydia."

"Me neither."

They did not release their grip on each other's arms as they went slowly from the foyer into their father's study and stared down at his dead body. Dorcas moaned and began to weep at the sight of the corpse of her sole remaining parent. Lydia's emotions were more ambiguous, for what he had done to her was unspeakable; and yet he was her father, and he was lying dead at her feet, killed by . . .

Killed by . . .

"What the *hell* is going on?" Lydia repeated frantically.

Dorcas wiped the tears from her eyes and frowned. "It's as if . . . as if . . ." She paused and then gasped with sudden understanding. "We both saw it. It was real." She spun Lydia around and stared hard into her eyes. "I *did* see Vernon, I *wasn't* hallucinating, and neither were you. I *did* see him, and he *did* kill Mr. Schilder, and he *did* take Mr. Patanjali to that cave. . . ." Though her hands were trembling, her voice was hard and even as she saw the pieces of the puzzle fall into place. "Lydia, listen to me. That day, the day Sarah was killed, I was with Mr. Patanjali. He was trying to explain his religion to me, and he was looking right at Vernon when he told me that Shiva, the god of death, has avatars." She waited for her sister to respond, and when she did not, Dorcas shook her and yelled, "Don't you get it? Shiva has avatars! That's what he must have been trying to tell me in the cave when . . . " Her eyes went wide. "I never did what he told me to do! That's it, that must be it!"

"Dork, what the hell are you talking about?" Lydia whined. "What the hell is an avatar?"

"Call the police," Dorcas yelled over her shoulder as she ran up the stairs to her bedroom to begin searching for the napkin upon which she had written the prayer.

"Call the police! Are you nuts?" Lydia shouted after her. "Call them and tell them what? Dorcas? Dorcas!" Her sister did not reply. From upstairs a moment later came the sound of a drawer being pulled free from a bureau and dumped hard onto the floor.

Rebecca Saunders rolled over and gazed at Sean Brenner through bleary eyes, and then jabbed him in the side. "Hey," she muttered.

"Hmmm?"

"You're snoring. Cut it out."

"Hmmm?" He opened his eyes slightly. "What?"

"Stop snoring," she said. "You woke me up."

"Sorry, Becky." He yawned. "What time is it?"

"Who cares?" she asked, and rolled back over to bury her head in the pillow.

Sean got out of bed, yawning and scratching, and walked out to the kitchen to look at the clock. Seven o'clock. Only been asleep for a couple of hours. He rubbed the sleep from his eyes and then went to the refrigerator to see if he could find some juice. I hate it when I wake up with cotton mouth, he thought.

He found some tomato juice and drank it down straight from the can. "That's better," he muttered aloud, and then looked out the window at the car that was pulling up to the base of the hill at the bottom of the driveway. "I wonder who . . . ?" he said, and then he saw Alex Brown step slowly and painfully from the car, a shotgun cradled in the crook of his left arm. "Oh, shit," he whispered, and then ran to the other bedroom, where Clayton Saunders was sleeping the untroubled sleep of the innocent. Sean shook him roughly. "Clay, wake up! Wake up!"

"Wha-what? Huh?" Clayton mumbled.

"Wake up, man! That crazy old fuck Alex is here, and he's got a gun."

Clayton sat up in bed and shook his head to clear it. "What did you say?"

"Alex, man, Alex. He's here with a gun."

Clayton grimaced. "Great idea, beating the shit out of him, Sean. Real good way to avoid any more trouble."

"Okay, okay, so I was still fucked up on the drug and I shouldn't have been drinking, okay? Come on, man, we gotta do something!"

"What do you mean 'we'?" he asked. "You're the one with the problem, not me. Alex ain't gonna kill a paying customer for his broken-down old bar."

Sean stared at him, astounded at his callousness. "I don't believe this!"

"All right, all right, don't get so upset," Clayton said, climbing out of bed and pulling on his dungarees and boots. "I'll go talk to him. Jesus. Gotta solve everybody else's problems for them. . . ."

He donned a sweater and then opened the front door of the trailer. "'Morning, Al. How's every—" and then he jumped back inside as Alex leveled the weapon at him. His motion was well timed, for the shotgun blast ripped a hole through the door right where he had been standing. "Holy shit!" Clayton exclaimed.

Rebecca ran out from the bedroom, clutching a sheet to her body. "What the hell was that?"

Before Clayton could answer her, the door he had neglected to lock opened and Alex rushed into the room. His face, swollen and bruised and cut from the beating

he had received from Sean, was suffused with an irrational, vengeful fury, and he screamed incoherently when
he saw Sean standing in front of Rebecca. He swung the
gun in Sean's direction, but Clayton grabbed the large
brass hookah from the floor and slammed it down on the
barrel just as Sean jumped out of the way and Alex
pulled the trigger. The blast struck Rebecca in the knees
and the lower portion of her body flew backward,
sending her crashing face first onto the floor. The blow to
her head sent her reeling into unconsciousness, and then
the agony in her shattered legs roused her from it.

She lay writhing and moaning in a rapidly expanding pool of her own blood as her boyfriend dropped
down beside her on his knees and her brother, knowing
that both barrels had been emptied, fell upon Alex in a
murderous rage.

"Becky," Sean moaned, "oh no, Becky . . . " She
lapsed into unconsciousness and Sean erroneously assumed that she was dead; and in that instant he saw all
his dreams of ease and perpetual self-indulgence die
also. He fell to his knees and wept, mourning not for the
shattered girl beside him, but for his shattered fantasies.

Clayton threw Alex physically through the trailer
door and began to beat the older man with the butt of his
own shotgun. Alex tried to fend off the blows with his
arms, but Clayton's fury was mightier than Alex's fear,
and he fell to the ground on his stomach beneath the
barrage of blows. Clayton dropped the gun and jumped
on him, rolled him over, and began to pound his face
mercilessly with his fists. Alex tried again to defend
himself, even tried to fight back, to dislodge Clayton,
but he was unable to.

Clayton looked up to see Sean stumbling out from
the trailer, tears cascading from his eyes. "Is Becky
okay?"

"She's dead!" Sean wept.

Clayton blinked, and then looked down at Alex. He stared hard into the older man's bloody, swollen face, and then he stood up slowly. Alex just lay there, immobilized by pain, watching as Clayton picked up the shotgun and raised the heavy butt above him, preparing to bring it down on Alex's head. "You goddamn fucking bastard," he muttered.

But the thick stock did not descend. Clayton saw a motion out of the corner of his eye, and then he turned to look down the long driveway at the two indistinct figures that were moving stiffly, slowly toward them, the second one trailing the first by a few hundred yards. He dropped the gun as the closer figure came into the range of clear sight, and then he screamed, and Sean screamed, and as he struggled to his feet in slow agony Alex screamed as well.

The thing that was shuffling up the drive could not have been described as a skeleton, for the bones had largely decayed into dust years before; but the bits of dust and bone had been drawn together into a semblance of their previous shape, and it was as if a skeleton molded of dirt was approaching them slowly. Sean and Clayton drew back against the side of the trailer as the thing shuffled up to Alex, stopped, seemed to gaze at him from its empty, dusty eye sockets, and then held out its arms to him as if inviting him into its embrace.

"No!" Alex cried. "No! Go away! Get away from me!" The thing bore neither facial nor physical resemblance to any living human being, even the hair having fallen out over the long years since burial; but Alex Brown recognized Paula's wedding dress, the dress she had worn when they lowered her into her grave. He recognized the tarnished cameo brooch that dangled from the narrow neck bones, and he recognized the wedding ring he had placed upon her finger three decades before, the wedding ring that was still encircling the gray bone. "No!" he cried again. "No!"

And then the thing cocked its head just so, and in that simple gesture, a gesture he had seen so often in his wife's lifetime, that gesture of love and sympathy and understanding and concern, in that simple gesture Alex saw the years roll back and all the warmth and happiness of those distant days return to him. "Pau . . . Pau. . . ." he said, his voice choking. The thing took a step forward and he fell into its arms, weeping like a child as it stroked the back of his head and pressed his tearful face onto its bony shoulder, and then slowly began to rock him back and forth in its embrace. "Paula," he wept, "Paula, Paula."

The thing did not release him from its gentle grip as it turned and began to walk back down the drive toward the road. Alex stumbled along beside it, weeping, mumbling incoherently, his body racked by pain and his broken mind racked by sorrow. Sean and Clayton watched silently, their eyes wide with wonder, and then both screamed again as the second figure drew closer and quickened its pace and stretched its arms out toward Clayton.

Sarah Ostlich had been buried less than three months before and the chill of the season had inhibited the process of decay; but her flesh was greenish-black and cracked and broken, and her dead eyes stared ahead of her, unblinking and wild, and when she smiled at Clayton, her lips split open all along their length, and maggots crawled out of her mouth.

Clayton began to run. Sarah Ostlich began to chase him.

Sean watched them disappear into the forest, and then he heard Rebecca's voice from within the trailer, moaning, "Sean, Clay . . . help me. . . ." He paused for less than an instant as he weighed money against survival and sanity. He found the choice an easy one to make. "Sorry, sweetheart," he muttered, and then ran to the jeep.

Clayton sped through the woods, stumbling and falling every few feet, screaming madly as the corpse pursued him. He hopped over fallen trees and slipped on the snow, he leaped across frozen streams and slammed his head against low-hanging branches. He ran and ran and ran, and still the corpse followed, and when he caught his foot on an upthrust root and his weight propelled him forward, he heard his ankle snap like a thick twig, and he lay helpless in the snow.

Sarah jumped on top of him, and no effort he made served to move her. She seemed to be attempting to laugh as she ripped open her dirty burial gown, grabbed his hands, and pressed them against the rot of her water-sack breasts.

"No!" he shrieked. "*Nooooooooo!*"

His mouth was open long enough for her to lean forward and thrust her desiccated, worm-infested tongue into his mouth. Clayton gagged and began to vomit, but she did not seem to care. As she held him motionless with her right hand, her left hand reached down and tore open his dungarees. She grabbed hold of his penis and testicles with her thin, cold, hard, sharp fingers.

"*Lov . . . er,*" she croaked, and then ripped his genitals from his body.

By the time Sarah Ostlich was forcing the bloody chunks of flesh down Clayton's throat, Sean Brenner was already speeding through the town of Beckskill in the jeep. Got to get help, cops, somebody, anybody, this is nuts, this is nuts. . . .

Everywhere he looked he saw the walking dead, corpses ringing doorbells, skeletons tapping door knockers as casual as you please, coming to say hi hi hi hello to friends and neighbors and relatives whom they had not seen in a pig's age, and family reunions were abounding. Michael Imhof's dead parents dropped in for Sunday dinner, and Frank Bruno's grandmother just hugged her grandson to death.

Thank God I got wheels, Sean thought as he sped out of Beckskill. And then the jeep ran out of gas.

"Help me, Jesus," he whispered as he jumped out of the jeep and began running up the road. He ran for half a mile, and then heard a car approaching him from behind. He turned to see Nancy O'Hara in Russell's Beetle barreling down the road from the other direction. Nancy pulled over to the side and unlocked the passenger door, and Sean hopped into the seat, closed the door, and locked it. "Thank God!" he said breathlessly.

"Sean, what the hell is going on around here?" Nancy asked. "You won't believe the shit I've been seeing."

"Yeah, tell me about it!" He laughed, trembling with fear and joyful relief. "Where are Russell and Peter?"

"Back there a ways," Nancy replied as she pulled back onto the road and began to drive into Beckskill. "Russ was changing a flat and . . . I'm not bullshitting you, man, honest to God . . . and Grogo the Goblin attacked us!"

"I believe it," Sean said. "Sarah Ostlich just chased Clay off into the woods, and that old asshole Alex just went off with a skeleton."

"Sarah Ostlich!" Nancy exclaimed. "Lydia's sister? But she's . . . I mean, Sarah's dead!"

"Yeah, right, I know," Sean replied. "That's the whole point, man! And whatever the hell it was Alex walked off with sure looked dead, too."

"Holy shit," Nancy muttered.

"Where're Pete and Russ?"

"They ran off into the woods, with Deirdre and Artie. I got into the car and got the hell out of there."

"Hey, real brave," Sean spat.

"So what do you think you're doing, helping Clay?" she rejoined hotly. "If Clay's being chased by some dead chick, what the fuck are you doing here?"

"Yeah, yeah, all right, all right," he said, urgency in his voice. "Let's just get the hell out of here."

"Shouldn't we go back to the trailer?" Nancy asked. "I mean, we have wheels, you know? What if Clay and Becky need help?"

Sean pictured Rebecca lying wounded and helpless on the floor of the trailer and remembered Clayton dashing off into the woods. "They're okay, I know they are. Becky managed to get into her car and get away, and Clay probably got to the police station already."

Nancy was skeptical. "You sure?"

"Yeah, I'm sure, I'm sure, okay?" He glanced at her angrily. "Besides, why are you so worried about Clay and Becky? What about Russ and Pete? What if Artie and Deirdre need help?" She had no answer to this, so he went on, "Now turn the car around and let's get the hell away from here!"

Nancy hesitated for a moment, and then she slowed down and made a U-turn in the middle of Route 42. She drove back in the direction from whence she had come, muttering, "This has been the most fucked-up weekend I've ever had in my whole life, so help me."

"Nuts." Sean nodded. "Absolutely nuts."

"And I thought nothing could ever be worse than Woodstock. Sitting in piss-soaked mud for two days, trying to ignore all the assholes bumming out on lousy acid. . . ."

Sean had heard Nancy's litany of complaints about the Woodstock weekend before, and he ignored her. They drove for a few miles, turned on to Bennets Road, and then Nancy slowed the car again. She pulled over onto the shoulder and gazed out the window to his right. "What are you stopping for?" Sean asked.

She indicated a direction with a nod of her head. "Look at that. Jesus, this is crazy!"

Sean looked at the entrance to the Beckskill Rural Cemetery, and he swallowed hard. It seemed that each and every grave had been dug up and emptied, and large mounds of earth skirted long rectangular holes capped by upthrust markers and toppled tombstones.

They were still looking out at the desecrated grave-yard when Sean saw movement on the road up ahead. He turned to see the thing that had once been Paula Riasanovsky shuffling toward them, the weeping Alex Brown still in its arms as he stumbled along beside her. Sean frantically checked the lock button on the door, but there was no need for fear, for the reunited couple walked past the car and into the cemetery, completely ignoring Sean and Nancy.

"Sean . . . isn't that . . . that's the old bar-tender, isn't it?"

"Yeah," he whispered. "And I think . . . I mean, like from the way he acted, I think that thing was his wife."

Nancy started to respond to this, but she seemed unable to think of anything to say. They watched as the gray, dusty skeleton led Alex forward into the midst of the cemetery and then down into one of the gaping holes. Their heads disappeared behind a mound of earth, and then two skeletal hands reached up and began pulling the earth down upon them both. A moment later one trembling human hand reached up also and joined its fleshless companions in their labor. Sean and Nancy watched with morbid fascination as the mound grew lower and lower, until at last the grave was filled. The earth shifted slightly as it settled, and then it was still.

They looked at each other and shook their heads simultaneously with disbelief. Then Nancy drove back onto the road and sped farther away from Beckskill.

They had gone four miles when Nancy slowed the car again and asked, "Is that Peter down there?"

"Down where?"

"There, in that ravine," she said, pointing off beyond the edge of the road.

As Nancy pulled the car to a stop Sean was able to see Peter Geerson standing about four hundred yards away from the road, back in the woods near what looked to be a dried-up stream bed. "Yeah, it's Pete. I think I see Artie, too. I don't think they see us. Honk the horn, Nancy."

"Horn?" She laughed glumly. "What horn? This is Russell's car. Nothing works on this fucking thing." She paused. "Look, we gotta get everybody in the car and then like lose this town, you know? You go get them. I'll wait here."

"I ain't getting out of this car!"

"Damn it, Sean, just go get them, okay? Somebody's gotta stay with the car."

Sean knew that concern for the car had nothing to do with it. "Okay, so you go get 'em and I'll stay with the car."

Nancy sighed with exasperation. "Look, neither of us wants to be alone, right? So let's both go get them."

"What about the car?"

She switched off the engine and pulled the key from the ignition. "Okay? Nobody's gonna steal the car, okay?"

"Okay," he agreed glumly as he stepped out onto the road, "but keep the key handy, just in case."

They began walking from the shoulder of the road down into the woods toward the ravine, and they saw Russell and Deirdre join Peter and Artie below. All four were shouting at them, their hands cupped around their mouths, but Sean could not make out their words. "What are they saying?"

"I don't know," Nancy replied.

They drew closer as the others kept shouting urgently, and Sean was able at last to understand what they were crying out to him.

"*Sean, that isn't Nancy. THAT ISN'T NANCY!*"

Sean heard laughter beside him, and he turned to see the dagger teeth bursting from Nancy O'Hara's mouth. "Pay no attention to that man behind the curtain," chuckled Grogo the Goblin. And then he attacked.

From the nearby ravine Peter, Russell, and Deirdre watched a replay of the same sickening spectacle they had seen a few hours earlier. They had fled into the woods as Grogo rushed at them, but Nancy had slipped on an ice patch and then had fallen victim to the demon's fangs. They had watched as Grogo burrowed into the back of her head, as the shapechanger's body melted and twisted and shifted into the form of Nancy O'Hara. The creature had donned Nancy's clothes and then had run back to the car and had sped off, laughing maniacally.

And now it was happening again. Sean tried to scream, but his brain was sucked out and swallowed so quickly that his open mouth was silent as the life fled from his eyes and he fell shuddering to the ground at the feet of Grogo, whose body had taken upon itself a form identical to his own.

The Brenner-thing laughed as he began to run toward the others. "Hey, you guys," he called out. "Wait for me!"

They began again to run into the woods and the Brenner-thing chased them, relishing the hunt and amused by the attempt of the living to escape death. Who shall be first? he mused as he pursued them.

Whose shape shall I take next, before I become Vernon Sweet again, as I have decreed I always shall? Peter might like to become one with the elemental forces, I would think. But surely Russell will bravely sacrifice himself for the greater good. Ah, but Deirdre's flesh would be so sweet, so sweet. . . .

" . . .MUJEY SUNO BHAGAWAN VISHNU . . . "

The Brenner-thing stopped abruptly in his tracks as he heard frighteningly familiar words echoing from a distance, echoing not in his ears, but in his mind.

"MEYRIY MUHDUHD KUHRO, BHAGAWAN VISHNU . . . " He looked around him wildly as if searching the air for the source of the voice that was intoning the hated supplication. "No!" he cried. "No, you must not, you must not!"

" . . .MEYREY SAREY ACHEY KURUM, MEY APHEY UPIYOG . . ."

He forgot his quarry and ran back to the car, jumped in, started the engine, and began to drive wildly back to Beckskill. With each passing moment he felt his power ebbing and his consciousness disintergrating as the hated words reverberated and enveloped him.

". . . IS JAN WUR KO NIRBUL BUNA KUR ISKIY . . ."

Just as he reached the outskirts of town, he lost control over his shape and dwindled down into the form and mind of Vernon Sweet, who had, of course, never learned to drive a car. He crashed into a pickup truck that was parked against the curb and was thrown forward through the window of the Beetle. He fell onto the ground amid a shower of broken glass, but he was not injured, for death is invulnerable; but he felt rage and hatred even though he was already forgetting its cause.

" . . .SUB JIYVIT PRANYO KIY OR SEY MEY THUMBARIY RUKSHA KEY LIYEY VINTHIY KURTHI HU . . ."

Hear me, Lord Vishnu.

Help me, Lord Vishnu.

All my good karma I surrender to you for your use. . . .

Weaken the beast and blind his inner eye. . . .

On behalf of all living things, I beg you to preserve. . . .

. . . preserve . . .

. . . preserve. . . .

The echoing words drew him to the Ostlich home, and he ran madly down the street. Everywhere were corpses and skeletons and piles of bone and dust that had been robbed of their unnatural animation and now lay dead and motionless upon the ice and the pavement and the snow. The last slender thread of his unearthly self-awareness snapped as he ran on and then trotted and then walked with nervous confusion until he reached the front door and knocked on it tentatively.

The door opened, and Dorcas smiled down at him. "Hello, Vernon," she said kindly.

"Dor Dor!" he chirped, smiling happily. "Hi hi hi. Hello!"

Chapter Nineteen

January 12, 1969 (continued)

The human nervous system is designed to be able to absorb just so much before it reaches overload, and Lydia Ostlich had passed that point hours before. During a very brief period of time she had seen her dead mother murder her father, listened to her marginally unbalanced sister explain how it all certainly made sense to her, tried to understand how some gibberish scrawled on a paper napkin was part of a divine plan, and sat watching in silence as her sister lighted a candle, sat down cross-legged in front of it, and began to chant in a language neither of them could understand.

Lydia was numb, she was short-circuited, burned out. Her ears had ceased to be conduits to her mind. They were impenetrable barriers, blocking out the tapping on the front door. Her eyes were blank as they followed Dorcas to the door, and no sharp intake of breath expressed any shock or surprise as Grogo the Goblin walked into the living room of the Ostlich house. I thought they killed him, she mused. They probably did. He's probably dead, just like Mom. But she dropped in for a visit, so why shouldn't old Grogo? Open house at the Ostlichs'. Come on in, and leave your coffins at the door. She giggled softly, but neither Dorcas nor Grogo paid her any attention.

"Sit down, Vernon," Dorcas was saying gently as she led him to the sofa. "I have to talk to you about something very important, okay?"

"Sit!" Grogo exclaimed, hopping up onto the cushions.

"That's good, Vernon." She smiled. "Now I'm going to ask you some questions, and I want you to try to answer them. Okay?"

He nodded. "Vernon do."

"Good, Vernon, good." She paused and took a deep breath before asking, "Do you know who you are?"

The little man seemed confused by the question. "Vernon!" he answered simply.

"Yes, that's your name," she said. "But do you know anything else about yourself? Do you have any other names? Have you ever been called anything else?"

He thought hard, and then smiled. "Vernon Sweet!"

"Yes, yes, I know. But do you have any other names?"

He thought again. "Grogo the Goblin?"

She nodded, staring at him. "Vernon, do you understand what happened in town today?"

Vernon's simple mind had never mastered the art of concealing thoughts or emotions behind carefully controlled facial expressions, and the intensity of his struggle to think and reason and remember was drawn clearly upon his pursed lips, his broad, furrowed brow, and his twitching fingers. "Car," he said.

"A car? What about a car?"

He thought harder. "Vernon in car. Bad car."

Dorcas was not certain what he was referring to, but whatever it was, it seemed unrelated to the topic of her question. "What about the people, Vernon? Didn't you see the people on the streets? Sick people, funny people?" She paused. "Dead people?"

"People," he whispered softly, trying to remember. He shook his huge head. "Car," he insisted. "Bad car."

She nodded. I've done it, she thought. He doesn't remember. He doesn't know. It worked. The prayer worked. "Never mind, Vernon. It isn't important. May I ask you some more questions?"

"Dor Dor!" He grinned.

She took that as an affirmative response. "Vernon, do you ever get hungry or thirsty?"

"No," he replied.

"Do you get cold in the winter, or hot in the summer?"

"No."

She nodded again. "Do you remember what happened the day you and Rinda were hurt by . . . by the mean faces?"

He sighed. "Vernon 'member."

"Can you tell me what happened?"

"Mean faces come," he replied. "Rope, rope, tight tight tight. Vernon sleep, wake up all brightness."

She considered his words for a moment, trying to make sense of them. "Did the rope make you go to sleep, Vernon?"

"Sleep!"

"Yes, but did you go to sleep all by yourself, or did the rope make you go to sleep?"

"Sleep!" he repeated, petulantly.

She paused. "Do you sleep at night, Vernon? Do you go to bed, and go to sleep at night?"

"No."

"You don't go to sleep at night?"

"No."

"So the rope made you go to sleep that day?"

"No."

No, she mused. He doesn't sleep. Of course he doesn't. He isn't human. So what did he do? Why did he seem dead to the lynch mob? She thought for a moment, and then a possibility occurred to her. "Vernon, did Rinda ever teach you to meditate?"

"Med . . . ?" He could not even say the word.

"Meditate," she repeated. "Sit very still and quiet and get rid of all your thoughts."

"Good-sit!" he exclaimed, suddenly understanding her. "Vernon good-sit!" Then he made the connection. "Vernon good-sit tight rope tree. Vernon good-sit tight rope tree."

She understood his oddly phrased explanation immediately. That explains it, she thought. Maybe it was fear, maybe it was rage, maybe it was confusion; but for some reason, he put himself into a trance while they were trying to hang him. A ploy, maybe? Or an instinct? Or . . .

"Vernon, why did Rinda teach you to good-sit?"

"Rinda say good-sit always."

"Yes, it's always good to med . . ." She paused. "What do you mean good-sit always?"

"Rinda say good-sit always."

"Did Rinda ever say he might . . . go away, Vernon?"

The little man started to cry. "Rinda go 'way," he wept.

"Listen, Vernon," she said, squeezing his hand, "this is important. Did Rinda ever say he might go away someday?"

"When Lord want." He sighed. "Rinda say Lord call, Rinda go, Vernon good-sit always."

It all seemed to make sense now. The old yogi knew he was approaching the end of his life, Dorcas reasoned. He had been creating a . . . what was the phrase he used that night in the cave? . . . a psychic link, that was it . . . he had been expanding some sort of mental control over the creature for decades. When Ashvarinda died, Vernon was to have followed some sort of conditioning, some sort of training. He was supposed to sink into a meditative trance and never emerge from it. Vernon good-sit always. Forever. For eternity.

But Ashvarinda didn't have enough time. Thanks to Clayton and Alex and everybody else, he didn't have enough time. All he could do was teach me the prayer, and try to explain things to me, and hope that I believed him.

"I believe you, Mr. Patanjali," she said softly. Then she looked back to Vernon. "Let's take a walk together, okay, Vernon?" she asked, rising to her feet and leading him to the door. He went with her willingly, and together they began walking toward the River Road.

She had not spoken to Lydia at all since she had begun praying, and now she departed without giving her sister so much as a glance. Lydia watched her leave, and then released the breath she felt she had been holding in for the past hour. A thought had been rambling around in her mind ever since the previous evening, and the events of the day had given the thought form and substance and had then transformed it into determination. I can't trust Clay . . . I couldn't even look at him again, I don't think . . . my parents are dead, one sister is dead, and the other one just eloped with a goblin.

Nothing's holding me here anymore, and I'm getting the hell out.

Lydia walked over to her father's body and went through his pockets and his wallet, and then went upstairs and began to go through his bureau drawers. All together she found just over four hundred dollars and some jewelry. She took that, his car keys and registration, and then got into his car and drove out of Beckskill, toward the thruway, toward New York City.

The hell with Beckskill, she thought as she sped

down the corpse-ridden street. The hell with all of you.

Dorcas and Vernon walked hand-in-hand through town, ignoring the old and recent dead whose bodies lay everywhere. They walked out of Beckskill and continued on in silence until they came to the River Road. Vernon smiled as he looked at the morning sunbeams dancing upon the icy surface of the river, but then the little man's cheerful expression sank into one of misery and sorrow. "Rinda go 'way," he moaned.

"I know, Vernon" she said softly, "but he wanted you do something for him. He told me about it that night when you brought me to the cave."

"Favor for Rinda?"

"Yes, a favor for Rinda. Will you do what he wanted you to do? Will you do a favor for him?"

"Vernon do, Vernon do!"

"Good." She smiled. "Rinda was very worried that after he went away, all the mean faces would be very bad to you, so he told me that he wants you to stay away from them. You remember the cave where you took me that night?"

"Remember."

"Rinda wants you to go to that cave and go inside and stay there by yourself, and never come out again."

"Never come out?"

"Never, Vernon. You never get hungry, do you? Or cold or hot or thirsty?"

"No."

"Then you never have to leave the cave, and you'll always be safe. And just to make sure, Rinda wants you to good-sit always. Do you understand me? Rinda wants you to good-sit always."

Vernon tried to understand. "You visit?"

"Yes, Vernon, I'll come to visit you sometimes. Do you understand me? Will you do what Rinda wants you to do?"

"Rinda friend for Vernon."

"Yes, your best friend, and he loved you very much. And now I'll be your friend. Is that okay?"

He grinned up at her. "Dor Dor friend."

"Yes, I'll be your friend now. Will you do what Rinda wants you to do?"

He looked at the woods that stretched out on the other side of the River Road. "Vernon do," he said, and then scampered off. "Vernon do!"

She watched as he went a little ways and then turned and called out, "You visit Vernon!"

"I will, Vernon, I promise," she called back.

"Rinda want, Vernon do," he cried as he ran deeper into the woods. "Rinda want, Vernon do."

She sighed and whispered, "Me too, Mr. Patanjali. I'll do what you wanted. Every sunrise and every sunset, for the rest of my life."

Dorcas stood motionless, her braids fluttering in the cold wind, watching as Grogo the Goblin disappeared into the forest.

By Way of an Epilogue:
From Arthur Winston
to the Reader

April 15, 1990

    The manuscript ended with the words you have just read, and I must admit that the final scene, with Grogo slinking off to his cave, reminded me a bit laughingly of the end of "Puff the Magic Dragon." I was amused at the way the author took many events that I still recall with great clarity and wove them together within the plot structure of a rather bizarre story; I must also confess to a few pangs of nostalgia and not a little embarrassment at the portrait of my younger self. But as I noted in the Preface, the author's letter in which reference was made to her impending death struck me as being characteristically self-indulgent and melodramatic, and I ignored it. I made a mental note to write to the author as soon as I had a few spare moments, and then promptly forgot to do so.

    A week after receiving the manuscript I received a letter from my old friend, which made me rethink my nonchalance. The text read as follows:

Dear Artie:

You're still alive, I'm sure, and so am I, for the moment. After I shipped the book off to you I had every intention of ringing down the curtain on myself, but the more I thought about it, the angrier I got about the whole idea, by the waste. I don't mean the waste of life, because I've already wasted my life; I mean that I got angry about the idea of wasting my death. Oh, I still intend to die, and quite soon, but not by a handful of pills (à la Monroe) or a hefty dose of smack and liquor (like Janis and Jimi) or a belt looped like a noose over the closet door (that's how Phil Ochs did it). No, I've decided to let my death serve a purpose, and that purpose relates to everything you've just read.

You see, I hate you, all of you. I hate you for what you were and for what you are and for what you did to me, and the only thing I hate more than all of you is myself. I hate myself for what I was and for what I am and for what I have done to myself. So I'm planning to die quite horribly, and I think that after I'm dead I'll be able to kill you.

Are you catching my drift?

I haven't seen Dorcas for ten years, but I know that she has been saying that prayer, or chanting that spell, or whatever you want to call it, faithfully twice a day. I'm not sure where she is, though I know she doesn't live in Beckskill anymore. Of all the people we knew, I think only Becky Saunders is still there, a bitter old alcoholic cripple. Anyway, I have an old address for Dorcas, so I think I'll be able to find her; and when I do, I'm going to get her to go back with me to Beckskill. I'm going to go to that cave at the base of Clayton's mountain . . . I guess it's Becky's mountain now . . . and I'm going to see if Grogo is still there, which I think he probably is. Then I'm going to kill Dorcas and wait until Grogo realizes who he is and what he is. I figure that she'll say the prayer to Vishnu that morning, and I can kill her in the afternoon, so the shit will hit the fan at sundown.

I have a pretty good idea what will happen then. He, the Shiva-demon or whatever the hell he is, once chose Grogo's body as a permanent home because it was so hideous. That's why no matter what shape he took, he always went back to being Vernon Sweet. So I figure that when he awakens, he'll kill me and then become me; and when he realizes how much hatred I have inside, he'll keep *my* form forever. Do you get it? *I'll be the new Vernon Sweet, the new Grogo the Goblin!* And then what a bloodbath there will be!

I'm telling you this because I want someone to know. Don't ask me why. And also because, of all the assholes I knew twenty years ago, you were the least obnoxious: but don't get a swelled head about it.

Nothing else to say but this: remember the *tandava*. It may comfort you as you wait to die. It has comforted me somewhat over the years.

So I've told you everything, and that's that, and now I'm off to find Dorcas and go to Beckskill. It's a bit like the old Rip Van Winkle story, isn't it! Grogo has been sleeping for twenty years.

And I'm going to wake him up.

Lydia

I prefaced this book with the comment that you, gentle reader, would find my comment about its veracity an amusing if hackneyed literary device. ("The story you are about to read is true," etc. etc.) I don't know if it was amusing, but it certainly was hackneyed. Well, here comes another exercise in well-worn prose.

As I write these words to close the book on this tale I am sitting with Peter and Russell over a pitcher of beer and a few shots of bourbon in the Greenwood Tavern in Beckskill, New York, the bar that once in my youth was called the Browns' Hotel. They are sitting pensive and quiet, lost in their own personal reveries as I pen this closing chapter. I am remembering the events of twenty years ago, and I am attempting to reconcile them all with what I read in the manuscript.

I know it sounds silly, sounds so Raymond Chandler or Dashiell Hammett. You know what I mean. "As I sat in the same old bar, swilling cheap rotgut and smoking stale cigarettes, I thought back to those days in the past, and I remembered . . ." etc. etc. etc.

I can almost see the editor wince as she reads this.

But I can't help it. It's true. I'm in Beckskill, sitting with Peter and Russell in the same place I sat the night Alex went after Sean with a knife, and I'm trying to remember it all, trying to make sense of it all. (I was there when that happened, by the way. I don't know why the author left me out of that scene in the manuscript, but I can't ask her about it. She's dead. Besides, I am present in appropriate scenes in the rest of the book.)

Anyway, this is what happened over the past two days:

When I received the letter, I dismissed it as more foolishness from a strange and unbalanced person, and I tried not to think about it; but it bothered me more and more with each passing day, to such an extent that I wasn't thinking about anything else and was unable to get any work done, and I finally decided that I had to do something to get it out of my system. I recall thinking that I had to exorcise the demon. An odd phrase, in retrospect.

My wife was taking our daughters to visit her family up near Syracuse for a week anyway, so I was being left to my own devices. (I married Deirdre Duell, by the way. It's been twenty years since we met, and she is as beautiful today as she was when she was nineteen.) I don't usually have much time to myself without commitments or obligations, so I figured that it would be fun to spend a weekend up in New Paltz, where I went to college. Might just take a spin up to Beckskill, too, while I was in the area, just for the hell of it, you understand.

Sure.

I called up Peter and Russell and invited them along for the ride, and they both agreed readily. Peter is a lawyer now, and a good lawyer at that. He doesn't lie, cheat, steal, or kill, which as I understand it makes him a unique member of his profession. He became very involved in the legal side of the environmentalist movement about sixteen, seventeen years ago, and wound up in law school. We lived in the same neighborhood on Long Island until a year ago, when he and his wife and kids moved about three miles away. Russell still teaches high-school social studies, and he lives a bit farther away from me, about ten miles. Hop, skip, and a jump in both cases, though I don't see either of them that often, what with kids, careers, and so forth. You know how it is.

Peter's wife, Janice, is an understanding woman, so she didn't object to his going off for a weekend with his old friends. (Hell, she treated him to a solo week in London as a birthday present a few years ago.) Russell's wife, Debbie, encouraged him to join us, for a different reason. They had a child about six months ago, and Russell keeps tossing the kid up into the air screaming, "My son! My son!" until the poor little thing vomits all over the place. I think Debbie wanted Russell to go with us just to give the baby's stomach a chance to settle.

Russ is still far to the left politically, but like most of us he has abandoned any faith in utopian panaceas. He was a genuine Marxist back in the 1960's, while the rest of us were what I can only describe as half-assed socialists who didn't think about it very much. Today Russell is sort of halfway between being a liberal and being a cautious radical, while the rest of us swing back and forth between apathy and resignation, occasionally mustering up enough enthusiasm to vote for somebody. Peter and I both voted for Reagan. I voted for Carter in '76. I even voted for Nixon in '72, God help me. (But he ended the draft, didn't he? That was a major selling point to a twenty-two-year-old kid who had just graduated from college and had thus lost his student deferment. And anyway, my moral credentials are intact. I was clean for Gene in '68.)

There was a saying back in the sixties, "We are the people our parents warned us against." Well, we have become the people we used to despise in our youthful, arrogant ignorance. We have lawns and barbecue grills and kids and dogs and mortgages. We talk about pension plans and interest rates and taxes. And the funny thing is, life is pretty good this way.

Ah, well. *Sic transit gloria mundi.* But I digress.

I knew as I passed the New Paltz exit on the New York State Thruway and then pulled off exit 19 that I had to go and speak to the police about the letter I had received. Of course, I had no intention of saying anything about the sixties or about Grogo the Goblin or about a vengeful avatar of Shiva or anything like that, not only because I didn't want to end up in the drunk tank, but also because I knew that the person who had written to me was not, shall we say, a paragon of emotional stability; but the letter bespoke an intention to commit suicide, and I felt an obligation to report it to the local authorities.

As we drove up toward Beckskill I gave Pete and Russ a thumbnail sketch of the contents of the manuscript and the letter, and they agreed with my decision. "She was never really well, you know," Peter said. "She always had problems which I guess we didn't really think too much about."

"Yeah," I agreed. "None of us really gave much thought to the emotional side of things, especially the emotions of a girl as weird as she was."

"Bunch of sexists," Russell said.

"Precisely," I said. "Think we still are?"

"Probably." He laughed, and Peter and I joined in his laughter, knowing (or at least hoping) that we were not.

I paid the toll at the thruway exit and then headed my Datsun 310 for Route 28, which would take us to Route 42. "I guess we were sort of thick and callous back then," I said. "I mean, it should have been obvious to us all that something was wrong with her."

"Sure," Russell agreed, "if any of us cared or were paying attention. All we knew"—and he dropped into an absurd parody of himself twenty years earlier—"was that she was like one really fucked-up chick, you know?"

"That's like really heavy, man." Peter chuckled.

"Like wow," I added, asking myself if we ever really sounded this stupid.

"What are you going to tell the police?" Peter asked.

"The truth," I replied. "She wrote and told me that she was going to kill herself."

"That isn't exactly what she said."

"No, but that's what she meant."

Peter nodded. "I haven't heard a thing about her in years. Have either of you?"

"I have," Russell replied. "Suzie Kosloski still sees

her, or at least still saw her, talked to her on the phone now and then."

"Suzie Kosloski!" I exclaimed. "You still see her?"

"Not exactly," he said. "She teaches special ed over in Kings Park. We met at a mainstream teachers' conference a few months ago."

"Small world," I mused. "So what did Suzie have to say about her?"

He paused before replying. "It isn't a pretty story."

"I think we can take it," I said as we drove through the little town of Catullus on our way to Haddlyville.

"Well," he said, "we all stopped going up to see Clay after he sold that land to the town, and apparently she left Beckskill at about the same time. Went down to New York City. She didn't have much education or any skills worth speaking of, so she got mixed up in the sex industry. Peep shows, one-on-one booths, stag films, that sort of thing."

"Jesus." I sighed. "That's a damned shame."

"Should be illegal." Russell nodded. "Anyway, she got involved with heroin and cocaine, got hooked on both of them . . . the kids call people like that smack 'n crackers, I think . . . and the last time Suzie talked to her she had just stopped working in a house. You know, a brothel."

"She was a prostitute?"

"That's what Suzie told me. She also told me that she stopped doing it when she got sick."

I took my eyes off the road for a moment to look at him. "Don't tell me she has AIDS. . . . "

"Yeah," he said. "According to Suzie, anyway."

I shook my head. "That's horrible."

"Tragic." Russell nodded, and then asked, "What about those references in her book you told us about, the stuff about incest with her father. You ever hear anything about that before?"

"It was news to me," I replied. "I have no idea if it's true or not."

"Probably is," Peter muttered from the backseat.

Russell turned to him. "Why would you think so, Pete?"

He shrugged. "Why would anybody make up something like that?"

"Well, " I said, "if it's true, it makes the whole thing even worse." They both nodded, sharing my thoughts about a life so terribly ruined. Molested by her father, abused by her lover, ignored (I blush to say it) by her friends, unable to pull herself out of the drug swamp in which we had all waded so foolishly, forced by circumstances and personality to live off her body, and at last falling victim to that horrible, horrible disease.

"Poor kid." Peter sighed. We were quiet for a while after that.

The state police station is in Haddlyville, about ten miles south of Beckskill, and Russ and Pete remained in the car while I went in to tell my story. John Bauer, the trooper behind the desk, listened to me carefully and politely and then said, "Well, sir, I can file a report on this if you like, but I don't know if we can assign someone to do any investigating on the basis of some vague reference in a letter. The lady sure sounds ill, but—"

"Officer," I broke in, "there may be a human life at stake here. If she has gone to Beckskill to kill herself, she has to be stopped, confined, given help."

He tapped his pen on the desktop and thought hard. "You think you can find this cave she talks about?"

"I can try," I replied. "That is to say, I know generally where it would be, if it exists. As I told you—"

"Yes, she has a very active imagination," he finished for me. He thought again and said, "I tell you what. I get off duty in a half hour. We'll drive over to Beckskill and have a look. But I really don't think we'll find anything.

The lady could still be in New York City, or in Los Angeles or Paris, for all we know. This may even be some sort of sick joke."

"Maybe," I agreed. "But I don't want to take the risk that it isn't."

He nodded. "Okay. Come back in a half hour, and we'll see what's what."

Peter, Russell, and I had a few cups of coffee at the Haddlyville Diner and soon thereafter followed behind Officer Bauer's patrol car and drove to Beckskill. It is difficult adequately to describe the peculiar sensation I experienced upon entering that town again after twenty years. I had remembered Beckskill as the site of many adventures, many sorrows, and many joys, and reading the manuscript had reminded me of so much; and now, back in that town again, I felt as if twenty years ago had been just last month. Beckskill seemed larger than I remembered it, but my memory may have shrunk it over the years. The old general store was gone, replaced by a 7-Eleven, but Alex Brown's bar was still there. Different color paint, different name, different owners, same dumpy little town.

"And just where was it," Peter asked with a smirk, "that Grogo the Goblin was supposed to have chased us off into the woods?"

"I don't know." I laughed, and then said, more soberly, "But we did get a flat tire that morning, and Nancy did get killed when she went into the woods to take a leak."

"Yeah, she got killed by a bear or a bobcat or something," Russell reminded me. "Not a Hindu demon."

"That's what the police inferred from the wounds on the body," I replied, and then added after a pause, "when they got the time to attend to it. After they had gotten all the corpses up off the streets and back into the cemetery."

They looked at each other with amusement. "Artie!" Russell laughed.

"I know, I know," I said, laughing with them.

Peter took a toothpick from his pocket and started chewing on it. He stopped smoking fifteen years ago, and he's been chewing on wood ever since. "It is funny, though, that we never saw any of the people after that weekend."

"What's funny about it?" Russell asked. "We left right when Alex was calling the police, and I sure had no reason to ever go back. We were all angry at Clay about the land, and after what Sean told us about moving that girl's body, I wasn't crazy about seeing him anymore either."

"People do just drift apart naturally anyway," I said.

"I suppose." Peter nodded.

I parked the car on the shoulder of the River Road and we followed Bauer into the woods. There was no way to get to the foot of Saunders Mountain except by walking through the forest, and whatever path there had once been had long ago been obscured by nature, making it something of a hike. We had been walking for a half hour before I asked Bauer, "Who owns this land now?"

"Miss Saunders," he replied. "She lives up there, on that mountain. She's something of a recluse."

I nodded. "She wouldn't be crippled, would she?"

He glanced at me. "Yes. Shooting accident or something, a long time ago. How did you know that?"

"I think I remember her," I said weakly. "Does she still live with her brother?"

"Doesn't have a brother, not that I know of."

"Look." Peter nodded ahead of us. "The house is still there."

We entered the clearing and stood for a moment, looking at the old Sweet house. I remembered it as a rotting old ruin in the first place, more a cabin than a house, and the years had not treated it well. The burned-out barn looked pretty much the same as it had twenty years ago, but then I suppose there isn't much more damage could be done to it. It had been flat on the ground when last I saw it.

Peter was staring at the house. "Brings back memories," he muttered.

"Yeah," Russell said, "and I'd like to forget a lot of them." We walked on into the woods on the other side of the house, and as we walked I was thinking back on it all, on the big party Clay threw that weekend, the would-be séance in Grogo's house, the problems in Alex's bar, the hasty flight from Beckskill in the wee hours of the morning, Nancy's death.

"Hell of a weekend," I said softly.

"Hell of an understatement," Peter observed, sharing my thoughts.

It was the same weekend, of course, that the local cemetery was vandalized by person or persons unknown. The police decided that it had probably been drunken bikers or stoned-out hippies who had dug up all those bodies and left them all over the place. The whole story was reported in the local papers, and in the *Daily News*. Didn't make the *Times*, though, as I recall.

We came to the upsweep of land at the foot of Saunders Mountain and walked slowly along its edge, peering through the scrub, looking for the cave. I wasn't surprised when we found it. There are caves all over the place in the Catskills. Officer Bauer switched on his flashlight and went in. We waited outside. He came back out a few minutes later, and I asked, "Anything in there?"

"A lot of bat shit." He laughed.

I hadn't said anything to him about the manuscript,

so I lied a little and said, "I seem to remember that there was another cave around here someplace. I think we'd better keep looking, just for a while."

He shrugged and we walked on. "Officer," Peter asked, "wasn't there supposed to be a factory or something like that built in this town, on the banks of the river?"

"Not to my knowledge," he replied. He was about twenty-five, so he wouldn't remember anything about that anyway. But then he added, "I don't think there could be a factory in Beckskill. The EPA keeps a close watch on the small rivers that feed the Hudson."

"Thank God for the EPA," Peter said.

I decided to needle Russell. "Yeah, good old Nixon, setting up an agency to protect the environment."

He glanced at me wryly. "We'll discuss this later."

And then we found the second cave, and Bauer switched the flashlight on again and went in, while we again waited outside. He did not emerge for a long while, and when he did, his face had a greenish tint to it. "Do you have that letter with you, sir?" he asked.

"No," I answered. "Why?"

He coughed. "Well, sir, this has just become an official police matter. There's a body in there, a woman. Been dead two or three days, looks to me." He paused. "If you don't mind, I'd like you to come in and see if it's your friend."

I breathed heavily. A few years ago my uncle died in a fire, and I had to go to the morgue to identify what was left of him. The image of his face tormented me for months afterward, and I prayed that I would never have to go through something like that again, but I guess my prayer had been answered no. "Okay, sure," I said reluctantly.

"You'd better brace yourself," he warned me. "It's been pretty warm, and she isn't far enough back in there for the cave's cold to do much preserving. She's in pretty bad shape. Looks like an animal got to her, too."

I swallowed hard. "An animal?"

"Yeah. Chewed the back of her head clean off."

I looked at Peter and Russell. Their faces were white.

Bauer went back into the cave and I followed him. Perhaps it was my imagination, but I think the stench of rot hit my nostrils the minute I entered, and it grew worse with each step. We went about ten yards and then Bauer shone the light down on the ground. And there she was, lying on her side, her slit wrists caked with dried blood, fragments of her skull lying on the ground behind her. Even though her face was badly decayed and my eyes were watering heavily, I had no trouble recognizing her.

"Is that your friend, sir?"

"Yes," I said, and then felt my breakfast struggling to work its way back up into my mouth.

I went outside quickly, and the nausea subsided. Russell put his hand on my shoulder. "You okay?"

I nodded. "I'm okay."

"Artie," Peter asked. "Is it . . . ?"

I nodded again.

Officer Bauer took a small notebook from his belt pouch and clicked open a ballpoint. He checked his watch, noted the time, and then said, "I'd like to get some preliminaries right now, if you don't mind, sir, and I'd like you to come back to the station later on today so we can make out a full report. I have to see to the removal of the body first."

"Sure, I understand." I coughed.

He put the tip of the pen to the paper. "What was the lady's name again, sir?"

"Ostlich." I sighed. "Karen Ostlich."

* * *

It all makes sense to me now, of course. It's right out of Psych 101. A sensitive young girl is sexually abused by her father, her mother commits suicide when she learns about it, and the poor kid just can't handle it all. Her personality splits, and Karen Ostlich no longer exists. In her place are someone she calls Dorcas (quiet, shy, nervous, guilt-ridden) and someone else she calls Lydia (loud, outgoing, solid as a rock, and willing to do anything). The stronger of the two personalities is the one able to handle the strain caused by the abuse, and so it is Lydia, not Dorcas, whom her father molested. But the emotional strain is an undeniable reality, the pressure mounts, the pain and the trauma and the irrational guilt persist, and so it is Dorcas who has a breakdown and slits her wrists, not Lydia.

I began to suspect what must have happened to her soon after I started to read "Lydia's" manuscript, as I realized that "Karen" is only mentioned in "Dorcas's" psychotic musings, as soon as I saw that "Dorcas" and "Lydia" were together time and time again. Physically impossible, of course; but as far as she was concerned, that was the way it all happened, because to her (that is to say, to Karen), Dorcas and Lydia were indeed two separate people. She must have had two distinct memory perspectives of everything that happened, a Lydia memory and a Dorcas memory. But except for a brief moment while she was tripping in Grogo's house, there are no Karen memories at all.

And none of us ever really noticed or understood.

Sure, we all knew that when she was in a partying mood, she insisted that everyone call her Lydia; and when she was depressed or quiet or nervous, she said her name was Dorcas. But people assumed and abandoned names easily back in the so-called psychedelic sixties, and damned peculiar names many of them were.

My first roommate at college was a guy everyone called Aardvark, and we lived down the hall from two other guys named Dwarf and Duck. I mean, good grief, Frank Zappa named his kids Dweezle and Moon Unit! Grace Slick named her son God, and then changed it to America because God seemed too pretentious! Children born back then were given names like Sky and Gazelle and Woodstock. So if she wanted to be called Lydia sometimes and Dorcas other times, what difference did it make? Who cared?

That explains the whole business about Clayton raping her that night in the trailer. He probably did, without realizing it. He thought she was Lydia that night, and he was always having sex with Lydia. But at that moment she *wasn't* Lydia, she was Dorcas; and in her Dorcas-memory of the incident, she was raped. As for Clayton raping and murdering Sarah, I don't know if that's the truth or merely one of Karen's paranoid fantasies. Sarah was indeed found dead, I remember that; but I don't remember rape being mentioned, and to the best of my knowledge the crime was never solved. For all I know, Karen killed her and then engaged in guilt displacement by assigning the crime to Clayton.

It was only as I stood there in front of the cave, giving what information I had to the trooper, that the pattern, which should have been obvious to us all back then, became clear. Dorcas and Lydia, Lydia and Dorcas. Dorcas when she was a good little girl, and Lydia when she was bad. Dorcas when she obeyed her father and Lydia when she didn't. Dorcas didn't do drugs, but Lydia did. Dorcas was virginally chaste, and Lydia slept with anybody and everybody. Dorcas pined with romantic innocence for Peter, and every orifice Lydia had was open to Clayton at his whim. In her letter Lydia said she hadn't seen Dorcas in ten years. Of course she hadn't.

Dorcas would never be a prostitute, and Lydia had always thought of herself as a whore. Lydia wrote and told me she was going to kill Dorcas; but inasmuch as Lydia was Dorcas and Dorcas was Lydia and they both really were Karen, what could she have been talking about other than suicide? She was a textbook case of multiple personality. I mean, like one really fucked-up chick, you know?

I found myself weeping.

We sat around the police station in Haddlyville for a few hours and then I gave my statement. Officer Bauer wants me to send him the letter, and I'll do that as soon as I get home. He said the manuscript isn't needed at the moment, but that I should hang on to it. I told him I had every intention of doing just that.

What had been supposed to be something of a nostalgic weekend had turned into a nightmare, and Peter was all for going back to Long Island as soon as we left the police station, but Russell wanted to go to New Paltz and have a few beers at P & G's, one of the bars we used to hang out in when we were in college. It fell to me to cast the deciding vote, and after giving it some thought, I said, "I want to go visit Becky."

"Becky Saunders?" Peter asked. "What the hell for?"

"I just want to talk to her."

"And ask her if Grogo the Goblin was a Hindu demon?" Russell asked with a laugh. "Come on, Artie!"

"When was the last time you saw Clayton or Sean Brenner?" I asked them, and then answered my own question. "It was twenty years ago, wasn't it? And not a word about either of them since. You, me, Buzzy, Gary, Danny, none of us has seen or heard about them for twenty years."

"Why would we?" Peter asked. "After that weekend, none of us wanted anything to do with them."

"Well, I want to talk to her," I insisted. "Look, you guys take my car. Just drop me off at the Saunders place and then go to New Paltz for a few beers. It's only a half hour away. I'll meet you back at Alex's bar in about four hours, and if you want to go home then, Pete, it's okay with me."

They agreed, and soon thereafter I was back in Beckskill, walking up the still-unpaved dirt driveway that led up to the trailer. I was wondering if she still lived in it or rented it or got rid of it, but my first view of the trailer told me that it had been uninhabited for many, many years. I looked off to the left and saw the big house that Clay and Becky's parents had built. It looked fresh and clean and painted, and I figured that she must have moved there after . . . after . . .

After what? What the hell happened up here?

I walked to the house and rang the doorbell. After a minute or so the door opened and I was confronted by a behemoth of a woman, a nurse or paid companion or something like that, who stared at me coldly and said, "Yes?"

"Hello." I smiled, as affably as possible. "I'm Artie Winston, an old friend of Becky's, and I was in the area, so I—"

"Miss Saunders doesn't receive visitors," she snapped, and began to shut the door.

"Wait a moment, please," I said hastily. "Please just tell her who I am. I'm quite sure she'll want to say hello."

The woman stared at me with irritation and then muttered, "Wait here." She shut the door again.

I tapped my fingers on the doorframe impatiently, mentally reviewing everything I wanted to ask Becky.

Did they ever solve Sarah Ostlich's murder? Where are Clayton and Sean? What happened to Alex Brown? How did she get injured? Was there really a lynching out by the old Sweet place?

And whatever happened to Grogo the Goblin?

The door swung open again and the female Gargantua said, "She doesn't want to see you." She started to close the door again.

"Wait," I said. "Did you tell her my name?"

"Of course I did. She doesn't want to see you. She says to go away and not come back." The door slammed without further exchange.

This, of course, left me in something of a quandary. I had expected to sit around talking to Becky for a few hours, and then call a radio dispatch cab from the bus station in Haddlyville to get me back into town. Now I was left without transportation, without access to a phone, and no option other than to walk.

And more importantly, I had not been able to ask Rebecca Saunders any of the questions that were on my mind.

I walked down the drive to the paved roadway, and then followed that for four miles until it bisected the River Road. To the right, two miles away, was Beckskill. To the left was the forest in the center of which stood the old Sweet place. I went to the left.

I don't really know why I wanted to go back to Grogo's house. Curiosity, perhaps, or nostalgia, or sheer perversity. I don't know. But I walked along the River Road until I came to the spot where we had parked a few hours earlier, and then I walked into the woods. It was only about four in the afternoon on a clear spring day, so I had no trouble seeing and no problem finding my way back to the clearing.

In one of his books, *Salem's Lot* I think it was,

Stephen King has one of his characters say that horror writers are usually more skeptical and less superstitious than the general population. That's probably true for writers, and it's most definitely true for people like me, actors. Our whole business revolves around fantasy, remember. I've made my share of horror movies, worn my share of ghoulish makeup, seen how special effects work, and I know nonsense when I see it. Keep this in mind as I relate what happened next.

I entered the old house and walked to the center of the large main room. The interior smelled like time, like age. If you have ever haunted the dark downstairs stacks of secondhand bookstores, you will know the smell I'm referring to, the smell of dry brittle wood and long-undisturbed dust.

I looked down at my feet and saw an empty beer bottle, and discovered to my surprise that it was a bottle of Old Peculiar, a dark and tasty Yorkshire ale that Gary Mercier used to drink back in college. Then I remembered that Gary had brought a few of them with him to the would-be séance, and I'm quite certain that he had not taken the empties with him when he left. What this meant, of course, was that this dust-covered bottle had been sitting there for twenty years, resting in the same spot where Gary had placed it when we all left the Sweet house to go to Alex's bar.

I saw a pile of papers resting in the corner and picked them up. They were worm-ridden and rotten, but a few of the central sheets were still legible, and I was surprised to find that they were a stack of Vernon Sweet's sideshow handbills. I leafed through one of the readable copies, and an old photograph fell out. I picked it up and looked at it.

I had never met Vernon Sweet, but the little man in the picture could not possibly have been anyone else. He stood beside a small, frail, elderly man with dark skin; Ashvarinda, I suppose. I smiled sadly and muttered, "One hell of a story, Karen."

And then I heard the floor creaking in the next room.

I shivered and commanded myself to stop acting like a child. Houses creak, especially old ones. I listened carefully and heard nothing more for a few moments. And then, very soft, I heard the sound of a woman laughing.

Perhaps my imagination had taken control of me, perhaps I was tired or overwrought from the terrible experience of the day, or perhaps the wind made an odd sound as it drifted through the forest. Already the moment is fading in my memory, and it was only a few hours ago. I guess I don't really know what I heard; but at that moment, I thought I heard laughter. I turned and looked at the doorway; and in the other room, a shadow moved.

In a movie, the hero would have rushed in to investigate. So would the protagonist of a novel. But I am neither a hero nor a protagonist, and this is not a novel in the conventional sense of the term, so I did what any normal person would do in real life. I got the hell out of there, and ran like mad through the woods and back to the River Road. It was only a matter of a few minutes before I reached the center of town, and I can tell you exactly how it felt to find myself once again in the midst of the real, substantial, no-nonsense world: I felt like Ichabod Crane making it safely across the bridge.

So here I sit in Beckskill, in what was once Alex Brown's bar, jotting down words in a notebook while Peter and Russell sit and brood over their beers. I told them what I experienced in the Sweet house, and they think that I've just let this all get to me. Maybe so. There's an awful lot in this manuscript that is true, that

I remember. There's an awful lot I can't possibly verify at this late date, and a lot that must, simply must be fantasy.

Reader, you can make up your own mind. I know that you bought this book expecting to find just another horror novel, and if that's how you want to think of it, that's okay with me. I've seen to it that the story has been told, and that's all I wanted to do.

I have one final thing to tell you, and then I will put an end to the story of Grogo the Goblin.

In her letter, Karen Ostlich told me to remember the *tandava*, and when I first read that word I had absolutely no idea what she was talking about; but now, having looked it up, I think I understand what she was trying to tell me. The *tandava* is a very famous image in Asian art, so famous, in fact, that I'll bet you know what it is, even if you don't know what it's called. The *tandava* is the dance of Shiva.

In the artistic representation of the *tandava*, Shiva the Destroyer is standing upright, right leg bent slightly at the knee, left leg raised and held out horizontally in front of his body. The position of the leg gives the statue a suggestion of whirling movement. A ring of fire surrounds Shiva, and his right foot is crushing a child. Poisonous serpents grow Medusa-like from his head, and a cobra with a fully flared hood encircles his waist.

In the statues and drawings of the *tandava*, Shiva has four arms. In one hand he holds a dagger, preparing to strike. In the second hand he holds a fireball, preparing to throw it. The third hand is pointed downward in a gesture of denial.

Death, the destroyer of worlds.

Wherever the observer looks, he sees symbolic representations of death and destruction, from the all-consuming flames to the fanged serpents, from the threatening weapon to the pathetic figure beneath Shiva's feet.

But there is a fourth hand, and that hand is held upward, palm facing out, as a minister holds his hand when giving benediction. It is the universally recognizable gesture of peace.

Peace.

Don't worry about it.

It is all an illusion.

ABOUT THE AUTHOR

JEFFREY SACKETT was born in Brooklyn in 1949, and counts himself fortunate to have made it home from the hospital unscathed. After studying briefly for the ministry, he chose to pursue an academic career—this being preferable at the time to his alternative, which was a year in the Mekong Delta as a guest of the government.

He obtained graduate degrees in history from Queens College and New York University, and also studied classical Greek, Latin, and several modern languages. Being thus possessed of a vast fund of fascinating but unmarketable information, he became a teacher of history and English, which he has remained until this day.

He explored other career alternatives at various times. He worked for a while as a bank guard (during which time the bank was robbed) and as a finder of missing persons (most of whom had disappeared by choice, and threatened him with all manner of violent reprisals when he found them). He decided that on the whole, teaching was his safest bet.

The Demon is his fifth novel published by Bantam. His four previous horror novels are *Stolen Souls, Candlemas Eve, Blood of the Impaler*, and *Mark of the Werewolf*. He is currently working on a new novel about ghosts.

Sackett lives in a ridiculously overpriced house in New York, with his wife Paulette, an artist; their daughters Victoria and Elizabeth, children; their dog Paddington, a cocker spaniel; and their lizard Horatio, a seven-foot iguana. Theirs is the only house in the neighborhood with a sign saying BEWARE OF REPTILE on the fence.